BRITTAN

SHE LIKES

PIÑA COLADAS

*What if the one who got away
was the one you ran away with?*

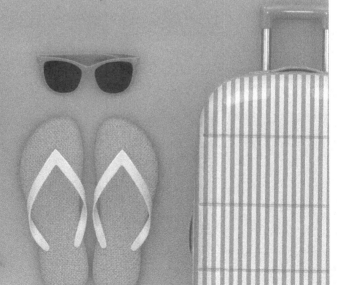

First paperback edition October 2021

Cover Design & Formatting by Cover 2 Cover Author Services

Editing by Happily Editing Anns

ISBN 979-8-4669-8606-8 (paperback)

BRITTANÉE
NICOLE
Romance with a Twist

Dedication

To my first reader, whether it was bedtime stories or my own books, you've always been by my side. Thank you for being my biggest supporter and sorry for all the sexy parts.

I love you Mommy.

Brittnee

CHAPTER I

Charlotte

Six Years Ago

I really shouldn't have had that last shot. The first one was a mistake. The second one felt like a good idea at the time, but God, that third one, after all the green beer...well, it was definitely a bad idea.

My eyes scan the room for my best friend, or her boyfriend, or really any one of the many friends we've run into today at the St. Patrick's Day parade. Where *is* everyone?

"Want another beer?" the voice behind me asks. I turn to look at the boy who bought me the last shot and grimace. If I have another beer, I won't be able to stand up straight. As it is, the loud music leaves my ears ringing.

Swaying unintentionally, I purse my lips as I try to answer his question. He's not unattractive, but I don't know him, and I'm pretty sure Steph would tell me that allowing him to buy me another drink would just be leading him on. Or it would result in a really bad decision where I didn't lead him on and instead led him back to my dorm room. We are in our last year of college, and Steph made me promise to let loose today, but I'm pretty sure this is not what she meant.

Pat's best friend was supposed to meet us at the parade. They swore it wasn't a setup, but Steph kept telling me his friend was hot and I would definitely want it to be a setup, and then he didn't show. Pat seemed super embarrassed, or maybe he was just upset because he got stuck with us all day. Either way it resulted in lots of drinking on my part, and now I can't find them.

I shake my head at the boy. "Nope. I'm okay."

He shrugs his plaid-shirted shoulders at me. "Okay, want to get out of here?"

Without hesitating, I reply, "No. I'm going to go find my friend, I think."

His shaggy head swings wildly as he walks off muttering under his breath. Pretty sure he called me a tease.

You've got that right, buddy. It takes a hell of a lot more than a few shots to find your way into my pants.

Turning away indignantly, I plop a twenty onto the bar and ask for another beer. Just because I didn't want plaid boy to buy me another drink doesn't mean I'm done drinking.

"Yeah, she's all set." A hand grabs the twenty off the bar and shoves it into my hand. What the hell? I turn my head around to give the rude stranger a piece of my mind and am greeted by a broad wall of muscle which is unmoving and daring me to trace my fingers against it.

Okay, maybe it's just that the man who belongs to the chest is unmoving, and definitely, probably not begging me to touch him, but that is precisely how my tipsy fingers feel. They do a twist up his stomach like the itsy-bitsy spider, and I bite back a laugh. Then I inch my chin up to look at the face which belongs to the chest. He has a strong jaw, chiseled cheekbones, a five o'clock shadow shading his face, and wide blue eyes with golden flecks which dance as he looks down at me, his brow slightly lifted as if he's daring me to fight him.

Yeah, I have no interest in fighting him. This beautiful man—he is definitely not a boy like the college guys I've been surrounded by for the last few months; he's *all* man—is someone I want to listen to. Which, for the record is an anomaly. I don't listen to anyone. Remembering that, I cock my chin up and ball my fists together. "Who the hell do you think you are?"

His lips pull up in a smirk, as if he were waiting for the fight and he's excited that I didn't give in right away, and then his deep voice rumbles, "The guy who's taking you home."

I bite the smile from my lips and prepare to go toe to toe with him. Without another breath, the man grabs my hand and pulls me away from the bar. As his arm goes around my shoulders and he pulls me to his chest, I find myself infatuated with the way he smells, like a rainy afternoon. Not the overpowering smell of

Abercrombie cologne like the rest of the guys here. He smells like he just stepped out of the shower. Embarrassingly, I push my head into his shirt and inhale again. His chest vibrates as he laughs, clearly amused by the crazy girl he picked up at the bar. How long until he realizes I'm delusional and he's in over his head? Hopefully not too soon, since I'd like to stare at him for a few more hours.

The cool air hits me when we breach the door of the bar. Spring in New England is cold. Especially here in Newport where I attend college because it sits on the water. My hands move to my arms, and the breeze brings me back to reality. I don't know this man, and I have no idea where Steph and Pat are. Pulling myself away from him, I ground myself in place.

"Are you cold?" he asks as he pulls me close again. Honestly, it's hard for me to think with his chest so close to my face. And his smell. I push back and keep my hand up, making it clear that I don't want him to come any closer.

"I'm not going anywhere with you." Yes. Finally, I've remembered how to act. I'm not going home with this stranger.

"You clearly have had too much to drink. I'm just going to make sure you get home safe." He holds up his hands as if to say he's harmless, but I'm not worried about him jumping me. It's the reverse he should be concerned about. I want to go home and climb him. Not a good idea and definitely not how I normally act. I don't do one-night stands. I don't do night-stands at all. I'm a girl who likes being in relationships. Someone who likes to be treasured. After all the drinking today, I can see myself making some *very* bad decisions.

And man do I want to because He. Is. Hot.

"I just need to find my friends." I fumble with my phone, trying to figure out how to make it work, but my thumb seems too fat, and I keep hitting the wrong numbers.

His lip inches up again. "How about we get you something to eat and then I can help you find your friends?"

Pancakes. Oh, pancakes sound amazing right now. I *need* pancakes like I need to breathe. I cock my eyebrow up at Mr. Mysterious again, trying to decide if I want pancakes as badly as I want to find Steph. Yeah, pancakes with the hot guy is totally going to win. "Name?"

His chest rumbles from that deep laugh again. "Mine?"

I nod. "Yes. I can't go get pancakes with you if I don't know your name."

His lips break out in a wide smile, and the butterflies flutter in my stomach. It's the most perfect smile that ever existed. And it's all for me. *I* made him smile like that. "Jack. And you are?"

Jack. *Ah.* Even his name makes my butterflies dance. *Jack.* I'm pretty sure I just sighed out his name a few times because his eyes crinkle, and he looks even happier than moments before. "My name is Charlotte. Nice to meet you, Jack."

He extends his hand out to shake mine, and I stare down in excitement. God, what that hand could do to me. My eyes grow large, and he laughs again. I'm making a complete fool of myself.

Without waiting for me to shake his hand, he pulls me under his arm and starts walking. "So can I take you for pancakes?"

My eyes light up. Yes, pancakes with Jack. Sounds like the perfect night.

Hours later, after I've eaten all the pancakes a girl could possibly eat and laughed harder than I have in years, I lie in bed with a smile. Ignoring my heavy eyelids, I focus instead on the man who shares my bed. I don't want this night to end. From the moment I met him, it's like the axis in my world shifted.

I, Charlotte Marie Chase, have met my soulmate.

No longer would I be the girl who is dateless on a Friday night—or the dreaded third wheel with Pat and Steph. I am now part of a couple. There will be double dates and wine nights in our future. I'll graduate college and won't have to listen to my grandmother mumble under her breath, "It's great the girl has a degree but what about a man?"

I have one!

Sure, we've only just met, and it's only been a few hours, but I am telling you, this is the *real* thing. I knew it as soon as I laid eyes on his tall six-foot frame. He might be even taller. My black boots gave me a few inches in height, and he was *still* a foot above me.

Blond hair is shaved tightly against his head, but that wasn't something I noticed immediately because he'd been wearing a Red Sox hat at the bar. It wasn't until we went to the diner and he took it off that I finally got a good look at him. His manners are something my grandmother will *love*.

I don't even know how old he is or what he does—I was far more interested in the way he made me laugh than his profession—but I'm sure it's something noble because he just *seems* like that kind of guy. During dinner I got lost in his blue eyes with the golden sparkles in them. I've never seen anything like it—they're not boring brown like mine—and he's got a freckle above his lip. When we curled up in bed, he whispered into my ear that he loves my "big, beautiful, brown eyes" and my face split open in a smile.

He sighs into my ear now. "You still awake?"

"Mm-hmm," I murmur, too tired to even use words.

His arms tighten around my waist. "This has been the most incredible night. Thank you." His voice is deep and husky, with an emotional undercurrent. There is no questioning whether these feelings are real. My butterflies tell me everything I need to know. Even if I couldn't rely on them, I can hear it in his voice—he knows tonight was *it*. The *last* first date either of us will ever go on. I feel like the luckiest person in the world. Most people never meet their soulmate, let alone at twenty-two. No more disastrous first dates. No more dating at all.

His lips brush against my neck, sending a shiver down my spine, and my entire body hums. I wish I had the energy to turn my head and kiss him, but that is something I want to savor— our first kiss. He'd been such a gentleman he hadn't even tried. "I just want to hold you," he said when we entered my dorm.

Grams would be proud.

I drift off to sleep in a love-drunken haze, hopeful for the future and content. I barely feel him shift a pillow closer to me as he slides his arm away, leaving my room and disappearing from my life.

CHAPTER 2

Charlotte
Six Years Later
January

"I swear, if I ever tell you that I think I've met a good guy, smack me. Just right across the face. Lay one on me, because I have the worst taste in men. *Ever.*" My best friend, Steph, stares back at me with an amused smirk on her face. Rude. The least she could do is hide her amusement and laugh about it later. But that's not Steph. Nope. She's going to enjoy this.

"I mean you met him at the grocery store. What did you think this was going to be? A fairy tale?"

"But his eyes," I say, batting my lashes at her. Her smile grows bigger.

"Oh, yes. You and his damn eyes."

They were the first thing I noticed about Ben in the grocery store checkout six months prior when he snuck in front of me while I was reaching for a pack of gum. I *almost* said something, but he only had a few things in his hand. Of course, it was the "under ten" aisle so none of us had much, and I didn't want to cause a scene. And like I said, his eyes were *so* blue. When the clerk announced Ben was the one millionth shopper in the store, and he'd won a hundred-dollar gift card, I couldn't bite my tongue. Fortunately, he took my tongue-lashing in stride and asked me out for a drink. The rest, as they say, is history. Or at least it was until today. Now we're history.

"So, what happened?" Steph asks, walking to the kitchen as I trail behind. On the couch sits her pug, Grover, and he barely looks up as I walk past. Lazy boy. Instinctively, my hand brushes against his soft ears, and I feel emotions start to bubble up from my chest. Swallowing my pride and my incoming tears, I snuggle close to his nose. What is it about dogs that makes everything seem better? Just sitting here, rubbing his soft black ears, my emotions soften, and I start to gain perspective about my entire day.

Steph returns from the kitchen with a box of wine in her hand and two glasses. Plopping them down on the coffee table, she doesn't hesitate to fill them both to the brim before taking a sip of hers.

"You brought out the box for me?" In awe, I finally take a sip and close my eyes as the red wine hits my throat and brings forth the emotions that the dog just suppressed.

"Yeah, I'm not wasting good wine on this conversation. I

can tell we'll be drinking a lot, and that's what she's good for." She pats the box like it's her child, and her chest swells with pride. Steph really likes her wine.

I laugh. "You do realize you just referred to the box of wine as a she?"

Steph doesn't even bat an eye. Her expression lets me know she's over the small talk. But where to start? I didn't begin the day with the intention of breaking up with my boyfriend. *Boyfriend.* Gah, I loved that word. What an idiot I was. Anyway, it wasn't my intention to break up with Ben today. Sure, he'd been grating on my nerves, but that was because he was always around, never giving me any space. That's all I was asking for— some space. But then he dipped his finger into the peanut butter jar and slurped on it. I shudder from the memory.

"I broke up with Ben."

Steph looks at me as if to say, *yeah, and?* We've been friends since the first day of college, and most of the time we finish each other's sentences. Right now, it would be great if she would not make me finish mine.

"Christmas break has just been, ugh, shall we say difficult." Wincing, I think of the last two weeks which I had looked forward to more than usual. Steph and I are both kindergarten teachers at the local elementary school. Ben works in finance and doesn't like kids. That should have been a red flag, but I only just found out that. "You know how Sam was having trouble with his letters?"

Steph's eyes crinkle but she nods. "I'm not sure where we are going with this."

I sigh. Sam is one of my favorite kids. He has two moms which he tells everyone about. It's completely adorable. He loves the color pink, can hit a baseball farther than any of the first graders—something he's never pointed out, but his best friend Cassidy says proudly all the time—and he has a lot of trouble with spelling. Last week he came into class and told me that Chris had called him the E word. My eyes bulged until I realized that I didn't know what the E word was. I sat him down at his desk and asked if he could whisper it—you never know what a kid is going to say, and if it was a bad word, I didn't want the rest of the class learning it too. Very seriously, he raised his eyes to mine and said, "Chris called me an idiot." I did my best not to laugh, and then called his moms and offered to tutor him over Christmas break. I didn't want him falling behind while he had two weeks off. Apparently, this was not the appropriate move. For Ben at least.

I tried to explain to him the importance of kindergarten, as it's a foundational year. "It's ABCs," he replied mockingly. "How hard could it be?" He followed it up with, "This isn't your job. Can't his parents help him?"

What he doesn't get is that I enjoy individual moments with my students more than I enjoy my time with him. Probably a bad sign. But still, I tried to keep him happy. Kept my time with Sam to a minimum and made sure I was available to spend time with Ben. Which, for the record, has been miserable.

Ben works virtually which means for the past two weeks he's been working from my apartment. He said it would give us more time together. Honestly, I wanted to settle on the couch and read a good book, not listen to Ben's condescending tone as he talks to his colleagues on Zoom. He's so loud. And jerky. Also, he looks ridiculous in the kitchen eating a bowl of cereal wearing a full shirt and tie tucked into his boxers—his work attire.

But today was the final straw. I left the house for my daily meeting with Sam. As soon as I arrived, I could tell something was off. The normally happy boy, who would greet me at the door with a big smile and some new toy, was looking rather gloomy. It took me the entire lesson to get him to reveal the source of his sadness—his grandparents were moving to Florida. His grandfather would no longer be picking him up from school. The way he explained that his grandpa was his best friend made me smile. It also brought tears to my eyes. It is something I totally understand because my grams, although always judgmental and quick with her snark, is my best friend too. But dementia is stealing her from me. Not quite the same as moving to Florida because I can still see her whenever I want, but it breaks my heart just the same.

Leaving Sam, I was an emotional basket case. I walked into my apartment hoping to find it empty, wishing for nothing more than to crawl into bed, have a good cry, and then head to Grams's nursing home to hug her tightly. Instead, I found Ben standing in the kitchen, in his boxers, scooping peanut butter out of the container with his finger and sliding it into his mouth.

When Ben saw my tears, he rolled his eyes and asked, "What's wrong now?" His cold stare hit me hard. I had braced myself for his indifference but certainly not his cruelty.

Shivering, I muttered under my breath, "Enough." I stalked into the kitchen and glared at him. "Ben, I need some space. Why don't you go back to your apartment today, and we can see each other over the weekend?"

He looked up surprised, but he didn't react. Instead, he went back to the jar and scooped another blob of peanut butter onto his finger. I watched in horror as he put it in his mouth and slowly sucked on it, making a slurping noise.

Something about the sound set me off. I didn't even want him to come back this weekend. I wanted him out. Gone. I staggered a breath and looked away. "Listen, Ben, perhaps that was a bit abrupt. But I think we should talk. Can you, uh, put the peanut butter down and come sit with me?"

And wash your hands.

He shrugged and put the container down, licking his fingers. Then he walked to the couch without washing his hands. In that moment, I knew I was done. He was a jerk, and he disgusted me. I don't even know what I previously found attractive about him, because in that moment there was nothing.

Definitely not the sight of his saggy boxers, or the doughy white stomach which hung over them. Certainly not the overgrown beard he developed once he stopped going in to the office. But most importantly, it was how he treated me. I wasn't even comfortable in my own skin around him. He needed to go.

"Listen," I started, but he was already looking at his phone. So rather than giving him the nice version, I plowed straight into the direct one. "I would like to break up."

"What? Are you on your period or something?"

I *hate* him. I don't even like him a little. And there was peanut butter in his beard.

"Ben, you need to leave."

He made no move to stand up. "Now," I said with finality. "I'm going to go for a walk. When I get back, I don't expect you to be here. So, uh, it was nice to meet you." I cringed at my choice of words. I've never broken up with someone. I've always been the dumpee, never the dumper. I was not very good at it. *Obviously*.

Finally, the reality of the situation seemed to set in. "Charlie, what are you talking about? Nice to *meet* me? I love you."

Okay, so the first time you tell someone you love them should definitely *not* be when you're being broken up with. Rookie mistake. Also, I hate being called Charlie. Ben knew how much it grated on me when he called me that. "Ben, you don't love me. And I don't love you. We had a good time with each other for a while, but I am no longer interested in pursuing this relationship."

"Well, where do you expect me to go?" he asked incredulously.

"Um, your apartment. Your parents' house. I don't care where you go. You just can't stay here." I flung my arms out in frustration.

His face turned beet red. "But I sublet my apartment because you asked me to move in. And now you're telling me you don't want me here."

I did what? Never happened.

"Wait, you moved into my apartment?" Obviously, this was some sort of misunderstanding. I would have noticed if he had *moved* into my apartment.

Ben walked to the closet and pulled out a suitcase overflowing with clothes. The closet, next to the front door and which used to house my jackets and shoes, was packed with boxes I didn't recognize. *Where are my shoes?*

"Ben, I did not ask you to move in. You *sublet* your apartment?"

He shrugged. "We were spending all of our time together. It made no sense for both of us to pay rent."

Oh, and he just decided he should benefit from the cost savings. How generous of him.

"Well, go to your parents' house then."

This was so not my problem. Mockingly, he replied, "Why don't *you* go to *your* parents' house?"

I mean seriously, what did I ever see in this guy? Just looking at him made me uncomfortable. I told him I'd go to Steph's for a bit so he could pack, and when I got back, I wanted him gone.

After recounting the story to Steph, I look up to meet her amused expression. "You broke up with him because he slurped the peanut butter?"

Glaring at her, I say through my teeth, "*That* is what you got from my story? The man moved into my apartment without me knowing! How am I going to get him out?"

She shakes her head. "Stay here tonight. Pat won't mind. It will all be better in the morning."

"How will it be better? Seriously, Steph, how do I keep meeting these losers?"

Steph taps on her chin as if she's giving this some real thought. "I mean this certainly isn't ideal. But you were never that interested in him anyway. Did you really even *like* him?"

Focusing on the stem of my wine glass, I ignore the tone of her voice. The tone that tells me she knows I already had one foot out the door with this relationship to begin with. The one that says, he wasn't *him* so you're not really that upset. "I *liked* Ben," I say quietly. Although, as I said before, I can't really remember what exactly I liked about him.

Steph puts her hand on mine, showing a softness that she reserves for special occasions. In class she's the one who keeps the kids under control. I'm the one who snuggles the kids close and whispers in their ear after they've done something wrong. My softness played against her tough gal demeanor makes us a great duo. "It's okay to admit that you want more. You deserve more, Charlotte. You just need to believe it."

Defensively, I pull back. "I believe I deserve good things. I just don't believe in that whole love at first sight mumbo jumbo. You meet a nice guy, you date, and you find out if you're compatible. I just seem to have very bad instincts when I pick guys. *Obviously*."

She shakes her head. "You need a spark. You need magic. You need to stop settling and wait for the real thing."

My mind flashes to the only time I ever felt that in my life—the spark. Undeniable chemistry with someone. It was as if my body buzzed simply because of his proximity. Emotion catches in my throat, and I roll my eyes as I squash the memory like a spider you find in the shower. It wasn't hard to forget. We only spent a few hours together and I'd been drunk. I barely remember his face and cannot for the life of me remember his name. Not that I've tried to remember or anything. "That stuff's not real, Steph. A dependable man that shows up? Now that's something to swoon over. But butterflies—magic when you kiss—that's the stuff of fairy tales."

"I can't help but think that the old Charlotte used to feel differently. That one perfect night ruined you. You need to let go of *him* and start believing in that spark again. You'll find someone that makes you feel that way, I promise."

I shake my head of the memories of that one perfect night, of the man who has only been a recurring character in my dreams, the guy I measure everyone else against, and the one who let me down just like the rest of them. With determination in my voice, I say, "Nope. I can't do this again. I'm done with men. Done with dating. Done with boyfriends. Done with it all!"

CHAPTER 3

Jack
April

"How did the date go?" Pat asks as he takes a swig of his beer, a smirk already pulling at his lips.

I consider throwing the basketball currently in my hand at his head but instead toss it into the air, swoosh, directly into the basket. His appreciation for my backwards shot is more rewarding than hurting him. "I blocked her phone number while we were on the Zoom call."

He laughs. "Brutal."

"You want to know what's brutal? Listening to her drone on about her kids the entire time and then having her introduce them at the end of the call. They were cats! She called her *cat* her daughter. *Mikayla* is such a good eater. *Mikayla* loves to dance with me in the kitchen. *Mikayla* had a hard time when her dad left, but now she's adjusting." I wish I was exaggerating, but Mikayla's "mom" had not even been the worst of the women I "dated" recently.

Hysterical, Pat spits out his beer and laughs loudly. "Where do you find these chicks?"

It's a valid question. "Not everyone is as lucky as you."

He shrugs his shoulders. "It can't possibly be that hard to meet someone normal. You dated plenty of girls in high school. Perhaps you're just too picky."

This time I don't hold back. I throw the basketball directly at his chest, and he falls backwards but holds his beer up like a trophy, saving it from spilling. "Ha! Keep it up and I'm gonna leave you alone again."

A cruel threat. I'd been working nonstop to fix up my house. I bought a fixer-upper, and Pat avoids coming over so that I don't rope him into any of my projects. This was probably a mistake—buying a house—or at least buying a house in *this* town. Being back in the town that held so many memories was almost as bad as being overseas. I could practically see my best friends and me riding our bikes up and down the street, my sister trailing behind us, as we set off to explore Colt State Park when we were ten. Or meeting up for lunch at Bristol House of Pizza. Bristol held every good memory in my life, and unfortunately now it also holds their ghosts.

My mind is constantly playing tricks on me. I'd even seen Charlotte. Or at least I imagined I did. A girl runs through my neighborhood every day, and I swear before she turns the corner onto my street the hair on the back of my neck rises, an electrical current letting me know she's coming. I watch her and imagine it's Charlotte. Impossible, of course, since she doesn't live here. Clearly, I'm losing it.

"I need to get out of this house. I'm going stir-crazy." Thank God, I still have work. And flying. Although, I miss going for drinks with the guys after training. There is nothing better than spending the afternoon in a jet, the engine and the wind drowning out all your thoughts, followed by a cold beer. Now all I do is come home to my own thoughts and this mess of a house. At least I have my dog to keep me company.

"I mean, this can't take much longer," Pat offers.

Right, that's what I said when I bought the place. But it was taking so much time. "I hope you're right, man. Doesn't Steph have any friends she could set me up with?" Pat chokes on his beer, laughing again. It is a bit desperate. *But desperate times.* "Seriously, you don't understand how lonely I've been. I never thought I'd say this, but I *need* a girlfriend."

"Jack, buddy, now is *not* the time for a girlfriend. This is how you get a stage-five clinger. She'll realize you have this beautiful house and think she can be the Joanna Gaines to your Chip. Then she'll move in before you even realize it has happened." He shakes his head.

"Sounds like you're speaking from experience." Pat couldn't possibly be talking about Steph. She is the least demanding woman I know. Steph is happy to sit by herself and read a book.

And she can play cards and throw back a beer with the guys. Pat literally has the best of both worlds.

"Not me, Steph's friend. Get this—she started dating a guy, and he moved into her apartment. *Without* telling her. She found out when she broke up with him and he refused to leave. She's staying at our house. So, believe me, you don't want a girlfriend."

Shit, that sounds awful. And like something that would happen to me. The ex-boyfriend sounds like he'd be perfect for Mikayla's mom.

But now I'm even more jealous of Pat. He's got *two* people to live with. "She hot?"

Pat smiles and nods. "You didn't hear that from me though. Strange how you guys never met. Although, with you being gone for so long..." he trails off.

That's the thing about being in the service. No one wants to talk about the reality of what happens when you're in it. I get it. I don't want to talk about it either. My reasons for staying away from this town for so long haunt me every day. I just want to be a typical thirty-two-year-old man, worried about meeting a girl, settling down, enjoying Saturdays at the park with my chocolate lab, my girl, and two kids. But the longer I'm in this town the more I think that is nothing but a pipe dream. Besides, at this point, I don't even know how long I plan to stay in this location, let alone find enough time to meet someone to settle down with.

Pat continues talking, even though I've essentially tuned him out. "Anyway, I'm pretty sure you'd say she talks too much.

And she does." He laughs at his own joke.

"Picture?"

Pat pulls out his phone, opens Facebook, and places her picture in my hand. Golden-brown hair and a wide smile accentuated by a dimple pulls at my memory. *Charlotte*. My one perfect night.

Wait…Pat knows Charlotte? How? And does that mean she's been in town all along? This feeling I keep having that she's here, the image of her running down the street, the force I feel pulling me toward her—is it possible it was actually her? That she wasn't another ghost?

She's really here.

Working hard to keep my emotions in check, I feign ignorance. "She's cute. You say she talks too much, but I'm sure I could tune her out." I wink.

Pat shakes his head. "Not gonna happen. Steph swore off introducing you to any more of her friends after that disaster with Astrid."

Rolling my eyes and running my hand behind my neck, I groan. That was not my fault. "Talk about a stage-five clinger." I throw the basketball again, feeling a rush of excitement when it sinks through the net. Three-point shot. I've already decided I'll be checking out Charlotte's profile when he leaves. Suddenly, I can't wait for him to go. "Damn, it's cold out here."

"Yeah, I gotta get home. I promised Steph and Charlotte I'd pick up wings from The Bean."

My stomach growls just thinking about food. I consider begging him to let me join him, but my phone rings before I have the chance. I wave him off as I pick up.

"Hello, sir," I say, taking in the familiar number as a pit settles in my stomach. Will I ever not feel anxious when I see his number?

"Jack, buddy, how are you doing?"

I stare at the unfinished front steps and imagine the disaster of a kitchen remodel waiting for me inside and shake my head. "Never been better. What can I do for you?"

"I was wondering if you've given any more thought to my offer?"

Not really, I want to respond immediately. Although, in all honesty, that would be a lie. Richard had called once a month for the last six months asking if I'd changed my mind. Was I ready to acknowledge that this life wasn't for me and join him in Las Vegas to train against Air Force pilots? A dream job for many people, especially someone like me who loves nothing more than sitting in the cockpit of a jet going five hundred knots day after day. "I'm not ready to give up yet."

I hear him grunt on the other side of the phone. "When are you going to realize that this is where you belong? Jack, this is flying against the elite of the elite. You'd get more flight hours than you'll ever have living in Rhode Island."

Of course, he's right. Richard operates a private company that helps the Air Force prepare for combat. One of the biggest gripes of all men in the Air Force is that they never get enough time in the air. In this contractor job, I could practically live in the sky. But I'm not sure I'm ready to be a civilian again. Besides, Vegas reminds me too much of the desert. Until I make a decision on what I want to do for a full-time job, I'm working with the National Guard in Westfield, Massachusetts and I still get to fly F-15s once a month. And, if I'm honest, after Pat just all but confirmed that I'm not going crazy—that Charlotte is *here*—there is no way I can give up a second chance to have something real with the girl I've never forgotten. "I've got to see this through, Richard. But I appreciate the call."

"Of course. When you change your mind, I'll be here waiting. There's more to life than your sleepy little town of Bristol, Rhode Island."

Chuckling, I reply, "So you keep telling me. Bye, Richard." I'd seen more of the world over the last decade than most my age. There was absolutely life outside of this town, but a life with Charlotte in Bristol, now that is something I would like to explore. Before I can do that, though, I need to do my background work. I screwed up the first time we met. I do not intend on missing my chance with Charlotte again.

CHAPTER 4

Charlotte
May

It's May. *May*! I feel like I'm living in *Groundhog Day*. I *am* Bill Murray. Every morning I wake up, positive I will be in my bed and this entire miserable existence will be a complete dream, only to roll over and find I'm sleeping next to Grover.

At least it's not Ben.

While Grover is adorable and smells far better than Ben, sleeping next to a dog is less than ideal. Okay, I'm being dramatic. But seeing how Ben kicked me out of my apartment, I don't have any calm left.

Ben left my clothes on the stoop and refused to let me in. He changed the freaking locks. I called the police, hoping they'd help me fix the disaster. "I'm sorry, ma'am, but he says he lives here, and you can't evict him without going to court."

Ma'am! Lives here! Evict! The entire sentence was a slap in the face of my entire existence. I am so not a ma'am—I'm only twenty-eight—and he doesn't live there!

It was hopeless though. There was nothing I could say. Apparently, he'd added his name to the lease by lying to the landlord, saying that he was my fiancé. I had no interest in going to court and having to hire an attorney. Absolutely not. The apartment wasn't that great. And honestly, the idea of returning to an empty apartment was depressing. Fortunately, my best friend had an empty room for me. So now I am sleeping with Grover and crowding Steph and Pat's marriage. It's kind of a mess.

I roll out of bed, kissing him on the snout, and up I go. "Come on, buddy, we can't stay in bed all day, even if there is *nothing* to do."

He raises his eyes, telling me to suit myself, he ain't moving. "Fine. Be lazy. But you're gonna miss out on the *bacon*," I sing in his ear as I rub the soft velvety blackness between my fingers. He bounces up and is out the door before I can react.

I grab my laptop to follow him down the steps slowly, catching myself on the top step, which is shorter than the rest, and almost stumble forward. "Watch the step!" Steph yells from downstairs.

Pat grumbles in his bedroom. I *need* to give them back their privacy.

"Coffee?" she offers, already handing me a steaming cup which is topped with frothed sweet cream and sprinkled with cinnamon, just how I like it. Why can't I find a man like Steph? She's the best date I never had.

"You're a peach." I offer her a smile and raise the cup to my lips to sip it slowly. Grover is already at my feet, wagging his tail in excitement. "I promised him bacon."

Laughing, Steph pads over to the refrigerator and pulls out the breakfast products. "So, what's on your agenda today? Going to visit your grandmother?"

It's Saturday. I have no plans. Normally, I spend my Saturday afternoons at my grandmother's nursing home. After she sold her house I had her moved to a nursing home close to me so I could visit her weekly. Unfortunately, they are on lockdown right now due to the flu. Same thing happened in the winter. All I could do was go to her window and wave. Sometimes, I draw pictures on the window with my breath. Little angels or snowmen, and for Christmas I even did a Santa. It's an exciting time to be alive. Now that the weather is nice, though, we normally sit and play cards or just walk around the property. It's a way to make sure she's stretching her legs. And sometimes I'm lucky enough that she mistakes me for her high school best friend and shares hysterical stories of her younger years.

Shaking my head, I reply, "No, they are on lockdown again."

Steph bites her lip. She and Pat normally spend Saturdays by themselves. I have to do *something*. Pat is going to kill me if I don't give them time alone, and I don't exactly blame him.

Blurting out the first thing that enters my mind, I say, "I've got a date."

This is a complete lie. I have no interest in dating. Or men.

It's been five months of no dating, and I can't say I miss it. If I had my way, I'd curl up in bed with Grover and a good book for the day.

Steph turns around with innuendo in her eyes. I'm not sure if she's thinking about me or the fact that she'll get to run around the house naked with her husband. It's probably the latter. "Spill."

"Oh, you know, online dating. I found someone really promising."

Shoot, now I'll need to create a profile, find someone to swipe right on—is that even the right terminology?—and shave my legs. I'm already exhausted.

"Pull him up." Steph walks over and motions to my computer. I freeze. Of course, she wants to see the guy. Opening the computer, I frantically search dating sites while she makes breakfast.

Dan is the first profile I see. Big blue eyes, blond spikey hair, and a huge smile. His arm is wrapped around a large Doberman. He likes dogs! Grover looks up at me with approval. "I think this could be a good one," I whisper to him. I click on his profile and start reading.

Life is like a penis. Simple, relaxed, and hanging freely. Then women make it hard.

I slam the computer shut. "I don't want to jinx it. I'll show you after my date."

Pat's ears perk up as he enters the kitchen. "Did I hear you say you've got a date?"

I can't stop the lies. They just keep pouring from my mouth. "Two! One for lunch and one for dinner. Maybe I can even fit one in midafternoon."

Steph eyes me oddly, as if she knows I'm full of it. Not Pat though—he's oblivious, looking at his wife like she's a snack. Which she is, by the way. With her long brown hair, brilliant blue eyes, and freckles, she's as beautiful as her personality.

"I'm gonna take my coffee to my room and read up on my dates." I nod at them both as I walk out of the kitchen, almost sprinting up the stairs, catching myself as I reach the top so I don't spill my coffee on that damn step again.

The problem is I'm not a liar. Not even a good little white liar. I am going to have to set up a stupid profile and go on dates because I told them I would. I roll my eyes and whip open the computer, determined to find someone worthy of a few hours.

Closing out of Dan's profile, my face scrunches at the sight of his words again. They can't *all* be this bad, right?

The next guy I click on looks more promising. He has a job. And while there is no dog in the picture, he does look very athletic, and I'm already imagining what it would feel like to have those calves next to mine. I have a thing for men's calves. Strange, I know.

Before I can swipe or click or do whatever I'm supposed to do, I need a profile picture. And a biography. I consider snapping a selfie and then remember the picture from my cousin's wedding last year where my breasts were on point, perky and sitting pretty in a low-cut black halter dress propped up from an amazing push-up bra. I plop the picture into my profile and consider witty commentary to make me seem interesting.

Teacher and lover of kids.

Er. That doesn't sound right. I scrunch my nose and rub my hand against my chin. *Hmm.* Should I start with my profession? That's not all I am. Surely, there is something more interesting about me than that…right?

I've got nothing. Not a single fact. I haven't won any big awards. No great talents to speak of. I was the quiet girl who read in high school. I was *really* good at beer pong in college. Is that a talent? I mean, my boyfriend at the time was always very impressed—no, definitely *not* a talent. I love kids. And dogs. I know a lot of useless facts. Like did you know pogonophobia is a fear of beards? I learned that one after Ben. I can recite almost every line from *The Office*. And I'm a teacher.

This is really depressing. I leave the biography blank and hit publish. Hopefully, my name and the slutty dress does the trick because my personality is evidently desperately lacking.

The dress worked! Calves messaged me and now we're chatting.

"So where do you live?"

"Rhode Island, how about you?" I respond, already feeling like my luck is turning. Thumb in my mouth, I bite on it while I wait for his response. I hope he lives close. Perhaps we'll meet and immediately know it's right. Then I'll live happily ever after

with Calves by my side, instead of Grover.

His message pops up. *"Pity your not here in sexy underwear spooning me."*

I slam the computer shut again. He doesn't even know how to use the proper version of *you're*. We didn't make it through pleasantries, and he already ruined it. *Ugh.*

I officially give up. I'll just take Grover to the park for some fresh air. I'll sit in my car for a few hours and pretend to be on a date. I can read a book in Colt State Park, stare at the ocean, and look at the stars. "You'll definitely be a better date than him," I whisper to Grover. He looks up at me with big droopy brown eyes as if he understands, and then licks me, affirming my belief he most definitely is better than every man on this site.

Grabbing Grover's leash, I holler to Steph that we'll be back, and I'm pretty sure I hear Pat already running her up the stairs and into the bedroom. Oh, to be in love.

Traveling the main road in our town, I get lost in the beauty. Although I've lived here since I finished college, it never gets old. With large colonials lining each side of the road, sailboats floating in the bay, and lobster boats idling with their morning catch, Bristol, Rhode Island is quintessential New England and as quaint as they come. Also, if I fail to mention that it's the most patriotic town in the country, they will probably disown me. Hosting the longest running Fourth of July parade in the good ol' USA, this town bleeds red, white, and blue. And in case you weren't aware, the town will make sure you know it. The main street, also known as Hope Street, is adorned with a red, white, and blue line separating each side of the road, instead of yellow. They repaint it yearly, and little flags are placed up and down the street in preparation for all the festivities. The Fourth of July here starts in June, although if I'm honest it never really ends—even during Christmas you're bound to find Americana décor.

Turning off our charming Hope Street, I make a left onto the road leading to Colt State Park. Grover leans up against the window, ready to play at his favorite destination. The road opens, and the houses are replaced by trees that shoulder together and reach across the road as if holding each other up. Glistening blue water in every direction leaves me grateful to live in such a beautiful area.

As I pull into a parking space, Grover looks at me excitedly. "Okay, buddy. Let's get some fresh air." I open the door, and he hops out, wagging his tiny pinwheel tail in eagerness.

The weather is a cool fifty-five degrees, but the sun is shining, and in New England a sunny spring day means only one thing—a crowded park. There are kids, dogs, and people in every direction. "Sorry, Grover, it looks like you're going to have to stay on the leash." He looks a bit affronted, but I give him as much slack as I can, and he takes off to the open field where we normally set him free.

Fortunately, his favorite spot only has one other person, but with that person is a large chocolate Labrador—not an appropriate companion for the small pug. As if taking my dare, Grover bounds toward the field, not fearing the large dog at all. Before he can go too far, I pull him close, lean down, and rub his head. We both watch as the man pulls his arm back to throw a tennis ball. The muscles in his back flex as he releases, and the ball flies toward the trees. Unlike me, Grover isn't interested in the man and his back muscles—he's got his eye on the ball and takes off in that direction, pulling me up from my stooped position. Before I can catch myself, I fall forward onto my face in the cold grass, and Grover's leash slips from my grasp.

I watch from the ground as Grover runs toward the Labrador who has already retrieved the ball and is bounding back to his owner. "He's friendly," I shout as I stumble to my feet and begin my chase. By the time I reach them, the man is petting Grover, and his dog is making his way over to me. "Hi, buddy." I pat his head, and he covers my hand in kisses.

With his Red Sox hat on, the man's eyes are shaded. Facial hair covers his lower face. Surprisingly, I'm not as affronted by it as I was by Ben's beard. Maybe I don't suffer from pogonophobia after all. "Charlie there is friendly too. Maybe a little *too* friendly," he says with a laugh as his dog covers me in kisses.

"Thanks for grabbing him for me." I reach out to take

Grover's leash, and when our fingers touch, electricity shocks me, scorching my finger, searing my heart, and singeing my body into submission. I'd be surprised if it hasn't left a mark. I whip my hand back in surprise. Our eyes meet, and for a moment I'm left speechless. He felt it too. Stuck in an alternate universe where it is just me and this man, the crowded park blurs, and the children's laughter and screams become white noise. The thump, thump, thump of my heart burns my ears. I swear I met him in another life. His blue eyes with golden starbursts of light are so familiar. I just don't know why.

Grover pulls on the leash, breaking the spell, but the man's eyes remain on mine. Uncomfortable, I lift my hand in a wave and awkwardly walk off. "Alright, Grover," I mutter under my breath, "we've had enough excitement in this park. Let's get lunch."

We arrive downtown only a few minutes later. The buildings nestle into one another like a Thomas Kinkade painting. I order myself a sandwich from the Wrap Shack and sit down on the sidewalk with Grover, waiting for them to call that it's ready.

My mind reels from the interaction in the park, and my heart pounds against my chest. I've only had that feeling once before. That electric connection with someone. It was years ago. I shake my mind of that night. If I've learned anything, it's that I can't trust these feelings. For years I've taught my students about the cause of lightning. That spark I felt is explained by science, nothing else. It's static current. When a positive atom meets a negative atom it will always release energy in the form of a spark, whether it be through an electric shock or a zap of lightning hitting the ground.

It's science, that's all. I stare at my finger and am astonished that there isn't an actual black mark there. I was almost sure I'd actually been burned.

A flyer on the travel agency window next to the restaurant catches my attention, and I shake away the swirling thoughts to focus on the intriguing words.

Escape and Travel to the Azores for the Summer.

The picture below it shows a large green mountain and a house which hangs arrogantly over the sea. *The Azores*. It sounds exotic. And it certainly looks it. I jump up to take a closer look.

Why does the Azores sound so familiar?

"If you could visit anywhere, where would you go?" I asked him, staring into those beautiful blue eyes, already hanging on his every word.

"The Azores. If I could go anywhere, hands down that's where I would go."

My heart skips a beat remembering Mr. Perfect's words. *Hmm.* The Azores. Sounds interesting. And obviously my interest in the place has nothing to do with *him*. It has everything to do with me. People who go to the Azores aren't boring—they don't date losers, they take risks, and they live exciting lives. Backpacking around Europe, traveling to faraway lands. Now that is something that would reset my stupid mind. Plus, I'd finally have something to write in my biography.

Traveled to the Azores. Swam in a cave. Jumped off a cliff. Surfed in the Mediterranean.

Oh, according to the flier it's in the middle of the Atlantic Ocean. Well, I don't surf anyway so that doesn't matter. By the time the waitress has called my name, and the chicken wrap is steaming in my hand, I have already made my decision—I am going to the Azores.

"What do you mean you're going to the Azores?" Steph stares at me incredulously after I've shared my grand summer plans. Even better, school is out in just a few more weeks so I can go soon.

Pat jumps in. "I think it's great!" Steph rolls her eyes at him, and I giggle. I know he is just saying it because I'll be out of their hair for a few weeks, but I appreciate the support.

"It is a *terrible* idea." Steph glares at her husband. He gives her a stiff upper lip and doesn't budge.

But this isn't their fight—it's mine. "It is a great idea, Steph. I have the time off. There is nothing to do here, the Azores look beautiful, and I *need* this."

She crosses her arms, ready to challenge me. "Fine. Pull up a map and show me where they are. If you're even in the right corner of the world, I will shut my mouth."

I bite my lip and make a face that says, *well, obviously, I can do that*. Even though I rely on GPS to get everywhere and never use maps. I'm not sure how she expects me to find a country I've never heard of in the middle of the ocean. Is it even viewable on a map? I think this a trick question.

Pat sees my struggle and hands me his phone. He places his thumb in the corner near Spain. *Ohhh, that's where it is.* I squint closely but can't find any islands in the area.

Steph pounces at my hesitation. "See, I told you. You are not going to the middle of the ocean when you can't even find the Azores while safely sitting in our house. How would you get around? Did you even consider they don't speak English?"

Steph appears very sure of herself. This only makes me more determined. And what does she mean they don't speak English? They definitely speak English. Right?

Pat once again rescues me. "Steph, stop trying to scare her. Half of Bristol is Portuguese, and they *all* speak English."

Ha! Vindicated!

The honk of a truck outside draws their attention. Saved by the honk! A rusted green truck, which appears almost teal from the obvious wear and tear of the sun, is idling outside the house. A man with a baseball cap sits in the front, and leaning across him is a chocolate Lab with his head out the window.

My heart races, and my hands grow clammy. I think it's the guy from the park. "Who's that?"

"Oh, that's Pat's friend Jack. Have fun, honey." Steph

offers her lips to Pat for a kiss while I turn crimson from their interaction. I have no idea why. I've been living with them for over five months, and obviously, they've kissed during that time. My body is acting strange.

"Jack." I whisper his name on my lips. A wave of clarity rushes through me but then it's gone. A moment of déjà vu, where I'm grasping through the water trying to locate what I've lost, but it's just too far out of reach in my mind. Why does that name stir these feelings? *Or that man.* I can barely even see his face.

Pat hops into the truck, and I move closer to the bay window, staring intently into the truck. *He's staring back.* Jack doesn't even look over at Pat. His eyes remain in my direction. I think he's the man from the park. I'm almost positive. I'm drawn to him, and I can feel in his gaze he feels it as well.

"Charlotte!" Steph waves her hand in front of my face. The man looks away, turning his attention to Pat, and I turn my eyes back to Steph. The spell is broken.

"Huh?" I try.

Steph pulls me by my arm over to the couch. "I've been saying your name over and over. Sometimes you're a space cadet."

The air returns to my lungs, the moment between myself and the stranger over. Maybe it never even happened. Just another figment of my imagination.

Or science. This strange connection with this man is all just crazy science.

"So, show me your profile on this dating website." Steph

pulls out her computer and hands it to me.

I stare back with disinterest. After my two interactions on that site, I can't possibly try again. "I think I'm over it."

Her lips purse, and she taps her foot against the floor. Just like my mother. She'll make an excellent one someday, but right now it just feels condescending. Probably because she's right, and she *knows* I lied about dating. "Charlotte Marie, you need to stop this."

I meet her eyes, trying to give her a cool stare that says *I have no idea what you're talking about*, but I think I'm failing because she definitely knows I do. "Stop what?" I ask innocently enough.

She sighs loudly. "Comparing everyone to the damn perfect man you made up in your head. There are good guys out there. You just need to give them a chance."

I huff, roll my eyes, and look away. "I didn't make him up," I mutter quietly.

"Then he isn't perfect. What man spends *'one perfect night'* with you and then disappears without a trace? Certainly not a good one."

When Steph puts it like that, I can't argue with her. But I still can't stop comparing every man I meet to him. But *this* wasn't about *that*. The men on the dating site were awful. I didn't even compare them to *him*. Okay, well maybe I did with Calves, because *his* calves were perfect. I just wish I could remember his name. Or his face. I have spent too many nights searching the faces of strangers in bars, hoping and praying I will see him again. And hoping I will recognize him if I do. Stupid alcohol left the entire night a bit fuzzy.

"Honestly, I'll show you the profiles—the men were awful—but I'd rather just look up the Azores and have you help me figure out my trip instead." I raise my eyes to her, begging to change the subject.

My scheme works, or maybe my face just appears so pathetic that she takes pity on me. "Fine. But if you're going to another country, you need to find someone who speaks the language to go with you. And you have to agree to make it someone of the opposite sex." Her tone tells me this is not up for discussion. Truthfully, I don't hate the idea. I wasn't crazy about going alone anyway. Although, finding someone willing to travel with a stranger will not be easy.

I glare at her. "Why does it have to be a man? Maybe I can meet a new friend?"

"No. You need a fling. You need to date. You need to get over the 'perfect man.' And if you won't do it here, and you're set on traveling to the Azores, then maybe you should at least try finding a man to go with you."

I don't even argue with her because it would be useless. I don't care if I travel with a male or a female, but if agreeing to her silly scheme gets her to focus on planning my trip, I'm all ears. "How am I supposed to find a man who wants to travel with me?"

"Is there, like, a travel website that matches people like

dating ones?"

I scrunch up my nose at her suggestion. None of the men I'd seen had given me any faith the Internet could help me find a companion, whether it be a boyfriend or just for travel. "Er, I have no idea. But seriously, you don't understand what it's like on the interwebs—it's scary."

"That's because you didn't have my help. I have an excellent eye. I picked Pat, remember." She smiles proudly. They are couple goals. God, I love them so much. He gets on her nerves, and she drives him up a wall, but even now when she talks about him, her voice changes into the same light tone she had back in college when she first told me she thought she'd met *the one*. Although, she'll kill me if I ever point that out.

I sigh. She's right. I need to stop comparing everyone to Mr. Perfect and focus on the future. "Fine. Let's grab some wine, and you can help me find my Jim!"

Steph lets out a loud laugh. She has a high-pitched obnoxious one that is such a huge part of her personality. Pat and I continually try one-upping each other to get her to make that glorious sound. "He's not even that hot! Why do you love him?"

I stare at her incredulously. How dare she insult Jim Halpert? "Take it back!"

Steph laughs harder now. "No. Seriously, you compare everyone to the mystery man from six years ago and Jim Halpert—a fictional TV character. You do realize no one is going to compare to these figments of your imagination. And like I said before, Jim Halpert is not even hot…he's *dorky*."

My mind tries hard to wrap itself around her horrible comments. Jim and Pam are like friends to me. Yes, I know they are fictional television characters—I'm not delusional. But through the years while I stumbled through one bad relationship after another, Pam and Jim made me laugh, smile, and swoon. They make me believe one day I will find someone who I can laugh with—a friend who will eventually become something more. It makes me believe plain girls like Pam—*good girls*—eventually get what they deserve.

Suddenly, I know how to win this fight. John Krasinski is hot, and I'll prove it to her. With a devilish smile, I say, "Have you ever seen Jack Ryan?"

Steph rolls her eyes. "I never said John Krasinski wasn't hot; I said Jim Halpert wasn't."

I shake my head. One man can have it all. Hot, funny, and kind. I'm not asking too much, am I?

CHAPTER 5

Jack

The house was finally coming together, and I gave myself permission to grab a beer with Pat and just relax. Also, I may have been interested in finding out how his roommate situation was going. "So, how's it going with Steph's friend living with you?" Making sure not to say her name, or sound too interested, I glance out the window and act as nonchalant as possible. I couldn't believe it when I saw her this afternoon at the park. Grover ran up to me like he always does when Pat brings him to play with Charlie. They are a funny set of friends, the big chocolate Lab of mine who runs circles around the small pug.

I knew it was her immediately. I wasn't sure what it would be like to finally see her again, but I certainly didn't expect to be struck by fucking lightning when I did. Probably should have known better. If anything, it confirmed my initial suspicion that what we had that night was real. She left me completely tongue-tied.

Mercifully, Pat is oblivious to my interest in his roommate. "Oh, Charlotte. She's fine. Can't complain. *Too much*."

The simple answers are pretty standard for Pat. He never expresses too many complicated thoughts. I try again, aiming to keep it light. "Any chance she'll be going back to her apartment?"

Pat laughs now. "Yeah, I don't think so. Although, she's been going on dates, so maybe she can steal one of those guys' apartments soon." He laughs louder at his own joke, and I join in. Internally though, I'm squirming.

Charlotte is *dating*.

I'd been trying to figure out a way to reach out to her, hoping for the perfect moment, but apparently, she was already dating. Of course, the gods, or whatever you believe in, had placed her right in front of me that afternoon, offering me my perfect moment, and I just stood there like an idiot. I try to sound cool, hoping my voice doesn't crack. "Oh, really? Has she met anyone good?"

Pat finally seems to realize something is amiss. He shifts his eyebrow up and shrugs. "No one who compares to the perfect leprechaun."

My nervousness forces out a loud laugh, the description of some mystical creature from Pat's mouth a bit too much to handle. "The perfect what?"

"Oh, man, listen to this story. In college, Charlotte had this '*one perfect night*'—St. Patrick's Day. She got way too drunk and got lost at the bar after the parade. Steph and I couldn't find her anywhere. Some guy helped bring her back to campus. But not before they spent the night talking, and he was '*everything*' she has ever wanted." Pat rolls his eyes as he puts the words in air quotes. "He brought her back to her dorm, and she fell asleep. When she woke up, he was gone."

I clear my throat. "Did she ever look him up? I'm sure he left his number."

I didn't. But I definitely should have.

"No, and she was so drunk she didn't even remember his name. She could barely describe him. Other than that he was perfect and had the most amazing eyes. For years she's been obsessed with the damn guy. Honestly, I feel bad for the ex-boyfriend, Ben. He never stood a chance. She compares every guy to some made-up fantasy."

Pat has no idea the effect this information has on me. And how could he? I'd never told him about that night. I was too young and naïve to understand how that type of lightning doesn't strike twice. Now I'm alone, and it's no one's fault but my own. Worse than that, she's alone because, like me, she remembers what magic feels like.

I can't even tell him now. He'll tell Steph, and she'll immediately tell Charlotte and then I'll never get a shot with her. I need a damn plan, and I don't have one.

I change the subject for the time being and push Charlotte from my mind. But now that he's brought up that night, I can almost feel her warm body snuggled against me.

After the parade we stopped at a diner. She ordered a *stack* of pancakes which she proceeded to cover in whipped cream and strawberries and ate ravenously. It was a welcome sight compared to the girls who would order a salad and not eat even three bites of their meal. If a guy is taking you on a date, he wants to see you eat the food he pays for, not twirl your fork in it.

Her observations on everything in life were hysterical. Charlotte couldn't keep a single thought to herself. She talked the entire night.

I remember there was a girl at the table next to ours droning on about her workouts to the poor shmuck she was with. The guy looked like he was going to fall asleep at the table. In his defense, it *was* after midnight. Charlotte looked at me with a gleam in her eye and started on a tirade about exercising. "Do you ever notice how everyone wants to tell you how often they work out? You'll never have that problem with me. It's a rarity that I'm caught at the gym. The last time I was there, probably over a year ago, I tried to compete with the person next to me on the treadmill. Of course, it ended in disaster. I glanced over at the girl's speed—six and a half and mine was only at four—and she was barely breaking a sweat. She was the same size as me, so I thought 'I could totally do that.' So, I jumped to the side, turned the treadmill up just as high as hers, and on the first step, my legs wobbled, threatening to snap, and then they flipped out from underneath me, causing my entire body to ricochet off the treadmill and onto the floor, landing in front of the hot gym instructor I had a crush on. Don't worry—it didn't hurt too much, just my pride. And yes, that's a true story. Even better, the girl next to me, the one running seamlessly, hopped off the treadmill without so much as a skip, helped me up, and then kissed the instructor. As it turns out, the girl and the hot gym instructor were dating, and I later heard he was so touched by the way she 'came to my rescue' that he proposed to her, like, the next week, so I guess my faceplant was good for something. Long story short, no one wants to hear workout stories unless you fall down and smack your face."

I mean, she wasn't wrong.

Then as I walked her home through the park, we saw a family of ducks. "Do you think they are all practicing their Instagram faces?" She pursed her lips like my little sister would for selfies, and I laughed out loud. I also had this overwhelming urge to kiss her. But I didn't.

She was obsessed with *The Office*. I'd never watched it before, but after that night I would watch re-runs and laugh out loud, wishing I could call her up and talk to her about the ridiculous things Michael Scott said.

I never kissed her, though, afraid that once I did, I wouldn't be able to leave. The magnetic pull between our bodies was almost impossible to combat. The fight just about went out of me when she walked out of the bathroom in her short shorts and Red Sox T-shirt, ready for bed. I still remember the way the shorts hiked up as she walked past me, giving me a preview of the perfectly formed peach below.

"Take off your pants," she directed without flinching. My eyes grew wide, and I stared at her. She took in my obvious surprise and laughed. "You can't sleep in jeans. I promise I don't bite."

We lay next to each other for hours. I didn't want to miss a moment of her talking. She pushed her body against mine, and I wrapped my arms around hers, holding her close. In any other world, it would have been the beginning of something real. But I was on leave, and my time was not my own. I belonged to the government and my life was too complicated for Charlotte. I knew I would just take her down with me if I was selfish enough to stay. So, when she finally drifted off to sleep, midsentence, I allowed myself five more minutes of inhaling her scent, a coconut vanilla mixture that reminded me of birthday cake, and kissed the nape of her neck before pulling away and quietly leaving.

"Dude, where are you?" Pat stares at me, waving his hand in front of my face.

I shake my head and dislodge the memories, trying hard to focus. "Sorry, work on the house has been crazy. I just remembered something I have to do later and was trying to mentally calendar it in. I need a vacation."

Pat nods. "Don't we all. Charlotte got a crazy idea. She wants to go to the Azores this summer. There is some crazy special the travel agency is promoting. I wish I could get Steph to agree to go. We could all use a break from the monotony."

The Azores? Is it possible she remembered me talking about it? I'm probably reading too much into this. No matter what Pat says, I'm sure she doesn't remember everything about that night. Not like I do. But I can't hide my interest. "By herself?"

"Steph? No, I don't want her to go by herself. With *me*."

Like I said, he's oblivious. "You said Charlotte is planning to go. I'm saying, is she going by herself?" I try to keep the interest in my voice down, but the squeak is not making it easy. I'm like Ross in the *Friends* episode where he keeps saying "I'm fine" in a high-pitched voice.

Pat eyes me warily and pulls on his neck. "You seem awfully interested in Steph's friend. Do you want me to introduce you?" He sighs now, clearly not excited by the prospect.

I wave my hands in front of me and laugh. "No, just trying to follow your conversation. You said she talks too much. I think I'll pass."

Apparently, I'm convincing enough. "Yeah, she was talking about going by herself. But Steph will never allow that. She's going on about how Charlotte needs to find someone who speaks Portuguese and who can read a map, which I mean, aren't terrible points. Charlotte can be a little ditzy if you know what I mean. She would probably have trouble navigating a different country. But she's an adult, and she's in my house. I could definitely use two weeks alone with my wife." He gives me a knowing smile, and I laugh.

"Yes. Sounds like she could use a guide. So, what kind of

wings do you want?" I change the subject, but in my mind I'm already trying to figure out how I can be that guy for her. Is it possible for lightning to strike twice without Charlotte realizing I am also the guy who disappeared without a trace?

CHAPTER 6

Charlotte

We've been at it for hours. Plugging in what I'm looking for in a travel companion.

1. Must speak Portuguese (obviously);

2. Can read a map (Steph's suggestion);

3. Must pay for own trip. (I'm a teacher, I'm not paying for anyone); and,

4. No funny business. No kissing, no romance, no sex. (Okay, I may take the last part off, since bringing up sex before you meet someone feels a bit presumptuous. Maybe my future travel companion won't even be attracted to me).

Steph thought she was really clever with the name she used for me: **Message me and Escape.**

"Looks good to me," Steph says as she scrolls through my profile. We decide to keep the slutty picture; it's like click-bait.

Besides, when we tried to take a picture now, they all came out scary. I haven't been to a salon to have my eyebrows done in so long that a caterpillar has moved onto my face. I really need to start focusing on my appearance again now that I am re-entering the dating world.

"Okay, hit publish before I chicken out." I close my eyes while she hits the button, praying that I don't end up with more Dans, Calves, or God forbid, Bens.

"What are you doing?" Pat appears out of nowhere and leans down between the two of us to stare at the computer, scaring me half to death.

"Jeez, Pat. Make some noise before you just appear like that!"

"Sorry, I do *live* here, you know." He rolls his eyes. He's definitely not sorry. Nor should he be. I've obviously overstayed my welcome.

"How was dinner with Jack?" Steph asks, giving Pat a kiss and pulling him close to her. I push away to give them their space.

"It was good." He sits down and pulls her onto his lap. "Bring that computer back over here. What are you girls doing?"

"Oh, I got a hit!" I yelp, throwing my hands in the air in excitement. *He's cute too!*

"A hit on what?" Pat asks now, moving Steph off his lap and trying again to peer at my computer.

I consider lying, but like I said before, I'm terrible at it, and then Steph tells him anyway. "We set up a dating profile for Charlotte to find someone to travel with."

She looks so proud, grabbing the computer and showing him her handiwork. They murmur to one another in appreciation, and she even smiles when he gawks at my picture, telling her she did a great job selecting it.

This is weird!

Covering my chest, which doesn't actually have the breasts that are splayed out in the revealing photograph, I huff. "Enough, you two! Can I have that back now?"

Pat looks up sheepishly and Steph giggles. "Don't be such a prude. You look hot!"

"My friend certainly thinks so," Pat says, eyeing me as he speaks.

"What friend?" I ask, far too excitedly. Fortunately, Steph is just as interested, and Pat doesn't bat an eye.

"Jack." He narrows his eyes. "Any chance you've met? He acts really weird whenever I mention you."

I think of the man who sat in the teal-green truck. Was he the guy from the park? What kind of things did he want to know? Did he feel the strange connection?

"Can't say that we have." I shrug nonchalantly. I'm trying hard not to jump him and ask that he spill everything that was said. Who is Jack? What does he do? What's he like? Please tell me he maintains his beard and doesn't eat peanut butter with his pointer finger.

But Pat seems to have moved on already. "So, who's the guy you matched with?"

Oh, right! I forgot about that.

I look down at the screen. Cory. Hmm, that sounds like a nice, wholesome name. "Says he speaks Portuguese, can read maps, and with a smile like mine he can't promise there won't be romance."

"Aweeee!" I hear Steph screech my thoughts. I'm smiling now. The big cheesy kind.

I write back to him. *"Would you like to meet to see if we would make good travel partners?"* Sounds so professional—which is probably good. Romance is fleeting, but memories of travel will last a lifetime.

"Yes, I'd follow those brown eyes anywhere."

Oh, shoot. With lines like those this is going to be more difficult.

"Where would you like to go?"

"I'll come to you. Name the restaurant." Oh, I like this guy already. The restaurants in town flash before my eyes like disks in a jukebox. Leo's. Roberto's. Quito's. Thames. The Lobster Pot. Aidan's. Christian's. Le Central. Café Central. The Bean. Bar 22. Portside. *Portside.* Yes, that is what I want. *"How 'bout Portside?"* I suggest, already imagining the glass of prosecco and plate of tuna sashimi in front of me.

"Sounds perfect."

We agree to meet the following Friday for dinner. I keep reminding myself that I've given up on dating. This is *just* a business arrangement. A means to an end. Travel. He is not going to be my soulmate. I no longer believe in those things.

But even as I say it, I hear the stupid voice in my head saying *what if*.

What if he's the one?

Is it so crazy to believe that I could meet someone wonderful, and we could spend a few weeks sipping sangria on the beaches in Portugal and kite surfing?

I'm really not into water sports, but you get my point.

"Looking forward to your date tonight?" Steph asks as she peeks into my room, watching me put the finishing touch on my appearance.

I stare into the mirror and take in my reflection. My golden-brown hair, which I work hard to maintain with regular highlights, falls in layers around my face and hangs at my shoulders. Cartoon dimples poke deeply when I smile, and my eyes are practically the size of Minnie Mouse's, brown and wide, giving me the title in my high school yearbook as "most innocent looking."

"It's not a date. It's like an interview." I give her a pointed look in the mirror.

Steph's signature loud laugh lets me know she's not buying what I'm selling, and I catch her rolling her eyes. "Whatever you say." Ignoring her tone, I give myself a final look in the mirror before heading out. As I trip on the top step again, she shouts, "That damn step!"

Fortunately, I catch myself. Look at that, my luck is already turning.

I arrive at the restaurant a few minutes early. I'm excited to see what he looks like in person and choose to sit in my car and wait until I spot him. A BMW pulls up, and I crane my neck.

Please, let it be him. *Please.* I could use a man with money rather than an apartment-stealing cheapskate.

Sure enough, he slides out of the car, and I notice strong cheekbones immediately. He wears a pair of dark blue jeans with an untucked light blue shirt. On anyone else it would look sloppy, but he appears like someone who doesn't have to try too hard. He doesn't need to. He's that sure of himself—with good reason. He's hot. I stare in the rearview mirror, checking my lipstick and eye makeup. Feeling I'm my best self, I hop out and walk toward him.

"Cory?" I ask.

Cory turns and his eyes scroll up and down, as if I'm an Instagram ad. I hope he's not regretting the date now that he sees the picture was a bit of a stretch, or at least as to my chest area. That push-up bra at the wedding worked wonders. If he's disappointed, he hides it well. "Charlotte, it's nice to meet you."

With the introductions out of the way, we make our way to the hostess stand and then follow her inside as she leads us to our table. Nervously, I bite the inside of my lip as I check out the view from the restaurant. The owner opened it the year before, turning a well-known German spot into the seaside staple. The floor is made from wooden planks, and there are actual portholes in the ceiling. With the view of the harbor in front, it feels like you're on a ship.

I look back to my date and find myself staring at his lips. The bottom one protrudes a bit, and as if feeling my eyes on him, he licks them in a non-suggestive way. "Safe to say your eyes do not disappoint," Cory says with a small smile.

My cheeks warm at his flattery. "Thank you. This is so odd. Have you been on a lot of these dates?"

He laughs at my question. Or perhaps my choice of words. "I've been on dates. Not sure any of them will compare to this one."

He's smooth. And I'm eating it up. "Oh, really. How come?"

"I can just tell you're different. You seemed so direct in what you want. Adorably so, if I might add."

I shake my head. "No, my friend actually made my profile."

He shakes his head. "I can hear you saying those words. No romance. No funny business. No *sex*."

Watching those lips say sex *does* something to me. Lost for words, I'm grateful when the waitress appears to take our order.

"So, have you ever been to Portugal?" I ask once we receive our drinks.

He settles into himself. "Great place to visit." And then he begins speaking Portuguese, and I'm lost listening to his words. Literally lost—as in I don't understand anything.

My face frozen with a smile, I nod. Is this what it's going to be like in another country? Steph is right. I can't go away without speaking the language. What was I thinking?

"You didn't understand a word I just said, right? I'm guessing that's why you're looking for someone to travel with?" He has a kind smile.

"Is it that obvious?"

He laughs. "Your face says it all."

Now I'm laughing too. It's so easy with him. "So, what did you say?"

His eyes darken as he looks at me. "I said that I love Portugal, but I have a feeling I would fall even more in love with it if I were to go with you."

I smile at his words, left speechless again. The rest of dinner is much the same—compliments, sweet talking, and laughter. By the time the waitress hands us our check—which he pays—I am already imagining how amazing the Azores will be if every day is like this dinner.

I think I might *like* him.

"So, would you like to do this again?" Cory asks as he walks me to my car.

"I would love that. This has been far more fun than I thought it would be."

He chuckles. "Had a few bad dates?"

"Maybe just a streak of unfortunate incidents. It's kind of the story of my life." Ben and his peanut butter-wielding finger pop into my head. I open the door to my car, prepared to say goodnight.

Cory moves closer to me and pushes my hair behind my ear, sending a shiver down my neck. "I hope your luck is about to change."

"I think it already has," I murmur, hoping he bridges the gap between our lips.

"Can I show you something?"

Interested in his request, I nod. Admittedly, I'm disappointed that he didn't try to kiss me. His face brightens as he retrieves something from his car.

My stomach somersaults when I see what's in his hand. *Yellow hair.* Is it a head? Did this kind man kill someone? *Is he going to kill me?*

Shut up, Charlotte. I'm sure there is some perfectly acceptable explanation why this man has a wig in his hand. Although, what it is I haven't a clue.

Cory pivots in my direction, and when I jump back, he winces. "What's wrong?"

Immediately, I feel bad. It's a wig. I'm being ridiculous. But *why* does he have a wig in his hand? Please don't let him be a cross-dresser. "Er, what is that?" I point at it like it's a rat.

He moves closer and attempts to place it on my head. I back away, bumping into my car door, and the wig falls precariously onto my shoulder. Rigid, my eyes dart back and forth as the straw-like pieces poke my neck. It's not even blonde—it's yellow—like a child's wig from a Halloween store. Why am I not throwing it at him and running? I can't get myself to move. My breathing is loud and harried.

"You're beautiful, Charlotte. Your eyes do something to me. But I prefer blondes. Would you indulge me?"

His voice is so sweet that I almost laugh. "You're kidding, right?" I pull it off my shoulder as my mind starts to work again. *Finally*. I hold it out, waiting for him to take back his chosen date.

Cory takes the yellow monstrosity and looks at me, as if trying to decide between us. Not willing to wait for the ultimate humiliation when he chooses the inanimate object over me, I back up against my car and slide into my seat, making sure not to turn my back to him. Certainly not allowing him the opportunity to put the wig on my head again.

"Dinner tomorrow night?" he asks, his eyes hopeful as he puts the wig behind his back, as if he could recover from that incredibly odd interaction by hiding it.

"Er, I'll be in touch." I stumble through the words and close my car door. I don't dare turn my head, wanting to avoid seeing the yellow shame again. I had been so hopeful. He *seemed* normal. The conversation had been so easy. There were no lulls, only laughter and warmth.

As I pull into the driveway and stare at Steph's house, laughter pours through me. I left this house thinking that a man I met on the Internet was going to somehow be my *soulmate*. And I began to believe he was because he complimented me.

It's hilarious.

The light above the door flashes, and Steph peers through the glass. I can't stop laughing. He brought a wig. A *wig*.

Steph runs out of her house, and although summer is just around the corner, it's still cool out and she rubs her arms as she reaches my car, not hesitating to hop into the passenger seat and stare at me quizzically. "What are you doing out here?"

I imagine the yellow pieces jutting out of the black mesh netting and laugh harder. "He brought a wig," I say between gasps.

Steph's eyes narrow, and her lips purse as she waits for me to explain, but I can't because tears are streaming down my face. "Okay," she says slowly, expectantly.

Finally, I catch my breath. "He told me he really likes me, but he prefers blondes." I pause, rolling my eyes as I remember the moment. I wish I had a better reaction at the time, rather than the doe in headlights look I'm sure I gave him. "So, he reached into his car and pulled out a wig, *for me to wear,* so that he didn't have to choose between me and what he really likes."

With saucers for eyes, Steph lets her jaw hang open. "No, he didn't."

I burst out laughing again. "He. Did," I say between fits of laughter. We both laugh so hard we're crying.

Pat taps on the window, shocking us both. I hadn't noticed him sneaking out of the house. I roll down the window. "What are you girls doing?"

Steph guffaws loudly and then covers her mouth, trying to

control herself. "Charlotte's date brought a wig for her to wear. He prefers blondes."

Pat stares at us both, trying to decide if the story is true, then he shakes his head. "Perhaps we should set her up with Jack. At least we know he's not a weirdo."

Rolling my eyes, I turn down his offer. "No more dating for me. Or Portugal. He started speaking in Portuguese—at least that much he didn't lie about—and I realized that I can't go to another country without knowing the language. I'm destined to stay in Bristol."

I turn the car off and get out. They both follow me and probably roll their eyes behind my back, which is deserved. I constantly make these proclamations, and they know I'll have another scheme tomorrow. But for now, I'm tired and really believe that I'm never going to date again. That was just *too* humiliating.

CHAPTER 7

Jack

I shift uncomfortably in bed and consider forgetting about sleep to focus instead on my plan. I rarely sleep most nights. The nightmares are far too real. At least while awake I can remind myself that it is only a memory. At night in my dreams, I can feel the scorching sun in the desert, blistering my skin even under my full uniform. I can hear Peter's screams and startle awake only to realize they are my own.

I don't want to feel that way tonight. I'd rather focus on Charlotte. Earlier this evening, I talked to Pat, and he told me about Charlotte's profile. He sent a screenshot, and my eyes practically doubled in size. *"Nice picture, right?"* he teased in his text. When I saw her screen name, "Message me and Escape," my mind started spinning.

"Who's she out with tonight?" It's odd how interested I am—Pat certainly realizes it. But considering that all I do is work

on my house and go fly once a month, there really is nothing to talk about. Even sports are out of the question, as all the New England teams are pretty terrible this year. So, this seems to be the new thing we follow—Charlotte's dating adventures.

"No idea. But I'm sure there will be a story to go along with it. There's always a story with Charlotte."

I wrote back with a laughing emoji and put the phone away. The phone pinged a few moments later, and excitedly, I pulled it out.

"Check out this new jet! Just say yes and you could be flying it next week!" The text from Richard was in bold font to get my attention. Attached was a photo of a plane that dreams were made of. Had to give the guy credit, he was persistent. But I wasn't ready to give up on this life yet. I owed it to my family to try to make this work, to try to be the son they said goodbye to at eighteen, the happy-go-lucky All-American kid who had big dreams and a bright future ahead of him. I owed it to Peter to try to be happy. He and I always planned on returning to Bristol, raising families together, coaching our kids in baseball. I know it's a lot of pressure to put on one person, but I honestly believe Charlotte is the key to making all that come true. I don't get to do it with Peter, but I can do it *for* him.

I pull her profile up again, re-reading her words. I can practically hear her speaking the words as I read them. *No romance, no funny business, no sex.* I stare at her photo, her big eyes wide and her lips turned up in a cheeky smile. God, I love her smile.

Before I can stop myself, I create a profile. Thinking I'm being clever, I choose the name "Piña Coladas." I wonder if she'll get it. Under likes, I write—rain, midnight cuddles, and the Cape. Then without hesitation, I message her. *"Message me and Escape, interesting profile. How's the search going for a travel companion?"*

My stomach clenches as I wait for her to respond. It's after midnight. Why would she be awake right now? Hell, she might still be on her date. I really hope not. That would mean it went well.

I turn over in bed, counting backwards from one hundred, as my therapist taught me to do at night. "Do something you can control—and *breathe*." The vibration of the phone surprises me. I look down and find I have a new message.

Charlotte?

"Just swimmingly. If only I had blonde hair it probably would have gone better."

Hmm. Pat said there was always a story. *"His loss?"*

"Obviously. I've given up. I'm not even sure why I'm responding to you right now."

This makes me laugh. Which I tell her. *"Haha. Well, I promise not to steal your apartment or complain about your hair color."*

"How do you know about the apartment?"

"I'm friends with Pat. My name is Jack." I go all in. I missed out on my chance years ago, and I'm not going to do that again.

She doesn't respond for a moment. Maybe I freaked her out. But then another message appears. *"Oh, well, hi."*

"Hi."

"No pic?" she asks.

"Just made a profile to talk to you. Haven't uploaded a picture. Based upon your dating experience, I think I'll keep my pic off this site."

Also, I don't want her to figure out who I am just yet.

"Haha, smooth. First you compliment me—I think—and then you insult me."

I smile. *"Definitely a compliment. It's not your fault there are a bunch of wackos on the internet."*

"True! How's your dog? I saw him in the truck with you when you came to pick up Pat."

I look down at Charlie and smile. *"He's good. Currently lying in bed next to me."*

"I've got Grover in bed with me too."

I'm immediately jealous of that pug. What I would do to be lying in bed next to her. *"Lucky dog."*

"Haha, don't. One guy I messaged with on this site told me he wished I was naked in bed with him."

My eyes bulge. The thought of her naked in bed hadn't actually crossed my mind. Now that she's said it, though, I can't remove the image of her short shorts and how badly I wanted to take them off her.

"Wow! Guys really talk like that on here?"

"Haha. Yes! It's horrible. I'm taking down the profile."

"Good idea. So, when are you going to the Azores?"

"I'm not. Steph told me it was a crazy idea and she was right. I can't go by myself. It was a nice idea while it lasted though."

"So, don't go by yourself then."

"I can't possibly go on any more dates to find someone to come with me. I mean, who travels to another country with a stranger? It was a crazy idea."

Couldn't argue with that. But I had a plan now. *"Go with me."*

There's a significant pause—I hold my breath waiting.

And then she finally responds, *"You want to go to the Azores with me?"*

Yes, I cheer to myself with a fist pump.

"Could be fun."

"But you don't know me. How do you know it would be fun?"

"Pat says there's always a story with you. And Steph is fun."

"Haha. I'm not sure that's a compliment."

"To me it is. Who wants to hang out with someone who is boring?"

"Life definitely isn't boring with me."

"So, let's go to the Azores together." My smile grows. The idea of two weeks away with Charlotte is too good to be true. Is it possible the spark that was lit six years ago could still be there?

"Are you serious about this?"

"Yes."

"Shouldn't we meet first and see if we actually get along?"

I smirk. We get along. *"Let's meet in the Azores. It will be more fun."*

"When?"

My pulse races. She's agreeing. *"How soon can you go?"*

"School's out this week. Then I'm off for the summer."

"I can make that work. Next Saturday?"

"Okay," she replies. Then a second later she sends another message. *"Are we really doing this?"*

I don't hesitate. *"Yes. I have a feeling it's going to be great."*

"Okay. I'm going to bed. Let's talk tomorrow so we can figure out our plans."

My heart sinks a little. I don't want to stop messaging with her. I know my mind will return to the desert, and I just want to be back in her dorm room, but I can't force her to keep talking. *"Okay. Should we exchange phone numbers?"* It's what I should have done years ago. Get her number and follow up. I wasn't going to screw it up this time.

"Sounds good."

She sends me hers, and I shoot her a text immediately. *"Hi Charlotte, this is Jack. Now you have my number."* I add a wink emoji and then hit send before I reconsider.

"Hi, Jack."

All I want is to hear her voice. Before I can stop myself, I hit call. She picks up after one ring. "Hey."

"Hi, sorry. I just wanted to hear your voice."

Charlotte pauses, as if I've taken her by surprise. "Same…"

she sighs into the phone, sending a shiver down my back. "Was that you in the park? With the chocolate Lab?"

"Yes."

She's silent. I think we both know a moment passed between us in the park when she touched me. It felt so shocking it took both our breaths away. Unless you've experienced it, you wouldn't believe in the necessity of a spark in a relationship—but once you've felt it, you'll spend your whole life trying to replicate that moment.

Not wanting a lull in the conversation, I try coming up with reasons to keep her on the phone. "So, tell me about your date?"

Charlotte hums into the phone, as if considering what to say. I hear a jostling on the other end, sheets crunching perhaps as she gets comfortable. "It was great at first. There was no awkward silence, and it wasn't only because I talked the whole time. We had *good* conversation."

I shift my pillow uncomfortably, not enjoying the idea of her having easy conversation with anyone other than me. I never had the type of connection I had with her, and I thought it was special. Hearing her talk about it with someone else makes me wonder if it's just her that makes things easy.

"So, what went wrong?" I'm happy to focus on the bad part of the date—the part that made her come home, swear off dating, and agree to travel across the world with me.

"I wouldn't say anything went *wrong*," she says slowly, a low giggle escaping. "He brought a wig that he wanted me to wear." Her giggles overtake her words, and she sounds so joyful it cracks my face wide with a smile.

"He what? What do you mean a wig?"

Between fits of laughter, she explains, "He likes blondes,"— she pauses, a squeak of laughter interrupting her words— "and he wanted to see what I'd look like as one."

We both laugh, and I imagine her smile is as large as mine, and my stomach aches as uncontrollable happiness rocks through my body.

"Thank you," I say once I've finally stopped laughing.

"For what?"

"I haven't laughed that hard in a long time. It's lonely living by myself." I swing my arm behind my head and get more comfortable, no longer stressing about her date, reveling instead in the feeling of finally falling back into easy conversation with her.

"Tell me about it."

"At least you have Steph and Pat!"

She groans. "I'm pretty sure Pat is ready for me to go. Vacation probably can't come soon enough for him."

I laugh. "Don't let his rough exterior fool ya. He enjoys the company. But yeah, I don't think he will be sad to get a little alone time with his wife."

Giggling, she says, "Believe you me, they aren't lacking in their time together. I just have to witness all their PDA."

A jealous wave surges through me as I imagine what it would be like to openly have public displays of affection with someone. Especially the someone I'm currently talking to. "They are a great couple. I hope one day I meet someone who I can't keep my hands off of."

She murmurs into the phone, "Hmm, that would be nice."

Her softer voice makes me think she is getting tired, and I consider letting her go. But I'm not ready. "What made you pick the Azores?"

"A sign in a window."

"Seriously?"

Charlotte laughs again. "Yes. This entire thing has been a bit ridiculous. But honestly, I was making my dating profile and realized I'm not that interesting—I've never done anything worth bragging about. My life has been pretty ordinary. I mean, I want to be a person who says I ziplined in Mexico, or swam in a cenote, hiked to the top of a volcano—*something*. Does that make sense? I probably sound nuts."

Her words leave a smile on my face. If she only knew how extraordinary I found her. It doesn't matter what things she does; I knew the night I met her she was special.

"You don't sound nuts. It's what most people want—to live a life filled with stories. I'm going to make it a mission to find something there that you've never done."

"That won't be too hard. I haven't done much."

"Great, that will make this easy then."

"How about you? Why do *you* want to go to the Azores?"

I can't very well admit it's to spend time with her. When

Charlotte sees me, like really sees me for an extended period of time, without the hat and the sun blinding her eyes, she'll realize who I am. The six years had completely changed my life, but my exterior remained almost the same. A little bit longer hair on my head, scruff on my face, and the deep-set wrinkles around my eyes were not enough to make me unrecognizable—even if I wished they were. My only hope is that two weeks in another country by ourselves will provide the opportunity for her to accept my apology for disappearing that night and convince her to give me another chance.

"Honestly, always wanted to go there. But I need a vacation. It doesn't matter where you suggested—I just need to get away."

"Hmm, I haven't even asked you—what do you do?"

The question is innocent enough, and for almost anyone else it would have a simple answer, but for me the answer is as layered as a wedding cake. "I'm a contractor."

It's not a lie, but it is deceiving. I'm currently my own general contractor for my fixer-upper, and I am giving at least some consideration to Richard's offer to be a contractor flying for his company in Las Vegas. Even to my ears that sounds pathetic. It's a lie and I need to fix it. But when Charlotte doesn't question me further, I take the coward's way out. Eventually, I will have to tell her everything. I'm just not ready yet. I change the subject. "What grade do you teach?"

"Kindergarten." Imagining her in the classroom surrounded by little bodies all jostling for her attention, I smile. It is precisely where she belongs. With her long stories, and the exaggerated faces that go with every one of them, I can see how kindergartners would love her.

A yawn escapes her lips.

"You're tired. I'll let you go. We'll talk tomorrow?" I'm on pins and needles waiting for her to respond. Hoping that she won't change her mind when she wakes up and realizes that in her sleepless delirium she agreed to go on vacation with a stranger.

Charlotte whispers softly into the phone, "Tomorrow. Night, Jack."

With the sound of my heart loud in my ears, I lean back into bed and stare at the phone. I have one week to get my shit together. I've been alone for so long, facing demons that I no longer want to deal with. I would do anything to be the person I was before, the person that lay next to her in bed and talked all night, without a worry or a nightmare in sight. As much as I want to spend time with her, I also want to spend time with the old me as well. I just hope that I can be him again.

CHAPTER 8

Charlotte

"I cannot believe you are doing this," Steph says for just about the thousandth time today. It had been a week since Jack called and I agreed to travel with him. We've spoken every night, for hours at a time, while Steph peeked in the door, rolled her eyes, and sighed long exasperating sighs, indicating her annoyance at my teenager-like behavior.

Some of my favorite things I've learned about him so far:

He recently bought a fixer-upper so he could live closer to his parents who are still happily married after forty years. *Forty years!*

He backpacked around Europe in college and tried over thirty different pizzas in Italy.

He's jumped out of a plane—cue slap on the cheeks like in *Home Alone*.

I could talk to him for hours and never get enough.

Oh, wait, that's something about me.

I fold a yellow shirt, placing it on top of the shorts I picked to match. Each outfit has been pre-planned. There is no room for error when you are traveling with a stranger to a foreign country for two weeks with no idea when you will see a washer and dryer. They have them, right? I always see the Portuguese women in our neighborhood hanging their clothes. I really can't imagine having to hang my underwear next to Jack's at the hotel.

I pick up my cotton whites and consider a sexy thong instead. But who can hike in a thong? Well, I don't really hike so I'm not sure which would be worse. I consider asking Steph, but the look she is giving me makes me think that won't go over well. But really, when has that ever stopped me? "Stop huffing over there and help! Do you think they have a washer and dryer?"

Her eyes turn to the sky. "Lord, help you. And me. And *Jack*."

I grab a pillow from the bed and toss it in her direction, but I completely miss her, and it hits Grover. He looks up, confused, and Steph's high-pitched laugh shakes the room. "Nice try, girlfriend. Seriously, tell me again why you think this is a good idea?"

Pat appears in the door, and his eyes grow wide as he sees the disaster that is their guest bedroom, my clothes tossed about and shoes in every corner. He offers me a mock congratulations at getting Steph to laugh so loud. Then he turns to Steph and pulls her close. "It's a great idea." He nuzzles into her neck, and she pushes him back.

"Pat, it's a terrible idea. Jack is *so* not the guy for Charlotte."

Now it's my turn to roll my eyes, but the blush scampering up my chest and to my cheeks shows she's hit the nail on the head, and they both know it. "I'm not interested in him. We are just excited for our adventure. That's all this is."

Pat shakes his head. "That is not all Jack is interested in. Mark my words, you guys will come back a couple."

My cheeks burn, and I look away in the direction of my suitcase, so he can't see the huge smile that's breaking through my face. "I'm not interested in dating him. I'm not interested in dating *anyone*. Seriously, I haven't even met him." But in twenty-one hours I will. *Twenty-one* hours!

"Pat, can you please just have Jack come over now? They need to meet before tomorrow at the airport." Steph's annoyance with the entire scenario is a bit extra. I think she's just jealous that she won't witness the crash and burn that inevitably happens whenever I meet a new guy. But I'm not thinking of this like a date. So, no crash and burn. *Hopefully*.

Pat shakes his head again. "No can do. He was adamant that he didn't want to meet her with us around. It's too much pressure. This is about them, not us." Although I'm sure he's giving Steph some sort of guarded look, I pay them no attention. His words have me too distracted. Is that what Jack said? It's about us? *Is* it about us? Is there an *us*?

Steph sighs and rolls her eyes again. "Fine, pack thongs, not those granny panties, Char. Jack is hot. You can't wear those underwear if you're going to sleep with him."

The back of my neck flares with heat, and I squeak, "I am not going to sleep with him!"

It's no use. They both look at one another and shake their heads. I'm totally going to sleep with him. I hastily throw the sexier underwear into my suitcase and slam it shut.

An hour later we are all seated on the couch, Steph in between Pat and me, the same way we have been positioned for the last few months living together. "So, is there anything else I should know about Jack?" I sip my wine and try to silence the butterflies which are doing sprints in my belly.

Pat sips his beer and gives me a look. "What kind of things?"

Steph nudges him. "Like is he a serial killer, or is he into weird sexual things." She pauses then turns to me. "No, and I don't *think* so."

I laugh. "That was not what I meant. I just mean, how come you guys never introduced us before?"

Pat looks at me thoughtfully, no irritation or humor in his stare. "Well, first of all, Jack just moved back to Bristol. So, it's not like we had a chance to introduce you. He was…um, not in the country for a while. And before that, well, Jack had a tough time. I'll let him share with you if he wants. It's not my story to tell. But let's just say I didn't think he was ready for a real relationship for a long time. He had some things to work through. But he's good now." He adds the last part when he sees me eyeing him warily.

"Okay," I say quietly, trying to imagine what big secret Jack is hiding.

Steph grabs my hand, pulling me toward her. "Hey, he's a good guy. A *really* good guy. Don't stress. I know I've been giving you shit, but just go and have fun. He doesn't have to be *the one* for you to have a good time."

She's right. I'm just not good at this. The hopeless romantic is forever taking over my thoughts.

"Do you have any pictures of him? I barely know what he looks like." I'd only seen him that one time in the park, and his face was shadowed from his hat. And he was too far away when I saw him outside the house in the truck. I'm dying to know what his face looks like. What his lips look like. What *he* looks like.

Steph looks around. "Nope. He didn't come to our wedding. He was overseas. Right, Pat?"

Pat nods. "Yeah. Honestly, until this year I hadn't seen him since college. He's good-looking though. You'll be satisfied."

I shake my head and act affronted. "Satisfied? I don't need to be satisfied. We are *just* going as friends."

Clearly, Pat and Steph don't believe me. Neither do my butterflies. They start going crazy the minute I see his name come across my phone. I answer and slide off the couch, whispering, "Hi" as I sneak out of the room.

"Hey, are you excited for tomorrow?" His voice is husky, and the butterflies go nuts. Ever since he called a week ago, something inside of me has let loose and is going wild. My mind tells me to slow down, but the center of my chest makes it hard to breathe. There is just something about him. And we haven't even met. The only time I've ever felt this way was years ago with the stranger who disappeared, and I keep trying to squash these feelings. They didn't serve me well back then, and I don't want to allow these stupid butterflies to fool me again.

I try to contain my excitement. "Yeah, should be fun," I say casually. Or so I hope.

"I agree. Still good for meeting at the gate?"

"That's the plan."

I tried to get him to meet me at Steph's yesterday, hoping it would make it less awkward, but he said he was busy getting things ready for vacation, and there really wasn't time for him to do anything other than pack. Now, remembering what Pat said, I wonder if that was true or not. Did Jack want our meeting to be about us? Or was that just Pat's interpretation? I don't think men are that complicated, Pat even less so. It's probably verbatim Jack's commentary because Pat isn't the type of guy to read between the lines.

"You all packed?" Jack asks.

Looking at my suitcase, I sigh. It's shut, but I know I will be sneaking in some comfortable underwear. "Mostly."

"Good. Well, I don't want to keep you too late. I get you all to myself for the next few weeks." My stomach somersaults hearing his excitement.

"Okay. Have a good night, Jack."

"Charlotte…" He pauses.

"Yes?"

He lets out a soft breath. "It's just been really nice talking to you this past week. It's meant a lot to me. Just wanted you to know that." His voice sounds like he's trying to convey some secret message—it's deep and penetrating, but the message doesn't land.

"Me too." Without knowing what is bothering him, I just want him to know how much this has meant to me. I haven't felt this way in a long time. Which makes me nervous. The last time I felt like this it all slipped away in a matter of hours. But I don't want to make things weird by acting like this is more than we've agreed. No romance, no funny business, no sex. Those are the rules.

"Okay, I'll see you tomorrow at Gate 12. Sweet dreams, Charlotte."

I already know mine will be focused on him, so they certainly will be. "Night, Jack." I fall back onto the bed and kick my legs up in the air, staring at the ceiling as the excitement courses through me. "Shut up, you stupid butterflies!"

"Charlotte?" Jack's deep voice calls distantly through the phone as I stare at it in horror. *No, no, no.* I click the end button and throw it. Oh my God! What have I done?

The phone buzzes, and I hurl myself off the bed toward it. Lifting it up to my eyes, I laugh at his message. *"Be nice to those butterflies. I happen to think they are on to something,"* with a wink at the end.

Shoot. I'm totally going to break my rules.

CHAPTER 9

Jack

As I arrive at our gate earlier than we agreed, my stomach twists in knots. I need to get a handle on my emotions before I see her. I hope to spot her before she spots me, so I can really look at her before she recognizes the con that I am. I've turned the thought around every which way in my head, wondering if it's possible she could have forgotten what I look like, that perhaps my scars have changed me more than even I realize. But when I looked in the mirror this morning, I was met with the same blue eyes with yellow flecks in them. If Charlotte felt half of what I felt that night, there is no way she could have forgotten my eyes. I know I haven't forgotten her big brown ones.

I considered leaving the scruff I'd grown over the last few weeks while working on the house, but at the last minute I shaved. The scruff might have given me a little more time of her not recognizing me, but that was the point of this entire trip—to show her who I really am. I hope she still likes what she sees.

"Jack?" Charlotte's soft voice interrupts my thoughts. I hold my breath trying to decide what I'm going to do. It's now or never. Make a decision, asshole.

Breathing deeply, I turn around to find Charlotte standing before me, her golden-brown hair pulled back in a ponytail and a bright smile on her face.

"Charlotte." I wrap my arms around her, pulling her into a bear hug, which may seem odd, but after the conversations we've had, I don't hesitate. Charlotte doesn't seem at all fazed by my forwardness as she wraps her arms around my waist, as if we've known one another for years. I allow myself to inhale the sweet tangerine scent that must be her conditioner and try to remind myself that this won't be the last time I get this close to her.

She pulls away before I'm ready and looks me up and down. If she recognizes me, she doesn't give away her thoughts. Brightly, she smiles and says, "I can't believe we're finally here. I know it's only been a week, but the anticipation was killing me."

"Let's go grab a drink and a bite to eat." It's six p.m., and our flight doesn't take off until eight thirty. We wanted time to talk before settling on the plane next to each other and falling asleep, or as Charlotte put it, "Before I snore or drool on you, we need to have a meal."

"Lead the way," she says. Already, I can feel the knots working themselves out. This is going to be okay. Maybe I made a bigger deal of that night in my head. Maybe she's just excited to see me and isn't mad that I disappeared or that I tricked her into traveling with me now.

Somehow, I know that's wishful thinking.

Her arm brushes against mine as we walk, and a shiver goes down my spine. Slowing down, I don't force her shorter frame to match my long steps. I tower over her by at least a foot and remember when I last saw her she was in tall black boots which hid her height. It was only once she was barefoot in my favorite shorts that I saw her true size. I keep my eyes forward, knowing full well if I allow myself to stare, my eyes will explore her entire body in an obvious and inappropriate manner.

The waitress shows us to our seats and takes our drink orders—a glass of sauvignon blanc for her and a Sam Summer for me—and then I slip off my Red Sox hat. Charlotte stares into my eyes, and her smile falters.

Nervous, I blurt out again, "It's so nice to finally meet you, Charlotte."

She stares at me silently, her eyes meet mine, and in that instant it's obvious that she knows. Her voice catches in her throat and she squeaks, "Same."

The clock ticks in the background, imprinting this moment in my mind forever. The waitress drops off our drinks and takes our order. I watch Charlotte's every move as she looks at the menu, glances up at me nervously, and then picks something. Her long black lashes flutter up and down, her brown eyes peeking through. I mumble my burger order but never take my eyes off her. I want to convey how sorry I am and also that I want to give us another chance, but the words are stuck in my throat.

Nibbling on her bottom lip like a mouse attacks a piece of cheese, she looks at her glass of wine. "I may need a few more of these to knock me out on the plane. I'm too excited to sleep."

That's it? No confrontation. No acknowledgement of what happened between us. Nothing? I stumble through the conversation, trying hard not to growl in aggravation. "Uh, right. Well, bottoms up."

An awkward tension descends on the table, and I hate the feeling more than I can explain. To go from easygoing to this is almost unbearable. I'd take the quiet desert over this any day.

"I'm gonna run to the bathroom," I say, excusing myself from the table and dialing Pat's number into my phone.

"Hey, how's it going with Charlotte?" Pat says when he picks up.

"Did you lie to me?" The frustration drips in my voice.

Pat inhales on the other end of the phone. "Did I what? What are you talking about?" I can almost imagine him scratching his head now, and I want to throw the phone.

"You told me Charlotte was obsessed with the guy from St. Patrick's Day. Were you pulling my chain because you knew it was me? Are you laughing at me now?" I feel like a fool, and although I know I'm not making sense, I can't help but feel like he knew the whole time.

"Wait. *Wait!* You're the fucking leprechaun!"

Okay, so he didn't know. Well, shit. This just keeps getting worse. "You can't tell her."

Pat laughs into the phone. "You are the one with her. How would I tell her?"

I roll my eyes. "I'm serious. I need to be the one to tell her."

"So, get off the phone with me and do that. But seriously, Jack, what were you thinking?"

I shake my head. There really is no good explanation. This was a shitty idea, and now I'm not sure she remembers who I am to begin with. "I don't think she remembers me."

"She remembers you. *Trust me.* There is no way Charlotte would forget that night. It's all she talked about. *You* were all she talked about. Do you have real feelings for her?"

It's not even a question. "Yes. Had I known she was Steph's friend years ago, I would have gotten her information when I got back." I don't have to say back from where—Pat knows.

He sighs into the phone. "I'm sorry, man. I didn't realize. Makes more sense now—why you didn't leave your number and all. But seriously, if things were as *magical* as she says, you've got to be honest with her. You don't want to be compared to the mythical leprechaun. No one can compete. Not even you."

I laugh in spite of myself. Truth is, I'm not that same guy. So, he's right about comparisons. I just hope that I'm still enough. "Will do." I pause. "Sorry for yelling at you."

"Don't mention it. Now go make that girl happy. She's been waiting for you."

CHAPTER 10

Charlotte

Sitting at the table, I twist my napkin in different directions, trying to work out what just happened. It is him. Jack was Mr. Perfect. The leprechaun. He was my *one perfect night*. And he doesn't even remember me. It's almost too humiliating.

What was I supposed to say? Hi, I'm the girl that has been obsessing over our one amazing night six years ago, which apparently was so unforgettable that you asked me out on *another* first date. Wait, this isn't even a first date. This is a trip. A strictly friends, no romance, no funny business, no sex *trip*. Which for the record is even *worse*.

I glance in his direction and, seeing that he's disappeared, sneak a phone call to Steph. "Hey, how's it going with Jack? He's *hot*, right?"

"He's the leprechaun," I whisper quickly into the phone, hiding my mouth with my hand.

Confused, Steph asks, "The what?"

Now is not the time for her to lack subtlety. "The leprechaun. St. Patrick's boy. Jack is my perfect one night." My voice is desperate, but it is no match for my heart.

"*Oh. My. God.*"

My thought exactly.

"Right? What do I do?"

"I'm sorry. I'm really at a loss. Are you serious? Did you have some crazy moment where you both realized who the other one was, and you jumped him right there?"

I roll my eyes now, and then my stomach twists, because no, we did *not* have that moment. He didn't even remember me. "Yes, I'm serious, and no, he didn't recognize me. Obviously, the night meant more to me than him. He snuck off, remember? You always tried to tell me he wasn't a great guy or at least not 'my guy' if he didn't stick around to even get my number. And in my crazy indignant mind, I always thought you were just jaded. But Steph, I think you were right. Because now he's here, and he doesn't even remember me. I was *that* forgettable." A lone tear escapes my eye, and I brush it away quickly, feeling foolish for having believed for so many years that something special had happened between us.

"Oh, Charlotte. Who knows why he left—he's there now—and from the way Pat made it sound, Jack *wants* to be there with you. Maybe subconsciously he remembered you, or maybe you just had such a big spark that it's reignited again. You should at least give him the opportunity to explain."

I'm already shaking my head. Absolutely not. "No, it is too humiliating. If he doesn't remember me then I'll pretend I don't remember him either. Oh shoot, he's coming back. I've got to go."

"Good luck, my friend," she says into the phone, but I've already hung up before I can respond, watching Jack as he reaches the table, a smile on his lips which doesn't reach his eyes.

"All okay?" He stares at me, searching my face for an explanation. I hope my mascara doesn't give away the truth.

"Fine. Food should be here any moment. Everything okay with *you*?"

Turning the tables on him, I can see his face is just as strained as mine, if not more. Perhaps he does realize who I am, and now he's freaking out because he thought he ditched my overtalkative ass years ago, and now he's stuck with me for another two weeks.

Jack reaches his hand out to mine, delicately rubbing my thumb with his. "I'm good now that I'm with you."

Or maybe he's not disappointed.

The butterflies are back, flying haplessly around my belly, making it impossible to focus on anything other than the present. They haven't flapped like this in years. Even *they* know the truth. I bite my lip, and a small sigh escapes. "I'm glad I'm here too."

We settle into an easy conversation, turning to the topic of our plans for when we arrive in Portugal. The flight isn't terribly long—only five hours—and then we will be touching down on the small island of São Miguel. Due to the time difference, it will be six in the morning, but our bodies will still believe it to be two a.m. We've booked a hotel in the city for the first few days and are hopeful that we'll be able to check in when we arrive to get some much-needed sleep before our day begins.

Now that I'm finally back in front of him—the man I've dreamed about for years on end—it feels strangely right. He doesn't need to know who I am—my knowledge is enough. There's no one to compare him to, which is a welcome relief. I'd been doing it for years to other men. He measures up to the man I created in my mind—steady and strong in the way he approaches our conversations, not at all intimidated to say what he thinks, *or feels*. I just wonder if the feelings are one-sided like they apparently were so many years ago.

Even though the butterflies are dancing the tango, I am able to stay focused on his words and enjoy his company. "Are you excited to be done with school?"

Throwing my head back, I almost levitate. "Am I ever. I love my kindergartners. I love being in the classroom. Love watching the kids blossom by the end of the year, learning to read and talking up a storm. But by the end of the year, I'm spent. Especially when you add in the fact that I've been living with Pat and Steph for the last half of the year. There's been nowhere to really decompress, if that makes any sense." Realizing I'm the one doing most of the talking, I turn the conversation to him. "What about you? I would think as a contractor your busiest

94

time would be in the warm weather. How'd you manage to take time off?"

Jack's blue eyes shoot to mine, the golden bursts sparkling at me. He'd been wearing a baseball cap when I first walked up, but he took it off when we sat down to eat, just like in the diner. It was in that moment that I had realized who he was. It was like a montage of music playing, or the scene from *Friends* where Ross and Rachel finally kiss—he comes back to Central Perk, their eyes meet, and everything slows. In a perfect world, when Jack pulled off his hat and slowly slid his eyes up to mine, recognition would have flashed in those beautiful blue eyes of his while U2's "With or Without You" played. He would have slow walked toward me while I bit my lip, my eyes wide and hands trembling, waiting for him to fold me into his big arms, to pull me against that muscular chest, and kiss the life out of me. Instead, he blinked, and the waitress walked up smelling like incense while a kid whined in the background.

Focus, Charlotte—this isn't TV.

Jack's dirty-blond hair is longer than it was years ago, not cut tightly to his head. He shaved the scruff from his face, and I'm reminded of the boy I met so many years ago, instead of the man I'd seen in the park. He's so incredibly handsome without the scruff. Although he was hot with it too. He isn't good-looking like a Ken doll—his face is hard and weathered from the sun, with a scar slit across his top lip leaving me staring and focused in all the wrong places. The first thing I noticed, though, were his hands.

They are soft, not rough, as one would expect from a contractor. "Uh, I'm not the type of contractor you are thinking."

He doesn't divulge any more, and I'm not satisfied with the answer. "Well, what type of contractor are you then?"

"Government."

Oh, like Jack Ryan? He just keeps getting more interesting.

"So, what do you *do* for the government?" Surely, this question is tailored enough to get an actual response.

Jack's mouth turns up in an almost half smile, that little scar even more prominent, as if he's impressed with my inquisition skills. "Fly."

My eyes bulge. He's a *pilot.* Jack was hot before, but the fact that he's a pilot is making me weak in the knees—and I'm not even standing. I'm speechless—which he seems to enjoy, his eyes dancing at my obvious surprise. "You let me go on and on about my kindergartners, and this whole time you've had this cool career." I cover my mouth in embarrassment.

"*Stop.* Your job is not any less cool. It's just different." His smile is addictive, and the way he talks makes my heart swoon. The freckle above his lip brings an innocence to him, like the kids in my class, and his dimple flexes whenever I talk, as if everything *I* say is entertaining.

With my nail resting on my lip, I realize I must be staring at him like he's a snack—my mouth wide open and eyes agog. I stammer a response, pulling my hair behind my ear and straightening in my seat. "So, tell me, Maverick, what's the biggest plane you've ever flown?"

Jack's head falls back, and he laughs, causing people to turn and stare. It's deep and rumbles through his chest, his shirt tightening as the muscles below it expand and contract. Like me, the women at the table next to ours are taken in by this incredibly attractive, happy man. My chest rises in pride that I'm the one sitting with him. Will I feel this way the whole trip? Staring at him in amazement that he'd want to spend time with me. Tongue-tied over the man who I've been dreaming about all this time. No, I most certainly can't do that. I need to get ahold of myself before I break all my rules.

"Why are you laughing?"

He shakes his head, smiling still. "Just not used to a woman playing the who's bigger game." The fire in his eyes tells me that he would definitely win that game. *Shoot.* Now I'm thinking about his lower body part, which is *so* inappropriate. As my eyes drift lower, he catches me and raises his eyebrow. I look away quickly, blushing.

"Get your mind out of the gutter, Mav."

He shakes his head again. "First of all, Maverick was a navy guy; I fly fighter jets for the Air Force." His dimples are as big as his cocky attitude. "And I'm not the one whose eyes are dipped toward the gutter, Charlotte."

This time my head falls back and I literally guffaw. It is the most unladylike laugh that has ever escaped my mouth. Worse than that, though, is that in my exaggerated state, I feel myself pushing my chair backwards, and it gives out beneath me. As my back hits the floor with a thud, I stare up at the airport ceiling in complete mortification, pretty sure that the entire place is now staring at me, including the hot girls one table over. I'm brought back to the moment I fell off a treadmill, and the woman next to me kissed the instructor I was crushing on. *Please, please, please*, do not be a repeat.

Jack must have jumped as soon as I fell because he now kneels next to me, cradling my head, and asks if I'm alright. With concerned eyes, his once smirking lips are drawn out in a frown. I cover my eyes and moan, "*Ow.*"

"Are you okay?" he asks, his eyes darting back and forth, scanning my face. "Be careful; don't get up just yet. Let's make sure you don't have a concussion."

"Don't tell me on top of being a hot fighter pilot you're also a doctor?"

He smiles and pushes me back down. "Alright, Sassy, I see you're still a wiseass. You can stay there."

Sassy? I like it. Much better than being called clumsy.

I grab his hand before he can let go, and a spark ignites, sending an electric shock through both of us. Cue musical montage. I'm thinking Selena Gomez's "Can't Keep My Hands to Myself" would work right about now. Jack's eyes meet mine, and he licks his bottom lip. I imagine what it would feel like if he would move his lips only a few inches closer. It's something I've been dreaming about for years—how it would feel to kiss

Mr. Perfect and what he would *taste* like. I think I let out a keening cry, high in my throat. The butterflies must have pushed themselves all the way up in a synchronized song. He moves closer, his lips now barely brushing against mine, and then says, "Our first kiss cannot be on the floor of an airport." The smile on his face is gone, his eyes blaze, and his breath is hot against my lips. He lifts me to my feet, and I'm rendered speechless.

He wants to kiss me.

I have no wise retort, and I happen to agree. I've been waiting years, so what's another few hours?

The moment is interrupted by the announcement that our plane is about to board. The women next to us look at one another, murmur something, and hop up, heading in the direction of our gate. Excellent, it'll be just my luck that they'll be sitting next to us on the plane too.

Both women appear to be about our age, late twenties, perhaps even younger than I am. I actually don't know Jack's age, but I'm assuming he's the same age as Pat—thirty-two—which would mean he was twenty-six back when we first met. But this is all conjecture. I really have no idea how he and Pat know one another. "Hey, how'd you meet Pat?" I ask, never allowing a thought in my head to go to waste.

Jack has taken it upon himself to grab my carry-on as well as his own, and he is waiting for me to finish my last sip of wine before we leave the table. Like internal thoughts, I also never let a sip of wine go to waste.

"High school."

We're back to the short answers.

"Where did you guys go to high school?" I walk next to him now as we make our way to the gate. The women from the restaurant are in line for the plane, and my stomach clenches again. Why do I feel like he'll be interested in them? There's no rational reason for my concern. He hasn't looked at anyone but me. More than that, I have rules for this trip, and Jack is allowed to look at whomever he wants. But I already know that my rules are going out the window very quickly. He's not *just* some stranger I'm traveling with—he's my one perfect night.

"We went to La Salle," he says, taking my hand in his as we walk, calming my nerves about the other women.

My hand fits within his big one in a way I've never fit with anyone before. The thought is dizzying and distracting—neither of which I can afford to feel. "When did you graduate?"

Jack lets out a soft chuckle. "Are you gonna look up my high school photo, or do you just want to know how old I am?"

Pink colors my cheeks. "The latter."

"I'm thirty-two. Almost thirty-three, actually. Too old for you?" His smirk makes me smile.

I push against him with my shoulder. "Stop teasing me."

Jack pulls on my hand as I continue walking forward, and I boomerang into his chest. He stares down at me, his bottom lip dangerously close, and whispers, "You're enjoying it, Sass, don't kid yourself." I can't respond. The butterflies move between my legs, and I bite my lip, begging my mouth not to betray me. "I told you no airport kisses, but you're making it incredibly hard," he whispers against my lips.

I remain perfectly still, willing my body to listen and wait for the mind-blowing once-in-a-lifetime kiss somewhere sexier than Logan airport. Like on the beach in the Azores, in the middle of the Atlantic at sunrise. Yes, I can absolutely wait because I *know* it will be worth it.

Pulling him close, I take a fist full of his shirt, surprising him. "Don't make promises you don't intend to keep."

He drops our bags and wraps his arms around me, but he keeps his lips inches away from my own. "Good God, woman, you're driving me wild. Let's get you to the Azores so I can finally do what I've been thinking about all week."

There is nothing for me to do but let go—if I wait another second, I'll stick my tongue in his mouth and devour him right here. Unlike him, I've been waiting a lot longer than a week. I need to get away from him before I get ahead of myself. Unfortunately, sitting next to him on a plane for several hours is not going to help my plight.

I do everything to avoid looking at him, staring instead at the massive plane which sits behind the glass to my right. We make our way down the long walkway, and I nervously glance behind me—yup, he's still looking at me like he wants to devour me.

Jack allows me to move into the window seat, and he takes the aisle. As expected, we are seated in the same aisle as the two women from the bar. They keep glancing in our direction and snickering. Normally, I'd be self-conscious around women like that, but as the plane starts to accelerate and excitement courses through my body, Jack takes my hand in his and rubs circles on my thumb, his eyes turned in my direction, watching my every move and looking completely enamored with me. Not even giving the women a second glance. Still unsure if I trust all these feelings swirling in my stomach or the man sitting next to me, I turn toward the window and close my eyes. Of course, even in my dreams I'm met with the image of Jack and the eyes that have haunted me for years. However, safe to enjoy him in my dreams, I fall asleep.

CHAPTER 11

Jack

As promised, once the plane takes off Charlotte's eyes flutter closed, and a soft snore escapes her lips. I welcome the sound because her head tilts toward me and rests on my shoulder. I'm left with the perfect view of her face, able to stare at her without shyness. My eyes focus on her peach-colored lips, and I ache to kiss her—her bottom lip is all I can think about, imagining when I can nibble it the same way she does whenever she's nervous. Obviously, her eyes are closed, so I am robbed of staring into them, but her soft caramel skin and the various shades of golden-brown hair fall across her face.

I shift in my seat and lift up the armrest that sits between us so I can pull her closer to me, laying her head on my chest. She murmurs something but doesn't wake. In all my thirty-odd years I had never been one to like cuddling, much to the chagrin of high school girlfriends. My chocolate Lab has been the only one I've ever snuggled on a couch. It's so different with Charlotte though. I can't help but hold her close, swimming in her tangerine scent and the softness of her skin and the silkiness of her hair.

The women in the seats next to us look over and smile, taking in the way I cradle Charlotte. They'd been watching us all night but even more so since the moment Charlotte fell backward in her chair. I nod in their direction but turn to face the window, wanting our embrace to be as private as an airline snuggle can be. They don't seem to take the hint.

"You been together long?" the blonde with the long legs asks, motioning to Charlotte. In another world she would have been my type—blue eyes, long lashes, and breasts falling out of her shirt. After deploying, when I couldn't handle anything serious, I dated quite a few women who looked like her.

"Only in my dreams," I reply honestly.

Both women turn to one another, and I hear the other one say *"aw"* under her breath.

The blonde is not deterred though. "You mean to tell me you're not even dating?"

That is a hard question to answer. In my mind we are. Since I spotted her a few weeks ago I haven't thought of anyone else. And after our conversations last week, when we planned this trip, it was all but settled that we would come back a couple. But first we have to get past the obvious problem—my disappearance six years ago. Until I admit I was that man, I can't consider her my girlfriend. It's an unfair assumption—something she may not be able to move past. "I'm trying to win her over," I admit.

Both women look at one another again. "Do you have a brother?" asks the brunette, laughing.

The blonde is not happy. "Don't take this the wrong way— you're hot. Like really *hot*. And she's a klutz. Why are *you* trying to win her over?"

I roll my eyes now and pull Charlotte closer to my chest, if that is even possible, protective that she may have heard the bitchy woman next to us. "Some women are just worth the effort," I reply, turning my head away from them and kissing Charlotte's hair. Once again, a sweet moan leaves her mouth, and I feel my stomach twist. I've never felt this content, or this excited, about anything in my life.

In a few hours I will finally be able to kiss her. I made a promise to both of us that I'd wait for the perfect moment which I've already planned in my head. I've been researching the island we are traveling to for the past week, trying to ascertain where this moment should take place.

São Miguel, the island where our adventure is starting, is often referred to as the Green Island. The landscape is similar to Hawaii although it is never quite that hot. The weather for the next two weeks is in the high sixties and low seventies. It is the largest island in the Azores and also where my mother's family emigrated from. This isn't information I have shared with Charlotte yet. It was quite fortunate that the island she chose to visit also happens to be one I've been dreaming about my whole life—or perhaps it's fate. God, I have it bad for her. I'm not a man who ever talks about fate.

Distant cousins of mine still inhabit the island as well as my grandmother's sister, my Aunt Maria—a woman who never married nor had kids but is the matriarch to the entire family. Sadly, I only get to see her when she travels to the United States, which was often when I was a child but less frequently the past few years. The last time I saw her was before my last deployment—the one that changed me. I wonder if she'll notice the difference—if she can spot the scars that are invisible to most.

Our first stop will be in Ponta Delgada. We are staying in a hotel on the water—separate rooms of course. This is the city where I imagine I will first feel her lips against mine—where I will finally get to *taste* her. Would she taste like the tangerine that was swirling lazily around us now, or like the vanilla cupcake that I've come to know as her natural scent, or something different that I have yet to experience, a combination so sweet I'll never want to give it up? I imagine that will be the case, and I'm already growing restless with concern that she'll never forgive me, and I'll forever wonder what flavor I'm missing.

Ponta Delgada is famous for the black and white stone walkways which circle the city, designs of flowers and zigzags, working their way through as if an artist had painted them when he got bored with all the greenery. I close my eyes and imagine walking down those very sidewalks, holding her hand in mine and leaning down to kiss her whenever I want. It's a dream I am not prepared to let go of, and I drift off to sleep focusing on the moment it will finally be a reality.

Charlotte stirs next to me, and I open my eyes to find hers piercing mine. "You're still here," she murmurs as she nuzzles her head into my chest.

Of course I am. Where would I have gone? My chest tightens. Had she realized I was the guy who disappeared years ago? If she has, she doesn't seem upset, only glad to have me still by her side. I kiss the top of her head and pull her closer. "Nowhere I'd rather be."

"The sun is rising." Charlotte points to the window. Around us people begin to wake up and coo over the sights. There is something incredible about seeing the sunrise while on a plane, the red sky blanketing the green island. "It's beautiful," she whispers.

The bubbles in my stomach clench in a nervous excitement. Soon we will touch down on this island, and the adventure will begin. And I'll have to get up the courage to tell her the truth. Not just why I left six years ago, but who I became after I left her. It's not someone I'm sure she wants to know—let alone spend her life with.

"I hope I didn't snore or drool on you." Charlotte lifts herself up and stretches her arms.

My body misses having her close, but I take the time to stretch as well. My arm fell asleep wrapped around her. "Only a little," I tease with a wink.

Her eyes grow wide in horror. "I didn't?"

Laughing, I can't help but continue to goad her. "It was cute. Fortunately, you didn't drool too much, and your snores sound like a baby sheep." I mimic the noise, and she hits me.

The blonde woman next to us mutters under her breath, "It was anything but cute." Charlotte's cheeks redden, and I immediately regret teasing her at all.

Deciding there is no fix to that conversation, I change it. "So, I arranged a taxi to take us to the hotel. Then we'll see what we can do about getting into our rooms."

Charlotte takes the bait and appears relieved by the plan, her shoulders visibly releasing the stress. "That was a great idea. See, this is why Steph said I needed to travel with someone. I never would have thought of that, and I'd be stuck at the airport at six a.m. trying to figure out how to get to the hotel."

"Hopefully, I'm better than traveling with *someone*," I tease again as I lift my hands in quotation marks. The teasing is a coping mechanism to calm my jealousy over the fact that had the blonde-loving man not been so strange, I would likely not be the one sitting next to Charlotte right now.

Batting her eyes, she calms my nerves instantly. "You are the *only* someone I'd want to be here with."

That's it. I need to get her off this plane now. If we were in a restaurant, I'd be yelling, 'check, please!' and carrying her out on my shoulders. Unfortunately, that's not how this works. It's another twenty minutes before we land, and then we have to deal with the disaster known as customs. I don't dare divulge to her that I have a Portuguese passport—something that would allow me to avoid the long line filled with Americans simply because of my grandmother's heritage. Not that I want to hide this fact from her, but I know she'll push me in that direction and force me to leave her by herself with the bitchy blonde behind her, who will likely be whispering negative comments about Charlotte the entire time.

When it's finally my turn, I do show the agent both passports, and he looks at me oddly, asking why I stood in this line.

I nod back in her direction, and he smiles and says in Portuguese, "Ah, young love." Some of the few words that I understand. Most of the time I can follow a conversation, but speaking is a bit trickier. I stumble my way through the conversation and then wait for Charlotte so we can pick up our luggage.

The airport is small, but the views are incredible. Maybe some of the best from the island. The sun sits low on the ocean and a pink haze lies across the sky. Inside though, the walls are beige, and it looks like any other sterile airport. The room is stale, and I don't believe there is air conditioning, but I could be wrong. May just not be turned on because the temperature outside does not yet warrant it.

"How many bags you got?" I look for my big duffel which is army green. Living the Air Force life for almost the last decade, I learned to pack tightly and lightly. Anything that couldn't fit in this bag, I didn't need.

A bright pink suitcase comes out, and Charlotte points to it. "There's one." By the sound of her response, that is not all that she packed. As it is, she is already wearing a backpack and carrying a large duffel-style purse.

"There's more?" I ask, trying to hide the judgment in my voice.

She laughs. "*No*. I just wanted to see how you'd react if there was. The car I rented is tiny. Any more luggage than this, and we won't fit in it."

She's perfect.

"Alright, Sassy, let's head out and find our taxi." I grab my duffel and reach for her luggage.

"I can get it." Charlotte shifts the duffel from her shoulder onto the suitcase and starts wheeling it forward. The bag goes sideways and almost takes her five-foot frame down with it. She's adorably tiny. I watch in amusement, waiting for her to acknowledge she needs help. Fortunately, she's smart enough to accept defeat. "Fine, could you please help?"

My lips curl up and I nod, grabbing her luggage. I walk without saying another word. Her hips sway in front of me, and I focus on her very fine ass, happy that her luggage is no longer trailing her and hiding it—very sneaky on my part.

"Oh my God, look at this place!" Charlotte spins when we walk outside, looking in all different directions and enjoying the views in front of us. The muggy air and the smell of the ocean tug at my lungs.

"There's the car," I say as I spot the sign with my name on it.

"Whose João?" she asks pointing to the sign.

I laugh. "It's Portuguese for John. Jack isn't a popular name on the island so I figured I'd use John, or João."

"Oh, my God! It's like I've traveled here with a stranger. A dream come true." Winking, she puts her hand over her heart.

Shaking my head, I grab the carry-on from her hands, making sure to smack her ass as I walk by. "Sassy. So, so Sassy."

She feigns offense and hops in the car.

"On your honeymoon?" the driver asks in Portuguese. Charlotte looks to me, wondering if I understand.

I respond in English, "Not yet. One day, I hope." He raises his eyebrows in the mirror in understanding, and Charlotte looks at me quizzically. Not quick enough to think of a lie, I pull her hand into mine and look out the window.

The driver departs the airport, and we both turn our attention to the sights. I'm silent as excitement bubbles. The road twists before us, and the car enters a roundabout. The roads are paved beautifully, which is a strange thing to notice, but there are no potholes like home or dirt roads like the desert. It's like we've stepped into an alternate universe where the vegetation is greener than in the *Sound of Music* and yet there are the modernizations of civil society that don't seem to belong.

When the taxi veers onto a cobblestone street, the car begins to shift and sway with the black and white artwork. "This is insane," Charlotte whispers, reveling at the designs. To the right of us is the ocean and a marina with boats of varying sizes, while to the left is the city where large hotels and restaurants line the street.

"It's nice, yes?" the driver says, realizing that Charlotte won't understand his native tongue.

"Yes," she murmurs excitedly.

"You picked a nice hotel. You will like." We pull up to a large building which is grey and unassuming. The driver hops out and helps us with our luggage, and I hand him money, thanking him for the ride. "Make sure you call me next time, when you come back on that honeymoon," he says with a wink, reverting to Portuguese again.

I laugh and give a wave.

"Bom dia," the clerk at reception says when we walk in.

I respond back in English, "Good Morning."

Fortunately, the man smiles and changes his tongue. It's amazing how in Europe, Americans can rely on the hotels to cater to our lack of understanding but in our country, we would never be as kind. I appreciate the hospitality and ask if our rooms are ready.

Charlotte stands next to me gazing around the room. We are staying at the Azor Hotel. There is a pool on the roof which overlooks the marina, something she was very excited about when we made the hotel reservations. But the interior is what has me buzzing. The walls are wood, and there are big Edison lights wrapped around a chandelier above our head. Huge empty wine and whiskey barrels are strewn about as tables. Tires, old bicycles, and a large old-fashioned plane finish out the lobby. It is eclectic but stylish. The room doesn't feel cluttered in the least but instead each piece seems strategically placed to take you back to a memory. Like the typewriter that is sitting at the coffee table which Charlotte is now staring at in awe.

"I'm sorry. Your rooms are not available yet. Hopefully in a few hours?" Exhaustion overwhelms me, but I sigh at the response. What choice do we have? "There is a café in the square up the street which is opening now. Also, you're more than welcome to relax on the couches." He points to the area where Charlotte is already sitting, and I nod in appreciation.

"Is it alright if you take our luggage?" Charlotte's bag will not transport well on the cobblestone sidewalks.

"Of course." He begins to take the bags from me, and I motion to Charlotte for her to get what she needs.

A few minutes later we are outside, both staring out at the ocean and silent in our exhaustion. "Let's grab a coffee and then we can find a place to sit."

I turn to Charlotte and lose myself in her big brown eyes, suddenly happy that we aren't going to our own rooms just yet. I'm not ready to let her go. I don't know if I ever will be.

CHAPTER 12

Charlotte

My whole body is tired. The kind of tired where everything aches, your stomach turns, it even hurts to keep your eyes open. But somehow, because Jack is next to me, holding my hand and walking me down the streets of a foreign city, I am completely content and able to keep moving.

Everything about the last twelve hours has been amazing. First, the way he greeted me in the airport, and then promised that our first kiss couldn't happen there, and how he then held me on the plane all night and whispered how he cared about me to those horrible girls. I heard everything; I was just too tired to move. But he said I was worth it. That he *dreamed* of me. What is this life I'm living? I'd stopped believing in fate years ago, but now that we've been reunited it feels as if fate stepped in and told me to start believing again. I'm still blown away that the man I had been dreaming about for years was the one to answer my travel ad. It's fate. Kismet. For the first time in six years, I'm going to let go and enjoy.

Jack holds me close, as if he can't wait to spend every minute with me, and all I can think about are his lips on mine and when our first kiss will happen. We passed the promised restriction time. Now is free game. Anytime from now until we get back on the plane.

Two whole weeks. When will he make his move? The butterflies are screaming.

"You feeling okay?" Jack wraps his arm around me as we walk in sync down the cobblestone street.

"Are you kidding me? This is a dream. Pinch me, please?" I pinch myself just to prove my point. He laughs and I smile. It may be delirium from the lack of sleep or from the excitement over being back with him, but my entire body is giddy.

"Good. It's nice to see you smiling." We continue in silence, soaking in the views. How did a simple sign on a door bring me here? This is the most incredibly surprising place. The air tickles my lungs, the sea and salt washing over me like a cold shower, awakening all my senses. As we wander down the street I check out each shop. Most are tourist related, with stuffed whales and dolphins sitting in the windows for children to take home in pinks and purples saying Azores on them. But there are also plenty of restaurants with food that I can't pronounce listed in the windows, or cafés, which seem to be a staple all over Europe. We pass a few of them, but the hotel clerk told us to keep going until we reached the square, and I am sure to listen because I want to experience everything as the locals do.

We come upon a square with three arches. "The City Gates," Jack says. The white stone arches tower above us, approximately sixty feet high, with dark accents running the entire exterior, the middle one with a crown-like design on top the color of rust. Below our feet, white and dark cobblestone is laid in beautifully detailed zigzag designs. Behind us, the ocean, and in front, a town where matching white buildings stand with the same dark roofs. It is as if one person designed the whole area to match. We walk slowly under the arches and stop directly below the one with the crown. "I think it's time for our first picture," I say, cautiously optimistic that this will not be the last.

Jack waits patiently while I take out my phone and then he smiles at the camera when I put it in selfie mode. The image looking back at us is two people whose heads are tilted toward one another, smiling brightly, both with dimples indented happily, and tired but vibrant shining eyes. The perfect first picture. Jack looks at it appreciatively and then takes my hand in his. "Let's get you some coffee."

The town is quiet with only a few people milling about. Likely tourists without hotel rooms, like us, and workers getting ready for the day. A woman with dark, unruly hair, wide hips, and a long blue skirt that billows around her as she walks, sweeps around the tables in front of us. She looks up as we approach and drops the broom next to a table, flattening her skirt a bit before looking up with expectant eyes. "Bom dia, quer um café da manhã?"

Huh? I look at Jack to see if he knows what she's said. He has been communicating with everyone today, and I'm pleasantly surprised that at least one of us knows what's going on. This time he just nods at the woman, and she grabs us two menus and points to the patio as if to tell us to pick whichever table we want, which makes sense since the place is desolate. "What did she just say?"

Jack smiles. "She said good morning, would you like some breakfast."

Hmm. Reasonable enough.

"Bom dia," I practice quietly.

His smile grows. Apparently, I said it correctly. I'd say it over and over again to keep the happiness in his gaze on me. The way his eyes travel my body and stare at my lips, as if they could cure cancer or star in a music video, is making me dizzy. As I nibble on my bottom lip while trying to discern what the menu says, he is laser focused on me. The tension between us has grown since we stepped off the plane, both waiting for the promised kiss. Or at least I know I am.

When will it happen? Hopefully, after we are both rested and have access to a toothbrush and a cleansing shower. The staleness from the long flight and wine the night before is not the least bit sexy—on me at least. Jack still looks like a sexy fighter pilot. God, that is such a hot profession. And it totally fits him. The blond hair on his arms is unruly and yet so tame on his head, his blue eyes with the golden freckles dance as he watches me, and his calves, *shoot,* they are all muscley and delicious. They're covered in the same unruly blond hair, which laces its way up to beyond where his shorts cover, an area I can't keep my eyes from.

What is *wrong* with me? The lack of sleep and the hot man next to me are making me like a sex-crazed teenager.

"What you looking at, Sassy?" Jack teases with a smirk in his eye. He knows *exactly* where I was looking.

Fortunately, the waitress returns, and I'm able to avoid his gaze and his question. Jack is kind enough to order us both coffees and then says, "I'd suggest a bolo sandwich."

I agree, and he orders us two. When the waitress disappears, he explains, "It's similar to an English muffin is the best way I can describe it. With a hint of lemon, but softer."

I giggle. "Jack, I've lived in Bristol for the last six years. Clearly I've had a bolo before."

The town we live in has a large Portuguese community, and bolos are in almost every store. He shakes his head sheepishly. "Of course, you have."

Embarrassment crosses his face, and I reach out to grab his hand. "Thanks for watching out for me though. I'm going to need those little tidbits throughout this trip. How did you learn to speak Portuguese?"

Jack relaxes as he settles into his chair. "I'm half Portuguese."

He pulls out his travel wallet and shows me a passport, which indicates he's a Portuguese citizen.

I take it in my hand and study it closely. "Wait, you're a citizen? Of Portugal? But you walked through the foreigner line with me." My eyes crease in confusion.

Jack reaches across the table, taking back his passport. "I didn't want to leave you alone."

Someone get us a room!

Not only is Jack hot, but he's sweet. He's everything I thought he was six years ago. And he obviously cares about me, which I don't really understand. There's little time to comment on it, though, because coffee is placed in front of us, and I take the opportunity to focus on the hot liquid which fills the air with a sweet aroma. As I take a sip, my stomach rumbles. My entire body aches from the flight and jet lag, but my stomach is the worst, empty and not used to being awake at this time. It is still only four a.m. at home.

Stop, if you keep changing the time back, you'll never adjust. Get out of your head and focus on the *blond god* in front of you!

Jack's eyes never leave mine; it is as if nothing in the world matters as much as my face. Or maybe he is just zoned out like me, and I'm giving his tired gaze too much weight. Food is placed before us, and we both turn our attention to eating in silence.

Oh my goodness. Jack perfectly described the bolo. The ones at home do not compare. This is pillowy soft dough with more than a hint of lemon, perfectly buttered and topped with a fried egg, white cheese, and bacon. *It is heavenly.* "This is incredible," I say between bites.

"So, tell me about your family," Jack says.

Hmm. My family. Where to start?

"Well, I have a brother, Shawn. And my mom and dad are pretty awesome. And then there's my grandmother..." I trail off thinking about Grams. I visited her before I decided to go on this trip. And by visit I mean I stood outside her window, and we each put our hands up to the glass and stood palm to palm, the closest I've come to her for the last few weeks since they put the nursing home back in lockdown. A tear escapes which I try to wipe away quickly, but Jack doesn't miss it.

He reaches across the table and with his thumb, caresses the tears from my face. Instinctively, I turn my face into his palm and close my eyes, focusing on the feel of him. "Hey, it's okay, talk to me."

Whatever reservations I have left crumble at his words. The breath burns as it comes from my chest. I'm trying so hard to keep the rest of the tears at bay, but my tiredness is making it difficult. "She has dementia. But she remembers things, you know? Like she instinctively calls me Princess when she hears my voice on the phone, but if I ask her who I am, she falters. And now with all the restrictions for nursing homes I worry that I'll never get to hug her again. That she'll...disappear completely."

I wipe away the tears that are freely falling, and Jack

pushes his chair close to mine, pulling me into him. Everything is overwhelming. My emotions are on high alert. Part of me can't believe I'm sitting here. A week ago, I was teaching my kindergartners, holed up in my friend's house because my boyfriend stole my apartment, and I haven't been able to see my Grams because of her nursing home rules. And yet here we are, in this little slice of heaven, and I'm reunited with a man I met six years ago, who I knew even back then was incredible. It's fate. There is no other way to explain this. How else could this have happened? I have tried for the past six years to explain away these feelings, to discount our chemistry, to say it was nothing more than a chemical reaction. But sitting next to him, I can't help but think that maybe college me was right all along. Butterflies are real, and they are telling me to hold on to him a bit tighter this time.

When we finish eating, Jack looks at me expectantly, after having already handled the bill over my protestations. "Do you think you can handle a walk after this, before we go our separate ways and sleep for a few hours?"

My stomach knots. I'm not looking forward to sleeping in my own room. Being cuddled up with him on the plane spoiled me. I nod. "Yes, I think I can handle that."

Jack pulls out my chair, takes my hand in his, and leads us through the square. No longer concerned with my staleness, I just want to feel his body close to mine, to taste his lips which keep turning in my direction. I sneak a piece of gum into my mouth, just in case. My lady parts are tingling, and I don't think I'll last much longer.

The marina is apparently our destination. There is a stone wall where we sit and stare out at the Atlantic Ocean, not a single building or landmark in sight. The water is dark blue, almost black, and splashes around excitedly as it laps against the wall. Every now and then drops of it land on my leg and mist me in saltiness. I rub my eyes trying hard to stay awake, but the warmth of the sun and full stomach are coaxing me to sleep.

"You're tired," Jack says. An obvious observation.

I shake my head and lean into his shoulder. "I just want to sit here with you for a few minutes longer. I'm not ready for this to end." I look up at him, eyes wide and begging for him to put me out of my misery.

Kiss me, please.

Jack's fingers push the hair back out of my face, sending warmth to my stomach, and he grazes my bottom lip with his thumb. "God, you are beautiful. *Once in a lifetime beautiful*," he whispers as he moves closer to me, causing every nerve in my body to stand on end. He pauses, staring at my lips, seeking permission. Before I can finish nodding, his lips crash into mine, and his arms pull me closer. My heart pounds as he nibbles on my bottom lip and kisses me harder. My body hums, and I'm completely lost to both the feeling of his hair which I run my hands through and the taste of his tongue in my mouth.

I pull away from him and just stare, afraid that if I don't, we'll tumble off this wall and into the ocean. "How could you forget me?" I ask without thinking, the insecurity in my mind overtaking my mouth.

His eyes crease, and he moves his lips closer to mine, as if the sheer force of gravity is controlling his every move. "You think I forgot you? I could never forget these incredible lips, or the way your every thought constantly slips out of them, or these big brown eyes which make me want to *do* things to you, or this," he says as he palms the side of my ass. "I've been thinking about doing *this* since the night in your dorm room when you wore those dangerously short shorts to bed."

He what? My mind goes blank. Jack's eyes implore a response, but I have nothing. The most perfect words just left his lips, and my heart wants me to leap into his arms and never leave, but my mind nags that something isn't right. Inhaling loudly, I force air into my lungs and hope the oxygen makes its way to my brain so that I can think.

Think.

I turn away from him to break the spell that his blue eyes have on me. "You remembered me?" I say weakly. My stomach turns, an uncomfortable feeling settling over me.

"Charlotte, how could I forget the most perfect woman who I had the most perfect night with?"

I stumble over his words. Jack's eyes glisten with sincerity. Or maybe it's just the way the sun hits the golden flecks, because he's leaving a large part of the story out. The most glaringly horrible part.

"You left. Before I woke up. You *left.*" As I say the words, I finally absorb how horrible it was. Steph had been saying it for years, and I never allowed myself to get angry about it. Assuming that perhaps I'd made up the magic in my mind, and he didn't feel it. *But he did.* He's now telling me he felt all those feelings and yet he *still* left.

Jack sighs. "Yes, I did. And I'm so sorry about that, Charlotte."

Trying to make sense of his words, I flounder for an excuse. "Was there some note you left that I didn't find? One with your phone number and an explanation?" I look at him, hoping he'll say yes. Even if it's a lie.

But he just shakes his head. "I wasn't ready for what we clearly had. *Have.* But the moment I found you again, I knew I had to make it right. We have something, Charlotte. *Something real.* I can feel it."

Anger courses through me. Anger for twenty-two-year-old me who woke up confused as to where he had gone. The girl who for months searched the faces of strangers in bars, wondering why he left. The girl who still believed for a time in fate and butterflies. The same one who at twenty-four met someone who stirred some similar feelings—not quite as strong, but the guy was good-looking and a guidance counselor at school. He said all the right things, and the tiniest of butterfly flutters made me believe that he was worth it. But after I finally slept with him, the flirtation stopped, and he never so much as looked at me again. After two encounters with men like that, I put my walls up. Stopped waiting for butterflies, stopped trusting my own intuition, and settled for people who were reliable. Men who didn't make my heart flutter but who I could depend on. All because the man sitting across from me wasn't ready. *Seriously*?

He caresses my bottom lip again, but the magic is gone. "The moment you found me again. When precisely was that?" I'm hoping he says when he saw me at the airport—that like me he was just as shocked and excited about our unplanned reunion. That it really is fate that intervened. But for some reason I'm already getting the sense that is not the case.

He finally seems to recognize that the aura has changed, and he pulls back a bit, giving me space. "Pat showed me a picture of his new 'roommate,' and I recognized you immediately."

"Pat knew about this all along?" The ground falls out below me. I knew Pat wanted time alone with Steph, but even for him this plan is cruel. I guess I really had been cramping their space.

"No. Charlotte, you've got this all wrong. This wasn't some hoax. I didn't know the right way to approach you until he told me about your plan to find someone to travel with."

"So, you tricked me into coming on this trip?" I jump up now, needing to put as much space between us as I can.

Jack gets up far more gracefully than I, his calves that I can't take my eyes off of pushing him up in one fell swoop. His hands take both my arms, and he looks me in the eye, forcing me to hear him. "No. Well, yes. I hid the truth of who I was. But I knew we needed time to move past what I did. And we weren't going to get that in Pat's backyard if I had him re-introduce us. You'd immediately have recognized me and not given me the time of day. Here, we have two weeks for you to realize what I've known all along—that we are *meant* to be together."

He has no idea how I would have acted if he'd just been honest. Told me the truth. Instead, he tricked me into coming on this vacation with him. Allowing me to believe for a moment that fate had intervened. Why did I let myself believe in this feeling again? Why did I fall for the idea of fate? It's nonsense. Something adults tell children so they sleep well at night. Speaking of sleep, that's precisely what I need. "I need to go to bed."

"Charlotte, please, we need to talk about this."

I hear myself scream and don't recognize the sound. "No. We keep doing things at your speed and your preference. You weren't ready for *us* back then, so you walked away. You're now ready and so here we are, on an island, kissing. Well, now I'm not ready. So please, Jack, if you care about me, give me some space."

I turn on my heels and walk away, afraid that if I look at him for even a moment longer the tears will sting my eyes and flow down in front of him. It's something I don't want him to see. I run back to the hotel, entering breathlessly, and beg them for the key to my room. Fortunately, it's ready, and I'm pretty sure the clerk can see from my expression that I don't want to be told where the pool is or what time breakfast is daily, so he hands me the key and points me to the elevators. As the door closes, I see Jack walk into the lobby, looking around, but he doesn't spot me. I lean back against the cold metal wall and stare at my luggage. I'm in a country with the man of my literal dreams for two whole weeks, and all I can feel is anger. And humiliation. I'm a complete fool.

My fingers tremble as I try to get the key into the door. Pushing forward, I leave my bags unpacked and flop myself onto the big white bed. The tears finally escape, falling freely down my face. "No. No. No. I don't want to cry." I turn over and look at the ceiling.

It was him. He's here. And he kissed me. And it was *amazing*. Hands down the best kiss of my life. Not even a competition.

So, why did you run?

The little voice in my head won't leave me alone.

Because you're scared, you idiot.

I'm scared. And I'm hurt. For years I thought I had it wrong. Believing that the butterflies I felt back then couldn't be trusted, because clearly he didn't feel the same. I dated one guy after another, never waiting to feel that magical feeling again because I didn't think it was important. And now he tells me that he felt it all along. *Ugh.* I could scream.

Trying to get myself grounded, I pick up the phone and dial my grandmother's nursing home. I told her I'd call when I landed, and since it's now almost seven at home, I think it's safe to call.

The phone rings once, and my grandmother's voice comes over the phone, sending all sorts of emotions running wild through my body. A sense of home because that's what she's always been to me, dread because her memory keeps getting worse, sadness because I haven't hugged her in so long, and calm because she relies on me to be that for her.

"Hi Grams, how are you feeling today?"

"Hi, Princess," her voice squeaks. Her nickname for me sends me over the edge. She remembers. "I'm good. Just woke up, I think."

"That's good. I just landed in the Azores, and I wanted to let you know I made it okay."

She's quiet on the other end of the phone. Maybe wondering who I am or what I'm talking about, so I continue talking. "The island is beautiful. You would love it." I find myself rattling off facts about the island, even though I haven't seen much of it yet. It calms me to be able to provide her with information, to just be able to talk to her about anything. Even if she doesn't know who I am, treating her as if she does gives us both some semblance of normalcy.

I squeeze my eyes shut after we hang up, feeling a bit more grounded from our conversation. I still don't know what to do about Jack. But if speaking with Grams has done anything, it's reminded me that life is too short to be scared.

CHAPTER 13

Jack

Well, I really fucked that up. Pretty sure that couldn't have gone worse. Charlotte took off before I could react—or take back everything I said. What I would give to have just kept my mouth shut and kissed her, letting her believe that this was all some way for fate to reunite us. But no, I had to go and be honest. Lot of good that did me.

Turning my eyes to the sky, I breathe and count backwards, controlling the anger and desperation swirling around me. *100, 99, 98…* It's no use. I'm not calming down. My hands shake, my palms sweat, and this feeling won't end until I make sure Charlotte made it back to the hotel. This is a foreign country, and she doesn't speak the language.

Fuck.

I can't very well chase after her. I'd be like a stalker. As it is, I've already followed her to another country, without her knowing my true intentions. Turning the corner, I see her walking into the hotel.

She made it.

My shoulders relax, and I breathe a sigh of relief. It doesn't last though as I realize Charlotte didn't even turn to see if I followed her. Instead, she was solely focused on getting *away* from me. I really screwed up.

Hanging back, I give her time to get her key as the town comes alive. When I make my way inside it's just in time to see her hit the elevator. I pause, not daring to look her way, and instead focus on the plane on the ceiling. I'm not sure which gives me more anxiety, the idea of these old planes which are a staple in the Middle East or seeing how much I've hurt Charlotte. It's probably a tie.

"The young woman you were with, she just went upstairs. Room 312," the clerk behind the desk says, eyeing me with concern. Apparently, heartbreak is a language understood by all.

I nod, appreciating his understanding and the information he has provided. "I screwed up." He hands me my key and sends me on my way. When I get to my floor, I stare at her door—the one next to mine—contemplating what to do. Charlotte asked for time, so I have no choice but to give her that.

Opening the door to my room, I am pleasantly surprised by the view—the ocean I'd just left where Charlotte and I shared our first kiss is sparkling a brilliant blue. Closing my eyes, I'm back on the docks, staring into Charlotte's eyes when my lips finally touched hers. I'd bitten her bottom lip as I'd seen her do all day and lit a fire in both of us that I hope won't go out anytime soon. If I thought our fingers touching had caused a spark, our first kiss could have started a fire with wet wood. What we have is magic, plain and simple. It is what Taylor Swift songs are written about. I allow this to calm me, recognizing that now is not the time, but *our* time is not over.

The bathroom to the left is all black with silver sparkles on the walls—it's shiny and so very different from the world back home. Even the toilet is black as is the sink which hangs on the wall, like an illusion, without a stand.

I reach into the shower and turn on the water, allowing steam to overtake the room and hopefully provide an appropriate fog for my mind. As I strip and stare at myself in the mirror, I imagine Charlotte is here with me, stumbling into the shower as we kiss. Before long, my hand takes over, and I release the tension that has built up since I first saw her. Remembering the taste of her lips, I moan. I lean my hand against the wall in shame—this is not how I expected this day to end. What I wanted, what I'd hoped for since the first time I set eyes on her picture on Pat's phone, was for a second chance. An opportunity to make things right. It appears now I'll be looking for a third chance. How many times does fate toss you a bone?

I finish my shower and crash into the crisp white sheets. Sleep hits me fast, and I'm transported back to the docks with Charlotte—the only place that feels safe to think about and exactly where I want to be.

When I wake, the sun is blaring into the room because I never shut the curtains. My head pounds, and my mouth is dry. But nothing is worse than the feeling that takes over when I remember Charlotte's face as I told her the truth. A blank stare which then led to understanding, her eyes turning to sorrow before the anger took over and she grew red-faced with her fists clenched. Add in the pouting lip and her chin raised high—well, let's just say if I hadn't known how badly I hurt her, I would have scooped her up and kissed her right there, her anger be damned.

That's probably what I should have done. Maybe the brooding, sad, introspective man who spilled all his feelings wasn't what she needed. Or wanted. She seemed more interested in the hot, sexy fighter pilot she kept making me out to be. Maybe if I'd just pinned her against the wall and kissed her, showing her precisely how I felt about her, that would have done the trick and shut her up.

But you didn't, so now you have to apologize and figure out a way to get through to her.

The clock on the table indicates it is already evening. I can't believe how long I slept. Anxious to see what Charlotte is doing, I dress quickly, grab the room key, and head out to find her. When I reach her door, I stare at it silently, trying to work up the courage to knock. This is a bit ridiculous; I'd been less nervous overseas. At least in the sky my training kicked in. My mind would go blank, and my confidence could take over.

This felt more like the first time I sat in a cockpit or barreled toward landing my first jet. There was no option other than to do it, but that didn't stop my stomach from slipping, seizing, and spinning. Breathing out, I garner some courage and hit my fist against the door. Tiny footsteps pad across the floor and stop in front of it. I can almost hear her hesitating and trying to decide whether to open or not. When she finally does, I lose my words. Her hair is down, spilling golden-brown strands loosely on her shoulders, her face is makeup free and glistening, as if she just stepped out of the water, and she's wearing a yellow V-neck top which exposes more than a little skin with white shorts that make my heart pound.

"Yes?" Charlotte folds her arms across her chest and looks at me crossly.

I stutter, "Er, I know you were upset with me before, but you need to eat." I sound like a bumbling idiot. Fumbling my hands in my pockets, I nervously twist the inside of my pants and barely look at her.

Charlotte glares at me. "I'm an adult. I'm very capable of finding food on my own."

Of course, nothing I say comes out right. Nor does my demeanor express the man I want to be for her, not a bumbling idiot but the hot sexy man she'd apparently thought I was before this morning. "I'm going to say I'm sorry once more and then I won't bring it up again. I promised you a memorable trip, and I intend to keep my word." I raise my eyes to hers, daring her to defy me, finally acting as the man who could pilot a jet and easily take her down with a stare. Or at least that's what I think until her chocolate-brown eyes melt me, and I look away again.

"You're released from your obligation. I'm going to get the next flight back home." Her eyes are steel, and her lips don't waver.

I can't back down. If she gets on the plane, I'll never see her again. "Charlotte," —I try reaching out my hand to touch her cheek, but she pulls away— "please, I know I screwed up. I promise I'll follow all your rules. No romance, no funny business, no—"

Before I finish the sentence, she puts her hand in the air to stop me. She can't even bear to hear the word sex come out of my mouth. "I get it. No need to go further."

Apparently, I'm not the only one affected here. She's nervous for me to talk about sex. She still *likes* me. I keep the smile from pulling at my lips, forcing them to remain neutral. "Let's go get you sustenance, and we can discuss the platonic trip we are going to have."

Charlotte looks away from me and focuses on the black closet next to her. Her clothes hang neatly in color coordination. She unpacked—she has no intention of leaving. This cheers me even more. Charlotte watches my eyes turn to her clothes and looks back at me, her face registering defeat. "Fine. But only because I'm very hungry and our hotel reservations are non-refundable."

I nod and wait for her to grab her things then watch as she

stalks past me. Charlotte may think the silent treatment and not holding my hand are punishment, but she hasn't been privy to staring at her ass in those white shorts. When she reaches the elevator, she turns to look at me. "Where to, travel guide?"

I point my finger in the air. "The rooftop. There's pizza on the menu and a dazzling view of the entire marina." At the mention of the marina, Charlotte's eyes close, she breathes in slightly, and balances herself against the wall. Gently, her fingers press against her lips, and she looks up at me with a fire in her eyes. We're transported back to only a few short hours ago—our kiss, my hands on her face, hers in my hair, my biting of her lip, and her limitless desire. The marina *does* something to her. It is precisely what I need to keep wearing her down. I'll remind her that we have something special and worth fighting for. I will literally fight with her all day if it means showing her how I feel. If it makes her look at me like *that*. Clearly, expressing my emotions doesn't work, but I'll do anything to figure out what does.

"Okay," she says simply, turning to the elevator and hitting the up button. My eyes fall to her white shorts again. From the mirror in the elevator, I see the smirk on Charlotte's face as she catches me eyeing her ass. It takes everything in me not to pin her against the wall and slide my hands up her shorts, but I need to let her brood for a little longer. Seeing as how she is already smirking, I know this game won't last.

CHAPTER 14

Charlotte

What is wrong with me? I can't hide my smile no matter how hard I bite the inside of my lip to keep it from moving. I'm so angry with him for leaving years ago, but he says there was a reason. I tried to call Steph when I woke up, but I didn't reach her. Is his reason worth sticking around for? Also, he lied to me and tricked me into going away with him.

Ugh. I'm so beyond frustrated.

I keep my eyes on the mirror in the elevator and try hard not to watch him explore my body. He is so obviously interested, which makes this even less fair. The first man who literally lived up to my dreams, and he had to go and ruin it with his stupidity. The elevator dings as it opens, and we are greeted by an incredible view. A black infinity pool sits to our right. Black and white is everywhere in this country, and while the stark contrast is certainly enchanting, I can't help but see the irony that nothing else about this trip is quite so black and white.

The water flows over the side and appears to fall straight over the building. Another mirage, just like Jack.

To our left is an indoor restaurant with a bar, and in front of us there are lounge chairs looking out to the sea. Jack mumbles something to the hostess, and she leads us to the seats in the sun and hands over menus. I sink back into the soft white cushion which is atop the black wicker lounge chair and close my eyes for a moment, imagining what it would be like if I still didn't know the truth, and I could just sit here lazily with Jack and hold his hand.

"What do you want to drink, Sassy?" That damn flirty nickname breaks me from my hazy dream. My head remains on the cushion, but I turn, drinking in the man next to me. Jack is fresh-faced and his hair is blowing ever so slightly in the wind. He wears khaki shorts that reveal his best feature, those calves, and a navy-blue polo shirt that exposes his neck which is covered in light golden freckles, just like the golden specks in his eyes.

Involuntarily, I moan. *Damn butterflies.* A smile plays on his lips. "Prosecco," I respond, turning away from him and closing my eyes. I'm not normally a prima donna who relies upon a man to order my drink, but I'm afraid if I try to speak, I will spill all my pitiful thoughts which are wracking my brain, telling him how badly I want his body on top of mine.

He orders our drinks and allows me to rest, or at least to

pretend. We both know I'm not sleeping. Pretty sure he doesn't mind as I feel his eyes roaming my body, scorching each inch as if he's dragging a lit match across my skin, something he wouldn't dare do if my eyes were open.

Giving up the charade, I open my eyes with a huff. As suspected, he is staring directly at me and doesn't turn to hide it, not even a tiny bit of embarrassment crossing his face. I hold his stare, refusing to be the one to look away. I have done nothing wrong—he should at least have the decency to let me win this round.

He doesn't. Instead, his eyes warm with desire. I want nothing more than to snack on his top lip, the freckle above it teasing me in the same way his eyes do.

Shoot. Someone please help me. I'm going to sleep with him.

The spell is broken by the blessed waitress who brings my Prosecco and places it next to me, surprising me with an orange slice on the side. "Squeeze it in and you'll be in heaven," she says with a smile. I do as told and am perfectly content, finally enjoying my vacation in the middle of the ocean with the hottest man by my side.

Although, to be clear, I'd happily trade him for someone who *wasn't* him so that I could focus on this vacation and not on my currently twisted heart.

Since he's not going anywhere, I sigh and accept my fate, turning to look at him. He's got a piña colada in his hand with an umbrella, and I burst out laughing. "That is *so* not what I pictured you ordering." The man is over six feet and all muscle—with his chiseled cheeks and the knowledge that he's a fighter pilot, something does not belong.

Jack slides back on his seat, crossing his feet, and takes another sip, the cocky grin pulling at his dimples. "Oh, Sass, I'm perfectly confident in my manhood." And now we both know precisely where my eyes go again. Jack grins wider, proud of himself for making me look.

Rolling my eyes, I shake my head and look out at the ocean, inhaling the salty smell mixed with the Prosecco and a hint of garlic that I imagine belongs to the restaurant sitting adjacent to us. The alcohol works its way to my toes, leaving me tingling, or maybe it's the way he stares at my body, as if I'm the only thing he wants on the menu.

If I could figure out a way to lose myself in him, without getting wrapped up in all these feelings, I know it would be an incredible trip. But he's not looking at me like I'm a one-time thing. His eyes make it very apparent he has real feelings for me. That scares me more than I'd like to admit. If I allowed myself, I know I would fall head over heels in love with him, and there is nothing more dangerous than that because I don't trust he'll be there when I wake up.

"So, what do you say? Should we order a pizza?" he asks as he peruses the menu. If I don't eat soon, I'll be drunk, so I nod, telling him I'm not picky. He places an order for a margherita pizza and a pepperoni pizza, and a salad for us to share. "Will you have some sangria if I get it?"

Throwing all my willpower out the window, I say, "Why not."

We sit silently, and I can't speak for him, but for me at least, I enjoy the cool breeze coming off the ocean as I sip my cocktail. I watch one boat after another enter or exit the port. One of many useless facts pops into my head. "Did you know that where we are sitting used to be where whale watchers would spot the whales for the fishing captains?"

Jack raises his eyes to me. "Really?"

A surge of pride hits me. I love imparting new facts on others; it's one of the reasons I love teaching. "Yes. This was once the whale capital of the world. Did you know that?"

"How did they communicate? I'm guessing not through cell phones…" He fingers the yellow and pink umbrella stick in his hand, twisting it around.

Happy to be back to having easy conversation, I allow myself to relax. "No. Definitely not cell phones. They banned whale hunting in the eighties. So, unless it was on a Zach Morris cell phone, I'm pretty sure they had to communicate some other way."

Jack laughs, and I picture the ridiculously huge cell phones that used to exist. Then he glances up at me with tension in his eyes. "You talk to Steph at all?"

"Nope. Not that I didn't try."

His shoulders sag. "They didn't know, Charlotte. Don't blame them."

I absorb this information with a nod and let the topic go. I don't feel like having heavy conversation. Fortunately, the waitress appears with our food, and I sneak a piece of pizza and change topics. "So which side of your family is Portuguese?"

He chuckles. "My mother's. Obviously not my dad's since my last name is Fitzpatrick."

I laugh now too. That should have been obvious. "So, your dad's Irish and your mom's Portuguese. Have you ever been to Ireland?"

He shakes his head. "Maybe our next trip."

I feel the butterflies react and yell at them to be quiet. "I've never been there either. Although, as you know, I haven't done a lot of things. Unlike you, obviously."

"What's that supposed to mean?" A sly smile spreads across his face.

So much for killing the sexual tension. The fire spreading between us burns my throat. Nibbling on the inside of my mouth, I say, "I'm sure a guy like you has had plenty of women." Now my stomach twists in jealousy. Why did I mention other women? The last thing I want to do is think of him with anyone else. Or make him believe I'm thinking about him in that way at all. Although, the way my eyes keep darting glances at his pants probably leaves no doubt about what I'm thinking.

He laughs again, his head falling back. "Oh, Sassy, you're the one that was going on all the dates."

I roll my eyes. "Please, you think I believe for a second that a man who looks like you hasn't had plenty of girlfriends?"

I don't know why I can't drop the topic, but now I need to

know, and I find myself staring at him, waiting for him to deny it.

Jack puts the pizza down and takes a sip of his sangria, glancing at me out of the corner of his eye, then he turns to meet my gaze. "There have been women, yes. But not girlfriends." His eyes remain on me, and I'm not sure how to react. Does he have more to say?

Before I can stop myself, I ask, "Why?"

He looks away from me now, focusing on the sunset, and says nothing. When he looks back, I can tell he's been somewhere else, his eyes no longer focused on me. "That's not an easy answer. Or at least not a short one. I guess I was always comparing everyone I met to you."

I snort. "Me? The girl you left after one night together?"

He sighs. "I know. I was an idiot."

Insecurity gets the best of me. "Then why? Why did you leave?" I hold my breath still, waiting for him to answer.

"It's hard to explain. I wasn't ready for this. But I never met anyone like you again. Nothing was ever as easy as it was that night. Or maybe I just changed. Probably both." Jack's eyes meet mine now, and there is a vulnerability there, a pain I hadn't noticed before. There is a bigger story, but I can tell this conversation is hard for him, so although I want to know more—*need* to know more—I accept his explanation.

"What about you? I know you had the apartment-stealing boyfriend and the guy who wanted you to have blonde hair. Anyone else I should know about?" His jaw tightens as he waits for me to answer, as if he's afraid I'll tell him about some great guy that got away.

Newsflash, it was him.

"Honestly, aside from Ben, the apartment stealer who liked to eat peanut butter with his finger,"—I shudder from the memory—"there hasn't been anyone that mattered." The smile on Jack's face is almost comical as he grins from cheek to cheek. For some reason this makes me blush. "That doesn't mean there weren't guys that *didn't* matter though," I say defensively, and suddenly wish I hadn't because his eyes grow dark.

"I don't like thinking of you with anyone else." His voice is husky, and he's staring at me with longing in his eyes again.

"There's nothing to be jealous of. None of them have ever…"

What am I saying? I almost told him I've never had the big *O* during sex. Which is a truth that he doesn't need to know. No one *needs* to know.

Oh, Charlotte, control yourself.

The smirk pulls on his lip. "Clearly, you haven't been with anyone worth your time."

I huff, annoyed with myself and with him, because now I'm wondering if he would actually be able to do it. And if he wants to. It is *all* I can think about now.

Changing the subject, I ask, "Can we go for a walk to get ice cream? I saw a place this morning by the water."

Jack nods with the smile still playing on his lips and once again refuses to let me pay for dinner. We walk next to one another down the cobblestone street, focusing on the dark water which is lit up by a golden moon. This has been the longest day of my life. We started in Boston and now we are under a star-filled sky walking together in Portugal. Jack's hand continues to brush against mine, and I can feel him intentionally swiping my pinky with his own.

Unable to relax with his body so close to mine, I start nervously chatting. "Do you know what the biggest planet is?"

Jack chokes on a laugh and looks at me sideways. "I do." I raise my eyes waiting for him to provide the correct answer. "Jupiter. Do *you* know how much bigger it is than the other planets?"

Oh, turning the tables on me. I like it. I shake my head no.

His eyes light up. "It is almost two times as big as all of the other planets combined."

My eyes grow as wide as Jupiter. "My students are going to love that!" I clap my hands together, already thinking of how to incorporate this into our space curriculum.

Jack's face breaks out in a genuine smile. He's proud of himself. "Bring in some grapes and a basketball. Earth would be the grape and the basketball is the size of Jupiter. Really puts things into perspective how we are such a small part of it all."

"That's amazing. Thanks, Jack. How do you know so much about space?"

Still sneaking swipes of my pinky, he stretches his other hand behind his neck as we walk. "I like to read. And considering I spend so much time in the sky, it's an interest of mine."

Right. Pilot. Sky. The butterflies flutter awake.

We reach the ice cream trucks I saw earlier. The area is louder now, with tourists and restaurants all lit up for the evening crowd. We both order vanilla which makes me smile—so few people appreciate the simplicity of my favorite flavor. On the way back, Jack takes my hand in his, and maybe it's because of the salty evening air, or the ice cream, or the fact that I have barely touched another human in months, but I allow it. Under the stars, we stroll back to the hotel, hand in hand, each eating our ice cream in silence.

Back at the hotel, Jack pulls me to his chest before I can react. "Would you like to grab a nightcap?"

I shake my head. "I'm pretty tired. I think I'll just head up, but feel free to stay down here."

There is quite a crowd at the bar in our hotel lobby. Several beautiful women look over at Jack, and my stomach clenches. He can do whatever he wants—we aren't anything. And if he does stay down here, it will make it easy to move on, realizing that everything he said today was just words. That's not what Jack does, though. He nods at me and steps into the elevator. My heartbeat quickens, and I blurt out, "You don't want to stay at the bar? I saw some pretty ladies that could join the list of women, *not girlfriends*." I blush and curse myself. Why am I trying to push him to be with someone else?

Jack moves closer to me, taking me by surprise, and presses me against the wall in the elevator. My insides flip, and the butterflies sing *Hallelujah*, but I stay perfectly still, focusing on his mouth. "I made a promise to you that I would keep this platonic. But let me be very clear, Charlotte. There is only one woman I am interested in, and she is you. So, unless you have changed your mind, please stop talking about me having sex with someone else, or I'm going to be forced to find another way to occupy that beautiful mouth of yours."

With his lips hot against mine, our mouths touch as he speaks, and my legs grow weak. I'm grateful for the wall behind me which is the only thing keeping me upright.

Our eyes lock, and I consider for a moment just giving in and kissing him, allowing him to make my body scream in pleasure.

The sangria is going to my head.

When the door dings and the elevator opens, I push past him, walking quickly to my room. I don't turn around, refusing to witness his reaction, aware that if I don't get inside, I will never leave him tonight.

CHAPTER 15

Jack

I stare at the door which has now closed and realize that the elevator is going back down to the lobby again. I'm not interested in the bar though. There is no one I want to talk to other than Charlotte, and I'm not going to give her any reason to doubt my intentions by sitting at a bar with a bunch of women who could obviously fill my time but not my heart.

Back in my room, I undress and lie in bed, thinking of all the things I learned today. Charlotte is angry, but her resolve is weakening. It is only a matter of time—I hope. Although, if she keeps talking about sex or staring at me like she wants to do dirty things, she'll regret it, because I won't be able to hold back forever.

The ringing of my hotel room phone takes me by surprise. "Hello?"

"How do you know your girlfriends weren't faking it like I

did with my ex?"

What? I choke on my laughter before realizing she's giving me an opening. I'm not going to screw it up by talking about feelings again. "Oh, Sassy, they weren't, I promise. Now is that really what you called to talk about?"

"I...I..." she stutters.

She's so damn cute when she's tongue-tied. Unable to stop myself, I goad her on, sure the next thing I say will leave her speechless. "Tell me what you're wearing, Sass." I feel myself growing hard as I wait for her response.

She replies sternly, "What does that have to do with anything? *Ugh*, I knew I shouldn't have called."

"Charlotte, take off your pants."

This time she chokes on her surprise. *"What?"*

"What?" I tease. "I promise I don't bite."

She laughs, finally remembering her words to me so many years ago. "Oh, Mav, I see what you're doing. Nice try."

"No, seriously, take *off* your pants. I promise I won't touch...yet."

She inhales sharply, and the hiss is so high-pitched it has a whimpering sound. A few seconds pass, and I wonder if I've pushed too far. Then I hear her wriggling around, seemingly giving me what I want. I pull my boxers off as well and whisper softly into the phone, "Now, what are you wearing?"

A sigh escapes her mouth. "A tank top and underwear."

"What kind of underwear?"

Charlotte's voice cracks through the phone in a whisper. "Black lace ones."

Groaning with desire, I picture her in the bed which is on the other side of my wall. We're only separated by some plywood. What I wouldn't do to be lying next to her, hips touching, legs intertwined, my hands on her ass, rather than in separate rooms. "Charlotte, I promised you a platonic trip. I'm about to break that promise. Is that okay?"

She returns a murmured, "Okay."

"Breaking a few of your rules now too," I tease. "You know, the no funny business one, no—"

She stops me before I can say it. "Shh, it's fine."

Her impatience gets me more excited. "I was going to say romance, Sassy—mind out of the gutter." I laugh softly when she hisses at me. "I'm teasing, baby. If I was lucky enough to be with you, I'd give you everything. Romance, sex…all of it. All of *me*."

She sighs into the phone.

"If I was with you right now, I'd slide the strap off your shoulder and slip that tank top off your body, never taking my eyes off yours. God, you're so beautiful, Charlotte. Do you know that? You're so damn beautiful it actually hurts."

Her breathing hitches. I picture her top coming off and her nipples hard from the cool air. "Are you okay?"

She murmurs, "Yes."

Groaning, I grip myself tighter. She's doing things to me

with her sounds. "I'd nibble on your breasts, biting down just hard enough to make you moan, then sneaking kisses from your lips because I can't decide where my lips would rather be." My voice is husky, and Charlotte moans.

"I'd lower myself between your thighs, kissing you softly first, and then harder because I know I wouldn't be able to get enough of you."

She sucks in her breath at my words.

"Oh, baby, you're so perfect. There's nothing I want more than to touch your soft skin, to lower myself between your legs and to feel you all around me. To taste your sweetness. I've been dreaming about that moment for longer than I'd like to admit."

On the other side of the phone, she groans in pleasure at the mention of me tasting her. Her soft, whimpering sounds in my ear are almost as erotic as the things I want to do to her.

"I'm crazy about you, Charlotte. I'd do anything to be with you right now. To see your beautiful brown eyes, to bite that bottom lip that you are continuously teasing me with by nibbling on it. I want to take your lips in my mouth, and for a moment just stop, forget about everyone else in the world, so it's just the two of us and the way you make me feel. Like you did by the docks, kissing my memories away, sending shivers through both our bodies, making it so I can't even remember my damn name. The only thing that matters to me is you and your lips and the way you make me feel. I can't get enough."

She's crying out now, and I know she's close—so am I. A

girl like her deserves to be treasured, to be told how wonderful she is, to feel secure enough in a man's feelings to be able to relax and let go. I want to give that to her. I want to be the man to send her spiraling into ecstasy.

Her breathing is labored, and the sounds escaping her throat, as if she can't control them if she tried, make me want to jump out of bed and go be with her. I'm lost to her sounds. "Jack," she cries in a soft whimper, begging me to speak, to take her over the edge.

"Come with me, baby." A pleasure-filled moan reverberates over the phone and leaves me throbbing with her. We're both silent, breathing heavily. Envisioning her lying in bed as sated as me, her body relaxed and her cheeks heated, leaves me lonely. I want nothing more than to join her in bed and do that all again—together.

Finally, she speaks, "Oh. My. God."

"That's what she said."

A surprised, throaty laugh escapes her. "Okay, Michael Scott."

"Do you still watch *The Office*?" I'm not ready for her to hang up. "Wait, hold that thought. I'll be right back." I pause, making sure she doesn't hang up. "Charlotte?"

"I'm here." Her voice is tired and spent. I jump to clean up and practically dive back into bed to talk to her.

"I'm back."

Her shyness practically hits me over the head through the phone. "Hi."

"Hi. So do you still watch *The Office*?" I fold one arm behind my head while cradling the phone with the other.

She murmurs a yes, "Mm-hmm."

"I never watched it before I met you. Spent a lot of nights in the desert watching it after that though. So, uh, thanks for the good show recommendation."

Back to a bumbling idiot. Great.

"Desert?"

Shit. Didn't mean to say that. Not at all what I want to talk about now. "Yeah. Flying. Government." I'm not even capable of putting together a sentence.

She sighs softly into the phone. "You can talk to me, Jack."

I roll my eyes at myself. This conversation has gone off the rails. "I was in the Middle East."

"When?"

I run my hand through my hair. "When wasn't I is probably a better question. For the better part of the last decade of my life, I was deployed somewhere."

Breathing on the other end of the phone matches my own, and then she sighs loudly. "Wow, so the nickname I gave you was pretty accurate then, huh?"

Ha. Maverick. Right. I consider pointing out again that I'm not in the navy but let it go. She's looking for honesty, not cockiness. "In a lot more ways than you realize." And one of the walls falls down. She keeps knocking them over and soon I'll be left bare.

Fortunately, she doesn't push. "So, what's your favorite episode?"

I chuckle. "Um, any of them with Michael Scott in them. I was so mad when he left."

"Yeah. So, you just like the show for the inappropriate commentary then, huh?" There's no judgment in her tone, just an honest question.

"Yup. Me and the rest of America."

I can practically hear her eyes roll. "Yeah. No."

"Let me guess, your favorite episode was the wedding one?"

She laughs. "Obviously. What else would a girl who loves a good happily ever after want?"

"Bet you they never had phone sex."

Charlotte seems almost shocked by my change in topic. She's silent, probably in her head trying to come up with a retort. "I can't believe we did that," she finally says, the embarrassment evident in her tone.

In a voice barely above a whisper, I say, "Don't. Don't be embarrassed. Don't spend a minute thinking about this. You're beautiful, Charlotte, and I would do anything to bring you that kind of pleasure myself. Go to bed and know that I'll be thinking about you all night. And those noises you made."

I can hear her smile when she whispers, "Night, Jack."

Putting the phone back on its cradle, I lie back down on the bed, completely spent. I can't believe I told her about the war. That was a slip of epic proportions.

But if you want her to get to know you then you have to let her in.

I can practically hear Peter's voice in my head, urging me forward. Easy for him to say. He doesn't have to open up and spill all his feelings.

Nice one, asshole.

Okay, he has a point. But not one I feel like discussing any further. I'd rather focus on kissing Charlotte again.

Can't do that if you don't open up to her.

Throwing the pillow over my head, I try to silence my thoughts, because that's all this is, not Peter. But it's probably what he'd say. And he'd be right.

CHAPTER 16

Charlotte

My body tingles just thinking about our conversation the night before. What was I thinking? Calling him up and asking him about orgasms? Not that I expected him to do what he did. Although, if I'm honest, what was I expecting? I just wanted to keep talking to him—to keep fighting with him. Our banter is like a tennis match that I can't turn off, and both of us scored last night.

What I really want is to talk to him about his career, find out why he disappeared all those years ago, get us past this sexual banter that he keeps throwing at me, and figure out if what we have is real. But when I open the door to him, I'm greeted by a shit-eating grin on his face, and I know any chance of a serious conversation is all but lost for now. I want that smile to remain on his face. I could live in that smile. Do cartwheels in it. So instead of overthinking, I revert back to our banter. "Don't look at me like that," I warn, stalking past him and his flirtatious gaze.

"You better stop walking in front of me if you don't want me to keep undressing you with my eyes," he sings after me.

Turning around on the balls of my feet, I take him by surprise and slice him with my eyes. "Not another word."

Jack throws his hands up in the air as if to say he's surrendering. "My lips are sealed. So what time is the car going to be here?"

The rental company is dropping off the car and then we are going to Mosteiros which has hot springs and a lunch spot that we've been told is heavenly. "Should be any minute."

"Okay, we should put both our names down as drivers. The roads around here can get dicey."

I shake my head. I am perfectly capable of driving around this small island. Honestly, this whole protective role he plays over innocent doe-eyed me has got to end. "I'm sure I can handle it."

Jack shrugs his shoulders. "Whatever you say, Sassy."

But when filling out the forms, I second-guess myself and ask for his license anyway. "Just in case," I mutter to him as his dimple pulls inward.

We walk outside to inspect the car, and I burst out laughing. Most men in Portugal are slight in size, skinny, and a respectable five feet, eight inches or so. Jack clearly has his father's Irish heritage to thank for his height—which is not going to fit into the Mini Fiat Panda I selected. The car looks like someone smushed the back, and the ceiling is bulbous. Thank God for that because at least when he gets in, he doesn't have to hunch down too low.

"Are you ready?" I ask, preparing to put the car in gear. Only then do I realize my tragic error. I rented a stick shift. *Shoot.*

The realization must be written in red all over my face because Jack smirks again. "Everything alright?"

Ass.

I lie through my pink-stained lips. "All is fine."

My father taught me to drive stick as a teenager. Obviously, that was *years* ago, though. Not the smartest idea to take my first spin with a stick shift on unfamiliar roads, but what choice do I have? I am *not* giving him the satisfaction of knowing I can't do it.

We jolt forward, and he lifts his hand to the window to brace himself. "Are you alright?" I ask in a sugary voice, hiding my fear with sarcasm.

Jack shakes his head at me and remains braced. The navigation leads us toward town, not exactly a place I want to go. The roads in the city are narrow and populated with people and other cars. I already regret my asinine attitude. Drivers dart in and out of the tiny side streets without looking, and I slam on the brakes, causing us to catapult around like we are on a carnival ride.

"Jeez, Charlotte," he mutters under his breath, and I can't even blame him. *I'm terrible.*

We continue in silence until we reach the highway, thank the Lord. As the road opens up, I get a handle on the drive, enjoying the smooth road and green mountains that surround us.

Jack relaxes his arm and settles the other one on the back of my seat. My neck tickles, feeling him so close, and I remember his words from the night before. "What are you thinking about?" he asks huskily.

Shoot, he knows me so well. And yet he doesn't. We've just barely met. "Just focusing on driving."

He chuckles. "Well, I'm trying to *not* focus on your driving. So, take my mind off it before I start talking about things you don't want to hear."

My nerves make me bold. "Who says I don't want to hear what you want to say?" I brave a look at him, and my insides turn to mush. He's giving me the look that says more than his mouth.

"Oh, Charlotte, do you want me to tell you how all I'm thinking about is the way you taste? Or how I can't focus on anything when you speak because your lips tantalize me, making me want to suck on them while my hands explore your *other* lips."

My stomach burns and I can't respond. I don't want him to stop. He moves himself closer to me, and his hand trails lazily on my neck, making me tingle all over. A sigh escapes my lips.

Jack chuckles and pulls himself back. "I don't want to die, so I'm going to stay over here in my seat."

Feeling naked without his hands on me, I moan in despair,

and he laughs harder. It was a good decision on his part though, as I could hardly focus on anything with him so close, let alone keeping us alive while I drive.

When I turn off the highway, my stomach drops. "Oh no," I mumble under my breath. The road narrows and winds to the left. Worse than all of that is the cliff which drops off to the sea. I've seen roads like this in movies, but they were always in Italy, like the Amalfi Coast, or in Hawaii. I never expected to encounter anything like this here. It's terrifying. As we round the corner, a car swoops from the opposite direction, pushing me even closer to the edge. I curse under my breath, white-knuckling the steering wheel the entire time.

"It's okay, Charlotte, you've got this. We've got plenty of room," Jack says softly trying to calm my nerves. It doesn't work. I can't breathe, and I just want to close my eyes so I don't see the death trap before me. The road swoops in the opposite direction and now my side is close to the ledge. I want to puke.

"I can't do this!" I scream, completely aware that I sound ridiculous and have absolutely no choice but to continue forward.

"As soon as we get to the next town, we can stop, and I'll drive. You've got this."

"No, I don't think I do," I say shrilly, unable to focus on the gorgeous views in front of us. I don't want to become a sinking dot within the view which is exactly what I think will happen if I focus on anything other than the black winding asphalt.

The road descends quickly, and I feel as though we are

nearing the town. For a moment I breathe and take in the scenery, which for the record is absolutely spectacular. To my right, a flowering rock wall stands in great contrast to the asphalt, the bright pink and yellow screaming for attention. To the left is the ocean, in varying shades of dark blue to teal, depending on the depth. In the distance I see the landmark this area is famous for. Off the coast are islets made of volcanic rock which tower in size over two hundred feet above the sea. Settlers of this area thought one of them looked like a church, and thus the area got its name, Monastery, or Mosteiros in Portuguese. Another fact I've needlessly acquired. Although focusing on the useless knowledge calms me. Sighing, I loosen my grip on the wheel. "Please tell me our destination isn't far."

"Just a bit farther," Jack says calmly. We finally enter a more open road, and although we are still high above the ocean, there are proper barriers and it's all one level. Cars are parked on the side of the road and people are milling about. We are close enough to where we need to be, so I zip into the first parking spot I see and stop the car.

With my stomach in knots, I stare straight ahead, waiting for my breathing to return to normal. "You did good, Charlotte." Jack reaches over and puts his hand on mine. His touch brings me back to the docks yesterday when we kissed. After the ride we just had, and the steamy conversation before that, it all seems like a hazy dream.

I remove my hand from his grasp and push the hair behind

my ear, as if that is the reason for my movement and not that I can't handle his touch. "You can drive home," I say, rolling my eyes with a laugh and trying to break the tension.

Jack hops out of the car, seemingly ignoring my slight of his hand, or maybe because he doesn't care, and shuts the door. I'm left staring after him wondering if I will ever feel comfortable in his presence. Jack stretches his legs and looks around. My eyes stupidly remain on his calves, and when he catches me looking at them, an excited glint enters his eyes. "Hope you brought your bathing suit." Jack motions to his board shorts and to his calves where I keep looking.

Cocky. He is so very cocky.

I hide a smile as I look in the other direction. Bright sun doesn't compensate for the cold wind around us or the fact that the beach is located a jarring distance down the cliff. "I don't think we'll be swimming right now." I point down to the ocean but don't dare look over the ledge, the sheer thought of the drop making my stomach clench.

"The hot springs, Charlotte." Waves pour over the seawall onto the black rocks where several small ponds have formed, and I see people swim in them, or more like holding on for dear life because the crashing water is violently knocking them around. It must be how crabs feel in a steaming pot. *No, thank you*, I want to say to him. But he looks so excited I just follow along. "Did you bring a bathing suit?" he asks again.

I point to the straps of my bikini sticking out the top of my shirt and nod.

Jack shakes his head. "What a pity. I was hoping you'd have to strip down to your black lacy thong."

My mouth hangs open at his statement. Recovering quickly, I quip, "It *is* a black bikini."

Jack stops short and turns around, and since I don't expect it, I walk right into him. His hands move to my hips, and he holds me steady, piercing me with his eyes. "Don't flirt with me unless you want *this*." Momentarily lost in what he's doing, I simply stare, and he takes my silence as acquiescence, grazing his lips against mine. As his tongue slips into my mouth, my body takes over, and I pull him closer to me, moaning with desire. Remembering his words from the night before, I allow my hands to travel his body, landing on his butt, which I find is grabbable and round. He cups mine as well, and we both laugh into one another's mouths.

I start to pull away from him, aware of the onlookers' stares, but he pulls me back to his chest, hugging me tightly. "Just give me a moment, please," he whispers into my hair. The hardness in his shorts makes me laugh as I realize why he needs a moment. Relaxing against him, I wait for him to regain control and smile realizing that I have the same effect on him as he does on me.

"I'm not ready for this yet," I say honestly.

We need to talk. Not sexy talk, not flirt, not kiss, but really talk. I need him to open up further before I can trust that this is real. But I don't pull away. Instead, I lay my head against his hard chest and immerse myself in his smell which has now become familiar to me after only one day—fresh like he just stepped out of the shower. He doesn't wear cologne, so you can't smell him unless you are close, but now that my head is against him it is almost intoxicating.

Jack looks down at me, and an understanding passes between us. *Not yet.* It doesn't mean never. Our mutual recognition of this buoys us forward. "Okay, let's get you into a hot spring then. We've got life experiences to add to your bio." He winks as he walks forward, and part of me wants to grab his hand and feel his fingers wrap between mine, but I follow along instead.

"So, are you sure this is safe?" my inner scaredy-cat asks.

"You can continue to live your life on the sidelines, or you can jump in," he says with a wink as he catapults his body over the ledge onto the black rock. Jack turns around to wait for me to come down, and his speech must have gotten to me, or maybe his body just has a gravitational pull because I jump over the side too, right into his arms.

"Thanks." I steady myself on the hot stone, grateful that the concierge told us to wear water shoes. The rock is slippery, and I bend my knees a bit to steady myself, not wanting to ask Jack for any more help. We walk forward, and my nervousness only grows stronger. What was I thinking coming down here? Have I lost my mind? There are areas with signs on them saying HOT! And poofs of steam seem to be coming from them. "What's that?" I ask him, pointing in their direction.

"Kind of like little volcanoes, I guess," he says with a quizzical look on his face. "Okay, I really don't know." He laughs now, finally accepting that he doesn't know everything.

"Okay, we will just stay away from those then." I stare off in the distance at the people in the hot springs, and it doesn't look at all peaceful. "I'm thinking I'll just watch."

Jack moves toward them, his calves flexing as he takes each fluid step in a manner that is both slow and deliberate, likely because of how slippery it is. I remain still, mesmerized by his body and by the way the ocean is perilously tossing people inside the cauldron. I really don't want him going in there, but I also don't want to miss out on this once-in-a-lifetime experience. My body is pulled in two different directions, kind of like my heart, and I don't know what to do. At the last minute I push myself forward—hoping the reward is worth the risk.

When he reaches the edge, Jack pulls off his shirt, exposing his chest to my ogling eyes. It's firm and muscled—to be expected I guess, because of his career—but I've never seen a body like his in person. How does someone maintain that, and can I touch? *Please*. The freckles which were visible on his neck go all the way down his stomach, and I wonder where they end. Lowering himself into the water, his eyes hold mine until he flinches when the water comes up and hits against his chest. "Is it hot?" I ask, worrying that he's burning.

"Cold." Jack laughs.

One of the men in the water yells out to him, "That's only

the ocean water you're feeling. Give it a second once you get in, and you'll feel the thermal waters rising."

I watch Jack's face to see if it changes when he enters the hot spring. He's treading water but moving about almost violently. There's a rope on the side and I move quickly to throw it to him. "Don't be a hero, you dummy. Hold on to this." He grabs on and moves closer to the side. The water continues to flow in from the ocean waves and I stare in awe and fear. The white caps are ferocious.

"Come on, you don't want to miss this. It's only cold when you touch the top. It's warm now on my toes."

"I'm scared," I admit, glancing nervously again at the raging ocean.

"Do it anyway," he yells.

I don't know what comes over me, but suddenly I'm slipping my T-shirt over my head and shimmying my shorts off my hips. In one quick movement I jump into the hot spring, afraid if I go slow I'll never get in. The water thrashes me about, and for a moment I can't find the surface. My body goes down and down, and fear catapults my mind to dark places. The water in this area is hot, and I'm pulling my arms up searching for the cooler ocean water. Finally, I feel a hand pull me to the surface, and I choke out a breath. "Dammit, Charlotte, you're not supposed to cannon ball into a fucking hot spring."

Jack pulls me against him and holds me with one arm while hanging onto the rope with the other. My weight, topped with the strength of the waves, takes a toll on his forearm which strains to hold us. I reach up to grab on to the rope as well to provide more stability.

Our bodies thrash against one another, and his smooth skin grazes against me, as the warm water pushes and pulls around us. Fear dissipates and I'm overcome with thoughts of sex. His body rubbing against mine and his concern for my well-being bring a desire I can't explain. The saltwater dripping from his face leaves my mouth aching to taste him. Without thinking, I look up, offering him my mouth, and he leans down in understanding, kissing me quickly and granting me my wish.

With Jack's tongue in my mouth, I hold on for dear life, unable to break away from him, and I savor the rush of exhilaration coursing through my body. We're salty and hot. I'm kissing Jack Fitzpatrick in a hot spring in the middle of the Atlantic Ocean. Talk about life *freaking* experience.

Completely lost to my body which has taken over for any part of my mind, I continue to move in a way I don't recognize, as if my body does things just because of his proximity. My head tilts, my teeth bite his lip aggressively, and my hands roam until he groans into my mouth. I'm like a sex goddess, and it's all because of him.

Jack pulls away first, leaving me breathless and wanting more, and pushes us to a small railing. I hadn't even considered how we would remove ourselves from the hot spring, and I'm glad I hadn't seen this first because I never would have jumped in.

"How am I going to get up on that?"

Nervous would be an understatement.

"You just do." He hoists himself up in one easy leap.

Did he just leave me in here by myself? I don't have ab muscles that ripple all crinkly like him. I'll be stuck in this cauldron forever.

Laughter pulls me back to his face and I glare at him. "Crinkly muscles—what does that even mean?" Jack's eyes turn up in a smile.

Shoot, I said that out loud.

"Are you gonna help me out of here or just stand there and laugh?"

Jack reaches down and pulls me up in one fell swoop, leaving me no time to notice his wet, slick, crinkly-muscled chest dangerously close to my body.

"Th-thanks," I stammer, as chills course through me now that we're out of the water, with no towels, and the cool air blows around us. Jack's eyes explore my body as if he's memorizing my every curve.

"Come here, you." Jack pulls me to his chest and moves his arms up and down mine, causing the goosebumps to disappear. "Why don't you use my shirt to dry off?"

Jack hands me his shirt, and I shake my head. Our towels are in the car—rookie move—but I'm not using his shirt as a towel and having his chest remain bare all day, because I'll never stop staring at the wall of muscles and beautifully freckled soft skin.

"I am *not* taking your shirt. What will you wear?"

Jack ignores my concerns and starts toweling me off with it anyway. "I have a spare in the car." His hand moves slowly down my back as he lazily rubs me dry. My breath hitches when his arms move down the back of my legs and over my curves. Leaning into his neck as he continues to work, I inhale his dewy scent, and my stupid lips purse as I lay a kiss on his chest. *What is wrong with me?* Jack's chest rumbles in laughter. He's completely aware of the effect he has on my body.

It's involuntary, I swear.

I push him away in jest. "I see what you're doing here, Maverick. First, you get me naked, then you save me, and now you're trying to seduce me with your touch."

He smirks again. "Seduce you? Pretty sure you are the one who keeps kissing me, Sassy."

I breathe out, picturing the incredible kiss we shared moments earlier. The other swimmers got quite the show. "I think it was the hot water. It went straight to my head."

He laughs. "Don't joke around. I'll throw you back in there if I can get you in my arms again."

"Nice try, Mav, but I'm starving. Let's get food." I walk off leaving him staring after me, and I know precisely what he's looking at. I'm not going to lie. I'm enjoying this as much as he is.

CHAPTER 17

Jack

Being with Charlotte is like being in that hot spring. The hot and cold keeps throwing me around, and I can't quite get a hold on what she wants. But I'm having fun—and I believe she is too. It's all surface level though, the banter and the teasing. I can't quite get her to take me seriously, to take *us* seriously. It's clear she's scared of being hurt. Which I understand, having given her plenty of reasons not to trust me.

Watching her walk away from me and staring at her peach of an ass, which she swings for my benefit, leaves me pining for her. Obviously, I could get her into bed and likely will this trip, and if that's all I was interested in, I'd be a happy man. But that's not what I came for.

A few nights with Charlotte aren't enough...I want a lifetime.

The thought stops me dead in my tracks. No doubt I sound crazy, even to myself. I can't possibly tell her how I feel. That will only make her retreat further into her head. I've got to continue to play the long game—keep her interested and hold my cards close to my chest until she learns that she can trust me.

Now who's the one in his head?

Shaking myself from her spell, I move quickly after her. The concierge told us to try the Sunset bar at the beach—it is really a glorified food truck with a few tables inside and several outdoor tables overlooking the islets and the incredible views. We make our way to the front of the line and grab menus.

"What do you want to drink?" The Sunset passionfruit lemonade calls my name. Charlotte will definitely have a wiseass comment. I'm already excited to spar with her.

"I'll try the lemonade, I guess," she says, and I smile, ordering two lemonades along with sandwiches. We take our drinks and sit at one of the tables overlooking the water. When I take a sip, the explosion of flavor takes over my senses. It isn't too sweet, and the passionfruit balances out the tartness of the lemonade.

Charlotte sighs in appreciation as she tries her drink. "Wow, this is good."

"Yes, I'm surprised you went for it though."

She laughs. "Well, I didn't want you to feel self-conscious about your girly choice in drinks."

Piercing her with my eyes, I smirk. "I told you, Sassy, I'm very confident in my manhood."

She laughs louder, and the sound makes my heart swell. For so long I dreamed of that laugh. Remembering how freely she offered that sound the night we met. Imagining spending time with her again, making her laugh, wanting so badly to experience the ease of that night. It was a light in the darkness that was my life for so long after Peter's death. I'd spent the last six years surviving on that sound, on that smile, which is why my heart causes my stupid mouth to blurt out what I really want. "I'd like to introduce you to someone."

So much for taking things slow.

Charlotte eyes me as she twirls her straw in her drink before taking another sip. Say something, please. My throat closes waiting for a response.

"Who?"

I breathe. "My aunt. She lives on the other side of the island in a tiny village. Would you be willing to go there after we leave the city? I know we made plans to stay at the hotel in Caloura, but my aunt has a large house in that area, with a pool on the water, and we could stay there instead."

In my gut I know this is where we need to go. If I want to show Charlotte who I really am, and explain to her why I disappeared that night, we can't be staying at a ritzy hotel. That will just keep everything surface level. I need to dive in like Charlotte did with the hot spring. Being around family will help me do that.

Anxiety plagues her face. This is taking the trip in a different direction—meeting family is not the light vacationing with a stranger she planned. Her finger twists tighter around her straw, and her eyes turn to the ocean, avoiding my gaze. "I don't know, Jack."

I graze my thumb against her hand and squeeze her fingers gently. "I know I'm asking a lot. You don't have to decide now. But I want to give us a real shot, Charlotte. I love the playfulness, and the kisses, and the late-night calls," I say huskily, my voice cracking a bit, "but I want more than that."

Silent, she eyes me but doesn't pull her hand away. It's as if she's taken my heart hostage while she considers. "I'll think about it."

My heart races. "Thanks, I really think it will be good for us."

Jumping up, Charlotte takes me by surprise. "I need to make sure to get pictures of the hot springs. My kindergartners will love this." She walks toward the rocks to take a few shots with her phone. I suppose it's possible the idea just came to her, but I have a feeling it's more likely that she wants to avoid this conversation. I've freaked her out. My jaw clenches. Why the hell did I have to go and ruin our perfectly easy conversation with such a heavy request? I asked her to meet my family. What is wrong with me? Since meeting her, I'm either a pool of emotional mush, spewing eighties rom-com ideas, or I'm a cocky asshole. I can never just *be* because I'm trying too hard to get this right. It's infuriating, because around anyone else I'm a leader, calm, someone who commands a room—but with her all rational thought goes out the window.

When Charlotte walks back over, she slides her phone in her pocket and sits down. I look at her expectantly, hoping I read the moment wrong and she isn't as freaked out as she appears. When she looks away from me again, I have my answer. She can't even look me in the eye. "Maybe I should plan a project for the kids to make their own volcanoes." Pulling out her phone again, she begins typing. I see we're playing the avoiding game. Very mature.

"I'm sure the kids will love that," I offer.

When she looks up at me with a smile, my heart slams into my chest. It's the first genuine smile she's had all day—not a flirty one, not a nervous one, just pure joy. With her hair still wet from our swim, natural waves appear, the same way they did many years before after we got caught in the rain. There is a kindness in her eyes when she talks about her students. Her kindergartners must love her. I'll play whatever game she wants.

The chef shouts my name, and I jump up to grab our food, grateful for the interruption. If I keep staring at Charlotte, I'll probably tell her I'm falling in love with her.

We settle into quietly eating, commenting only that everything is delicious. After lunch, I offer to drive and suggest we do more sightseeing. "Honestly, I could use a little nap," Charlotte replies, looking away from me. "Do you mind if we take a break and maybe meet up later?"

I shrug off my concern that it has more to do with us and less to do with her lack of sleep and tell her it's not a problem. But as we drive the windy roads back to the hotel, and Charlotte doesn't make so much as a peep in fear or concern, I suspect I may be right to be worried. Clearly, I spoke too soon and pushed for too much. The spark is gone—we don't even have banter.

"Thanks for a great day," Charlotte says as we get out of the car.

"Sure thing." I stuff my hands into my shorts uncomfortably. *Sure thing*? Ugh. What is wrong with me? Why did I tell her I wanted her to meet my family? What was I thinking?

We walk into the hotel together, and she turns to me as if she has something to say, but then she just stares. I can feel the stress radiating from her skin.

"You okay?" I don't dare reach out to touch her. A guy can only take so much rejection.

She nods. "You going to your room?"

I look around the lobby and see the bar has quite a few empty stools—and quite a few women. While only one thing at the bar interests me, I know she will think otherwise. But I need a drink and time to think. "I think I'll hang here, actually. Enjoy your nap." I turn and walk to the bar before I can see her disappointed reaction. She likely believes I'm proving her point—she can't trust me. I'm just a player. For now, I just don't care. I can only handle so many of her disappointed looks in one day. I've reached my limit.

CHAPTER 18

Charlotte

Slamming my head against my pillow, I stare at the ceiling and wonder if Jack is talking to any of the women at the bar. That's clearly why he stayed downstairs. It was beyond obvious. Almost like he wanted me to know that if I continued to pull back from him, there is a long line of women willing to step into my place. As if I don't know that already.

I have eyes. I'm not blind.

Jack is the type of guy women fall all over themselves for. Women who haven't even been privy to the feel of his lips, or the way his chest feels as it bucks against them in the water, or the dirty way he speaks.

Although if I'm honest, none of those things are why I'm so torn. Nothing compares to the way he looks at me. *Nothing.* And the way he expresses his feelings. Any other woman would fall into his arms in two seconds if they experienced it. So why am I hesitating?

Picking up the phone, I dial his room. Maybe I have it wrong. Maybe he didn't stay down at the bar. But as I listen to the phone ring and ring, I know I pushed back too hard. There are only so many times a guy is going to put his heart on the line and have a girl reject him. The reaction I gave to his request to meet his family was lukewarm at best. And then I was cold the entire ride home. The worst part is that he was giving me what I wanted—he was trying to take things to a deeper level, take us past the banter. Why, when he offers me everything I want, do I pull back?

Shoot. My chest tightens and saltiness rises behind my eyes.

I slam the phone down and dial Steph's number quickly. "Hey! How is Portugal?"

When I hear her voice, the dam cracks open, and I sniffle into the phone, trying to control my tears. "I'm totally messing this up."

Steph sighs and Grover whines, likely annoyed that I'm hogging her attention. "What do you mean you're messing this up?"

I roll my eyes at myself, because really, I am beyond annoyed. I was supposed to go on this exciting once-in-a-lifetime trip, and instead I'm crying to my best friend. "*Jack.* The Azores. You name it, I am messing it up."

Steph growls, which is not a sound I'm used to hearing. For a moment I actually think Grover took the phone, but no, it is indeed Steph because she is also yelling at me. "Charlotte Marie Chase, you have got to be kidding me!"

I mean, really, I'm crying over here; she could have *some* compassion. "What?" I ask meekly.

She huffs, and I can practically see the little hairs falling into her face as she blows them up out of her eyes. Her freckled cheeks are probably red in aggravation, and she's likely walking to the kitchen to pour herself a glass of red wine to calm down. "Charlotte, *please* do not take this the wrong way, but give me a freaking break."

"Huh?" So much for the pep talk.

She sighs into the phone, and I hear her uncork the wine. I was right about that. Next, she sets a glass down on the counter and the liquid sloshes in. A few more seconds and she's sipping and humming in appreciation. I count to five waiting for her to get to her point. I'm about to lose my mind.

"For six years I have had to hear about the perfect man who you were sure was *the one* and who slipped through your fingertips. News flash, he's now standing in front of you, and he's interested in you. So, Charlotte, maybe everything in life *isn't* fate. Hell, maybe Jack isn't even your person. But the two of you are on an island, in the middle of the ocean, in *Europe*, for two weeks, and you are *blowing* it!"

Silently I sit, taking in her words. Flipping them over in my mind. "I know," I whisper. "But I don't know how to stop." And this is precisely my problem. This is what I do. I get in my head.

So much so that I can't even enjoy the moments while they are happening. Who wants to live like that? It's exhausting.

I hear the relief in Steph's voice when she speaks again. "Oh, girlfriend, you just need to get out of your own head. *Stop thinking*. Stop sitting in that room and trying to decide what you want. Go get it. You deserve to have fun. And that much I know Jack is good for. He's a hot man, and he's interested in you. Drink him up until you're so intoxicated by him that you're seeing stars."

I laugh, thinking of how he made me see stars the night before. Groaning, I divulge a few of the details. "He *is* a very good kisser."

"Well, duh. Have you seen his mouth? He's like stupid hot."

It must be the scar on his lip, or the freckle. His mouth is meant for kissing. I lean back against my pillow and laugh. "Don't even get me started on his abs. Each one has a twin. There are eight of them, Steph. Eight! I could seriously trace them daily and never get bored."

"Thatta girl. Now go make mama proud and sleep with him. Or don't. Do whatever makes you happy. Just don't cry. You're too pretty to be cooped up in a hotel room."

Smiling into the phone, I feel much better. "Thanks Steph. Give Grover a kiss for me." She agrees, and we hang up the phone, my mood already exponentially lighter.

Hopping out of bed, I walk to my closet with big plans. No more hesitating. No more living in my head. I am going to put on my hottest outfit, go after that hot man with the eight pack, and go out tonight.

CHAPTER 19

Jack

Two drinks in and I'm starting to relax. I've mastered the *I'm not interested* look, so most of the women steer clear of me. I switched to the hard stuff—no more fruity drinks for me. They seem to be making me far too expressive in my emotions. It has become abundantly clear that Charlotte doesn't like the sweet, nice guy routine. Whenever I try to open up, she pulls back. I can do broody detached as well as the next guy. Probably better.

My phone buzzes in my pocket, and the screen indicates its Pat. *Excellent.* I'm sure he's calling to yell at me. "Hi."

"What the hell is going on with you?"

Right on target.

"Nice to talk to you too, buddy. Miss me?"

He scoffs. "You don't get to do that."

I interrupt him. "Excuse me? Do what?" People turn toward me as my voice goes up a few decibels.

"You're screwing with Charlotte, and you need to stop."

I make a strangled noise, something between a guffaw and a, *you've got to be fucking kidding me*. "I have done nothing but try to make everything right. I've been respectful, well, okay, not totally respectful—we did have phone sex last night." A look of horror sweeps across the faces of a couple sitting across from me. *Whoops*, the alcohol is going straight to my head, and out of my mouth. Loudly.

"Save it. She called Steph crying. Whatever you're doing...just stop."

Crying? "Fuck," I whisper, massaging my temple and trying to sober myself up. I throw some money onto the bar and walk outside with the phone, craving the fresh air and quiet. "She was really crying?"

"Yes. Listen, I know you have feelings for her, or whatever, but she's like the girl you bring home to meet your mother, not just someone you date for a short time. And she's Steph's best friend."

I kick my shoe against the stone wall. "I know that. I wanted to bring her home to meet *my* family. That's why she's upset. I think."

Pat laughs. "I don't know what the hell you two are doing there. Phone sex? Family introductions? It's been two days. Maybe you are meant for each other. Both of you are moving at warp speed... No, wait, Steph is shaking her head at me. You are *not* meant for each other."

A ruffling noise scrunches in my ears and Pat yells, "Don't listen to her!"

"Jack, what the hell is going on there?" It's Steph, and her voice is all growly and short.

"Hi, Steph, lovely to speak with you."

She stabs me with her words. "Cut the shit. What did you do to her?"

"Oh my God. Why does everyone assume I did something wrong? I told her I'm crazy about her. Told her I wanted to give us a real shot. Asked her to meet my family. Yes, I know, I'm a terrible person and scum of the earth."

Steph screeches, "You did what?"

"Yes, Steph, despite your apparent belief that I am trying to take advantage of your best friend, I am literally trying to do the exact opposite. I could have had her in bed last night if I wanted, but I don't want just one night with her."

"Well, what do you want then?" she asks suspiciously, though I can hear a smile in her voice.

I sigh. These women are driving me nuts. Am I supposed to ravage Charlotte or woo her? Could someone please clue me in? "I want her. All of her. For all the days of our lives." I mumble the last part and kick the wall again. I sound like such a pathetic fool.

"But how?" Steph asks, obviously dubious of my ridiculously strong feelings.

"*You're* her best friend. You should know. It's *her*. She's amazing. It's so enraging how amazing she is. But after I met her six years ago, no one ever compared. And the moment I laid eyes on her again, I knew the feelings were real. I'm crazy about her, and I can't stop telling her. I keep *trying* to stop. And if you tell me that is what will work, then I'll stop emotionally vomiting how I feel about her every time I see her. Honestly, Steph, tell me what I can do to make this right."

"Shit." Yes, that about sums it up.

"I know." I sigh again.

"No. *Shit*. I told her you weren't her person."

My jaw clenches, and I pull on the back of my neck. "You did what?"

Steph groans. "She's been obsessed with the idea of you for years. The idea of you was getting in her head. I thought I was doing the right thing. I told her to be bold. Sleep with you. But to stop this fantasy of falling in love."

I laugh. "Well, *thanks*. I mean getting laid is awesome, but yeah, I want more than that."

"Pat, we need to go to the Azores." Her voice is muffled as if she's holding the phone away from her mouth.

"Woah, what are you talking about?" I say, trying to get her to respond.

"We need to be there. She needs me." Steph says it with such finality, I'm already resigning myself to the fact that our romantic trip for two is about to turn into a couples' trip.

"Listen, I'm going to go try to talk to Charlotte." I still haven't worked out what I'm going to say, but I don't want her crying, and I definitely don't want her believing Steph's bullshit that we aren't meant to be together.

"No!" Steph practically screams into the phone. "No more

baring your soul. No more emotional vomiting. *It's not working.* She's overthinking everything—which if you knew her, you'd know that she does that with everything! Let her lead. Just enjoy her until we get there. It's all she can handle."

Realizing that she won't take no for an answer, I agree.

"I'm not kidding, Fitzpatrick. Don't you dare smooth talk her or tell her you love her. It won't end well."

I laugh. "Okay, okay. I'll just sleep with her—no emotional Olympics."

"I never thought I'd say this but yes, please, just get her to let loose and have fun. It's what she needs. The love stuff will come later. Stop *rushing* it."

I smile now that we have a plan. "Okay, thanks, Steph. Let me know when you guys are heading this way."

Pat takes the phone and whispers, "I can't believe you convinced my wife to take a vacation with me, and she told you to sleep with her best friend. What is happening?"

"Haha, you are very welcome. And you owe me an apology. All of you keep thinking the worst of me." My ego is starting to feel a bit bruised. I may have gone through a few women over the last few years, but I never led anyone on, and I'm not loving this apparent reputation I developed.

"Sorry, man. Good luck with Charlotte tonight."

"Thanks, man. I have a feeling I'm gonna need it." We hang up, and I throw my head to the sky. Somehow, I will convince them they are all wrong about me.

CHAPTER 20

Charlotte

First, I slip on my silky red dress—by far the hottest one I packed—but as I stand looking at myself in the mirror, it is all wrong. My body doesn't yet have the sun-kissed tan that I need to pull this off.

Not in my head, I promise—I'm just being honest here.

The fabric slides off my body, and I place it back on the hanger, promising myself I will wear it by the end of the trip, once there are tan lines to go with the strappy number.

Flipping through the other hangers, my eyes land on a dark purple chiffon dress. It has a halter top and reaches my toes. A bit fancy for an evening with no plans, but I don't intend to keep it that way—I am going to find my hot sexy man date and force him to have fun with me. No more overthinking, no more talk of love, hopefully little talk in general. All I want is to feel him cling to me like the soft fabric of my dress, caressing every curve of my body.

Next is jewelry. I am done being the girl next door with the sweet innocent doe-eyed look. I stack gold bangles on my wrists, attach long dangly earrings on my lobes, and spray my body with a shimmery mist which makes me sparkle. Dabbing a little extra between my breasts, I stare at myself in the mirror. Radiant. I add mousse to my hair, creating a wet crinkly curly look, and leave it hanging on my bare shoulders. Straight hair begone. I imagine my strait-laced personality is also flying out the window and smile, tossing my hair over my shoulder.

Topping my eyelashes off with mascara and my lips with a plumping gloss, I look like I just came out of the hot springs—or how I imagined I looked then—hoping to remind Jack of our hot steamy kiss and how his body reacted when it slid against mine. Finally, I throw a black shawl into my clutch and head out the door, walking quickly to the elevator.

Slow down, Charlotte, I hear Steph's voice in my head. I slow my walk, swinging my hips like I know he'll be waiting for me. When the elevator opens on the lobby floor, Jack is nowhere to be found. So much for a grand entrance.

You do not need a man to be happy. Repeating the words in my head, I saunter over to the bar, grab a stool, and daintily plop down—okay, no one can daintily plop, but work with me here.

"Boa noite, linda," the bartender sings in his beautiful dialect. From my limited understanding of the romance languages, I believe he said, "good evening, beautiful" and I am going to rock it even if I'm wrong. I smile broadly and accept the drink menu.

"May I have a glass of pinot noir?"

In a thick accent, he responds in English, "May I suggest Monte Velho instead?" I look at him quizzically, and he continues. "It's a bit heavier but from our local vineyards. With fruits—plum and blackberry."

What the heck. I'm in another country, might as well try their wine. "Yes, thank you," I reply, already feeling myself relax.

The bartender places a plate before me which has a soft white cheese on it, something that looks like jam, and a piece of bread. My stomach grumbles as I realize I haven't eaten since lunch. Even that I barely touched because of my nervousness over Jack's proposition. The bread is warm and crispy on the outside but doughy in the middle. With my mouth watering, I slather the cheese and jam on it generously. The bartender watches me with appreciation, and I place a bite in my mouth, biting it seductively, as if I'm a sex goddess.

Oh my God. The jam burns my tongue like a thousand fire ants. My eyes tear up, and I search the bar for a glass of water. This can't be how I die—in a foreign country, dressed sexily, choking on a piece of bread, before I even get to sleep with Jack.

The bartender's eyes remain on me as he pours my wine. I try hard not to react, but the heat rises to my face, scorching my cheeks, and then slowly burns its way down my throat, into my chest and singes even my toes. Every inch of my body is on fire.

Finally, the bartender slides the wine glass across the bar and waits for me to try it. Sipping is not an option. I down the wine in one gulp, craving the cool liquid and any flavor that is not that mouth-burning jam.

"I take it you liked the wine?" Jack whispers into my ear, appearing from nowhere. His warm breath takes me by surprise and makes my already frayed nerves stand on edge.

"How long have you been standing there?"

I feel my tongue again, just in time for Jack to make it throb.

He sits down and smiles his beautiful-dimpled smile. Why does he have to be so painfully good-looking? "Long enough to watch you stumble your way through a conversation in Portuguese, flirt with the bartender, and jam your mouth full with hot peppers."

Hot peppers. That explains it. The bartender approaches us with the wine and offers a refill. I nod in appreciation, and he gestures to ask Jack if he wants a glass. Jack shakes his head. "I'm all set. I'm going to shower." As he gets up from his chair, I almost grab him. Where is he going? I'm hot, like literally on fire, but also dressed solely for his reaction, and he seems uninterested.

Jack places his hand on my bare back, sending shivers down my spine, and tickles my ear when he whispers, "Relax. I'll be back. Enjoy the wine. Flirt with the bartender. *I'm not concerned*. I know you'll be going home with me tonight."

Goosebumps slide up my neck. The butterflies scream.

I moan as he releases me and turn to watch him walk away,

focusing on his calves. Tonight, I will feel his body against mine, and every inch of my skin aches for his touch.

As he gets in the elevator, Jack catches me drooling over him, and he raises his eyebrows with his cocky smile, no innuendo left between us. We both know what will happen tonight. Somehow knowing we have to sit through dinner before we can have dessert is almost better. The looks we'll share all night will be hot with anticipation.

I take another sip of my wine, finally appreciating the flavors the bartender told me to expect. It's smooth with undertones of spice, and I taste the blackberry he mentioned. The alcohol works its way through my body, setting my senses on overdrive.

"Your boyfriend?" the bartender asks, raising his eyes to me. This is the first time I've really stared at him. He's got dark black, curly hair atop his head, which is messy from running around, and a kind smile. His black shirt is unbuttoned at the top revealing muscles and black fur. Definitely not my type, but I don't hate the attention.

I shake my head. "Nope."

His eyes light up. "Your lover, then?"

A loud laugh escapes my lips. I've never had a *lover*. What an absolutely glorious European concept that is though. Yes, I think I shall have a lover on this vacation. I practice the word on my tongue, "*lover*," rolling it around and exaggerating the word. The bartender laughs.

Whoops, I did that out loud.

"I think you are not the type to take a lover, only to fall in love," he says, appraising me and nailing my persona on the head.

But I don't want to be that person anymore. I sip my wine again, swirling it around with my tongue, and close my eyes. "Maybe I can be both."

CHAPTER 21

Jack

Don't tell her you love her, don't tell her you love her, don't tell her you love her. Repeating the words as I ride the elevator away from her sweet citrus scent—does she bathe in tangerines?—I can't help but think that the words will eventually slip out of my mouth. Especially when she looks like she just came out of the hot springs, all dewy and glowing. What is this woman doing to me?

I promise this is not the man I've been for the last thirty-two years. The last time I was this obsessed with a woman, I was probably four and she was my mom. But here I am, following her around like a helpless puppy, crying out for her attention.

In my heart I know Steph is right. I was pushing too hard. There is a reason men play hard to get—*it works*. Women like the chase. And anyone who tells you different is lying. I like the chase too—which is why I'm falling all over myself for

Charlotte. She's not making it easy.

Part of me wants to release all this built-up tension in the shower, but the other part wants to hold it all for Charlotte, not wanting to waste any of the feelings she's stirred in me. So, I leave the black bathroom in the same ball of nerves that I entered, clean-shaven and fresh for a night that I hope won't end anytime soon.

Based upon her outfit, I throw on a pair of navy-blue slacks and a white button-down shirt. Tonight I will take her downtown to a small restaurant on the water I spotted on our drive back to the hotel earlier this afternoon. The marina with bars and restaurants dotted with twinkling lights will be breathtaking at night.

Our first real date. Because that is what I'm doing. I'm going to date this girl—and she's going to have no choice but to fall hard, *but slowly*, I promise myself again.

After slicking my hair to the side, I pat some aftershave on my cheeks—I'm going all in here—and then I'm ready to go.

It's only been thirty minutes, but I find Charlotte at the bar, looking flushed from the wine and a bit impatient. "Gosh, I was starting to get nervous that you stood me up." Her cheeks blush. "Not that this is a date. I just mean—"

I cut her off, lifting my finger to her lips. "Shhh. That is precisely what this is. Will you go to dinner with me, Charlotte?"

Her lip between her teeth, she ponders the question. I remember Steph's instructions and the promise I made. "Stop analyzing, Sassy. Let's go." I offer her my arm, and she smiles as she nods at the bartender and grabs her purse off the bar.

"Amor," the bartender shouts after her, and she turns around and shakes her head.

"Amante!" Her eyes light up as she winks at him and looks back to me with a mischievous smile in her eyes.

"Amante?" I ask. This is not a word I'm familiar with.

She hums in happiness and allows the word to roll off her tongue, "*Lover.*"

I close my eyes. Every cell in my body begs me to throw her over my shoulder and carry her upstairs to my bed.

Slow. Down.

Willing myself forward, I ignore my impulses. Besides, just having her body tucked close to mine as we walk out onto the cobblestone street is enough for me right now.

We aren't fighting, she's not crying, and we are together.

"Did you have a good nap?" I ask, very aware that she didn't get any rest but not giving away that I've spoken to Steph.

She leans her head into my shoulder and murmurs an assent.

"Am I going to be carrying you home, Charlotte Marie?"

Her eyes dart up to mine. "How do you know my middle name?"

I chuckle. "Your passport. I'm in the military, I pay attention to details."

"Ah, yes, that elusive career of yours that you don't like to speak of," she teases. I don't detect the same irritation she had before, though, when I gave her little information in response to her many questions. She seems to have accepted that I won't talk about it. At least for now.

Changing the subject, I say, "So, I know you're not a fan of hot peppers. Is there anything else that we should avoid on the menu?"

My lips twist up in a smile, and she elbows me in the ribcage. I feign falling over, and she laughs and quips, "Stop, you big baby. Don't dish what you can't take."

Charlotte takes my arm again and we settle into a comfortable rhythm walking to the restaurant. Even in long sleeves, the cool night air is getting to me, and whipping off the ocean, it sends Charlotte's curls in all different directions. She's got to be cold. Pulling her close to me, I rub the goosebumps off her arms. So much for the long game. It's almost impossible to keep my hands off her.

An hour later we are seated at dinner, sharing a bottle of wine. Charlotte's cheeks are flushed and she's talking non-stop, entertaining me with stories of her kindergartners, adventures in the life of dating—a very disturbing story about peanut butter has her very heated—and just charming me with her observations on everything that comes to her mind. When a plate of pasta with a large shrimp on it is placed in front of her, she does little to hide her fear. Loudly, she whispers, "What the heck is this?" She pokes at the shrimp, like it's a foreign object. When a red blotchy substance squishes out of it, she screams, "Oh my God, it's still alive! It's *bleeding*!" Charlotte's hand flies over her mouth, and she looks like she may be sick.

I pull a piece onto my plate, inspecting it for her. It does in fact appear to be blood—but certainly that must just be our American eyes fooling us. No one else at the tables around us seem a bit upset about their shrimp, and it is on almost every table. "It's definitely not alive," I say with more conviction than I have. "Give me the shrimp. I'll take it apart for you like a lobster, and you can eat just the meat." This seems like as good of an option as I've got, but she does not appear interested.

"How 'bout you just take the living shrimp, and I'll eat my dead pasta."

I laugh now at her because really, she's so damn adorable in her stubbornness, and I kind of don't blame her at all. But now that I've acted like it's not a big deal, I do have to try it, and surprisingly, it tastes good.

When the waiter takes our plates, Charlotte asks about the shrimp, because she can't just be demure and say she didn't like it. "*Carabineros,*" he says, as if it's obvious.

"I guess we'll have to google that one," she laughs after the waiter is gone. Her eyes are glowing, and I'm not ready for the night to end.

"So, what do you want to do now?"

"Oh, you mean now that I've embarrassed myself with my ridiculous dating stories and my fear of food?"

I laugh. "You're not the only one who has had bad dating adventures."

Her eyebrows rise. "Adventures? That sounds scandalous."

Chuckling, I shake my head. "Okay. That did sound a bit cheesy. But seriously, I've had my fair share of crazies."

Charlotte's eyes dance, and her smile stabs at my heart. "Tell me more."

"I'll let you in on my *scandalous dating adventures* if you agree to let me hold your hand while we walk."

She laughs. "Okay, Maverick, you win, I'll let you hold my hand." Eyes rolling, she stands up and offers it to me as if I'm putting her out. But I know she's having fun.

Her fingers wrap into mine, intertwined, not just handholding. Far more intimate. Glancing down at them and seeing that we fit together perfectly, I smile. "Okay, spill," she says impatiently, pulling me from my thoughts.

"Let's see. First, there was Steph's friend, Astrid." Her fingers tighten in my hand, and I can feel the jealousy pouring from her.

"You *dated* Astrid?"

I don't think anyone would call it dating. But I love how jealous she is, so I egg her on a bit. "Yeah. Just for a little while. She was a special one there." A special kind of crazy.

Charlotte clears her throat. "Wow. Was it serious?"

I lean in closer as if sharing a secret. "So serious." I try to keep my face straight, but my lips pull up. Charlotte doesn't notice as she's facing the water and biting the inside of her mouth again. "It was so serious we started talking baby names."

Charlotte practically spits out her breath. "What? How long

did you date?"

I can't handle it anymore. My grin widens, and my dimples give me away. "Oh, just the one night."

Charlotte shoves me hard. "Jack Fitzpatrick!"

I laugh. "What? I told you it was serious for a little while. We went to dinner, and within the first hour she was asking me if I liked the name Tony. When I asked why, she said she wanted to make sure because she wanted it to be our son's name."

Charlotte's laughter rings out into the night, filling the air around us and my heart. "Stop it!" she cries.

"That's what I said!"

"Oh, my God. Then what happened?"

"Oh, you know she proceeded to text and call for the next week and wanted to know if the reason I didn't want to see her again was because I didn't like the name." Staring seriously, I say, "She offered to change it—we could do Jack, Jr. if that's what I had my heart set on."

Charlotte's eyes light up in laughter. "No, she didn't!"

I laugh. "She *did*."

Shaking her head, Charlotte grabs my hand again, and my stomach flips. "I'm gonna have to talk about this one to Steph. I can't believe she set you up with Astrid and didn't introduce us."

What would life have been like if I'd found Charlotte back then instead of Astrid? Probably a lot more dates. Although, I'm not sure I was ready. "Eh, she was probably right to wait. She probably thought you deserved better."

Charlotte leans her head against my shoulder. "And then we wouldn't be here right now. And I like where we are."

The air around me fills with her scent, and my lungs can't get enough. Speechless, I focus on her hand in mine, lost to the feeling of having her close.

"God, I wish we could go dancing," Charlotte whispers into the night sky.

Although a black shawl covers her shoulders, I spot her nipples standing at attention through her dress, and my pants tighten. Bringing her body close to mine, I sway her back and forth in my arms. "You like dancing?" I murmur in her ear.

She giggles and squirms away, but I pull her back even closer. Her eyes grow wide as she feels my hardness against her. Bringing her lips near mine as she speaks, she answers, "Yes, I like dancing. I wish we could go to a club and be in a room with people, the music reverberating around us, our bodies close."

"Then I'll take you dancing," I say into her mouth.

"You found somewhere that has dancing?"

I laugh. "No, but I have an idea."

Charlotte follows me back to the hotel, into the elevator, and up to our floor. The whole time she is staring at me, waiting for me to reveal my big plan. When we get to my door, she looks at me suspiciously. "Did you just con me into coming back to your room with promises of dancing? Damn, you are smoother than Maverick. You really earned that name."

Although that wasn't my intention, she doesn't seem

197

upset, so I just smirk. I hold the door open, and she walks inside, nervously looking around and probably waiting for me to pounce. I breeze past her and flick on the radio, which is a part of the clock, and the speakers blare loud Portuguese music which is a tad upbeat with lots of instruments.

I turn to her with a glint in my eye and begin shimmying my hips back and forth like "The Carlton," and she bursts out laughing but remains grounded in her spot. "I have no idea how to dance to this music," Charlotte says. She looks at me with those wide innocent eyes that I'd follow to hell.

"Neither do I. Dance with me anyway." The music continues in the background. I can't figure out the rhythm or the appropriate moves, but I keep jiving toward her until we are standing face to face. When she wraps her arms around me, pulling me close, I can see she doesn't have dancing on her mind any longer.

Running her hands through my hair and messing with the perfectly gelled style, she stares into my eyes and says, "I like your hair messy. You look more relaxed this way." And in that moment, I feel that she sees me as I am, a messy broken man who is crazy about her. She tilts her mouth up to me, offering me her lips which I greedily take, knowing there is no coming back from this moment.

CHAPTER 22

Charlotte

As Jack's mouth crashes into mine, every cell in my body stands at attention. This is really happening. I am making out with Jack Fitzpatrick—Mr. Perfect, St. Patrick's Day, the *leprechaun*—in his hotel room. Music akin to the polka is playing on the radio, though, and it is totally screwing with my mood.

"Turn that off," I whisper into his mouth as I pull myself away from him and drop my black wrap on the floor. He stares at me, drinking me in, but then does as told.

Only now the silence kills me. I hear myself gulp as I watch Jack slowly unbutton his shirt. The pounding in my chest replaces the musical instruments, and I sigh out a symphony. There is only one light on in the room, a lamp on the bedside table, which provides a soft flickering glow. Leaning against the bed, I watch as Jack continues to remove his shirt, biting my lip and pinching my fingers to keep myself in place. Wanting to savor every moment of tonight, I hold myself still, unsure when I will have a man this beautiful in my bed again. That's what Jack is— not a pretty boy, not a hot guy—he is a beautiful *man* whose eyes melt my panties and whose lips are swollen like pillows. I can't wait to sink into them again and lose myself.

"Are you just gonna stand there and watch?" Jack asks, his voice husky and filled with desire. His lips tilt in a crooked smile. He has all sorts of plans.

I gulp again and try to clear my throat, willing my mouth to speak, but my lips are parted in a silent *O*, unable to formulate a word. Gawking at him appears to be the only thing I can handle in this moment. "It's too quiet now," I whisper nervously.

Perhaps the bartender was right. I'm someone who falls in love—I'm *not* a lover. Images of women he's likely been with before me fill my head, and I bite the inside of my mouth, nervous of how I will compare.

Jack just smiles and picks up his phone, and soon Adam Levine is crooning the song from *The Wedding Date* as Jack walks toward me like Dermot Mulroney, all sexy and ready to jump my bones. I feel suspiciously like Debra Messing, a bit of a mess and yet wanting so badly to feel desirable, so I remain still and wait for him to lead.

His freckled chest appears soft, but the ripples reveal his dedication to his body, and I can't wait to see him dedicate some of that attention to me.

"You are the most beautiful person I've ever met, Charlotte Marie Chase," Jack murmurs into my ear, sending a shiver down my chest and leaving my nipples standing at attention. He reaches behind me and pulls on my halter, causing my dress to fall in one fell swoop. Stomach clenching, legs shaking, I know this man will be my undoing. But I seem to be his too. He's momentarily speechless as he realizes I wasn't wearing a bra under the dress, and my breasts are now standing exposed and pointing into his chest.

He groans and steps back to stare, and I stifle the urge to cover my breasts in embarrassment and act instead as the goddess he believes me to be. Moving into his arms, I distract him with my lips and tongue which have a mind of their own. Jack has other ideas though. He moves lower, pushing my chin up as he grazes his tongue against my collarbone.

I think I may have died a little.

My knees buckle, but Jack wraps his arm behind my back and holds me in place, providing all the stability I need. "I am going to kiss every inch of your body," he says as he moves down to take my breast in his mouth. He bites on my nipple gently, and I let out a soft cry. "Oh, baby, your sounds are going to be the death of me."

While the feel of his lips on my body is pure ecstasy, hearing him call me "baby" does things to me that I can't explain. I'm unable to control my need for him, fumbling with his belt and trying to pull off his pants as quickly as possible. He pulls on my wrists, pushing me backwards until my calves hit the edge of the bed and I fall into the soft white bedding. "As much as I want you, I want to take my time. Slow down, baby."

He said it again.

I stare into his eyes, memorizing the way the golden flecks light up for me—all I see is his complete devotion to worshipping my body. Throwing back my head, I allow him to take the lead. There's no point in fighting him—not only will I lose, but the fight only keeps me from experiencing all the pleasure he's raining down on me.

Realizing I've stopped trying to rush him, he whispers, "Thank you." Then he trails kisses down my chest, onto my belly, and around the line of my panties. "Oh, woman, you are damn near perfect."

I cover my mouth with my hand, hiding my smile and biting my lip to keep from laughing as he kisses the sensitive area between my thighs. "Oh my," I sigh loudly into the pillow.

Jack chuckles to himself. "Oh, Sassy, this is going to be fun. I am going to take off your underwear now and lick you until you scream my name. Okay?"

My stomach clenches, and I nibble harder on my lip as I nod my head. No one has ever spoken to me this way. No one has ever *touched* me this way. It is quite possible that I will never feel this way again. I lie back and allow him to show me precisely what I had been missing all this time.

The first time his tongue licks me, I literally buck my hips forward, my body taking over as a chill runs straight between my legs. "Oh, you like that," he whispers, becoming more aggressive with his kisses as if he is hungry for me.

My toes curl into the bed, but he holds my body still, forcing me to endure every wonderful stroke, until he shifts his fingers into me, and I can no longer remain subdued.

"I need you inside of me," I whimper into the sheets.

His head shakes against my thighs. "Not until you come for me." One hand slides under my ass, and he pulls me closer to him, holding me as I begin to throb and shake, until I reach a point where I can no longer take it. Grabbing hold of his head and controlling how he moves, I scream out for him as my body spasms in ecstasy.

Dizzy and panting, I literally see stars. I want to do this to him. I want him panting, screaming out my name, bucking against me like he can't control himself. I try to move around to reciprocate but he pushes me back down, telling me to relax. "There's no rush. I'm not going anywhere."

My cheeks are on fire, and my body is spent but I need to feel him inside me. I listened to him long enough—followed his rules—now it's my turn to be in control.

Before he can stop me, I slip down the bed and pull off his boxers. He groans as I take him in my hands, appreciating the manhood he keeps going on about. He seems surprised when I slide him into my mouth. I've never been so attracted to a man before, never wanted to taste him so badly, to the point where this is all I can think about. For once I'm not concerned if I'm doing it right; his sounds let me know exactly how he feels. Jack's hand slides behind my head and he plays with my hair as I move myself back and forth, getting more excited with every sign of pleasure that escapes his mouth.

Without warning, he pulls me up and presses his lips against mine. He takes a piece of my hair in his hand and pulls it loosely, watching it spring back at him. "You wore your hair curly that night too."

Momentarily lost, I stare at him confused. "Huh?" Why was he stopping? Am I doing it wrong? Impatience rips through me.

"That night…six years ago." His eyes meet mine, as if he wants to know that I accept his apology before we go any further.

"I did?"

"Yes. After the rain your hair curled, and honestly all I thought was that you were the most beautiful woman I'd ever seen. You still are…" Jack pauses as he looks into my eyes and brushes a kiss against my lips. As the kiss deepens, I moan against him. I'm inhaling him, living for this moment, and if I stopped breathing right now, I swear to God I would die a happy woman. This moment is everything I've been waiting for. My entire life. And then he says the words that are my complete undoing. "Charlotte, I've never wanted a woman in the way I want you. I *need* to be inside of you."

None of this is what I thought it would be—I wanted a fling—but maybe this is what I need, and it doesn't matter in the end because I know this is going to mean more than just one night. His every touch is attentive, and his kisses are filled with emotion. He's writing a love letter with our bodies, and I don't want him to stop.

He slips on a condom and lies down on the bed, waiting for me to mount him. I place one hand on his chest and the other on the headboard, lowering myself slowly, crying out as I tighten around him. Jack grabs my neck and pulls my mouth to his, kissing me as we move, our tongues saying everything we didn't during the daylight.

Then Jack Fitzpatrick does the impossible. He silences my thoughts and kisses me so hard that I can do nothing but live for this moment. Clearly, I've been living life wrong, choosing not to spend every waking minute in bed with this man. I want to do nothing else for the rest of my life.

When he finally comes apart inside of me, I almost want to scream in celebration because *I* did this to him. But then my own waves of pleasure take over again, and he watches me with such satisfaction, such adoration, that my mind can't focus on anything at all.

Collapsing on top of his chest, both our bodies slick with sweat, I listen to his heartbeat, transfixed in this moment. Emotions threaten to take over and spill out of my eyes—sex with Jack has literally been a life-altering experience. I'm sure every time he's done this before has been amazing because he is amazing, but I have never felt a fraction of what he did to me. Which is completely frightening. I can feel myself getting attached...too attached.

Biting down on my lip, I try to quell the emotional undercurrent that is pulling me out to sea. As if he can feel my mind turning over, he pulls my body up higher so that my head is resting on the pillow next to his. "Don't you start."

I sputter a cough. "Huh?"

"I see your mind working, your heart started to pound, and you're biting your lip like you always do when you're deep in thought."

Like I always do? We barely know each other. Although that seems like an inappropriate statement after what we just shared. And I'm still naked. Too naked. I sigh, giving up the charade. Removing my lip from my teeth, I start to speak, slightly annoyed that he can read me so well. "It's just...that was amazing."

He laughs, surprised at my comment. "Well, Sassy, that's kind of the point."

Squirming I lean back on the pillow, facing the ceiling. "Maybe it's always like that for you...but for me...that was, like, not normal."

Pushing himself closer to me and onto my pillow, his hand gently pulls my face to his, and he says tenderly, "It's never been like that for me before."

My heart does a little dance, and my eyes dart up in surprise. "No?"

His face cracks open in a big smile. "No." Pressing his lips to mine, he quiets my mind. "I'm going to get cleaned up and then I'm going to cuddle you...if you can handle that."

I smile again. "I think I can handle that."

I watch him hop out of bed, and my eyes widen as the muscles in his butt flex when he walks. It's not even fair that someone could look that good naked. Like, it should be illegal.

There is no way I'm walking around naked in front of him. I assure you there are not even invisible muscles in my ass let alone ones that flex. I wrap the sheet around me before he comes back so that I can go clean up too.

Jack's eyes dance, and the cocky smirk is back. "What are you doing, woman?"

I hop precariously through the bedroom and into the bathroom, ignoring his stares. Taking in my swollen lips and the bite marks he's left on my chest, I feel a surge of adrenaline.

I look hot.

Like incredibly hot. Not at all as I expected. I drop the sheet and stare in the mirror, daring myself to act more like a lover. I saunter out naked, and Jack's cocky smile is gone. "Get over here." He pats the bed next to him as I stare at him provocatively.

I'm not sure what comes over me, but I run at him without thinking about my jiggly parts, hop into the bed, and lose myself against his chest.

"Charlotte, I—"

Pushing my lips into his, I stop him from speaking. No more talking. No more worrying. I want an exact repeat of what we just did, because if there's a chance we only have one night, I'm not going to waste it.

CHAPTER 23

Jack

The sun filters into the room, waking me from my pleasure-induced coma. Charlotte's hair is the first thing I see, the sun brightening the golden strands which streak her brown hair. If there is a more perfect way to wake, I'm not aware of it. In the desert, sometimes the guys and I would wake up before the sun rose just to see it coming over the mountain—a spectacular miracle if you understood how the rest of the country looked. It was our one good thing, and that is what this feels like to me. For a few moments before she wakes—and I need to go back to holding my feelings in—I bask in this perfect moment, pretending we really are together, that she is mine, and all is right in the world. Just as quickly, the moment passes. She starts to shift her body, moving away from me, and I slip a smile on my face, a façade to mask the feelings of love stirring within.

"Good morning, Sassy."

Charlotte's hand flies over her face as she tries to look up at me, then she turns in the opposite direction, likely worried about her breath. Women always worry about that, men not so much. "Uh, what time is it?"

I lean over and kiss the back of her head. "Too early. Go back to bed. I'll close the blinds." I jump up, drag them closed, and darkness settles over the room. Then I make my way to the bathroom, where the light from the closet goes on when I walk by.

"Where you going now?" she yells into the pillow.

"Going for a run. I'll be back in a little bit. Just relax."

I brush my teeth and grab a pair of shorts from the drawer. Charlotte sits up, and I appreciate that she is topless. Even in the dark I can see the outline of her breasts. "You're going for a run?" Her voice is fretful, and I can almost see her bottom lip stick out in a pout.

I laugh. "Yes. I go for a run every morning."

"Even when you have a hot naked woman in your bed?"

Well, when she puts it like that, she does have a point. "I'm assuming I'll have a hot naked woman in my bed every night this trip, and this body doesn't look like this without work." I slap my hand against my chest, and she laughs. But inside, I am stewing over what she said. Will this be the one time I have her? Am I wasting it? Refusing to believe that to be the case, I dash over to her, lean down, and kiss each one of her breasts before placing another kiss on her forehead.

"Fine. I'll go to my room and rest. Call me when you're back."

Charlotte begins to stand up, and I lunge at her in the bed, pinning both her arms against the sheets. "If you leave this bed, I am going to start tickling you."

Holding her mouth firmly shut, Charlotte nods. *Women and their morning breath.* I laugh. "Fine. You can brush your teeth and make yourself comfortable, but when I get back from my run, I want you naked again."

Charlotte's eyes grow wide as she realizes I know why she's acting so strange. Or maybe it's because I'm talking about her naked. All I know is if I do not get out of this bed now, I never will, so before I lose my nerve, I sprinkle kisses on her neck and release her arms.

When I hop out of bed, she turns with a mischievous smile and then smacks me on the ass. "Hurry back now." I groan at the innuendo in her voice and stride to the door, determined to run off this feeling she is stirring inside me.

It took everything in me last night not to whisper over and over into her hair, into her breasts, and into her mouth how much I love her. Instead, I focused on pleasuring her, using my body to express how I feel. But never before had sex felt like such an out-of-body experience—like we had come together with a greater purpose than just those few hours of bliss. Because that's what we had—hours of making love. I'm not sure what time we even fell asleep.

As I sprint down the road, and the salty air stings my oxygen-starved lungs, all I can think about is Charlotte. In truth,

I want her out of my head. It would be a lie to say that she is only on my mind because we are vacationing together. She'd been on my mind for the past two months since Pat showed me her picture, reminding me of the one that got away.

Before that day she was on my mind more randomly. I would be sitting with the guys in the desert playing cards, or watching a movie on my iPad, or, God forbid, on a date with someone, and something from *that* night would pop into my head, and people would stare at me like I was an idiot because I was smiling for no apparent reason. I would picture her eating the stack of pancakes with gusto or walking out of her bathroom in her short shorts before bed. It's like she had settled into the back of my mind that night and refused to move out. Which makes sense since she's so stubborn. Although, perhaps a more accurate description was that she'd stolen my heart and refused to give it back. And it was only now when we were reunited that I realized she'd taken it. She'd been holding it all this time, and now that I'm with her I can finally *feel* again, no longer able to hold back all the emotions I'd become so good at conquering these last few years. My therapist would be proud. She always wanted me to talk about what happened in the desert— Peter's death—and my emotional detachment to it all. Now that Charlotte had given me back my heart, I could feel his death as if it were happening today.

I feel the salty liquid sting my lips, and I try to brush away the sweat only to realize it won't stop. I am fucking crying while running, and no matter how many times I swipe at my face, the tears keep coming. So, I keep running, until I finally lean over panting, unable to move anymore.

My lungs burn, and I suck in as much air as they can take. The images of deployment keep flashing through my mind, flooding me with memories I can't handle.

100, 99, 98.... I follow the exercise laid out by my therapist, breathing as I count down in my head. This time it takes me all the way to fifty before I relax, my breath evening out, and the tears cease.

I can't see Charlotte right now. I shoot her a text letting her know I'm going to be longer than expected and head off in the direction of the marina, to sit with a coffee and recover.

CHAPTER 24

Charlotte

Throwing myself backwards in bed I groan, surrendering to these feelings swirling inside me. They are dizzying and intoxicating and make it as if every nerve in my body is aware of his departure from the bed.

Get a grip, girlfriend, I hear Steph say in my head. I can already see her rolling her eyes and telling me to slow down. "Not every man you meet is *the one*." Pretty sure those were her exact words yesterday—and at that point I thought she was right—but that was before. Before Jack had looked at me with all these feelings stirring in his eyes, before I felt his tongue expressing everything he wanted to say and I wouldn't let him, before our bodies joined together, and I knew there was no going back.

I am now living in A.J. times—*After Jack*. Or better put, ASJ times—*After Sleeping with Jack*. There is no going back. Sex before had never felt the way it did with him. It was imitation sex—like the bad crab meat you get at the grocery store.

I'd been going through the motions. It's pitiful that everyone else in the world is not having sex like we did. No wonder so many women tire of sex—they aren't doing it right. Although, to be fair they aren't doing it with *him*. And I'm pretty sure he is the only reason I feel this way. This is exactly how it's supposed to feel—your entire body singing, the butterflies permanently fluttering in your stomach. Does every woman in love feel this way? Am I in love? Or is it just that Jack is so good at what he does with his tongue that I've somehow convinced myself that's what this is?

It doesn't matter either way. The promise I made to both Steph and myself is that I wouldn't overthink it, and I intend to keep my promise. I will embrace these feelings—I'll swim in the refreshing Jack waters until I either come up for air or drown. His text interrupts my thinking—*thank God*—because I was doing precisely what I promised I wouldn't.

"Gonna be a bit longer than expected. Feel free to go grab coffee if you want. I'll catch up with you when I get back."

Frowning, I stare at the text. *Come again?* I thought he wanted me naked in his bed. He forbade me to leave. Did I do something wrong? Massaging my temple, I sigh. My inner Steph tells me to snap out of it. Get out of bed, go get a coffee. Or screw that, don't get a coffee—he told you to do that, and you should do what you want. Although, I do really *want* a coffee—

it's too early for me to think, let alone walk around without one. So yes, I will get a coffee and go up to the pool with a book, maybe do some laps and just relax.

Of course, now I have to locate an outfit to wear to get to my room. The purple dress does not look appealing, even if it is just for a few moments. But I also don't want to rummage through his drawers to locate anything. It feels oddly too personal— sifting through his stuff— despite the fact that he literally explored every inch of my body last night.

My stomach knots. The butterflies from the morning settle, and my body doesn't feel like it's singing anymore. I just need to get out of his room—and stop my mind from working.

Sliding the dress back on and tying it tightly around my neck, I run out of the room quickly, wanting to free myself from the memories of the night before and the way his text message makes me feel. I get to my room and reach down for my keycard only to realize I have nothing to reach for—there is nothing in my hand. No purse, no phone, no key card. *Shoot.*

Of course, on top of being dressed in my clothes from the night before, I also have to pee. I hop on one foot trying to decide what to do. I can't very well break down the door, so the only option is to go downstairs and get a new key.

Hopping as I try to contain my bladder, I appear at the front desk and try to ignore the stares people are giving me based upon my unruly appearance. "I got locked out of my room. Room 312. Could you please give me another key?"

The man looks at his computer and then looks back at me. "Ah, yes, Ms. Chase. Do you have a form of identification?"

No. How would I have identification? It's obviously with my keys and my phone and my purse.

I compose myself, or at least I try to. "No. Unfortunately, that is all in my room."

He doesn't flinch. "Then unfortunately I cannot help you."

My eyes grow wide, and my bladder threatens to spill out. "You've got to be kidding me. What am I to do then?"

A crowd is beginning to form. It's early, but people are on vacation and breakfast is only up the stairs from the lobby. A little girl whispers loudly to her mother, "Mommy, why is that woman dressed like that?" Others gawk and speak in Portuguese—I can only *imagine* what they are saying. I'm sure my mascara is smudged under my eyes, my curled hair is standing in different directions, and let's not forget, I'm practically dressed in a ball gown at eight a.m. *Ugh.*

I really need a sign that says I got locked out of my room. A banner perhaps? Or I could just scream it.

None of these are great ideas though, so instead, I turn and run to the lobby bathroom to handle at least one of my problems. Fortunately, no one else is in the stall, and I have a momentary reprieve from the humiliation.

I have no idea what to do. I can't sit in the lobby and wait for Jack. That's *too* much. Not only do I look ridiculous, but I have no idea when he will be back. Nor do I know what the hell his problem is, but clearly there is one. Obviously, he changed his mind about us, or last night wasn't as great as I imagined.

Yes, I am absolutely spiraling here.

Sadly, I have no other option—a walk of shame through the lobby cannot be avoided. "Amore," the bartender from the night before says, looking up with a smile, as he cleans and witnesses the leftovers of my debauchery.

I shake my head in dismay. "I tried...but I think you were right. I am not a lover." The word no longer plays on my tongue like magic.

He shakes his head. "Nonsense." And then he pulls a cup of coffee from behind the bar and places it in front of me. "Take this." I almost burst into tears at his kindness. I slump against the bar and take a sip of the warm coffee. "What happened, mi amor?"

"I'm locked out of my room, and I can't get a key because I don't have my ID. And my friend is off somewhere, doing who knows what, obviously not thrilled with my bedroom skills." I cover my mouth in embarrassment. It's morning, and I'm blabbering to a bartender in my dress from last night. This is definitely a new low for me. Fortunately, I don't think he understands, because he just keeps nodding. "I'm going to go to the roof. If you see my friend from last night, let him know I'm up there, please."

He nods as if he understands, but I can't be too sure.

When I arrive on the rooftop, I am no longer enamored with the view. The magic is gone—*from everything*. The chairs are empty, and the restaurant is closed so I saunter over to the lounge chair I occupied days before and settle myself down on it with a sigh. Somehow it feels like a repeat of six years earlier, when I fell asleep with magic and woke to find it was all a lie. So much for second chances.

CHAPTER 25

Jack

I'm having a harder time getting past this attack than normal. It's been three years since Peter died. You'd think this would get easier. But living a normal life, doing normal things like vacationing, dating, having sex, nothing is easy about this. It was easier being away, focusing on a mission, doing a job that required you to zone everything else out. Anything was easier than feeling this way—feeling all of these emotions—it's honestly overwhelming. For one extremely weak moment I consider texting Richard that I'm in. I'm ready to keep moving, to focus on another mission. Hell, I'd fucking go on another tour right now if it meant silencing all these thoughts. Instead, I dial a number I have for emergencies. One I rarely use because I don't like to admit that I need help.

"Jack, how's it going?" She answers on the second ring, no pretense, no small talk—exactly why she's the therapist I needed.

"Having a moment, if I'm being honest." Embarrassed, I run my hand across my face.

"Tell me three things you can see, Jack."

I breathe. This is what I need. "Um, a boat, the ocean, and uh, a bird."

"Good. What about things you can smell?"

Sucking in air, I close my eyes and focus. "Coffee, salt, the sea."

"You're painting quite the picture for me, Jack. Good job." This forces out a chuckle which further releases the tension.

"Thanks, Doc, I needed that."

I can hear her smile as she responds, "So, tell me what you were doing when you started feeling this way? What do you think triggered this?"

Sex? Realizing I'm in love? None of that makes sense. Why did sleeping with Charlotte trigger this? And what does it all mean? Will I never be able to be happy, or will I forever feel this vise of guilt when I start to forget? My chest seizes again. "I'm on vacation with a girl."

"Where are you?"

This seems like easier territory to navigate. "The Azores."

"Hmm, sounds nice. So, you are on vacation, enjoying yourself, and you feel guilty?"

Rolling my eyes at how cliché it sounds, I grumble into the phone, "Maybe."

"Why do you think that is?"

"Because I'm happy and he's not?" I ask, as if she's going to actually answer me.

"*Is* that why?"

I sigh again. I don't know *why* I feel this way. I don't know how to not feel this way. "I'm moving on. Or trying to at least."

"And you believe that your best friend, the man who grew up with you, who served with you, would want you to be miserable and mourn his death forever?" There's no judgment in her tone. Quite frankly, it's as if she is voicing my subconscious.

"No. Peter would want me to be happy. He would want me to live the life we both wanted. Which is what I am trying to do. But it's a lot of pressure—having to be the guy he always held me up to be." I kick at an imaginary rock and stare out at the ocean, wishing I could be having this conversation with Peter. Or with Charlotte.

"Can you do me a favor?"

I smile, knowing what she's doing. She knows I don't do things for myself; I do things for others. So if she asks me to do something, I'm not going to be able to turn her down. "What do you need, Doc?"

"Pick something to do today. Something that you will enjoy, and just focus on that. Don't worry about what this all means or try to plan for a future you think Peter would want you to have. Just live for today. Pick an activity and enjoy it. Can you do that?"

One day at a time. It's what she had been telling me since

we started therapy six months ago when I moved back to Bristol and felt the crushing pressure of being home without a mission to focus on. "I can do that, Doc."

"Okay, Jack, you know you can call me any time. But honestly, you have the tools to move forward. You just have to keep putting one foot in front of the other and *breathe*."

I let out an exasperated laugh. "Yeah, I'm trying."

After spending a good chunk of the morning sitting by the marina and working through my shit, I finally make it back to the hotel. I try calling Charlotte to see where she is, but she doesn't pick up. She's probably pissed I left her alone. Not that I blame her—I promised her a memorable morning, and instead I got caught up overthinking everything. Precisely what Steph told me to avoid.

We only have two more days in the city before we are supposed to head to the next hotel— it's located in Furnas which is famous for their sweets, food that they steam in the ground, gardens, and the rust-colored thermal pool. After that we are supposed to head to Caloura, or if I have my way, to Villa Franca where I can introduce her to my aunt. I don't have much time to convince her. Today I'm going to make up for going AWOL, and I'm going to take my therapist's advice and pick an activity for us to enjoy. I'm not going to focus on the future. I'm going to focus on sharing a moment with the girl whose smile grounds me.

While I was at the marina, there was a whale tour leaving which gave me the perfect idea. Her reason for this trip was so she could do something she'd never done before. My reason for the trip was to spend time with her. This seems like the perfect way to show her that I care. It is something different, but it isn't scary—like jumping in hot springs or driving on perilous cliffs.

But now I can't find her. *Anywhere.* I stand knocking on her door, apologizing to the black metal, begging her to open up. I don't even hear a peep on the other side. Should I just let her be? I'm really at a loss as to what to do. Before disappearing, I decide to try one last spot—the roof. As the elevator opens, I spot the purple chiffon out of the corner of my eye, and my stomach flips. This *cannot* be good.

"Charlotte?" Shielding the sun from my eyes, I walk in her direction.

There is no movement from the chair; it's like a mannequin inhabits it. I walk quickly until I'm standing in front of her, and I'm met with red puffy eyes, dark circles, and tear-stained cheeks. Dropping to her side and pulling her close to me, I whisper into her hair, "I'm so sorry."

Her body doesn't react to my touch, as if she's too drained to even respond. "Please take me to your room to get my key."

"Of course." I help her up and try to get her to look at me, but she avoids my eyes. "Charlotte, what happened?"

She turns, and her eyes remind me of a wild animal, about to attack. "*You* happened."

"Charlotte, please, I can explain. I—"

She throws her hand up, as if she can't even bear to hear my voice. "I need to shower. I'm not upset. I just want to shower, get dressed, and explore this city. No more talk of romance. No more apologies. Just, please...I can't take anything more."

She sounds exasperated, and I know not to push. Whatever magic existed this morning is gone. I destroyed it just like last time. I'm no good for her. Six years ago, I was smart enough to realize that. Why I thought I could do this I'll never know. Perhaps all we'll ever have is perfect nights—anything more seems out of reach.

I let her into my room, and she grabs her stuff and stalks out, leaving me to sit in the place where I last felt her body against mine, as she takes with her any hope I had for the future.

CHAPTER 26

Charlotte

I fall back into the shower and let it wash away every kiss, every touch, and all feelings from the night before. Then I scrub the tears from my face, wishing there was a facewash that could erase memories. Let's face it—it doesn't matter what I say— I'm not done with him. I'm hurt, really freaking hurt. And confused. But none of those feelings overpower the undeniable chemistry I feel when he looks at me. The love that his body emits. It's why I couldn't hug him back, *or pull away*—my body won't freaking let me. The butterflies seem to push me toward him, refusing to let my mind protect me from the inevitable heartbreak.

When I get out of the shower, I look at my phone and see the text messages and multiple missed calls from Jack. The ones he was making all morning while I was locked out of my room.

Shoot. Shoot. Shit.

Of course, he didn't just ditch me. Why don't I trust his feelings for me? Since we arrived he's been telling me how he feels. Showing me with his gaze, with his touch, with his adoration, that I'm all he wants. Yet I don't trust it. I don't trust *him*. Even worse, I don't trust myself. Years of bad dates convinced me that love isn't real. That my instincts can't be trusted. That I'll always be alone. In the end, insecurity got the best of me.

It was some sort of horrible accident that I would leave my phone in his room and get locked out of my own. Or let's be honest, it's a perfect example of the tragically dumb things that always happen to me. And then he couldn't find me. It's no one's fault. But after my tongue-lashing, I'm sure he'll want nothing to do with me, and who could blame him.

Embarrassed and angry with the situation, I stare down my appearance in the mirror. "You are worth it. Trust yourself, trust your feelings, and for God's sakes, Charlotte, trust him."

Vulnerable and determined eyes stare back at me. The only way I'll ever be happy is by dropping my walls and letting him in. It's possible I'll get hurt, but isn't it worth it? The alternative isn't an option. Holding myself rigid, protecting my heart, and forever alone. It's not something I'm willing to even entertain.

Putting on my big girl pants and grabbing my purse, which I've ensured has both my key and my phone in it, I make my way to Jack's door and give a little knock.

"Coming," he says. My stomach flips as I wait. "Hey." His

eyes grow wide when he sees me. He's paler than I remember, and his shoulders stiffen. He looks terrible. Did something happen while he was gone all morning, or is this worried frown only because of me?

"Hi." I stare at him now, itching for his touch but too scared of rejection.

Jack's fingers bounce on his sides, as if he's trying to hold himself back too. Unable to take his strained look, I throw myself into his arms, wrapping mine around his neck. "I'm sorry, Jack. I was just...*embarrassed.*"

His arms move around my waist, and he pulls me close, breathing me in and sighing into my hair. "Wow. That is not at all what I expected."

We stand in his doorway holding one another—both expressing how we feel through touch as we apparently do a terrible job of it with words.

Begging to be relieved of this awful feeling in my stomach, I ask, "Can we do something today? And not talk about this?" The lightness we had this morning feels like it is just out of grasp. If we just spend time with one another, the dizzying, humming, *I can do anything* feeling will come back and knock us both out.

A small smile creeps across his face. "I think I have the perfect afternoon for you."

Nuzzling my head into his chest, the air is lighter. *He has a plan.*

I am downright giddy with Jack's arms wrapped around me and his lips whispering into my ear, "Look that way."

We haven't seen a whale yet, but the staff keeps telling us that the number of dolphins we've seen is incredible. There've been hundreds. Watching them jump and follow our boat is quite simply one of the most amazing things I've ever experienced. All of them give me back my joy. Could anyone be sad while watching dolphins? But Jack's big excitement right now is the two blue sharks that circle our boat. Even the captain came out to see them. "Quite rare," he claims.

I can really understand why they call São Miguel the Green Island now. The lush greenery goes on for miles. There are peaks and valleys, most of it green, interspersed with hotels and beachfront homes which hang lazily off the cliffs, and purple, white, and blue hydrangeas sprout in every direction. "It's beautiful."

Jack murmurs into my ear, "I happen to agree." He's not looking at the island, though, he's staring at me. My cheeks redden, and a warmth travels into my chest. I turn around to face him and wrap my arms around his neck. Pressing my lips to his, I kiss him softly. The first kiss of the day. I'm not sure how I waited this long.

Jack smiles. "What was that for?"

"For being you. Thank you for this." I don't just mean the boat excursion or the sweet words. He gave us a gift by tricking me into coming on this trip with him—he gave us time. Something we clearly need. Both of us are sure to keep screwing this up, and without being stuck together for two weeks, I'm pretty sure we both would walk away at one point or another. I am going to try really hard to not walk away again.

The color of his eyes changes. They lighten and sparkle, or maybe it's just how the sun hits them, but I *feel* his heart brighten. "Thank *you*."

It's not some beautiful speech—no one expressed their undying love, and no promises were made. And yet the way we hold one another and the kiss that follows those simple words says everything. I float in it, allowing the feelings to lap around me, soaking in the happiness and hoping a wave doesn't come.

That night, we find a small restaurant tucked into one of the city streets, sit outside, and share a bottle of wine. Monte Velho to be exact. Dipping the soft bread into a spicy Mozambique sauce, I soak up every last drop with the warm crispy papo secos.

"Pop sik," Jack says, pronouncing it properly for me.

I test it out on my tongue, "Pop sik."

Jack grins. "We'll have you speaking Portuguese in no time." His eyes are happy, and I delight in his joy.

"Pop sik," I say again, loving how much he enjoys hearing me speak Portuguese. "I will admit knowing the word for bread will definitely come in handy."

"Hmm, what other words do you know, Sassy?"

The smirk on his face lets me know the answer he's seeking, but I tease him a bit. "Let's see, there's good morning—bom dia; thank you—obrigada; bread—papo secos…." Pausing, I tap my finger to my chin. "I think that's it."

Jack's eyes darken. "Oh, I think there's another one you know."

Biting my lip to keep from smiling, I shrug my shoulders. "Really? I have no idea what you're talking about."

Jack pushes his chair closer to mine and whispers in my ear, "Don't tease me, pretty girl."

Goosebumps trail down my chest. "I would never." Turning to him, I bring my lips close to his ear and whisper softly and with a flip of the tongue, "Amante."

"Check!" he shouts, holding his hand up in the air in exaggeration. I swat at him and nuzzle into his chest. When I look back up, he has the biggest grin on his face.

After dinner, he slips his hand into mine, and we walk slowly down the grey and white street, soaking in every ounce of the night air. We peruse the shops and enjoy just being with one another. There is something magical in the air—something has shifted—and I never want it to shift back.

"Dance with me?" he says gruffly as we enter his room and I slip off my shoes.

Jack starts his music app on his phone and leads me to the bed. As the music plays softly, I lean against his chest, swaying with his body. The air fills with his fresh scent, and my body warms from his touch, every ounce of me tingling and my toes barely touching the ground. The dizzy, intoxicating, *we can do anything* feeling is back. Closing my eyes, I memorize exactly how this feels, with his arms wrapped around me and his humming in my ear.

Tonight, the sex is excruciatingly slow—there is no rush to taste one another, and it isn't harried or nervous. We take our time, kissing, moaning, and crying out in a way that feels both sensual and joyful. As he moves above me, he twists his fingers into mine, and his eyes are so filled with emotion I almost can't breathe. This isn't sex. This is so much more. "Charlotte, I…" Jack whispers, but I stop him from saying it, kissing the expression from his mouth, afraid he'll jinx us.

In my head I respond though. *I love you too.*

CHAPTER 27

Jack

Everything about this morning is different than yesterday. As I open my eyes, I feel Charlotte's penetrating stare, her mind working and her heart pounding. It's apparent that she already snuck out of bed to brush her teeth because she's not covering her mouth, instead greeting me with a wide smile. She's already dressed, wearing a tank top and stretch pants—far too many clothes for my liking.

"Morning, beautiful."

With her skin pink from the sun yesterday and her face free from makeup, her wavy hair hangs over her face as her eyes remain on mine. "Morning, Maverick. You going for a run?" She looks at me expectantly.

Pulling her close to my chest, I reply, "Nope. Not making that mistake again." Her soft skin leaves me wanting to trace her entire body with my fingers, and her vanilla scent infiltrates my lungs.

She settles her head against me, which I can't help but kiss. "Yesterday was a fluke. Go for a run. I'm going to go read a book up on the roof and relax. I'll still be here when you get back."

I shake my head. "Not gonna happen. I'm not risking any more disastrous things happening—which for the record occur every time I leave you alone."

"Oh, so you think you're like my knight in shining armor protecting me from myself?" my sassy girl sasses me with a smile. God, I'm crazy about her.

"I just think life is better when we're together." I wink at her.

"Okay, Jack Johnson," she teases, recognizing the lyrics from one of his songs. I smile realizing that we have similar taste in music. "Let's go get some banana pancakes and snuggle." Chuckling at her jokes, I find myself infatuated with how damn cute she is. "But seriously, go for your run. I'll be fine."

My eyes rake down her body. "I'm pretty sure I could get a workout without leaving this bed."

Before I can react, she hops onto my lap, mounts me, and pushes my shoulders back against the bed. "Don't make promises you don't intend to keep."

This woman has no idea what she does to me. Within moments we're naked, working up a sweat, punishing one another for the snark, and I love every minute of it. Every moment I am with her—whether we're in bed, or walking next to one another in silence, or fighting, or dancing—is exhilarating. Intoxicating. Pure joy. There is not a moment I'm with her that I'm not happier than every other moment when I'm not.

That afternoon as we walk on the beach in Santa Bárbara, watching the surfers who dare to challenge the rolling waves which tower above them, Charlotte slips her hand in mine and pulls me closer. "What is it that we're doing?"

Although I know what she's asking, I never miss an opportunity to goad her. "I'm pretty sure we are walking."

"I'm being serious here." The vulnerability in her voice and written all over her face makes me want to tell her everything. That she's all I can think about, that I stopped feeling for the last few years and she woke me up, *how much I love her.* But Steph's warning holds me back.

"We are enjoying one another's company. *A lot.*" I lean down and kiss her, saying with my tongue everything my lips cannot.

Charlotte nibbles on her lip when we pull apart. I sense her nervousness, but I'm scared if I say anything more, I won't be able to stop myself from telling her how badly I want to marry her. That I know she's my future. That I can never go back to living in a world without her in it. That she's healing me, making me the man I want to be, the man Peter wanted me to be. It's too soon to tell her all these things though. I'll lose her.

A restaurant sits on the cliff overlooking the beach. We order limpettes which are small clams served in a white wine sauce and share a pitcher of sangria. A white one this time, which has peach in it. Charlotte beams when she takes a sip. "I think you're rubbing off on me with your fruity drinks."

Smiling, I stare at my girl, memorizing this moment, with the ocean raging in the background, the salty air blowing her wild hair in all different directions as she tries to tame it, and a smile on her face. The waiter tells us that the pasta is homemade, so we decide to order another course and enjoy the peaceful afternoon. "So tell me, what you were like in high school, Maverick?"

Running my hand behind my neck I consider her question, trying to keep the smirk from playing on my lips. "How do you mean?"

My sassy girl rolls her eyes. "Let me guess, you were captain of the baseball and football teams and probably prom king?"

Laughter rumbles through me.

"Oh my God, you so were, weren't you?"

I cock my brow at her. "Maybe. Although, you forgot basketball."

She lets out a loud huff in frustration and laughs. "Of course you were. Mr. Perfect would so have been prom king."

My jaw ticks at her choice of words. I'm far from perfect. But I've always aspired to be. It's a completely exhausting task and one I know I'm no longer capable of being. With Charlotte I don't feel like I have to be though. She is easygoing. Fun. She doesn't obsess over her makeup or the way her hair falls. Hell, right now her hair is so crazy I'm sure it will take an hour to get a brush through it. But her smile lights up her face and mends my battered heart. "No one is perfect, Charlotte. What were you like in high school?"

Remembering Charlotte at twenty-two, I know she was probably a good time in high school. The girl just about swept me off my feet the night we met with her laughter, stories, and proud chin. There is a fire inside her that lights me up. "Oh, I wasn't a cheerleader if that's what you're asking. I'm guessing you dated lots of them."

I laugh. "Why do you do that?"

"Do what?" she asks innocently, her big eyes genuinely confused.

"Put yourself down. Act like I have any interest in people who aren't like you."

Charlotte worries at her bottom lip. "I guess I'm just surprised that someone like you wants someone like me."

"Charlotte, I would have killed to have met someone like you in high school. But you're right, I dated the cheerleaders because they were the loud ones who came after me, and I didn't have to make an effort. I was always busy with school, sports, and yes, being captain of all the teams. It wasn't until I got older that I realized how stressful that all was. Being 'perfect' as you like to call it. It feels anything but."

Charlotte's eyes dart to mine, an apology written on her face. The last thing I want is for her to feel bad about her opinions of me. I just want her to know me. Or at least I want her to know the person I want to be. The person I've been isn't necessarily someone I think she would like, but maybe with her by my side I can become someone worthy of her. "I'm sorry, Jack. I guess I just always wished I was the girl that someone like you would have looked at back then."

"How do you know you weren't? We didn't know each other, but the first time I saw you the only one I had eyes for in that bar was you."

She smiles now. "I was…not dorky per se but just the quiet girl in the corner."

"You? Quiet? No way!" Not buying it. The girl never stops talking.

"You know how sometimes you meet people that help you become you? Does that make any sense?"

Sure does. The girl sitting across from me was doing it to me as we speak. I nod. "I think I have a faint idea what you mean."

"Well, for me, that was college. In high school I just didn't fit in. I mean I had friends and a serious boyfriend but no one that really *got* me. Until Steph. She broke me out of my shell and made me feel comfortable in my own skin. I think seeing her be so unabashedly herself made me realize that I could be too. And voila, now you've got chatty Charlotte with the big smile." She beams at me as if proving her point.

"Remind me to buy Steph a really nice gift to bring home."

Charlotte smiles. "Why?"

"Because if she helped make you, *you*—my favorite person ever—well, then she deserves a thank you present."

Charlotte's jaw falls open. "Did you just call me your favorite person?"

I laugh. "Yeah, I'm kind of a fan of yours."

"Oh Jack, you are *so* getting lucky tonight." Charlotte moves herself closer to me, and I pull her onto my lap, holding her face close and pressing a kiss to her lips.

"I don't know, Charlotte, I'm feeling pretty lucky right about now. I'm not sure how it could get any better."

The look on my girl's face lights me up inside. The fact that I can make her smile like that, make her feel treasured, make her feel even half of what she makes me feel, just about leaves me in a puddle of lust.

That night I make love to her slowly, taking my time to show her precisely how I feel. When we check out of the hotel, we both look at one another as if we have a secret. "It's strange, right?" she asks, as we close the door of her room.

"That you only spent one night sleeping in your room? Yes, it is strange," I joke.

She tries to smack my arm, but with her purse, the carry-on, and her suitcase she just about falls over, reminding me of the scene in the airport, when she was stubborn and trying to do it all on her own. I grab the bag from her, and she lets out an exasperated sigh. "I'm kidding, Charlotte. What's strange?"

Charlotte stops in front of the door, her eyes glassy. "This place, it feels like it's become a part of me. A part of *us*. It was the first place we…and I…I just feel like a different person leaving it."

I put both our bags on the floor and grab her hips. "Yes. It did change us. We came here separately, but I'd like it if we would leave as a couple." I say it as if it isn't a question, but really it is. We aren't fifteen. I can't slip her a note in science class and ask her to go steady. Although, after our conversation yesterday, I am pretty positive that I could have had her back then if I wanted. It feels odd, though, asking her to be my girlfriend—she already feels like so much more than that. But it isn't official, and I want it to be. My stomach twists in nervousness. I hope she understands what I'm asking.

A smile spreads across her luscious lips. "Are you asking me to be your girlfriend, Mav?" she says in a singsong voice, as if we are six.

I roll my eyes. "Yes."

Lifting up on her tiptoes, she places her hands on my cheeks and pulls me close to her mouth. "Then that is my answer. Yes, I will be your girlfriend."

I'm pretty sure my heart soars, and I want to shoot my fist up in the air, but instead I just smile cockily at her, as if I knew she'd say yes all along, and lift her up for a kiss. Her feet aren't the only ones not touching the ground.

As we walk out of the elevator, strolling past the bar, hand in hand, she stops and spins on her heels, pinning the bartender with her gaze. "You were right, Romeo, I am both." I stare at her quizzically.

He nods as if he understands completely. And I'm pretty

sure I hear him say behind the bar, "In love and a lover," with a twinkle in his eye as he chuckles and continues cleaning.

CHAPTER 28

Charlotte

I am floating. On a cloud, in the sky, with angel wings pulling me up, up, up, and I never want to come down. Is this what it feels like? Falling in love? Because if so, God, why did I wait so long? Oh right, because I was waiting for him. And he is *so* worth the wait.

Yesterday, we checked into the new hotel, forgoing our individual rooms. When Jack opened the door to *our* room, he got all cheesy and picked me up in his arms—like I weigh nothing—and carried me straight to the king-size bed, tossing me like he would a feather. "What are you doing?" I asked him, sitting up on my knees, ready to rip off his clothes.

"New bed. We need to christen it." His eyes were dark, desire written all over his face. We spent the afternoon in bed, missing out on all the sights. I'm starting to wonder if we will ever see the rest of this island. Not that I'm complaining. Exploring Jack is just as enjoyable.

Today we finally leave the room to explore Furnas. "So, what is the brown water?" he asks, as we both stare at the oval-shaped pool which is the color of rust.

Lying, I reply, "It's like a spa." I really have no idea. But all the brochures and articles say we have to go in it. I'm going to need to do a bit more research, since I'm slacking on providing useless facts. The only information I can provide is what the concierge told me this morning. "Apparently, the iron makes it like a clay mask for our entire body. I think it's warm."

Jack turns up his nose. "It smells funny." He isn't wrong. The smell of rotten eggs hangs in the air, so strong and pungent that it feels like you are actually breathing it in, instead of oxygen. It is thick, and I'm sure we'll be washing our clothes and bodies of the smell for days to come.

I huff. "Weren't you the one who said we needed to try new things? Your exact words I think were 'just do it' or some other feel-good statement that you stole from a commercial."

He eyes me. "Charlotte, do not jump in this thing. We can't even see the bottom."

I laugh. "I'm not *jumping* in." I stick a toe in, nervous now what it will feel like. Oddly, it doesn't feel any different than a warm bath. I stick my foot farther down. "It *feels* normal."

"Charlotte, it might turn your toe a different color. Don't do it." He grabs me, pulling my leg close to him jokingly, which unfortunately just makes me lose my balance, and I feel myself falling headfirst into the egg-smelling water. The last thing I hear is his scream, "Nooooooo!"

I hit the water with a splash. Warm water laps against me, and suddenly Jack's hurtling himself into the brown pool as well, lifting me out of the water and holding me above his head, like a hockey player holds the Stanley Cup or a raving throng carries a crowd-surfer.

What is wrong with this guy?

"Jack, put me down!" I hiss sternly. He lowers me into his arms and cradles me like a baby. "What the hell is wrong with you?"

"I'm sorry." He lowers his eyes sheepishly, and I can't help but laugh. People are staring at us—this is supposed to be a tranquil place—and this only makes me laugh harder. "Close your mouth!" Jack says, wiping the wet droplets from my face.

"Oh, Jack. It's pointless. I'm pretty sure my mouth was wide open when I fell in." I taste the putrid water and shake my head. "Hopefully, the benefits for your skin translate to my insides too—or I may need to get a separate room."

He eyes me warily. Only now does it occur to me the real problem with sharing a room—the bathroom. How could I have not thought of this sooner? It appears the same thought is running through his mind, and we both start laughing again. This is going to be a very awkward night if the waters do to my stomach what I'm imagining.

We get out of the "spa waters" and I notice his navy and white board shorts have turned a dirty orangish brown. "Ugh,

Jack, I've got bad news."

He looks at me, concerned. "Huh?"

"I think you shit yourself." I start to giggle again as I point at his pants.

Jack looks down and rolls his eyes. "Sassy, how old are you?"

The giggles continue as I dry off and wring the egg-infused water from my hair. "Serves you right. I cannot believe you threw me in there!" I take my towel and whip it at him. It flies through the air perfectly and hits his ass with a "thwack" and he shrieks. An actual, real shriek. Girly and high, like a thirteen-year-old who's just found out her crush likes her. I stare back in horror.

Then it occurs to me that I have finally mastered the towel whip. A tremendous amount of pride washes over me. My father used to chase my brother and me through the house after bath time with a towel. Is it like a special power you get as an adult? And why? Honestly, it's pretty cruel, but right about now I feel like a superhero.

Jack grabs me around the waist, pulling me close. "You enjoyed that *way* too much."

I laugh. "I did. Sorry. Are you okay?"

Jack rubs his behind, and I'm not sure if he's being overly dramatic or if it actually does hurt. Honestly, I think I may have really hurt him. I'd been on the receiving end of that from my father growing up, and it never *didn't* hurt. But then he raises his eyebrows in a cocky manner. "I did three tours in the Middle

East. I'll be fine."

A moment passes between us. He still hasn't told me about his time in the military. Speaking of it so flippantly, trying to establish his manhood in the cocky manner he does, feels fake. But standing half-naked in a park surrounded by people who all smell like rancid eggs does not seem like the place to ask anything more of him. So, I reach out my hand and pull him close, rubbing the place where I branded him. "Let's go get showered—and I need to brush my teeth and sterilize my insides with some mouthwash."

He lets out a slow breath. "Okay, Sassy." Then he relaxes into my arms, his weight pressing against my shoulder, and his quiet breathing reminds me that there is still so much I don't know about this man.

After showering and sterilizing my mouth, I suggest we take a walk around the property. The hotel is famous for the twelve acres of gardens, ponds, steaming pools, and quiet relaxation. Walking hand in hand, the silence between us a comfortable one, I think back to his comment about deploying and yearn to know more. "Was it horrible?"

Jack glances over at me, almost as if he knows what I'm asking, despite the fact that there was no context to my question.

His eyes flash, and I wonder if he'll feign indifference, but then they soften, and he says quietly, "Not always."

"What were some of the good things?" I wrap both my arms around his right one and lean into him, squeezing him tightly. The sound of a waterfall rushing down provides a sense of calm, and the palm trees on either side of us offer shade as we walk.

"Definitely not the food." He laughs.

"Got it. I'll keep that off my bucket list of things to try."

"The karaoke was fun."

"Oh, don't even tell me on top of looking like this,"—I gesture in his direction, pointing at the incredible body and face that is drool worthy—"you can also sing."

Jack's lip twitches up, and his eyes dart down shyly. I love when he's cocky, but when he acts shy, I'm just about a pile of putty in his fingertips. "I'm not terrible at it. How 'bout you?"

Laughter bursts from my belly. "I mean *I* think I sound great in the shower or in my car, but I'm pretty sure no one will be handing me a mic anytime soon and begging me to sing Adele."

Jack pokes my side and pulls me close to him. "I'd love to hear you sing. We could do a duet. Be a real force to be reckoned with, maybe the next Sonny and Cher."

Oh, I can already see the Halloween costumes in our future. "What's your go-to song?"

Jack turns to me with a memory in his eye, dreamy and happy looking. "Well, my best friends and I did 'Hurts So Good' for my friend Nate's proposal. That's definitely up there on a favorite memory, but I haven't sung that in a while, and it's more their song. I think for me it would be 'You've Lost That Lovin' Feelin'.'"

I wrinkle my brows seductively. "Oh, Mav, talk *Top Gun* to me." He laughs and pulls me close again, brushing a kiss against my head. "So, you were involved in a musical proposal? That's so romantic."

"Oh, you like that sort of thing?" he asks, looking curiously at me.

Flashing him my biggest smile, I reply, "Um, yes, have you met me? I love all things romantic and cheesy. Like a flash mob, oh my gosh, amazing! I can't dance, but I always wished someone would tap me on the shoulder during one of those, and I could be part of it."

Jack laughs heartily. "Noted."

"So, tell me what else you liked about deployment?"

"Flying." Jack looks to the blue above. "When I was in the sky, and the noise was so loud that I could silence my thoughts, that was something good." Lost in the moment, Jack smiles to himself, almost as if he's back in the sky, his apparent happy place.

"And now, do you still love flying?"

He smirks. "Outside of being in bed with you, it's my favorite thing."

I smack his arm lightly. "Be serious, Jack. I want to know about your job. I want to know more about *you*."

Jack pulls on my hand, twining our fingers again. "Yes, I

still love flying. I haven't decided my next step in my career. I'm considering my options right now and where they might take me. It's nice being home in Rhode Island and close to my family. But flying…it's who I am."

I ignore the way my stomach flips when Jack mentions having options that might take him somewhere else. Maybe it should have been obvious to me that it was a possibility, but seeing as how I didn't really know what his job entailed, I hadn't given it much thought. Swallowing down my nerves, I reply, "It sounds amazing. To be up in the sky, completely in control, flying a jet of that size. I mean I'm a scaredy cat so I don't think it's something I would ever have even thought to do—but it sounds incredible."

He shakes his head. "You're a lot braver than you give yourself credit for."

I frown. "How so?"

"You put yourself out there. Like *really* out there. I don't do that. I've never opened my heart to anyone—but you open your heart to everyone. You're eternally optimistic. You flew across the ocean with a stranger, you put yourself on an online dating app, and you weren't afraid to tell people what you wanted. When you set your mind on something, you go after it. That's brave to me."

My heart pounds in my chest, and I grip his hand tightly, looping our fingers together. I love that he sees me in that light, even if I don't see myself that way. "Are you willing to open your heart to me?"

Jack stops walking and turns to face me. Surrounded by bonsai trees and hibiscus flowering plants, we are in our own private paradise. Brushing his hand against my cheek, he says softly, "You make me want to be brave."

Dangerously close to having a life-changing conversation, my stomach twists with nerves. But the butterflies seem to be grabbing the twisting vines and untangling them, willing me to take the leap so they can dance again. "Be brave," I whisper.

Jack's thumb trails my jaw, and he lifts my chin up as he touches my lips softly, pulling them apart as he lowers his mouth close to mine. His warm breath intoxicates me, making me heady and dizzy. But none of it compares to his words. "I'm falling for you, Charlotte." As his lips crash into mine, and his tongue works its way into my mouth, the butterflies sing and the sound escapes in a moan. He smiles into my mouth. "Your sounds kill me."

Thank God he's holding me up, because the kiss is knee-shaking good. I lean against his chest, sighing in happiness. "Okay."

Jack looks down at me quizzically. "I don't think I asked a question."

I smile up at him. "Okay. I will meet your family."

CHAPTER 29

Jack

Forty-eight hours of blissful, mind-blowing, earth-shattering moments with Charlotte is not enough. Since we left Ponta Delgada and arrived in Furnas the smiles have not left our faces. There were no fights, no awkward moments—well, aside from dropping her in the dirty water. It's been nothing other than complete bliss waking up next to Charlotte, holding hands as we explore the area, and talking late into the nights about everything in between pleasuring one another and sleeping. I am so not ready to leave this place. Why did I suggest that we go to my aunt's again? We could be heading to Caloura now, for another week in a hotel by ourselves, and instead we are walking into a lion's den.

Some say Portuguese families are nosy or judgmental. Mine is both. The men spend their time outside working in the gardens or on the couch watching TV. But the women, with their signature black hair, round hips, and big personalities, stuff you with food while judging everything that comes out of your mouth. With a smile on their face. They'll gossip after you leave and tsk tsk about something you did wrong—and I am walking Charlotte right into the center of it all without the appropriate armor.

Which is why I am currently placing a call to my dad—I need to talk to someone about what I'm about to do. He had been in Charlotte's shoes, having to impress his wife's mother and aunts who were as judgmental as they come.

"You're introducing this girl to your mom's family?" he asks in quiet admiration. "You're either really crazy about her, or she's so crazy you're trying to get rid of her. Which is it?"

I laugh uncomfortably. "The family isn't that bad, Dad."

My dad whistles. "Wow. She must be something then, huh?"

I laugh again. "Huh?"

"If you aren't trying to get rid of her by introducing her to that crazy pack, then it must be true love. I don't think you've ever introduced a girl to me and your mom."

I breathe into the phone. "No. I haven't. Not like this anyway." Sure, there had been high school girlfriends that my parents had to meet because I lived in their house, but no one I brought home because I wanted my parents to get to know them. Now I couldn't wait for them to meet Charlotte. I wanted to show her off. My chest swells with pride—somehow, I convinced this amazing woman to be with me. "So, any tips?" I ask him again.

"Too late to cancel?" he jokes.

"Right. We are leaving in an hour."

"Just don't leave her alone with the women. They can be brutal. Especially when they start speaking in Portuguese, and she can't understand it."

I nod into the phone as if he can see me. "Thanks, Dad. I'll call you guys when I'm with the family. Give Mom my love." I hang up the phone, and my leg starts to twitch. What did I sign us up for?

"Everything okay?" Charlotte asks, staring at me with those big innocent brown eyes, turning my insides to mush. I'm not sure how long she's been standing there—I thought she was in the bathroom getting ready. I run through the conversation with my father, trying to remember what I said and if she could have heard anything problematic. Like that I'm in love with her.

"All good. You ready to head out?"

"Yup." She turns around to grab the rest of our toiletries and treats me to the view of her ass in those white shorts again. She has on a turquoise halter top which looks perfect against her now tanned skin. Long golden locks cascade down her back—even her hair has been brightened by the sun.

Unable to resist, I tap her on the ass, and she turns around and gives me a daring grin. "Don't start something you're not prepared to finish." With the challenge hanging in the air, I rush at her, tackling her onto the bed, and she lands in a fit of laughter. "Stop," she says breathlessly as she laughs harder. "I got myself all ready for your family, and we have to be out of this hotel room soon."

I lay kisses on her neck, savoring the taste of her, a vanilla cake flavor that I've become obsessed with. "Wanna just skip the family? Go to the beach instead and make love for another week?"

Charlotte lifts herself up so that we are now side to side, facing one another, and she leans on her elbow as she searches my face. Nibbling on her lip, she quietly asks, "Is that what you want?"

"Stop." Pulling her into my arms, I kiss her nose. "I see that brain of yours working. I'm not backtracking. I just don't want to share you. But you're right—let's hit the road before I start undressing you and we never leave."

Looking up at me she says, "I'm really happy, Jack. I'm trying to stay out of my head. I promise."

"Good. Because I'm really happy too. And your happiness is the only thing that I want. Let's go, baby." I see her eyes smile at my nickname for her, and her cheeks pink up. God, she is the cutest damn thing in the world. Lifting my hand behind her head I pull her closer to me, kissing her hungrily.

An hour later we are on the road, heading to my aunt's. I'm driving—thank goodness—and Charlotte's hand is resting on my thigh. "Tell me about your family. Who are we going to meet?"

"Well, like I told you, there's my Aunt Maria, my grandmother's sister. She never had kids so she's been like an extra grandmother to everyone. My cousin Isabella is staying with her for the summer, so she'll be there too. She lives in the US, but she can never get out of her own way, so her mom sent her here to live with my aunt so she could 're-evaluate' what she wants to do in life." Belle is a complete sweetheart—I have a feeling she and Charlotte will get along great.

"Okay. That sounds doable—two people," Charlotte mumbles to herself.

I laugh. "Oh, no, woman, those are just the important ones. I won't even try to name all my cousins and uncles. Just know most of the women are named Maria, and those who aren't won't be offended if you accidentally call them that, and the men are almost always Manny or José. When in doubt, say Maria or Manny and you should be fine."

Charlotte laughs, but I just stare at her. "Wait. You're serious?"

"Yes, baby. I don't joke about the name Maria." I give her a serious stare, and she nods as if understanding.

I squeeze her thigh. "I'm just kidding. It's not serious."

"Okay. So, tell me their names," she asks impatiently.

"No. I mean that is really all their names. Save for, like, three of them. You'll do fine."

"When was the last time you saw your aunt?"

My jaw clenches. Before is the answer. Before I met Charlotte. Before I went on the tour that changed everything. Before Peter's death.

Before.

But I simply respond, "It's been a few years." Then, changing the topic because I can't possibly talk about the before, I ask, "You close with your family?"

Charlotte's face brightens. "Yes. But I don't have a bunch of extended aunts and uncles with the same names." She laughs at her own joke. "It's just my immediate family and my grandmother."

"You have one brother, right?"

"Yup. Shawn. He's actually my half brother." Charlotte bites her cheek as she looks out the window.

"Oh, I didn't realize your parents were divorced."

Shaking her head, she replies, "Oh, they aren't. My parents are married. He's a few years older than I am. Shawn was the product of a teenage pregnancy—my mom's. He never knew his dad. It was actually years before I even realized my dad wasn't Shawn's. He never treated him any different. But I'm sure it affects him. I mean his dad didn't want him. I know it affected me. I always pictured this perfect family of four, and then suddenly I'm told one day that my parents aren't perfect, my mom wasn't perfect, and they'd lied to me about it all. I get now that they weren't lying. I mean you don't tell your baby when she's born that her older brother is another man's child. And when's the right time, right? But when I finally learned about it, well, I must admit it definitely took off those rose-colored glasses, you know?"

Squeezing her hand, I nod. "Makes sense. Are you and your brother close?"

She nods. "Yeah. He's a good brother. Although, I always wanted a sister. Someone to play Barbies with would have been nice. Instead, I got stuck playing baseball with my brother, or really doing anything he wanted. I followed him around like he hung the moon. You only have a sister, right?"

"Yup."

"I'm guessing you forced her to play sports with you too?"

I laugh and shift uncomfortably. Once again we are getting dangerously close to discussing the truth. "I mean, Ames definitely played sports with us but not by my choice. I had my two best friends, Nate and Peter—they lived on my street—and we did everything together. Ames just followed us around."

"Ames?"

"Yeah, Amelia. We called her Ames though. I guess I'm the only one that still does." It was actually Peter who gave her the nickname.

"So, Nate and Peter, your best friends. Will I get to meet them when we get home?"

My knuckles turn white from the way I'm gripping the wheel. I clear my throat trying to garner the words that I know I need to say. *Peter's dead, so you'll never meet him.* But I can't get it out. I can't force myself to utter that statement. Fortunately, the GPS tells us to turn right, and we pull into the driveway which leads to my aunt's house. Charlotte bounces in excitement. "Oh, we're here!"

I've seen pictures of my aunt's house all my life but never been here. It's magnificent. Hydrangeas line the entire driveway, and there is a view of the Atlantic beyond.

Calming my nerves, I squeeze Charlotte's thigh. "You ready for this?"

She raises her eyebrows and looks at me. "Ready as I'll ever be."

As we get out of the car, I spot my cousin running in our direction. Her dark black hair flows around her face, and her blue eyes light up when she finally reaches me. Throwing her arms around my neck, she screeches, "Jack! I can't believe you finally made it here!"

I let go of Charlotte's hand and wrap my arms around Belle. The last time I held her was at Peter's funeral. The memory burns my chest. Somehow, I manage to whisper the words, "It's good to see you."

She smacks my shoulder. "I cannot believe you have to come across the ocean for me to actually spend time with you." Turning to Charlotte, she raises her brows. "And who is this?"

"This is Charlotte. Charlotte, this is my cousin Isabella."

Charlotte extends her hand to shake Isabella's but like a good Portuguese girl, Belle leans in to kiss both of Charlotte's cheeks. "Jack here lives in the same town as me and can never make time to see me, but when I come to the Azores for the summer, somehow I get to see him. Go figure."

"Wait, you're from Bristol?" Charlotte asks.

She laughs. "Yes. You ever been?"

My mind swirls trying to bring me back to the present. But my memory replays the trumpets and the sobs of Peter's family.

I shake it from my head. "Charlotte is from Bristol too."

Belle's eyes light up. "Oh, when you said you were traveling with a stranger you met on the Internet, I figured she lived in another state. How crazy!"

Charlotte turns, likely waiting for me to tell Belle she's my girlfriend, but the words remain trapped in my throat. Peter's face dances in my memory, and the air stills around me, getting hotter and making me feel like I'm spinning.

Out the door of the house comes my aunt. Time has not done her any favors, and I feel terrible that it has been so long since I last hugged her. She is at least forty pounds lighter; her dark black, long hair is now short and gray. The skin on her face hangs with wrinkles, but she still has the same smile and beautiful grey-blue eyes. "Titia," I whisper into her ear as I fall against her, grounding myself for a moment in her arms.

Slowly, more and more people filter out of the house, kind of like a clown car—uncles and cousins I'd never met but had heard about all my life. Their voices come out muffled to my ears, and since I'm not making the introductions, Belle introduces Charlotte to all of them. Charlotte smiles and greets everyone, but I can tell she's uncomfortable since I've yet to introduce her as my girlfriend. I feel like shit about it, but I can't make my mouth work. My tongue feels heavy, and my heart pounds.

"Jack!" A woman with long black hair like Belle's comes through the crowd and throws her arms around me. It takes me a moment to register who she is, and unfortunately, it isn't long enough for me to grab Charlotte and warn her. "What's it been—like six years?"

My chest grows tight. This just keeps getting worse. "Katalina, how are you?" She still hasn't let go of me, holding my hand even as I pull out of her hug. Charlotte's eyes burn holes in my face.

"Oh. Much better now that you're here. I couldn't believe it when your cousin told me you were coming. It's like kismet." She stares at me like she wants to eat me for dinner, and I know I'm in trouble.

I clear my throat, finally getting my body under control as panic sets in. "Charlotte, this is Katalina. Katalina, this is Charlotte."

"Oh, you must be the girl he's traveling with. What a crazy idea. Did you guys really meet online and agree to come on a trip together sight unseen?"

It was uncomfortable how many people knew my business. This has my sister's name written all over it. Amelia and Belle are best friends, and she clearly told her everything. Well, the everything that I shared with everyone else, which was obviously not the truth. No one knows who Charlotte really is to me—the one who got away.

Finally, Charlotte speaks, "Yup. We really did. So, how do you guys know each other?" The steam pouring off Charlotte is unmistakable. She's furious.

Katalina grabs my arm, linking hers with mine. "Oh, Jack and I met a few years ago when I was visiting Belle on spring break. What was it, six years ago now, Jack? We had one wonderful week and then I had to come back here, and he was deploying. But I always knew one day we'd be reunited."

I pull my arm away from Katalina and look at Charlotte. I watch as she connects the dots, but I can't stop the train wreck that is occurring. "When was spring break? March, April?" Charlotte asks, as if it is an innocent question.

Unfortunately, I know better.

"Hmm." Katalina looks at me. "Do you remember, Jack? I'm guessing March."

"After St. Patrick's Day?" Charlotte asks, still not looking at me, her fists balled up and her chin defiant.

"I don't really know. We don't celebrate that here. Jack, do you know?" They both turn to look at me, Katalina with no real interest in the answer and Charlotte with righteous indignation.

"After." I meet Charlotte's eyes and try to convey my apology, but I know that it's no use.

"Right. That's what I thought. Jack, do you mind finding out where I'm going to stay? I need to lie down for a bit. I'm wiped from all the traveling."

That will likely be the last time Charlotte speaks directly to me. This is about as big of a fuck-up as they come. I should have told her the truth about everything before we got here. Although, I had no idea this was how it would all turn out. Why didn't I remember Katalina lived near my aunt? Truth is, even if I did, I wouldn't have remembered that night we spent together.

She's overdramatizing the relationship—we hung out with Belle while she was in town. Yes, we hooked up, but it meant nothing. It was one night. Also, I never thought I'd see Charlotte again. And it was six *years* ago.

My breath catches in my throat when I see the hurt in Charlotte's eyes. It doesn't matter if it was six years ago or yesterday. I hurt her. *Again.* I'm so fucking angry with myself I can't see straight.

Seemingly sensing the change in mood, my aunt offers to take Charlotte to her room. I try to follow but both Charlotte and my aunt give me a look that tells me to stay away. "Come on, Jack, you've got to tell Belle and me all about your trip so far. Let's go down by the water and catch up." Katalina links her arm in mine and leads me down the path, and like an idiot, I follow.

Every inch of my body screams for me to get up and go talk to Charlotte. But I stay grounded in place, listening to Belle and Katalina prattle on about who knows what.

I don't know what to say to Charlotte. There are no words to properly explain that this is just a big misunderstanding. I know in her mind she thinks the reason I didn't stick around six years ago was because I didn't care. That I was a playboy who bounced from woman to woman. But it's not true. It's because I cared too much. I knew I was deploying in April. I didn't want her to have that life, waiting around for me to come back from a never-ending war. Even more than that, I didn't think I could actually leave her if I ever kissed her.

Damn, was I right about that. Now having tasted her, I know it would have been impossible.

So, I left. In all honesty, I thought when I came back, I would be able to find her. I knew where she lived...I knew her first name. How many Charlottes who went to Salve Regina and stayed at the Founders Hall dorms could there be? I *would* have found her.

Katalina had been a warm body the week before I left. Nothing more. Then Peter died, and I couldn't think about anything else—let alone find the girl whose memory kept me company while I was in the desert.

"Jack, are you listening to me?" Belle waves her hand in front of my face.

I shake my head. "I'm sorry. I think I screwed up, and I'm just trying to figure out how to fix it."

Belle's eyes meet mine in understanding. "I thought that was the case."

Katalina stares blankly at us both. "I'm lost. Screwed up what?"

"Charlotte's your girlfriend, isn't she?" Belle asks me. Katalina glares at her and then looks to me to refute it.

"Yes." I can't find the words to explain anything further.

Belle sighs. "So, what are you doing sitting here with us? Go talk to her."

I run my hand through my hair. "She doesn't want to talk to me. I'm giving her space."

"I'm seriously so confused," Katalina says exasperatedly.

Belle glares at her. "Jack's in love. It's clear as day. And like any dumb man, he probably hasn't told her how he feels about her, and you walking up and acting like you guys were a thing probably didn't help."

I shake my head. "This isn't your fault, Kat. It's mine. I met Charlotte six years ago—*before you*." They both look at me confused now.

Belle especially. "Wait. You've known her for six years?"

Certainly feels like it. "Not really. We met and had one perfect night together. But it was before I was deploying. I didn't want to be distracted. I wasn't ready. Like an idiot, rather than telling her that, I just left in the middle of the night." Belle's eyes grow wide at my betrayal. Saying it out loud really does make it sound so much worse. Or maybe it was actually that bad.

"Well, surely she understands what happened to you when you deployed." Belle reaches out and touches my hand.

No one really understands—but I appreciate that they all try.

"I'm sure she would understand. But I haven't given her the opportunity. I haven't told her." I look down at my hands now, embarrassed and ashamed. Also sad, because I should be having this conversation with Charlotte. I know I love her. I know she's the one I want to spend the rest of my life with, and yet I didn't trust our love enough to give her the whole truth. I didn't really let her know me.

"And I thought I was the naïve one when it came to relationships," Belle says, wringing her hands together. "Come on, Kat, let's give Jack here some time to think. He needs to come up with a plan to explain all of this to Charlotte." Belle gets up, and Katalina remains seated, staring at us both. Please tell me she's not upset too. I can't take another woman's disappointment.

"That was a pretty terrible thing you did," she says with fire in her eyes. I know what she means. Kat realizes I used her back then. I hang my head, acknowledging her accusation.

"Yes. Yes, it was. I'm sorry, Kat." She doesn't look at me though, just gets up and stalks off, leaving me to stew in my thoughts.

"Don't worry about her. She's a bit dramatic," Belle says, squeezing my hand.

"You should go after her."

Belle shakes her head. "Nah. I have all summer to cheer her up. You're only here for a few days. And we need to figure out how to fix this issue you have."

I look at her sadly. I don't think there is a way to fix it. How many times could I let Charlotte down? How many second chances was she going to give me? It seemed all I did was disappoint her—and there is no one to blame but me.

"Do you use TikTok?"

Tik what? I give her a look letting her know I have no idea what she is talking about.

"It's an app. Seriously, it's hysterical. It always cheers me up when I'm upset." She pulls out her phone, and suddenly, videos of talking dogs and cats and people dancing synchronized moves take up the next hour of our lives. I find myself laughing with Belle which just makes me feel worse. Up in the house is the woman that I love, and I know I've broken her heart.

CHAPTER 30

Charlotte

Squeezing the tears back and clenching my shaking hands, I somehow put on a fake smile for Jack's aunt and follow her through the house. For the record, it's gorgeous. The tile is beautiful Azorean blue and white, and the walls are white stucco with huge windows that open to the sea.

Leading me up the stairs, she speaks softly, as if she's aware of my aching heart. "I'm going to give you my favorite room in the house. It's called the Lovers' Quarters. Legend has it that if you stay in this room with your one true love, you will be married the rest of your days—happily, of course."

I hold a rigid smile on my face. The word lover no longer holds any magic. "Oh, you don't have to give me the nicest room. I'd be happy to stay anywhere." What I really mean is that I will not be needing any Lovers' Quarters. Perhaps Jack and Katalina can reunite there.

"Now, sit here." The old woman sits on the bed and pats the spot next to her. Unable to refuse, I sit down. "I was never lucky enough to find someone to share my life with. But everyone in my family—they honeymooned in this room. It will bring you good luck. Yes?"

I appreciate her ability to speak English and the warmth she's showing me. I don't have it in my heart to turn her down. And since my mind always controls my mouth, I can't help but engage her in some questions. "Did Jack's parents honeymoon here?"

She nods. "Yes. And one day Jack will too. I think that's why he brought you here though, no?"

I shake my head, fighting back tears. "Jack and I are just friends."

Aunt Maria places her thin hands on my knee and pats. "Once I was young and beautiful like you. And I thought I had all the time. I pushed away someone who loved me, and look at me now—we don't have unlimited chances at love." She appears to have said her piece and stands up ready to leave me with her wisdom.

"Obrigada." I say thank you as Jack taught me. She turns and smiles before walking out, a sparkle hitting her eyes. I lean back against the bed and cover my head with a pillow, screaming my frustration into it.

The second I started putting all the facts together about Katalina it was like I was back there again—in my dorm room bed—waking up and looking around for Jack only to find that he was gone. No note, no phone number, nothing. Alone and left to wonder if I imagined everything I felt. Questioning if he was even real—if what I felt was real.

Just when I finally begin to trust him and become the hopeful person I used to be, it turns out it's all a lie.

How did I let him do this to me again?

I try calling Steph, but her phone goes straight to voicemail which leaves me wanting to scream. No one else in my life knows Jack. I need to talk to someone who knows him, because if I tell any of my other friends what he has done they will just think, "*Poor stupid Charlotte did it again, believed a guy was the one after only a few nights.*" Which is *so* not what happened. Or at least I don't *think* it did.

Steph told me to do this. Said he would be good for fun. Although, she told me not to fall for him, and I went and did it anyway. Dammit. Stupid Charlotte. So, so stupid. I'm not Sassy. I'm not quick-witted. I'm the stupid girl who falls in love with the wrong person. What is wrong with me?

My heart hurts. But I can't very well stay holed up in this room all night. I go into the bathroom and clean up my tear-stained face, spray my hair to create some loose waves rather than bed head, and spritz myself with perfume. If I'm going to face Jack, I am going to look damn good doing it. He'll regret playing with my heart—he'll regret having ever met me.

Okay, I don't look *that* good. But I lie to my reflection and give her a searing glare.

There are French doors leading out to a small balcony. I tug at one, and it opens easily. The salty air mixes with a floral smell, tickling my throat. The property has a green hill with gardens spread throughout, and the ocean beyond sparkles gloriously. There is an empty picnic table at the end of the hill, right where the cliff breaks down to the water. It's probably an incredible spot to sit with appetizers and a glass of wine and watch the sun sink down into the ocean.

Maybe if you hadn't gone and fallen for Jack, you could be doing that with him right now. Instead you were a fool. Again.

I sigh loudly and leave the balcony and my dreams of a romantic night behind. We had a vacation romance. Nothing more. We presented the vacation side of ourselves. The light, easygoing person that you become without the worry of work, or the necessity to clean, or the drama of life. For a few days when you're on vacation anyone can be carefree—they can drink too much, dance like a fool, and laugh for no reason at all.

At home I don't wear shorts like this, or halter tops. It's almost laughable. God forbid my students, or their parents, saw me dressed like this. I'm the teacher who wears long skirts, whose hair is always nicely styled, and who wears a light pink gloss on her lips. I'm never flashy—more the girl next door. Never the seductress that I'd been portraying to Jack. And who knows who he is at home. I don't know him. And he doesn't know me. Here I let my hair curl, swing my hips wider, and tease Jack as if I'm actually the sassy woman he craves, rather than the clumsy disaster that we all know I am. If I wasn't so broken over losing him, it would be comical that I actually thought we'd fallen in love. I'd presented him with vacation Charlotte, not real Charlotte. The relationship was bound to fizzle in the real world. Which is precisely what happened. As soon as we entered a world where one of us knew other people, we failed to exist. *I* failed to exist. I'm not his girlfriend. I'm not anyone to him. My heart seizes in pain.

Dialing Grams's number quickly, I wait for her to pick up so I can check on her. But in all honesty, it's me that needs her right now. I just need a reminder that I'm not a complete screwup. I'm a good granddaughter, a good teacher, and I have wonderful friends. So what if I'm a bad judge when it comes to men—that isn't all that matters in life.

As soon as I hear her voice my resolve crumbles, tears spilling down my cheeks. "Hi, Grams," I offer weakly.

"Princess, it's good to hear your voice. How's your trip?"

She must be having a good day. They are so few and far between that I know this is a gift. "It's good, Grams. You would love the Azores—it's beautiful."

"Your grandfather and I went there many, many years ago."

"What?" I practically shout my surprise.

"Some of the loveliest people I ever met. Although, at the time, we were dating, and I must admit, I was jealous of every beautiful woman that walked by. Those Portuguese women with their dark hair and hips for days can be quite intimidating."

If you've ever met my grandmother, with her gorgeous red hair, amazing hourglass figure, and the voice of an angel, you would understand my complete shock at this admission. My grandfather basically ate out of her hand. I remember him following her around even when I was a young child, and they were in their sixties. I'd never seen a man so in love. "Grams, I can't imagine you being intimidated by anyone. Besides, Pop Pop only had eyes for you."

She laughs—it's girlish and carefree, a laugh from another era—and my heart soars. I live for her stories and thought I'd all but lost a chance at learning new ones because of her dementia. Like I said, this is a gift.

"Your grandfather is the one who made me this way. His love for me allowed me to stop being so insecure. Charlotte, for so long I was like you, unsure of myself, untrusting, and unbelievably scared to get hurt. That trip though…I learned something about myself."

I lean in closer to the phone, not wanting to miss a single word, hoping that if I get close, the magic will come through and sprinkle over me like the fairy godmother did for Cinderella with her wand. "And what was that?"

"That I had to love myself the same way he loved me. I had to see myself the way he saw me. And as soon as I tried—as soon as I saw the woman he saw—well, I stole the swing in my hips from the Portuguese and believed that with a smile and a little bravery, I could have anything I wanted. And I did,

Charlotte. I had a wonderful life. A life filled with memories. Which is what I want for you."

Another tear slips down my face, but I'm smiling now. That's what I want too. And I want to hear more about her memories. "Grams, tell me, what was your favorite thing about the island?"

She pauses. "What island?"

My eyebrows pinch together. Not yet. Please, give me more time. "The Azores, Grams, when you went with Pop Pop." I try to bring her back, to restart her memory.

"I...I..." she falters. It hurts to even breathe. I can't bear to confuse her anymore.

"It's okay, Grams. Go rest. I'll call you tomorrow. I love you."

She's quiet on the other end of the phone. She has no idea who I am. I hear the phone disconnect and know she probably looked at it like she didn't even know why she was holding it and then put it down without another thought. It's happened before. But that doesn't make it hurt any less. I try to focus on the fact that I was granted a little gift instead of on the disappointment that it's already over.

Kind of like my relationship with Jack.

Sighing, I give myself a pep talk and head out of the room. Making my way down the steps of the house, I hear loud voices and laughter in the kitchen. Not sure what I will find, I brace myself for a tension-filled evening. "Olá!" Jack's aunt says to me when she spots me standing in the door watching everyone.

"Olá," I say quietly.

Looking around the room, I find that Jack is nowhere to be found. Instead of this being a relief, it makes me sad. Annoyingly, I miss him. I still care.

Jack's cousin Belle holds two glasses of wine in her hands and turns to me with a friendly smile. "Come. The sunset here is magnificent. Let's drink some wine by the water, and you can tell me all about your trip so far."

My shoulders relax at leaving the crowded kitchen which is filled with four older women with black hair all staring at me. As we head out the door, I hear them begin talking again in loud excited voices and wonder if they are discussing me. In America, they'd at least have done it in hushed tones, but since they know I can't understand a word they are saying they don't bother whispering.

"Don't pay any attention to them. It's been a long time since these walls were graced with a young couple in love." Belle hands me my wine, and I follow her steps as she leads me to the picnic table.

"Oh, Jack and I aren't a couple," I say unconvincingly.

She gives me a look that tells me she knows I'm full of it. "You may not be a couple, but Jack is most certainly smitten."

I blow out the steam that is running through my body and sip the wine. Plum undertones pull me back to the night in the bar when I finally decided to throw caution to the wind and pounce on Jack. Closing my eyes for a moment, I remember how good it felt to be in his arms. "I don't know what we are. I just know that he keeps hurting me with his half truths." It's the most honest assessment of our relationship to date.

Belle turns around and squeezes my hand with her own. "*Men.*" Her tone leads me to believe she's had her fair share of relationship issues. I suppose heartbreak is something all women deal with, even women as beautiful as Belle. She towers next to me with her long legs, and her figure is the kind that people work to attain all their lives. Large breasts, tiny waist, and generous hips. With black hair which reaches her waist and an olive skin tone, anyone would be jealous. But it's her eyes that do me in—they are as blue as the sea before us. She's also extremely kind. I find myself relaxing in her company and letting my guard down.

"Where did your friend go?" I flinch just thinking about the fact that her friend had so obviously had something with Jack. Katalina was as beautiful as Belle. Jealousy courses through me. Jack hadn't hidden the fact that there had been women before me—I'd be naïve to have not known even if he hadn't. But somehow being presented with it and knowing it occurred so soon after our own meeting years ago was hard to reconcile with the way Jack said he felt back then.

Did he really have those feelings then? Is he lying now? I'm trying to get out of my own head, but it's kind of impossible.

"Oh, Kat? I sent her home. It's none of my business— although, that's never stopped me before—but it was six years ago, and it was only one night."

What Belle doesn't understand is that her statement could apply to either Kat or me. It hurts that he'd been attracted enough to sleep with her, and he hadn't even attempted to kiss me. It stings more than I'd like to admit.

I change the subject to keep the tears from starting. "So, Jack says you're staying here for the summer?"

Belle sighs. "Yes. I'm trying to figure out my life. I have no career, no boyfriend, and I'm twenty-eight. So, essentially, I'm useless according to my family. Although, I guess I don't so much disagree with them. I just don't know what I want to *do* with my life."

I totally get where she's coming from—at least I have a career I love. I scrunch my nose in understanding. "I get it. But you only have one life, so it's good that you are really considering it. I mean, I am a teacher, but I feel like that's *all* I am. That's why I chose to come on this trip—I wanted something more than to just be a woman who works, watches *The Office*, and goes on bad dates." I laugh now at myself. It was pathetic that this could actually have been my biography for a dating website. I'm actually pretty sure it was.

"But look at you—you did it! You're here. You're taking a chance."

Did I? If I'm honest, I've had my walls up since Jack admitted he remembered me. Did I ever really give us a chance?

Instead of psychoanalyzing myself, I focus on Belle. "So are you."

Belle shakes her head, and her dark black hair swings in the wind and her blue eyes light up. "No, I'm hiding at my aunt's because she's the only one who ever understood me. She had a career—her life didn't depend upon meeting a man, or God forbid, her ability to procreate. She bravely has lived her life on her own terms. And she has a fantastic shoe collection."

I remember Aunt Maria's words to me earlier—that you don't get unlimited chances at love—and think that perhaps Belle doesn't know everything about her aunt. It doesn't appear that she lived her life completely on her own terms. Like both of us, she was too scared to take what she wanted, but she did seem to embrace what she did have—a beautiful home and nieces and nephews who loved her. And, apparently, good shoes.

She did sound like someone who had a few regrets, though. I don't want to look back on life and feel that way—but I'm not sure if allowing Jack another chance to break my heart will be a regret or not.

Not that any of this matters, because Jack isn't here. He disappeared and didn't even come find me to apologize. No sense in stressing about a decision on forgiving him since he never asked.

Belle stares at me, and I realize I haven't responded to her proclamation. "Thinking about Jack?" she asks.

"Sorry. I'm not the best company right now."

She reaches out her long fingers to touch me. They wrap around my short ones as she squeezes. "Give him a chance. Jack has been through a lot. But he's a *really* good guy."

I sigh and blow the hair off my face. "That's what everyone keeps saying. I wouldn't know what he's been through. He hasn't opened up to me about any of that." I try not to sound bitter, but I definitely feel that way. Jack wants me to believe that he's fallen for me, and he keeps telling me we have some special bond, but he hasn't opened up to me at all. Everything feels very surface level with us.

Other than when he kisses me. There is nothing surface level about that. It's almost like we have deep conversations with our lips. My cheeks turn pink just thinking of kissing him.

As if on cue, the sky sighs in pleasure, the hazy blue fading to light pink with yellow pops of color. The sun sinks into the ocean, winking before it dips below the surface. What a very flirtatious sunset.

I close my eyes and try to breathe. We've only known each other for a week. *A week.* And yet everything felt more beautiful because of him, and without him, now it seems so tragic.

Feeling heartbroken over a man not opening up after a week sounds like old Charlotte, a person I swore I was leaving behind—the one who falls hard and quick. I promised myself that wouldn't happen, but I'd be lying if I didn't admit that is precisely what I did. I jumped the gun. Fell for Jack before I knew him. Which really means I didn't fall for him at all. I fell for the idea of him and the idea of getting married and having a happily ever after. It's unfair to put all of that on Jack. That's on me too.

I so badly want what my grandparents had. I think back to my conversation with my Grams—she finally trusted how he felt and that gave her the ability to trust herself. Somehow, I think it's the reverse for me. I need to learn to love myself before I can ever expect someone else to love me.

"Give him time. He's worth it. I wish I could find someone like my cousin. What I would do to find someone who talked about me like he talks about you."

I look out at the ocean, trying to keep the tears from my eyes. "Where is he anyway?"

"He had to run an errand. He'll be back soon."

I finish my wine. "Then I think I'll need another one of these." I lift the glass up to her, and she laughs.

CHAPTER 31

Jack

"I can't believe we are in another country! This is insanity! How did you sneak away from Charlotte to pick us up?" Steph is talking a million miles per minute which is normally Charlotte's MO, not Steph's. Now I get why they're such good friends.

I glance in the rearview mirror and meet her eyes. "I just left. I don't think she wants to talk to me right now, anyways."

"Dammit, Fitzpatrick. What'd you do now?"

If steam could come out of her head, I'm pretty sure it would. Pat glances at me nervously and whispers, "Don't screw up her mood. I'm looking forward to vacation Steph, not angry Steph. I *need* this."

I shoot him an apologetic smile. Steph is not pleased. "Um, hello! Don't ignore me. What did you do to Charlotte?"

"I didn't introduce her as my girlfriend, and I slept with someone else six years ago." I think that about sums up my fuck-up today. Quite frankly, while I completely understand her being hurt—it *was* six years ago!

"That makes no sense," Steph mutters to herself.

Thank you, I agree.

Okay, it did make sense. I just don't want to admit it.

I huff. "I didn't introduce her as my girlfriend to the person I slept with six years ago."

Pat whistles now. "Yup. You fucked up."

"I know," I grumble angrily under my breath.

Steph is silent in the back, and I'm hoping it's because she is concocting some magical plan to make everything better. "Say something," I say gruffly into the mirror.

Steph meets my eyes, and I only see defiance in them. I am not getting help from her. She appears as angry as Charlotte was hurt.

We drive in silence back to my aunt's house. I had cleared it with my aunt before inviting all these people to stay with her. But now I really wish that we were going to a hotel. I don't want her to see how dysfunctional my life is. The tension in the house is going to be too thick to dispel with some wine. Even the homemade kind which could grow hair on a five-year-old's chest.

One perk of my aunt's house, though, is the view—even Steph can't stay angry when she sees the property. "Holy crap! This is incredible." I see her reach around Pat's seat and squeeze his shoulder.

At least someone will have a romantic weekend.

Pat and Steph get out of the car before I do. I stay rooted in my seat, my eyes glued to Charlotte, who is down by the water with my cousin. How am I going to face her? What am I going to say? Her head turns at the sound of the car door slamming, and she meets my eyes. Even at a distance I can feel her look penetrating my soul. In my gut I can feel how much I hurt her—continuously—and wonder if she would be better off if I let her go.

With my eyes on her, I open the door to get out. All I want is to hold her. Charlotte looks to Steph and Pat and then back to me, her eyes offering a bit of a reprieve from her anger. "What is going on?" A smile spreads across her face.

"Surprise!" Steph shouts as she holds her hands up and walks into Charlotte's open arms, hugging her. Pat looks to me and then turns back to Charlotte and chooses to embrace his wife's best friend. I don't blame him—Charlotte is prettier, smells better, and choosing her will give him brownie points with his wife. I stand back, watching them all catch up from a distance, with a fierce jealousy over how they can all bring Charlotte such joy.

Belle walks over and introduces herself, offering to show them to their room. Then she winks at me and motions her hand toward Charlotte. Time to face the music.

With her hair blowing in the wind and her brown eyes glistening, Charlotte looks beautiful. Black shorts perfectly accentuate my favorite asset, and a cherry-red halter top that is tied just like her purple dress forces me to avert my eyes. It's almost like she planned the outfit to get back at me. I'm probably being vain, but if she did then I salute her gumption because I certainly deserve it. "Charlotte," I say, but her name sounds more like a sigh as it's stolen in the wind.

She eyes me expectantly and then bites the inside of her mouth nervously.

"Can we go down to the water and talk?"

Charlotte nods her head in assent but says nothing. I walk next to her and try to think of what to say. What are the right words to express that I understand why she's angry, but that Kat meant nothing to me?

My hand swings next to hers, and our fingers graze against one another. Rather than allowing the momentary touch, she folds her arms across her chest as she walks.

A bottle of wine sits on the table, and there are empty glasses as well. "You guys enjoy the sunset?" I ask, trying to make conversation while pouring myself some liquid courage.

"Jack, please don't make small talk. Just say whatever it is you want to say, so we can get this over with and spend time with our friends." Her voice isn't angry; she just sounds defeated and tired. I don't blame her at all.

I try reaching out to her, but she pulls back and grabs her glass of wine, sipping and staring at the ocean. "I know you're upset with me. You have every right to be. I should have introduced you as my girlfriend. I knew six years ago I wanted you to be my girlfriend. I wasn't ready for it, but finding you again was fate intervening. I don't want to screw this up. Charlotte, I—"

As I am finally ready to tell her I love her, she interrupts me, holding up her hand in frustration.

"Jack, please stop. This isn't fate. We didn't miraculously find each other on some dating website after six years of losing touch. You disappeared six years ago and then *you* arranged finding me again. You sought me out and invited yourself on my trip. You won't tell me why you disappeared, other than some non-answer of 'I wasn't ready for this yet.' Although somehow you were ready to sleep with Kat six years ago, and you didn't so much as want to kiss me." Her voice is quiet, and I want to object but I don't interrupt. "If I believe in your ridiculous version of fate, then for the last six years I have wasted *my life* so that you could run around with all of your women, *not girlfriends*, and I moved from one miserable relationship to the next, comparing them to a guy I thought was incredible but turns out just didn't want me enough."

So much of what she said is wrong. She believed I didn't want to kiss her six years ago when it is all I wanted to do. It's the only thing I want now. But seeing the frown on her face and the despair in her eyes leaves me only saying, "I'm really sorry, Charlotte."

Sighing, Charlotte looks away from me. "Honestly, I don't want to fight. I appreciate you bringing our friends here. I thought we had a good thing going and that I could keep this light, but that's not who I am. I'm the girl that falls in love. Too easily. That's not your fault. Can we just be friends? Enjoy the rest of this trip, have fun with Pat and Steph, and leave it at that?"

Love. She loves me? My heart seizes. The feeling is fleeting as I focus on the depression in her eyes. They plead with me to just agree. I can't stand the idea of her being sad any longer. All I have brought to her life is disappointment. The selfish thing would be to take her in my arms and tell her how I feel. I won't be selfish anymore. "Okay. If that's what you want."

She exhales and turns to face the water again. We both sit in silence, stewing.

"Hi! This place is incredible! I'm so happy we came!" Steph says, practically skipping to the table. I've never seen her skip, and from Pat's surprised face, I don't think he has either.

"It's amazing, isn't it?" Charlotte says, a smile now on her lips. It actually hurts to see her so happy when only moments before I would have killed for her to look at me like that.

"How has the trip been? Have you guys done a lot of sightseeing? Please tell me there is stuff you haven't done that we can do now, because I want to see *everything*."

I risk looking at Charlotte again, and she darts her eyes away from mine. We've mostly explored one another's bodies—there are plenty of things we haven't seen yet.

"Oh. We've seen a few things, but there is plenty for us to do," Charlotte replies. "So, tell me, when did you all plan this?"

Pat looks to his wife to answer this one, and I hold my breath waiting for her response. "Well, when Jack told me about his feelings for you, I knew you'd need me."

Pretty sure all three of us look up at Steph in shock. I can't believe she just told the truth. Although, she's never been one to bullshit anyone. "Excuse me?" Charlotte stutters. "What are you talking about?"

Steph turns to me as if looking for approval, and I shrug. Maybe she'll have better luck. "Shortly after you called and I told you to ignore your feelings for Jack, he called, and I realized I may have spoken too soon. Listen, I understand things are... shall we say 'difficult' between you two?" She looks at me and I nod. Yes, difficult is the appropriate word right about now. "And part of that might be my fault for getting involved to begin with. Listen, Charlotte, I think you should hear Jack out. He cares about you...even if he is a bit boneheaded in how he expresses that."

Charlotte turns away from us all. I barely realize that she has started talking because the wind steals her words, so I move closer to hear. "I appreciate that you all think you know what is best for me. And Lord knows I have given everyone reason to doubt that I can handle my own love life. But I just want to focus on this trip and enjoy our time away. Jack, you're absolved of feeling bad. Steph, you're absolved of your bad advice. And Pat, you get to enjoy time with your wife. No more talk about feelings, okay?"

I nod, acknowledging that no one can fix this but me. I need to find a way to prove to Charlotte that I love her. I need to tell her everything that happened since I left her six years ago. In this moment, though, I simply need to respect her wishes and show her a good time. Steph looks like she is about to reject

Charlotte's request, like she believes she can fix all of this herself, so I change the conversation. "You all must be starving. Let's go into town and get dinner?"

Charlotte turns to me now, realizing I am moving on, and I'm not sure if the nod she gives is in appreciation of my acceptance of her request or if she has just resigned herself to accepting that we aren't going to be together. "Yes. Let's get food."

CHAPTER 32

Charlotte

I'm so unbelievably confused. My mind is all over the place. Across from me sits my best friend and her husband—compliments of a man who claims to care about me. It's hard to reconcile with the man who couldn't even introduce me as someone other than a stranger only a few hours earlier.

I was ready to accept his apology the second I saw Steph. Clearly, he cares about me. He arranged a surprise of epic proportions for me. But then he had to go and talk about fate. Which only reminded me of the real reason I'm angry—because he *lied.* And he continues to lie every time we talk. He said he couldn't keep me out of his mind for the past six years, but that is just a sweet thing he says—it's just words. I was gone from his mind quick enough for him to sleep with Kat.

I always thought I wanted a sweet-talking boyfriend, but now I realize I don't want a relationship that makes me swoon.

I want a real relationship, grounded in real things, like trust and memories and moments that you build together. Like my grandparents had. I want a relationship that makes me stronger. Not weaker. And that's all I feel with him. Maybe it's not his fault. Maybe it's just me. The old me wanted something like serendipity, but if I have learned anything from all of Steph's rants it is that I need a man who can prove to me through actions that he cares—not just empty promises.

Although, he did get my friends to fly here.

I silence my thoughts. This is not debatable. We aren't meant to be together. Even if his eyes watching me right now make the butterflies flap like crazy, and it is hard to breathe in his presence. That is all just a chemical reaction to him—my body betrays me, but my mind doesn't need to.

"What kind of wine should we have?" Steph asks, eyeing the wine list. We had walked down the street to a restaurant which sits on the water—almost every restaurant on the island is on the water—and the pink sky had turned black, leaving only the stars and the boats in the marina to light up the otherwise dark ocean.

At the same time Jack and I both respond, "Monte Velho." I look at him and smile. "It's a good red wine," I explain to Steph quickly. I feel Jack's eyes on me but turn away from him. "It's local to the area and has a nice, spicy, fruity taste."

Steph laughs. "I'm pretty sure that is not how a wine connoisseur would describe wine, but I appreciate the attempt."

I roll my eyes—she's such a snob—but I am pleasantly surprised when she orders the bottle for the table anyway.

Sipping the wine, I am back in Jack's arms, or at least in my memories I am. He watches me as he swirls the liquid on his tongue, and I know precisely what he is thinking about.

"So, tomorrow we're going to a winery. I figured you both would be a little jet-lagged so you could use the morning to rest. Does that work for everyone?" Steph squeals in excitement because a winery is right up her alley. I'm just happy it's not somewhere we've already been—I could use a new place with no shared memories.

Pat asks a bunch of questions, and I can tell he's just excited to be here. I'm happy to sit in silence and let them all talk. I sip my wine and stare out at the ocean. When it's Steph's turn to order I hear her ask for the pasta with carabineros on it.

"Don't do it!" I shout, and Jack laughs.

"The bloody shrimp," he says, looking at me. I nod and my mind goes back to that night again. I remember the way he took the food off my plate and how he offered to take me dancing. And then I remember the way he undid the tie of my dress and watched in appreciation as it fell to the floor. Our eyes remain on one another—it feels like he can see my thoughts. My cheeks grow warm, and I look away again.

"Don't get the shrimp," I say quietly, pushing it all from my mind.

"I wouldn't say everything about the shrimp was bad," Jack

offers, trying to get me to look at him again. When I meet his eyes, I see a man who is trying, and I allow myself to stare at his lips, remembering how they explored my body. But I also remember how those same lips were silent this afternoon when he had the opportunity to set things straight with Katalina.

Defiantly, I raise my eyes to his. "It wasn't what I expected. It pretended to be something it wasn't."

"Not on purpose." His eyes are full of remorse.

"I know," I whisper. *Dammit.* It's so hard to be angry at those eyes.

Pat interjects. "How come I feel like we aren't talking about shrimp?"

"Now is not the time to stop being oblivious," Jack quips.

I shake my head. "Steph, don't get the shrimp. Order something else. I promise, you'll regret it." I excuse myself from the table before I start to cry. I know it all seems pathetic. I'm crying over shrimp. But what I'm really crying over is the realization that we did have more than just words—we have memories, but they all hurt too much.

Steph follows me into the bathroom. "What the hell is going on?"

I wipe away my stupid tears. "I'm just an idiot. That's all. You told me not to fall for him and I did. But he isn't who I thought he was. He doesn't live up to the man I've created in my mind. Surprise, surprise."

Steph's blue eyes look at me with sadness. "No one can live up

290

to your expectations, Char. I don't say it to sound mean, but really, you are expecting some fairy tale in life. Jack is a *good guy*. It's my fault that you don't believe he is. And he did screw up. But give him the opportunity to make it right. I promise you there is a good reason for why he acted this way. But it's not my story to tell."

I bite the inside of my mouth, willing myself to listen instead of speak. The butterflies beg me to hear her out, as does the old Charlotte.

He's a good guy. Give him a chance. He could be the one.

I sigh and tell the butterflies to shove it. "I am going to enjoy this trip. I am not going to get upset again. I promise." I will myself to believe that I won't ruin everyone else's time.

You are on an island with your best friend—get out of your own head.

"I don't believe you. But I would really like you to try. For your sake."

"I will. I promise. Go out and order some food. But seriously, don't get the shrimp."

She laughs. "Okay, okay. I get the point."

After she leaves the bathroom, I clean up my face and give myself a pep talk in the mirror. "You've got this. Just don't look at his lips, or his calves, or his *hands*.... Shit, just don't look at *him*, period." I nod at myself in agreement and paint on some red lipstick. That's another thing I've learned from Grams—girls with red lips don't cry.

CHAPTER 33

Jack

"So, is there really something wrong with the shrimp?" Pat asks under his breath after Steph and Charlotte leave the table.

Rolling my eyes, I throw my napkin down. "Don't get the shrimp, man. Charlotte is right about that one."

"But that was actually about something else, right?"

I laugh. He is *so* clueless. "Yes. It's always about something else with women, isn't it?"

What is it like to walk around completely unaware that you're pissing people off? Since hanging out with Charlotte, I'm constantly thinking—overthinking quite honestly—but this guy can just sit here and have a beer completely unaware of what is going on around him. And it works. Steph just laughs at him, and they avoid a fight. I should take a few pointers from him.

Steph arrives back at the table and sits down with a sigh. "It's going to be okay," she says looking up at me.

Shrugging my shoulders, I reply, "If you say so."

"What's your plan?" she asks quietly. I look around to see if Charlotte is coming back, but I don't see her. Why is she whispering?

Rubbing my temple, I'm honest. "I have no idea. We were having a great time, and I screwed it up. I tried being honest about my feelings, and that didn't work. At this point I'm just going to smile and nod, show her a good time, and leave her alone if she wants me to."

Steph hisses at me, "No. Don't listen to her!"

I throw my hands up in the air. *Women.* Honestly, if I had ignored her advice to begin with, I would have told Charlotte exactly how I feel, spilled my guts about what happened six years ago, and maybe we'd be happy right now.

Before I can protest, though, Charlotte comes out of the bathroom and walks to our table. She's still wearing those little black shorts with the red top, and with the cold night air I can see her nipples poking through. I can't take my eyes off her. She doesn't seem to mind my stare. Walking by me, she swings her hips and stares me down. She's got fucking red lipstick on. Is this woman trying to kill me? I picture those perfect red lips doing dirty things and then scold myself. I don't deserve her in my fantasies if I can't treat her right in real life. But damn, she's doing this on purpose, and I can tell by the wicked smile she gives me that she's enjoying it.

"Everything okay?" I stammer, trying to hold her gaze.

"I'm good. Just had a bit of reaction to the shellfish." She winks at me, and I almost fall over.

Pat watches us with a confused look on his face. Steph is focused solely on the menu. "Okay, I'm thinking steak. That's okay, right?"

"It's perfect," I respond without looking at him. My eyes remain trained on Charlotte's lips. She bites down on her lower one and doesn't look at me. It's a huge "screw you" to me, but I'd rather have her pissed off than sad. At least when she's angry I have a chance to spar with her, to banter with her, to communicate with her. I'll take that Charlotte any day.

My eyes remain on her the entire dinner. When Pat starts to yawn, I curse the night ending, not ready to take my eyes off my girl. I've got to win her back. I just have absolutely no idea how. After we walk back to the house, Charlotte waves awkwardly as she sneaks up the stairs and into her room.

Unable to bear the thought of my single bed, I grab a bottle of red wine and walk down to the picnic table to stew in my thoughts. Or drink until I can't think anymore. I don't even bother with a glass, drinking it straight from the bottle. I shout into the wind, "What the hell am I supposed to do?"

You could start with the truth.

Peter's voice stirs in my head. It's just my mind screwing with me, and I tell him to be quiet.

You asked my opinion. I'm just telling you what you already know.

I throw back another gulp of wine. Of course, he's right. Or I am. Because obviously Peter isn't here, no matter how much I wish he were. I've always been a cocky asshole, but I've never been a liar, and that's all I've been to Charlotte. Hiding who I am, sneaking out of her room rather than having an adult conversation, failing to tell her why I never came to find her, not letting her know just how damaged I am because of Peter's death. How can I really believe that Charlotte had fallen for me when I'd never let my guard down and told her the truth?

She'd opened up to me. She told me about her family. About her fears in life. About her disappointments. And I've eaten it all up because I'm crazy about her. Seeing her vulnerable—I love that side of her. Sassy and brave—that also drives me wild. Talkative and full of ridiculous facts—that's when she makes me laugh the most. I never stop smiling when I'm with her. I feel whole when I'm with her. Like the man I was before I deployed. She's done that for me by just being *her*. She hasn't held anything back, and I've given her nothing.

The truth is I don't deserve her. She deserves someone who isn't damaged. Someone who can give her the life Peter and I both dreamed of having. It's not something I'm capable of. All I can offer is one day at a time, not a real future. I can give her a few more days of fun, a few lust- filled nights. They'll last me a lifetime. They'll have to be enough. I grab my phone and shoot Richard the text he's been waiting for. He was right. I'm not meant for this life. Las Vegas is my future.

"I'm in."

And then I let the sobs take over my body, crying for everything I've lost, the past that I can't change and for the future I'll never have.

CHAPTER 34

Charlotte

The wind on the balcony contained his scream, but I saw his breakdown loud and clear. Something more than just our fight was breaking Jack to the core. It was hard to watch without going to him, holding him, comforting him. The man I'd fallen in love with was broken. Was I strong enough to weather whatever storm was taking him down? Did I want to be? I knew the instant I watched him fall over in sobs that of course I did.

Everyone kept telling me there was something that was holding him back. That something *happened* to change him. That I should show him grace. And if I truly believed that going to him in that moment would have been what he needed, I would have jumped off the balcony to take away his pain. But Jack needs to open up to me in his own time. He's been struggling all along. He will confide in me when he trusts I won't run. When he believes that I can handle it. So instead, I put myself to bed, leaving Jack and his sorrow to mend themselves.

Proving to Jack that we are meant to be together is going to be as much an exercise in restraint as it is anything else. I wonder if that's what Grams meant. I need to see myself how he sees me. Unfortunately, what Jack sees is someone who is too in her own head to handle his breakdown. I need to prove to him that I'm strong enough. That I *love* him enough. Because I do. I'd been wrong when I said what we had wasn't real. It's the most real thing I've ever felt in my life. Maybe "Vacation Charlotte" is who I was always meant to be. Just like Steph helped me to become more me—so has Jack. Strong, confident, sassy, and yes, still talkative, clumsy, and unsure of myself. Maybe being with your soulmate brings out the best sides of you. I'm beginning to think that's what Jack has done on this vacation. Although, he's also brought out the worst sides of me too, because he keeps hiding the truth from me.

If I was brutally honest with myself though, every time I asked him what happened and he started to explain, I'd see the pain in his eyes and shut him down. Part of that was probably to protect him but also to protect myself. If I didn't know why he did what he did, my foot could still be one step out the door, protecting my heart.

I never let him open up. Not when we were down at the docks, not on the roof when we ate pizza, not the morning after we'd made love when I could see he'd been devastated about something. Instead of just asking, I used my insecurity as an excuse to breeze past the incident rather than asking him why he'd disappeared in the first place. And last night, when he tried to tell me what happened, I shut him down again, telling him it didn't matter. When it was clear as day that it mattered more than anything. Because he matters more than anything. Gah, what have I done?

The sun isn't even up, and I find myself tiptoeing out of my room and knocking on the door next to mine. I need to get all these thoughts off my chest.

The door swings open, and Steph's hair is almost as crazed as her face. "What?" she glares at me. Behind her Pat hides under the sheet, and he huffs as he stares out the window. Eek, he probably regrets reuniting with me after the latest interruption.

"Sorry, I need you," I whisper loudly, reaching to drag her into the hall with me. I hop on each foot nervously.

With her shirt on backwards and no pants, Steph folds her arms across her chest and glares. "Okay, get to it."

I bite my lip. "Well, I can't talk to you when you're like this." I motion to her aura.

"Like this?" she whisper screeches. "You just dragged me out of bed. If you didn't want me *like this* then you should have waited until a normal hour."

"I'm spiraling and Jack's hurting." My eyes plead with her for some compassion.

Came to the wrong chick for that. "Since when do you care about Jack?" Her tongue pushes against her cheek as she dares me to be honest.

"Since six years ago, okay? Since I love him, and I need to figure out what the hell is wrong with him."

Steph claps her hands together and a grin breaks through her face. "Fina-freaking-ly! Oh, there's the girl I've been waiting for! God, it's good to see you."

Rolling my eyes, I laugh. "Okay, can you go put on pants? I can't take you seriously like this." I motion to her outfit and hair, and she snorts.

"Fine, give me ten minutes and I'll meet you on your deck. But you better have coffee. And some type of pastry." She eyes me again like she's not fooling around. As if I would ever begrudge the girl her pastry.

"Of course. Thanks!"

I sneak down to the kitchen and am pleased to find it's empty. Of course it is, it's barely six a.m. I start the coffee and check out the options for Steph's sugar craving. We bought this special dessert in Furnas known as *Queijadas*. Similar to a tart, it is made with a few simple ingredients—eggs, milk, butter, flour, and sugar. All perfectly acceptable for breakfast. I'm pretty sure this will be a proper apology for interrupting what was clearly a steamy morning with her husband. I grab two of them and our coffees and sneak back up the steps. When I reach the top, I stare at Jack's door, and my heart hammers in my chest. Did he get any sleep? He'll probably wake up with a massive headache from the red wine and tears. I sneak into my room, grab the

Tylenol from my bag, and leave it next to his door. Then I set up our breakfast on the outdoor table on my deck.

"I've arrived," Steph says as she walks into my room with a smile on her face. "Now show me the goodies." Her eyes light up when she spots the powdered sugar on the treats. "Oh, what is this?"

Laughing, I hand one to her and watch as she takes a bite. Steph closes her eyes and moans. When she goes to speak, white powder puffs onto her lips. "This is so flipping good. I want to marry this. Like, can you marry a pastry? I'll divorce Pat if I can. I'm serious here, please tell me if you're single." Delusional, she stares at the pastry and talks to it.

"Yeah. They are good. No, you can't marry it. But I have an entire box downstairs, and if you are nice to me during this conversation, I'll even let you have mine."

Steph turns her head sideways, twists her lips, and looks at me out of the corner of her eye. "Nah, I'd rather tell you the truth then eat your food."

"Ha. Brat!" I laugh at her honesty.

"At your service. But seriously, this is like heaven in my mouth. It's so creamy. Take a bite. The sugar will bring back the color to your face. You look like you barely slept a wink."

I let out a long breath, pick up the treat, and bite into it. Jack and I had bought this dessert from every bakery we found in Furnas. But wow, this one really melts in my mouth. I smile and speak with a mouthful, causing the words to come out garbled.

"Okay, yeah, I want to marry this too."

She shakes her head. "It's mine."

We both laugh, and I feel myself relax a bit. "Thanks. I am so glad you guys are here."

With a sincere smile, Steph murmurs, "Me too, my girl. Now talk to me."

Sipping my coffee to wash down my treat, I think of where to start. "I think I'm in love with Jack."

Steph laughs. "Yeah, I got that much from seeing you together last night. And you *know* you're in love with him. Not just *think* you are."

I bite my lip. "Right. So, what do I do?"

Steph folds her legs up onto the chair and looks me dead in the eye. "What do you *want* to do?"

She's infuriating. That's why I asked her to come in here. Because I have no idea. Grudgingly, I admit, "I want to be with him."

Like a proud mama, she smiles. "Then be with him. Stop making it so difficult. Just *be*."

I sigh. "It's not that easy. Something else is going on with Jack. And there was that girl. I feel like I'm in love with one man, but there's a whole other side of him I don't know. Like the Jack that I'm with is one person, but when he's with other people he's someone else. Does that make any sense?" I twist my hands in nervous frustration.

"The Jack you know is the person I think he wants to be.

But are there some dark things from his past that he needs to explain? Sure. Did he do something really dumb six years ago? Absolutely. Does that disqualify him as someone worthy of your love? That I can't answer. Only you can. But if you stopped looking at this like a fairy tale and just looked at the man who is standing before you and has gone out of his way over the last few weeks to win you over, I think you'll realize that he's worth it. I mean, does it have to be that he was in love with you six years ago for you to make it work now? Or is it good enough that he's so obviously crazy about you now?"

My stomach flips, and I turn my eyes to the ocean. She's given me a lot to think about. The part I keep having trouble with is that Jack said he felt all those feelings years ago, just like me. And I never would have walked away. But he did. So, what will stop him now? Are his feelings strong enough now for him to stick around? Or will I wake up one day to find he's gone?

"Thanks for the Tylenol," Jack whispers into my ear, pressing himself against me as I stand at the kitchen counter refilling my coffee. For a moment I say nothing, allowing myself to relax against his touch, to soak in his dewy fresh-out-of-the-shower smell, and I sigh softly.

When he moves away from me, I roll my shoulders and

stretch my neck like a cat, my body arching for his touch. "How'd you sleep?"

I turn around to face him, and the dark circles under his eyes give me my answer. "Not great."

I squeeze his hand as I walk past. It's all I can offer right now with a room full of people. "Join me by the water?"

Jack's eyes light up and he nods. "Be down in a minute."

As I make my way down the path to the water, I can't help but appreciate the beauty around me. The property is absolutely stunning, with rolling green hills, flowers springing from the ground, and the water glistening before me. However, today would not be a great boating day; the water is rough and tosses a tiny boat in the distance precariously. My stomach turns just imagining how the sailor must feel.

Voices behind me steal my attention. Jack and Pat walk together down the path, a big smile on Pat's face and a strained one on Jack's. "Beautiful day, huh?" Pat says as he plops down in the seat next to me, much to my chagrin. Jack stands for a moment staring at Pat, willing him to get up perhaps, and then takes the seat opposite us.

"Yeah, it's gorgeous," I reply, turning my gaze to Pat.

"Did you work out your issues this morning with my wife?" Pat asks cheekily, a smirk pulling at his lip.

Jack's eyes raise to mine, and I nudge Pat in the side. "Issues?" Jack asks.

Quickly, I reply, "Yes, all worked out. Thanks."

"Great, so hopefully you can let me have Steph to myself tomorrow morning?"

I roll my eyes. "She's all yours."

"Who's all his?" Steph asks as she sashays down the hill, a big smile on her face. "Hope you're not talking about me, buddy. I've already promised myself to a dessert."

Laughing, I watch as Pat turns to Steph with a confused look on his face.

"A dessert?" Jack asks, raising his eyebrows to me.

I smile. "Yeah. I bribed Steph with the queijada."

"Oh Sassy, talk Portuguese to me, and I might jump you at this table."

My grin grows. "What time are we leaving today?"

Jack's eyes are still lit up when he replies, "Maybe in an hour or so. Everyone shower, and we can head off in the direction of the winery. We'll take the back roads so we can experience the views."

Eek. The word "views" reminds me of Mosteiros. I'm not sure I can handle more winding roads, but Steph is already clapping her hands in excitement. "Wine, views, my best friends all on vacation. Ah! Pinch me!"

Summoning the strength, I focus on flirting with Jack and getting back the magic. "So, Mav, what kind of winery is this?"

The grin on his face should have its own song. "Hmm,"—he pauses, tapping on his chin—"I'm pretty sure they use beets."

I break out laughing as Steph's mouth drops open. "You're taking us to a winery where they use beets rather than grapes?

Are you insane? That's disgusting." Steph fumes and babbles on, but Jack keeps his face straight. He's taken a page out of Dwight Schrute's farm in *The Office,* and I couldn't love him more for it.

"The Portuguese take their wine very seriously, Steph. I promise you'll love the beet wine." I have no idea how Jack is keeping such a straight face, but I'm trying hard to rein in my giggles so I don't ruin his fun.

Arms crossed, Steph lifts her eyebrows in defiance. "Forget what I said earlier, Char, this man is unredeemable. Beet wine! That's called juice."

Jack shakes his head and waves his hands back and forth. "Wait, wait, wait. You told Sassy over here I'm redeemable?" His eyes beam as he looks in my direction. My entire face hurts from smiling so much.

"Who the hell is Sassy?" Steph asks begrudgingly.

Shrugging, I smirk right back at her.

Jack points at me. "That girl. There. The one who is always sassing me. Driving me crazy with her snark."

Steph rolls her eyes. "Now that's something I'd like to see."

Pat laughs. "Sassy? Try more like chatty."

I elbow him again and murmur out of the corner of my mouth. "Shut up, he hasn't noticed that about me yet."

Jack laughs. "Oh, I know you like to talk, Sassy. I just happen to like listening to you."

Everything about this moment is perfect—my best friend

sitting across from me, the weather, the location, and the man I've not so slowly fallen in love with teasing me. This is what joy feels like, and it's written all over my face.

"Okay. So, to be clear, are you or are you not taking us to a regular winery?" Steph asks with her eyes pointed at Jack.

Jack stands with a shrug. "I guess you'll find out." Throwing me a wink, he walks up the hill and into the house.

"God, he's insufferable," she mumbles under her breath.

Ignoring her, I focus instead on the space he just occupied, wishing for more joy. More teasing. More Jack.

CHAPTER 35

Jack

I hold my lips together, trying to keep the laugh from escaping. Steph is beet red, and Charlotte eyes me with a cautious excitement, as if she's trying to decide if this is for real. Pat is completely oblivious and obviously thinks this is all normal.

"So you were serious? It's a beet farm?" Steph stares at the farmer in front of her who is holding up the bulbous plant and explaining to her the process of fermentation. I swear to God I've never been this sneaky in my life. But I know Charlotte is going to love the day I put together for us.

The farmer turns and begins speaking in Portuguese, "How long do you want me to go on about this?"

I wink at him and translate. Or at least I translate what I want her to hear. "So, next they want us to go into the back where they've set up some barrels, and you can dance in the beet juice."

Charlotte's cheeks inflate, and her breath escapes in a low guffaw.

Pat walks to the back, and Charlotte and I stare at Steph, waiting. "Dance in the juice?" she asks like I've asked her to strip naked.

Charlotte—God love her—replies, "Well, yeah, Steph. Isn't that what we did at the winery for your bachelorette party?"

With her hand on her hips, Steph refuses to move. "If I find out that you're screwing with me, Fitzpatrick, I swear to God you're dead. Dead. Do you hear me?"

Shrugging, I walk forward, stealing a glance back at Charlotte, who whispers in Steph's ear, trying to calm her down. When we get to the backyard, I see the three barrels I had Belle set up. This is our cousin's farm. I had Belle pick up cranberry juice which she mixed with water and placed in the barrels. Unfortunately, we couldn't find wine barrels on such short notice, so we got black trash cans instead. I swear to God I am going to die laughing if she actually gets in one.

Pat leans over to take off his shoes, and I almost fall over. "What are you doing, dude?"

Without hesitating, he replies, "Dancing in the beet juice. He said it's a traditional Portuguese experience."

God bless my cousin, he stands off to the side hiding a grin.

The other two barrels remain empty, but I help Pat into his and watch as he spins around slowly. "Am I doing it right?" he asks my cousin, who gives a thumbs-up and turns his head to cover his laughter.

We definitely need music. I grab my phone and type in "Portuguese classics" and when the upbeat music comes over my speakers, Pat starts to speed up his moves. "This is actually kinda fun. Wanna get in?"

I bite the inside of my lip. "No. Only three barrels. I'll let the girls try."

Charlotte sneaks up behind me and whispers in my ear, "Oh, Mav, you are totally getting in there."

Wrapping my arm behind me, I grab her back and pull her close, turning my head so I can look at her as I speak. "Oh no, Sass, this was all for you."

A grin pulls on her lips, and she whispers, "Best. Surprise. Ever."

Her lips sweep against my cheek, and I swear my heart jumps, along with other parts of my body. I can feel the air between us slowly shift and her forgiveness coming in waves. She leans her arm against me as she slips off each of her shoes and then asks me to help her get in. I gladly comply, taking her hips in my hands and lifting both her feet into the red juice. Swinging her hips, Charlotte lets out a laugh and smiles at Steph. "Come on, girlfriend, you're missing out!" Every time she spins, she reaches her hand up to high five Pat. Charlotte then adds an exuberant "Olé" as she turns her hands up like a belly dancer and snaps her fingers. When Pat follows suit, I almost lose it.

"Fitzpatrick, don't you want to join them?" Steph says as she watches Pat and Charlotte make fools of themselves.

"Ladies first," I reply, offering her an assist into the garbage barrel.

With no reason left to resist, Steph finally complies. Timidly, she steps her feet up and down, like one would do with an actual grape smashing. "I don't feel anything. What is the point of this?"

Pat replies, as if he has any clue at all, "It's tradition, Steph! First you dance in the wine then you drink it!"

Charlotte nods as she bounces around, the red juice splashing up onto her white shorts. God, I hope that doesn't stain. Charlotte doesn't seem too concerned at all, but it would be a shame if my favorite shorts were ruined. I love how her ass looks in them.

Watching Charlotte and Pat enjoy themselves, it seems Steph decides to throw caution to the wind, and she starts to bounce around more. "When in Portugal…" she says with a laugh.

I take out my camera and snap several pictures. These are pure gold. But rather than delighting in the prank I am currently pulling off, I find myself lost in the pictures I'm taking of Charlotte. Her face is lit up, her eyes bright and her smile contagious.

Bounced out, Pat looks to me for a hand which I happily provide. "That was actually a lot more fun than you'd think," he says with a laugh. "You wanna try?"

"Eh, I think I'm all set. We have to get to the next winery in fifteen minutes."

"Do we get to try the beet wine?" Charlotte says with a smile.

Coming down off her dancing high, Steph is ready with a quip. "I'm not drinking beet wine. Dancing in it was one thing."

Pat sighs. "Come on, Steph, what happened to embracing the whole experience?"

"Yeah, Steph, what happened to that?" I quip.

She rolls her eyes. "I'll try it after Jack does. You want me to grab you a cup of my foot juice?" She looks around for a ladle.

The gig is up. There is no way in hell I'm drinking that. "Alright Manny, you can dump the cranberry juice." My cousin jumps up with a smile, dragging the container that Pat just got out of. Charlotte and I lean toward the one she was in, sneaking glances back at Steph to see her reaction.

Red face, red legs, and steam pouring from her nose, she vows, "Fitzpatrick, you will be buying me a bottle of every wine at the next place. You hear me! Every bottle!"

Worth it.

The giggles from Charlotte turn to full-on hysterical cackles. She has trouble breathing she's laughing so hard. "Show…me… the…photos…" She reaches for my pocket where my phone is located and takes it out to look. "Oh my God! You got video! Priceless!" Tears stream down her face.

"You are dead to me, Fitzpatrick. *Dead*." Steph glares, but I can't take her seriously. Her legs are stained red. Even her hands have tinges of color on them from all of Charlotte's splashing.

Of course, Charlotte is red too, but on her it looks happy, jubilant even, while on Steph it reminds me of the devil.

Charlotte throws her arms around me, pulling me close to her chest as she continues to laugh. "Thank you so much. Best. Day. Ever."

Like I said, totally worth it.

"You are so lucky that this wine is good," Steph says between sips. As promised, she's plopped a bottle of every wine she can find on the counter. She's trying to figure out how to get it back to America, but if she can't, she says she'll drink it all before she goes home. Not impossible based on her wine consumption.

"This wine is good," Charlotte agrees. "But now I need food."

"Wanna head back to my aunt's house, and we can have an early dinner?"

Steph practically jumps at the idea. "Yes, then I can have an afternoon nap too!" Pat glances in her direction, and he does not have sleep on the brain. He better keep her from having any more wine, or her idea will win.

We all head back to the car, squeezing in tight for our ride home. Unlike Steph, I only had one glass of wine, and I'm certainly glad about that now. Everyone falls asleep on the ride home, and I'm forced to open the window for fresh air to keep my body from slipping into the warm cocoon that an afternoon nap would provide. Barely any sleep last night and all the planning to put the Beet Farm in action left little time to rest. Chuckling, I picture Steph in the garbage bin of "beet wine." Charlotte's eyes fly open as I let out a snort. "Great day, Jack," she mouths. I'm watching her in the rearview mirror in all her glory—sleepy eyes, soft skin, warm smile—the woman I've fallen head over heels for. I'm enjoying every minute while I have her. As soon as we get back to the states, I'll have to get the house on the market and head to Las Vegas. It kills me to leave her, but I know in the end it will be for the best.

I return her smile and bring my eyes back to the road just in time to see the chicken cross the road. No, that's not a joke. The chicken crosses the road, and I wait patiently, shifting in my seat as Charlotte's soft giggles roll over me. "Don't say it." I look up at her sternly, but the grin pops out easily.

"I'm just sitting back here. Not saying anything. Although, if I were to say something…" she trails off with a smile.

Smirking, I laugh. "Have at it—do your worst."

Turning my head to face her, foot on the brake, I wait for her to tell me a ridiculous joke. Her eyes grow wider though, and she laughs. "Why did the cow cross the road?"

I roll my eyes. "That's not how the joke goes, Sass."

Charlotte motions with her eyebrows for me to look. Turning my head, I spot the line of cows now entering the road.

What the…? Looks like we'll be stuck here for a while—it's a cow traffic jam. A cowfic jam? Ha, okay, that was bad.

"Okay, Sassy, why did the cow cross the road?"

Charlotte grins and lets out a loud snort. "Because he thought he was a chicken!"

The laugh bursts out of my mouth, waking both Steph and Pat who appear alarmed by all the cows. "What in the ever-loving hell is going on here?" Steph shrieks.

Giggling louder, Charlotte pokes Steph in the ribs. "Afraid of the little cow, Steph?"

Pat jumps in, "Eh, I don't think those are cows, Charlotte. They look more like bulls. They're bigger than this car."

I laugh and roll my eyes. "Everything is bigger than this car, Pat. Those are cows. Calm down." He wouldn't have made it a day in the military.

After the final cow crosses the street, we continue on with the banter, and I continue to sneak glances of Charlotte in the mirror, which she catches almost every time with a wink or a smile.

We spend the afternoon sipping wine by the water, relaxing with my aunt and cousin, and eating copious amounts of food. After sunset, Pat and Steph excuse themselves. I told them tomorrow we'll need to get up early to go to a famous spot on the island. It houses a massive volcanic crater, and there are two lakes that sit side by side in the crater, one blue and one green.

Not ready to say goodnight to Charlotte, I ask her to join me for a drink in town which she obliges. "You sure you'll be

315

okay?" I hear Steph whisper to Charlotte. It's a bit of a punch in the gut, but I understand why Steph's asking. It's the first time we've really been alone since everything went off the rails.

"I'll be fine," she says to Steph, smacking her on the ass as Pat pulls Steph back to the house with eyes on more than sleep.

Charlotte shoots me a look once they're gone. "It's just a drink, Maverick. No funny business." Her lips curl up in a smirk though.

I hold my fingers up in salute. "Scout's honor."

When we get to the restaurant, we both order espresso martinis and stare at the dark ocean. The waves are loud crashing against the shore. After laughing about the day, and rewatching the video of the garbage can dancing, Charlotte asks, "So, tell me about the place we are going tomorrow?"

"Sete Cidades," I say.

She repeats after me, saying it a few times and allowing the words to ripple on her tongue. I watch in amusement as her red lips tease me. "So, what does it mean?"

"Seven cities. There are actually two lakes that are separated by a small strip of grass and a bridge. They are two different colors, one blue and one green."

"Really? That sounds cool."

"Yup. Legend has it that long ago, the king of the village lost his wife and was left to raise his daughter alone. He was obsessed with her and refused to let her go into the world, wanting to protect her from everything. She snuck out into the fields and met a shepherd, and he fell in love with her at first sight. She brought him back to meet her father, hoping that her father would see that he was a good man and allow them to marry. But the father forbade it."

"That's terrible," Charlotte says, but she smiles. I can tell she's enjoying the story.

"Yes. So, she asked to say goodbye to him, and the father agreed. She went to him, and they cried over the fact that they couldn't be together. Her tears were blue, like her eyes, and his were green, like his. Hence, the blue and green lakes."

Charlotte eyes me. "And then the father saw how sad his daughter was, and he let her go be with him, right?" She's sure there's a happy ending.

"Hate to disappoint you, but the Portuguese are known for their depressing stories. The women wear black all the time. The men walk around with frowns. We're not exactly a happily ever after culture. This is kind of like Romeo and Juliet. No one ends up happy. But we do have these two beautiful lakes to look at now."

Charlotte kicks me under the table. "That's horrible! I hate this story! Stupid stubborn men ruin everything."

I laugh. "Right. But there is romance there. I mean, love at first sight and two eternally beautiful lakes."

Charlotte shakes her head. "I don't believe in love at first sight." Her chin is hard, and her fist tightens around her glass.

I want to reach across and touch her, but I keep in my corner.

"That's a pity. *I do*."

Charlotte looks up at me defiantly. "No more lines, Jack."

I lift my hand up again. "Scout's honor."

Charlotte stares me down, maybe trying to decide if I'm trustworthy. She releases her breath and smiles. "Let's get out of here. I'm tired of Romeo and Juliet."

"Her name was Antilla."

"Poor Antilla," Charlotte says as she stands. "There's nothing worse than a broken heart."

Maybe it's the way that she says it or the fact that she's now standing next to me, but I can't help myself. I reach my hand out to hers and take hold of it, starting to walk before she can protest. I'm not sure if it's because she doesn't want to make a scene or that she's cold, but she nuzzles into my arm and walks along silently, giving me the only thing I've wanted all day.

I look down at her as we continue walking. "I have another story I'd like to share, if you'll let me."

"*Jack*." She looks up at me expectantly, as if trying to decide if she's ready for things to turn serious. Whether she's ready or not, I need to get it all out in the open now. I want Charlotte to know everything. Despite the fact that I can't be the man she deserves, I want her to know that she's always been the girl that I wanted.

"Charlotte, I want to tell you *everything*. I want to tell you how I felt the first night I saw you. How I spotted you at the bar and the moment you smiled I couldn't look away. How I knew in that moment that something changed inside of me. For one night, I tried to forget that I was deploying in ten days. I knew what I was going to be dealing with there—I knew what families dealt with waiting at home. I made a decision. You were *too* good. If I kissed you and told you who I was and that I was going to be deployed, you would wait. You'd be like those families...and I just couldn't *do* that to you. In my mind, it was better to disappear and hopefully find you again. But Charlotte, I promise you, I didn't know you were right under my nose all these years. I had *no idea* you were Steph's friend. It wasn't until Pat showed me your picture that it all came together. I know I screwed up. I should have been honest. But last time I did what I thought was right, I lost you anyway. This time I wanted to be selfish—I wanted to do what felt *good,* and that was finding you, convincing you to give me a chance, and finally kissing you."

Charlotte's mouth hangs open as I speak. I don't know what to think. What is she thinking?

She stares at me for another moment and then without saying a word, she reaches up to my face and brushes her hand against it, as if seeing me for the first time. I stay completely still, afraid if I interrupt her thoughts she'll pull away. I turn my head and inhale the birthday cake scent on her skin that I've come to recognize as *her*, and the tangerine smell of her hair blows in the wind around me. I close my eyes, losing myself in the feel of her hand.

Since my eyes are closed, I don't see her coming closer, but

319

when her lips crash against mine, I moan in pleasure, tasting her sweet lips. The espresso flavor dances in our mouths as I wrap my arms around her, pulling her off her feet and closer to me. This isn't a first kiss—it's a hungry one, and an honest one, *a red-lipstick, keep you up all night thinking of all the things you want to do with one another* kiss. It's a forever kind of kiss, and I don't ever want it to stop.

Charlotte pulls away first, breathless, and she pushes me back so hard I almost stumble in shock. "Dammit, Jack. I told you no more sweet talk." I look at her, confused, and then watch with amusement as a smile spreads across her lips. "You are as bad as my kindergartners when it comes to listening."

Pulling her close, I kiss the top of her head. "Guilty as charged."

Her head turns up to mine and that defiant chin sticks out at me. "I'm still mad at you, ya know?"

"Oh yeah? How come?" I hold her chin with my thumb, keeping her eyes on mine.

"You kept me from kisses like that…*for six years*…" I stop her from speaking though, offering my mouth to hers once more. Time stops as I apologize with my lips, our bodies holding each other tightly.

When we come up for air, I apologize again. "I'm so sorry, baby." I apologize for the past and for what I know is our future. One without kisses like that. It sucks, but the next few nights are all I can offer.

Charlotte wraps her arms around me, and we stand in the

dark, listening to the waves crash, my head on top of hers, and I know without a doubt that it had been love at first sight six years ago.

"Walk me home," she says softly, seemingly accepting my apology. We walk slowly, holding hands, but we don't speak. The wind is so loud it would drown out our words anyway.

The area where my aunt lives is a tiny village with narrow winding streets that wind up and up and up, so that almost every house sits above another with views of the now violent ocean.

As we reach the gates of my aunt's house, Charlotte stops walking. "Everything okay?" I ask, looking down at the fierce beauty whose features I can't quite make out in the dark.

Pushing me back against the gate, the moon lights up her face, and I see a wicked smile. Her red lips are still swollen from our kiss, and my pants get tight just staring at them. "No more games, Jack. We walk back into that house with no more lies. This is your *last* chance." Her words are strong, but her eyes are vulnerable. The truth is this is our only chance. And I'm taking it. I'm taking every minute I can with her.

"No more lies." I lean down, and she lifts herself so that our lips meet. Wrapping my arms around her, I lift her up, and she wraps her legs around my hips as I cup her ass with both of my hands. Her soft moans move through my mouth. "Dammit, baby, your sounds again."

Eyeing me seductively, she says, "Take me to bed." She doesn't have to say that twice. I shift her body so I am literally carrying her down the driveway, and she starts to wiggle and laugh.

"Put me down, Jack Fitzpatrick!"

But now that I have her in my arms there is no way I am letting go. "Princess coming through," I shout, holding her daintily, and she laughs louder and tries covering my mouth with her hands.

"Shh, people are sleeping!" I consider her instructions and decide to listen because I don't want anyone waking up and interrupting our night. But I don't put her down. We reach the door, and I stumble to open it with her still in my arms, and she finally relents and turns it herself, giving me an evil look as I kick it shut behind me.

"So, where did my aunt put you?"

She smiles again. "Lovers' Quarters."

I groan. "Oh, you are killing me, woman. Don't say that word—don't roll your tongue like that—unless you are ready for the consequences."

When we reach the top of the steps, Charlotte points me in the right direction, and I walk through the door, tossing her onto the bed. It is a four-poster bed with a canopy, but the mattress has no give, so she lands with a thump and rubs her behind as if she's hurt. "*Ow.*"

I leap next to her and reach for her ass. "Don't worry, baby, I'll kiss it all better."

She swats at my hand though. "Stay on your side, Maverick."

I give her my best *you've got to be fucking kidding me*

look. She can't possibly believe now that I finally have her back in bed, I'm just going to sit on my hands and not touch her. "Seriously?" I croak.

Charlotte rolls on her back and looks up at the ceiling, as if she's trying to summon the courage to turn me down. "Your aunt told me the history behind this room...*it's sacred*," she whispers, as if speaking about the magical powers will make them disappear.

Genuinely confused, I roll over on my side but keep my distance. "Fine. Tell me about this special bed. But if it involves talking about getting naked, I'm just letting you know I am going to pounce on you before you finish."

She laughs and shifts onto her side, staring at me now. "Apparently, all the couples who have spent their honeymoon here have gone on to have long, happy marriages." Twirling her hair in a nervous manner, she is almost edible.

I push myself closer to her. "Okay. So, let's get to our happily ever after then." I grab her ass and bring her as close to me as possible.

She wiggles away from me. "Jack! Stop it. This room is sacred. You can't have S-E-X in here unless you're married," she whispers, covering her mouth as she speaks, as if the bed can hear her words.

"Okay, let's say our vows real quick and get to it then," I joke, taking the hair she is twirling in her finger into my own and mimicking her movements.

Charlotte smacks me. "*Stop,* I know that you're ready to worship my body, but you're not ready to obey me for the rest of your life, so get in your corner and keep your hands to yourself."

The truth is there is nothing I want more. If I could give her forever, I would do it in a second. But since I know the truth—that we only have a few more days left together—I move back a few inches and smile at her. "Okay. I'll stay in my corner."

A slow breath escapes her mouth, and I'm not sure if she's happy I listened or disappointed. She adjusts herself so she's lying down on her arm, staring at me. "Do you really remember the night we first met?"

Her hair falls in front of her face, and I push the waves behind her ear, wanting to see her as I explain exactly how I felt the first time I saw her. She closes her eyes at the feel of my touch, and I can see the goosebumps I've caused. This only makes me want to touch other parts of her, but I keep my promise and pull my hand back. "I remember every moment."

"Tell me what you thought."

I settle into the bed, making myself more comfortable, and turn my thoughts back to that night. "I had just walked into the bar. It was around eight thirty at night. I was pissed because I'd missed the parade and the day drinking. Belle asked me to help her move into her new apartment—*on St. Patrick's Day*—and I couldn't say no. I can never say no to her." Charlotte smiles and I continue. "I was annoyed because Pat had been texting me all day, and he told me to meet him at Buskers, but when I arrived, he wasn't picking up his phone or responding to my texts."

"*How rude.*" Charlotte's voice teases me.

"Exactly. I was only home for a few weeks, and I was heading back at the end of the month. I just wanted to have a beer with my friend and forget who I was for a little bit. But life had other plans." Her eyes soften at the mention of deployment. Her memories of the night are probably a lot lighter than mine—unfortunately, mine are mixed with all kinds of emotions which color the way that I felt everything all those years ago.

"I didn't know," she whispers softly.

I force a smile onto my face. "I know." I go back to the night though—and take her into my thoughts. "The music was so loud. Some wannabe band was playing *Drop Kick Murphy* and I felt my mood begin to lift a bit. I always loved their music. I walked to the bar to grab a beer, hoping a Guinness would make me feel like myself again. I wanted to be like any other normal, hot-blooded, twenty-six-year-old male who could drink a beer and flirt with a pretty girl and not the guy who had been changed so much from my time overseas. But really, I was in a battle with myself just trying to relax. I took a sip of the Guinness and closed my eyes, feeling like my world was resetting itself. When I opened them, you were standing beside me, like an answered prayer. Your hair was a mess, your big brown eyes were glassy, and you had a panicked look on your face."

She laughs. "Oh, lovely first impression I made. I couldn't find Steph—I was *freaking* out."

"I could tell. But I couldn't speak. You literally took my breath away."

A smile plays on her lips, as if she's back in the bar in Newport, clearly enjoying the memory. It seems like a lifetime ago, but I can almost taste the Guinness on my lips right now. "So, what did you do?" she asks, as if she doesn't remember. But I know she does.

"You asked the bartender for a beer, which I could totally tell you didn't need. I told the bartender, 'She's with me. Don't give her anything.'"

"And what did I do?" she teases.

"You balled your fist like this,"—I impersonate her—"and you looked up at me defiantly with your chin in the air and said, 'Who the hell do you think you are?' and I said, 'The man who's taking you home tonight.'"

Charlotte shakes her head, a big smile on her lips. "You were so cocky."

"Aren't I always?"

Charlotte hits my shoulder, and I grab her wrist, daring her to come closer. She stares at me defiantly again. "And then what happened?"

"I took your hand, threw some cash at the bartender, and dragged you out of the bar. Although, I don't remember you putting up much of a fuss. You just stared at me, shocked, when we got outside, like you couldn't believe I had the audacity to touch you or speak to you like I did."

"I *was* shocked. I also wanted to climb you. No one had ever told me what to do in a way that made me want to listen. And I *wanted* to listen. My butterflies were going crazy—they were literally flopping around in hysterics. I had never felt that way before."

"Your what?"

A giggle escapes her throat. "My butterflies."

"Oh. I *need* to hear more about these butterflies."

"Well, they only react to you," she whispers. I pull her closer to me, sprinkling kisses on her defiant chin—the one that made me fall so hard for her years ago.

"And where are these butterflies located, Sassy?"

She pushes me back. "Hey, you promised you'd stay on your side of the bed."

I hold my hands up in retreat. "Fine. But stop talking about butterflies then."

We both stare at one another silently, huge smiles on our faces. There is a buzz in the air between us—the chemistry—the flame that was first lit six years ago is still as bright as that night. "So, how come you didn't kiss me that night? If I left you so breathless as you now say."

"I was scared if I started I'd never stop."

Her face relaxes, the big smile releasing and making way to something even more beautiful—contentment. "That's a beautiful line, Jack."

"It's not a line. You and I walked to the diner. I couldn't

believe I got you to agree to go eat."

"I was starving," she interrupts. "Remember, I'd been drinking all day."

"Yes, I could tell. You smelled like a brewery."

She looks at me affronted. "Oh, God. That's horrible."

I move closer to her, taking her hand in mine and kissing it. "I'm just teasing. You smelled like coconut and vanilla—like cake—like you always do." Her eyes grow wide as I take her thumb in my hand and bite it.

"We got pancakes!" she reminds me.

"No. *You* got pancakes. And you devoured them. I'm pretty sure I had a coffee."

She shakes her head. "I would not have eaten pancakes in front of you while you drank a cup of coffee. Impossible!"

I laugh. "You were drunk. Believe me, my memory of the night is better than yours. You ate a stack of pancakes covered in whipped cream and strawberries. I've never seen someone so happy as you were when the waiter placed the plate in front of you."

Charlotte rolls her eyes. "Oh. Well, that is definitely not when you wanted to kiss me. So, get to the good stuff. When did you want to kiss me but held back because '*you wouldn't be able to stop.*'" She says the last part in a mocking tone, but I can tell that she really wants to hear how badly I wanted to kiss her. And I don't mind reliving this story at all.

"Well, the first time was when you looked up at me defiantly in the bar. If I'd had the balls, I would have grabbed you right there and kissed you against the wall."

My confession seems to get to her. Charlotte's eyes pinch together, and she furrows her brow. "But you just said I looked panicked, and was a mess, and you didn't even know my name. I don't think I'd said two words to you yet."

I laugh. "I know. Imagine how much more I wanted to kiss you after the diner when you didn't shut up." She glares at me now. "But yes, it was the way you looked at me, with a fire in your eyes, like no one could tell you what to do. I knew I had to have you."

"So, it was the challenge?" she asks coyly.

"No. It was your hair, and those big brown eyes, and *you*."

Charlotte snuggles in close to me, resting her head on my chest. "Keep talking."

I close my eyes and return to that night, happy that for once I'm thinking about it with her in my arms. "Well, we left the diner, and we went back to your dorm, but not before getting absolutely soaked in the rain. You danced around in it, throwing your hands up like it was the greatest thing to happen. And to me it was too. We didn't get a lot of rain in the desert. Right then I wanted to kiss you. I wanted to kiss the raindrops off your lips."

"I waited for you to do it. I put my lips so close to you I thought you wouldn't be able to resist…but you did." She bites her lip.

"Right, like I said. I knew I wouldn't be able to stop. So instead, I took your hand and walked you back to your dorm.

You disappeared into the bathroom, and I was just giving myself a pep talk to leave when you walked out in the Red Sox T-shirt and those short peach-colored pajama shorts."

She inhales loudly. "You remember what I was wearing?"

I kiss the top of her head. "I remember *everything*. Besides, you didn't match at all and so that kind of sticks out to me." She smacks me in the stomach, and I lean down to look at her, taking both her wrists in my hand. "You walked by me, and I saw that perfect round ass of yours peeking out from below your shorts, and it took everything in me not to grab you by the arms and pull you to me, like you are now, and kiss you." My lips take hers, and when I release her wrists, she runs her hands through my hair while her tongue explores mine. Breathless and needy, I want nothing more than the taste of her, taking the frustration I felt years ago out on her body, and allowing my hands to explore every inch of her like I wanted that night.

"So do you get it now?" I ask with a smile.

"Get what?"

"My profile. The one I used to con you into this trip?" I say it teasingly and she actually smiles.

Staring at me for a beat, I watch as realization dawns on her. "Oh my God, how dumb am I! The song."

I nod. "I wasn't trying to trick you. I was giving you a clue."

She laughs softly. "He puts out an ad and finds the person he loves...the one who had always been right in front of him."

I smile. "I had no idea you were right in front of me all along.

Just down the block. Living with one of my best friends. All those years we wasted not seeing one another. When Pat told me what you were doing, I couldn't do anything but think you and I both loved getting caught in the rain, you hated working out, and we had that amazing night holding one another in your bed. If I hadn't been so scared, we'd have made love at midnight."

"Take off your pants," she whispers into my mouth.

I choke on my words. "What?"

Her brown eyes glisten fiercely. "That's what I said next."

I grab her ass and kiss her again. "Yes, Sassy. That's what you said." And then softly I whisper, "You remember too."

She smiles. "But seriously, take off your pants."

"I thought you said we needed to be good."

Her smile turns seductive. "We will be good. You can't sleep with your pants on. *I don't bite, I promise*." She teases me with the memories of that night, repeating the words she said then, and I obey, because just like that night I am a prisoner to her every wish. We both get up from the bed, brush our teeth, and undress. When she walks out of the bathroom, I am pleasantly surprised to find that she is wearing a white tank top with the peach pajama shorts from years earlier. "You've got to be kidding me," I groan.

I walk over to her and cup her bottom. Charlotte raises her chin and looks up at me. "I didn't bring the Red Sox shirt, but I hope these will do."

"They'll do," I whisper, lifting her up into my arms and carrying her over to the bed. For a moment I allow myself to believe we can have it all. That I can be the man she deserves. Being with her makes me want to try. Before I can stop myself, the words slip out of my mouth, "Promise to wear these on our honeymoon?"

Charlotte stares at me, her open mouth practically hitting the floor.

With my heart racing, I make a promise I hope I can keep. One that I want more than I've ever wanted anything in my life. "I am going to stay on my side of the bed, and I won't do anything other than hold you, *I promise*, but one day I am going to make love to you in this bed, and we are going to have that happily ever after. Okay?"

Speechless, she just nods. We both get under the covers, and she pushes herself next to me, pulling my arm around her and bringing my hand to her lips. We lay there silently for a while, and I believe she's fallen asleep when I finally hear her whisper, "Okay."

CHAPTER 36

Charlotte

The moment the sunlight filters into the room, I turn over to make sure Jack is still there. Breathing peacefully, he sleeps soundly next to me, his arm tightening over my hip as I start to move. Letting out a sigh, I snuggle in close, happy that for once I didn't wake up with him gone.

The night had been eye-opening for sure, but his track record of disappearing keeps me guarded. How can I be sure that everything he said last night wasn't just words? Trusting him has become the biggest hurdle in our relationship, which doesn't bode well for the future.

But he explained why he disappeared, and he's trying.

With those thoughts in my mind, I snuggle closer and inhale. His warm body next to me feels almost too comfortable, as if I've finally found what I've been waiting for my entire life. Afraid to get too attached, I kiss his chest and sneak out of bed.

Every moment I spend in his arms makes it harder to leave him. Until he proves that he's a man of his word, I need to keep my head in the game and my body out of his bed.

I grab a pair of pants and a sweatshirt and sneak into the bathroom, replacing the peach pajama bottoms with black sweats. The shorts are far too inappropriate to wear in front of his family. My hair looks messy, so I decide to throw it in a ponytail and wash the red lipstick off my face from the night before. As I touch my lips, I'm reminded of the way Jack kissed me, with such passion that I swear they'll be swollen for days. I close my eyes and feel his mouth caressing mine.

You're getting too attached.

I shake the memories from my head and sneak out of the room, trying to ignore his shirtless chest which is covered in the light freckles I've come to adore.

The door creaks behind me, and I tiptoe down the steps. When I enter the kitchen, I spot Jack's aunt sitting at the Azorean blue table reading a book.

"Good morning, Charlotte. How did you sleep?" Her voice has a thick accent, but I appreciate her effort in speaking English. She wears a long pink robe which hangs loosely over her shoulders and makes her look even tinier. Without makeup to hide her wrinkles, she looks older than the day before. It suddenly occurs to me that she doesn't only look old, she looks frail, as if her health could be something of concern.

"Good morning. It was wonderful. Thank you so much for

allowing us to stay here. You have a beautiful property."

She folds her page down and closes her book, leaning against the table to provide her the strength to stand up slowly. I walk over to assist, and she smiles warmly at me. "I'm afraid getting old isn't something we can avoid. Here, let me get you a cup of coffee." She shuffles slowly over to the coffee maker, but I walk quicker to assist.

"Here. Let me. How do you take your coffee?" I reach for the cups and pour the coffee for both of us. She accepts hers with two cubes of sugar, and I drink mine black.

I glance out the window and see that it is an absolutely glorious day. There isn't a cloud in the sky, and the flowers look even brighter than the day before. "I used to like to sit by the water when I had my coffee, but now it's too hard for me to walk down there. Such a pity," she says as she sips her coffee.

"How long have you lived here?"

She shifts in her seat, and her smile spreads, as if she's replaying a happy memory. "Oh, my father built this house. I've lived here my whole life, except for a few decades when I lived in America while I worked. But I always knew I wanted to come back."

"That's why you speak English so well!"

She grins. "Thank you. I've worked hard at it."

"Do you miss it?"

"America? No. Not really. What's to miss when I have this view?" She looks outside again, and her face is serene. "But I do miss my nieces and nephews who still live there. Jack and

Belle's moms. All of their children. That's why having them here is such a blessing. I haven't seen Jack in person in so long. I was nervous I wouldn't..." She stops talking, and I have a feeling she was going to say that she was nervous she'd never see him again. I am almost certain that she is truly ill, but I am not sure of the right thing to say. So, I use the universal language of touch and place my hand over hers, squeezing and offering her comfort. She sighs, affirming my suspicion, and puts her coffee down, taking both my hands in hers. We sit silently for another moment before footsteps on the stairs steal our attention. Dropping my hand with a sad smile, she goes back to sipping her coffee.

Belle enters the kitchen with her black hair trailing behind and her face luminous even in the early morning. "Good morning! How are you both doing today?" She makes her way over to her aunt and kisses her on the cheek before looking up at me.

"Much better than yesterday," I admit.

Belle's face beams back at me. "Oh, thank goodness! Would you like to take your coffee down to the water with me and fill me in?"

I look to Jack's aunt who just picks up her book and goes back to reading.

"Okay." I follow Belle out the door and down the path through the garden. The aroma from the flowers seems stronger, and I wonder if it's because I'm happier today. The entire world seems brighter now that things are better with Jack.

So much for not getting ahead of yourself.

"Is your aunt okay?" My mind is still in the kitchen with Aunt Maria, and I can't shake the feeling that something is really wrong.

Belle studies my face and turns to the water. "I'm not sure. But I'm glad I'm not the only one who noticed. Or maybe I'm not glad. It certainly gives validity to my concerns, but I'd rather everyone told me she's fine."

I nod. Unfortunately, it seems we are both concerned. "Life can be so unfair," I say quietly.

"Yes and no. She lives on this beautiful land, and her family is here. I know there is nothing more she would want. And she has all those shoes..." she says with a dreamy smile. "We are all lucky. I can see you feel very lucky today too. Things went well with Jack, I take it?"

Pink colors my cheeks. "Yes. They did."

She sighs. "I *need* more information than that. Come on, give a girl a bone! I have to live vicariously through you all. I'm living with my elderly aunt, remember!"

I laugh. "He said all the right things. I'm just hoping he means them." The butterflies flap around as if trying to get rid of my nerves.

"Well, what did he *say*?"

"Yes! Please tell me what he said?" Steph shouts from a few feet away. I turn to see her walking toward us with a big smile on her face, a coffee cup in hand and a sweatshirt around her waist. She sets the cup down and pulls the sweatshirt over her head. "Jeez. It's cold by the water."

I rub her knee trying to warm her and buy time before I divulge all of Jack's proclamations from the night before. Part of me is nervous that it was all a dream—*or just words*. I guess that's my real concern.

"Spill!" Steph says impatiently, looking me in the eye and not giving me an inch of wiggle room.

Rolling my eyes, I finally speak. "Fine. He told me why he didn't kiss me the first time we met—because he was deploying, and he knew that if he told me that I would have waited. Which is true. I just wish he would have given me the opportunity to be there for him. It feels like six years of my life was wasted waiting for him, anyway."

Steph bites her lip, and Belle looks to the water. I feel like they have more of the story, which sets my nerves on edge. "What?" I look at them both, waiting for someone to clue me in.

When Belle turns back to me her eyes are glistening, holding back emotion. "You guys wouldn't have made it if he had kissed you." She says it with so much certainty I almost believe it.

Steph nods. "I actually agree."

I fold my hands over my chest, hating the feeling that once again people are telling me what I can and can't handle. "I'm a lot stronger than you think."

Steph's arm goes around me, which is quite a shock since she is the least affectionate person I know. "It's not about what

338

you could handle. It's about Jack. He would have dragged you both down back then. But he's good now. He's done the work. Just…just give him some slack. If he tells you he held back for your own good, believe him. I know I do."

Somehow hearing these words and seeing both of their expressions gives me the strength to believe him. I don't feel like I'm falling for someone's words, or a fairy tale, or just falling for the next guy who showed interest in me. I'm choosing to trust that the man who says he wants to be with me actually does. Buoyed by their words, I divulge the rest of our conversation. "He told me he knows I'm his future. He talked about our honeymoon like he was certain it would happen."

Steph whistles and Belle screeches. "Now that is what I was talking about. The good stuff! That's something to live vicariously for!" The three of us laugh, and I feel even better. We continue to chat and sip our coffee, enjoying the view and the company.

I notice Jack looking down at us from the balcony. He's still shirtless, thank you, and he's holding up his hand shielding the sun from his eyes. I offer a small wave, and his face breaks out into a big smile.

Steph hits me under the table. "Go get your man!" I smack her back and shift out of my seat, offering to take everyone's cups.

"Nah, I have to shower anyway. Jack said he wanted to leave early, right?"

"True. Belle, are you going to come with us to Sete

Cidades?" I attempt to say the name properly, and it seems I'm on track because Belle doesn't wrinkle her face in confusion.

"No. I've been there before. It's beautiful. I'm going to stay here with my aunt and help her cook for tonight. She wants to make you all a family feast. And don't worry—there won't be any shrimp."

Steph and I burst out laughing. I have no idea how Belle knows about the shellfish, but I'm glad we won't be having any bloody shrimp tonight. "Excellent. Let me know if we can pick anything up while we are out."

"Nope. She's got wine and more food than any of us will be able to eat." She shakes her head and mumbles something under her breath about the crazy Portuguese. I laugh and make my way up the hill.

Steph grabs me before we walk into the house. "So, you're really feeling okay today?"

"Yeah," I say as I nod, assuring myself as well. "I don't want to get ahead of myself. But I also don't want to *miss* this moment. I mean, every love story *has* to start somewhere, right? I can't keep pushing him away because I was disappointed last time. I'm choosing to believe that this is my chance. This is *my* story. Am I crazy?"

Steph's smile doubles. "No. Everyone's love story is different. Go get yours." She smacks my butt as I walk into the house, and I laugh all the way up the stairs.

Walking into my room, I spot Jack standing on the balcony lost in his own thoughts. I take this opportunity to stare at the muscles in his back, loving how they are also covered in light freckles. Sneaking up behind him, I wrap my arms around him, but apparently, I'm not quiet enough because he whirls around and grabs me in his arms. "Good morning, beautiful. I was nervous when you disappeared this morning. Thought maybe all my grand plans might have scared you off." He takes my face in his hands and looks down with a teasing smile.

"That's your MO, not mine," I say playfully. His blue eyes don't hide his insecurity. My chest tightens. Insecurity is my MO, and I hate the feeling. I nuzzle my head into his warm chest. "I liked all the things you said last night. I'm not running."

His chest relaxes, and he sighs into my hair, placing a kiss on top of my head. "Good. Let's get ready to go then."

I'm not quite ready to leave his arms though. "Hey, shouldn't we shower before we go?"

Jack shrugs. "We're just going to get all sweaty."

I give him an exaggerated pout. "It's just that I want a few more minutes alone with you."

He looks at me oddly, not understanding my insinuation. "Well, I'm not sure how a shower would fix that."

"It would if we showered *together*," I tease as I slip off my sweatpants.

Jack's eyes light up as he watches me slowly undress. "I thought you said no funny business in this room." But he's already slipping off his pants as he follows me into the bathroom.

I walk backwards and enjoy watching him stumble after me

as I lift up my sweatshirt, revealing the white tank top below. "I said no funny business in *that* bed." I point behind him to the four-poster bed.

Jack runs at me, hopping out of his boxers one leg at a time as he stumbles into the bathroom and leans me against the wall. He's completely naked, and I feel his excitement between my legs, but I'm still wearing panties and my top. "Slow down, baby, I'm not going anywhere," I tease him with his own words.

Jack grins and kisses me. Then he leans into the shower and turns on the water, causing steam to settle around us. "Is that how you want to play it?" He slips down my underwear with both hands and drops to his knees before me. "I'm going to take this nice...and...slow." His movements with his tongue are torturous, to the point that he leaves me begging for him to speed up, to take me into the shower, and make love to me.

"Please," I whimper, unable to say anything else, but Jack just shakes his head as he continues to pleasure me.

"Not until you come for me, baby." His whispers into my body send me over the edge, and I feel myself explode, my legs shaking and my body only remaining upright because he's leaning me against the wall. His face registers pure joy. "I love it when you listen."

Too spent to argue, I just smile at him. "Told you, there's something about you, I always want to listen."

My words appear to do something to him. His eyes grow

dark with desire, and his voice matches the look. "Get in the shower, Sassy."

Elated that I'm finally getting what I want, I do as told. "I want to watch you wash yourself," he says, as he steps in with me.

All I want is Jack inside of me, to feel every inch of him, and know that we're one again. But he has other plans. I play along hoping we'll both get what we want. I take the soap bottle and turn it over, pouring it into my hand, never taking my eyes off his. The way he is watching me makes me feel like the sexiest woman alive. Slowly, I lather myself, washing my breasts as he almost salivates. "I think you missed a spot." His voice is husky as he moves closer to me, preparing to take the soap and wash me himself.

I raise my eyebrows. "Yes. I definitely did." I take him in my hand and begin stroking him with my soapy fingers. "I want you inside me, Jack."

He groans. "Sass, we don't have a condom."

"I'm on the pill. And I *trust* you." He meets my eyes, and I know the words hold more meaning than just sex. I trust *him*. I believe in us. It's what he's been pushing for all along, a real chance for happiness. His lips meet mine and he lifts me up, entering me as I wrap my legs around him. My moan escapes into his mouth, and he returns the sounds of desire.

"Fuck, baby, you feel like heaven." He pushes into me harder, and I know neither of us will last long. Every inch of my body is tingling, and my mind has gone completely blank—the man has managed to silence my thoughts. The only thing I'm focused on is bringing him as much pleasure as he brought me. There's no barrier between us. Nothing separates us. We're one, and I've never felt so alive in my life. So full. So cherished. "Come with me, baby," he says finally, and we're both left panting and breathless, releasing the pent-up stress from the last few days. With steam billowing around us, we remain holding one another in the shower, our brains numb but our hearts full.

"Wow. Remind me to never disappear on you in the morning again," he teases as we towel off.

Stupid boy. He already forgot my towel trick which I now use, whacking him with the wet thick towel, leaving him screeching, "Damn, woman! It was a joke."

I walk out of the bathroom and yell behind me, "You're no comedian. Don't quit your day job, Maverick."

"So how did this morning go?" Steph whispers to me as we sit cross legged on our feet in the backseat of the tiny rental car.

"Okay."

My coy reply does little to stifle Steph's interest. "Spill, or I'll ask Jack."

"Ask Jack what?" he questions from the front.

"About our sex in the shower." I surprise them all with

my response. Jack's eyes dart up in the rearview mirror, a grin teasing the corner of his lips. *Bastard*. Instead of my words making him squirm, he looks quite proud of himself.

"Shut up!" Steph smacks me. "I need all the details."

Pat laughs. "I don't."

"It was incredible," I mouth and hold up two fingers to Steph.

"No way," she whispers.

I grin and give her an exaggerated nod.

"What are the two of you talking about back there?" Jack eyes me. I wink at him, and he shakes his head.

"Don't interrupt our conversations if you don't want me to embarrass you."

He shrugs. "Ain't nothing to be embarrassed about. I just don't normally kiss and tell, babe."

Steph looks at me and puts her hand up in front of her face, whispering, "He called you *babe*."

"I know!" I screech.

We are such teenagers.

"Will the two of you stop gossiping and look out the window? The view is incredible." Pat isn't wrong—but the roads are winding, and we all know I can't handle that. To make matters worse, I have no window to stick my head out of so I'm trying hard to focus on anything other than the twisting car and my stomach flipping.

As if Jack can read my mind, he turns off into a spot and stops. Once the guys are out, we untwist our pretzeled legs and push our bodies through the tiny door. But I don't think Jack properly explained to me where he was taking us. Whose cruel joke was this anyway? I look out and see nothing but the sky—we are legitimately above the clouds. "Don't look down," Jack whispers into my ear as he grabs me from behind. Of course, the sheer force of his touch scares the shit out of my sensitive self, and I almost fall forward. Jack grabs me and pulls me close to him. "Dammit, woman, what did I just say?"

I laugh nervously and lean into him. "Why did you bring me here?"

"Trust me." It's said as if it's a statement, but honestly, I'm questioning whether I do. He knows my fear of heights. I'm not sure I can trust him at all. Grudgingly, I accept the hand he is holding out and shuffle behind him, keeping my eyes on the back of his calves, which is not the worst way to spend an afternoon.

"I don't understand. It was so sunny before." A grey fog covers the area—it hangs around us like a cloud, which I now realize we are likely not above. Although we are *very* high. It's scarier being this high when you cannot see the area around you. I have no idea where the land ends and the volcanic crater begins. I certainly don't spy the beautiful lakes I'd been promised.

Everyone walks quietly—ignoring my whining—and no one else seems nervous at all. I keep my eyes down, focused on Jack's calf muscles and the feel of his hand in mine. There are clay steps that we keep climbing, and I mutter curses when I trip, leaving Jack smirking. We finally reach a landing, and Jack stops. "Okay. Do you trust me?"

My stomach flips. *No,* my inner scaredy-cat wants to scream. But that doesn't seem like the correct answer, and it's not the truth. I trust him completely. I bite the inside of my lip and nod. He pushes me in front of him a bit and points in the distance. "Look over there." As I finally lift my eyes to look at where he's pointing, my stomach whooshes. The green mountain curves inward, and the grass follows it all the way down, until it opens into the two lakes, one green and one blue, with the tiny piece of land separating them. For a moment I am breathless, remembering the story of Antilla and imagining her tears.

What only moments before was just a green mountain hidden in the clouds is now more colors than the eye can see. Flowers spurt from all over, pinks, purples, yellows, and blues blossoming from the mountain. The lakes are as serene as a picture. Jack has quite literally forced me to open my eyes to experience the beauty in the world—I know without him I would never have taken this leap. It's what he has been doing the entire trip—forcing me out of my comfort zone in our experiences as well as in our relationship. My body tingles, and I know it's not just from the nervousness of where we stand—it's the butterflies telling me to keep listening to Jack, keep taking chances.

"I want to take you down there," he whispers, pointing to the bridge between the two lakes. I nod, and we separate from Steph and Pat, allowing them some time alone as well. The ride down to the bottom of the crater is silent. I wonder if he also feels the tingles from the moment we just shared.

Jack takes my hand as we walk down by the lakes—the difference in color is no longer evident from the surface. Trick of the eye up in the clouds? I try not to read more into it—this isn't something for me to psychoanalyze. For once I'm going to take at face value what I've seen. Jack is crazy about me, we are walking hand in hand in the middle of one of the Seven Wonders of Portugal, and life is good. Of course, that's what I want to believe. But my stomach is already getting all flappy and I'm in my head again. "Was it really love at first sight?" I blurt out.

Jack bursts out laughing. "Are you in that noggin of yours again?"

I look up at him sheepishly and pull on his arm. "Seriously, I need to know the truth. Was it just a line? It's okay if it was. I know you're crazy about me now. I don't need it to be that you've always been."

"That's why I wanted to take you over here. To talk to you. To tell you everything."

I let out a breath that I didn't realize I was holding. He's going to tell me everything.

See, he is a good guy. He does care about you.

"Yes. The absolute truth is I fell hard for you that night. I don't think there is another way to explain it other than my butterflies were attracted to yours." He grins sheepishly now, poking me in the belly.

I smile back at him, but my brain is working overtime. "So,

why didn't you leave your number? Or come find me when you got back?" I'm so nervous for his response. I'm not sure there is a right answer—we are trudging into dangerous territory. Why does it matter if he loved me back then? If he loves me now, shouldn't that be enough?

"My intention was always to find you. I didn't know you were Steph's roommate, but I didn't think it would be too hard to find Charlotte Chase from Salve Regina. Obviously, it would be a lie if I told you I tried. Because I didn't." My stomach drops. So he hadn't been searching for me for years— he hadn't searched for me at all. My face must give away my disappointment, because Jack pulls my chin up to look at him. "Hey, don't do that. Let me finish before you judge everything."

I bite the inside of my lip nervously. "Okay."

"As you know, I was deploying a few weeks after I met you. Which like I said before was why I didn't kiss you. I know you say you could have handled it, Charlotte, but I couldn't. I had never felt the way I felt when I was with you. You made me feel like me. More me than I'd ever felt in my life. Like Steph did for you. And I didn't think it was possible—no, scratch that—now that I know what we have, I know it would have been impossible to leave you after I tasted you. This feeling, *us*, it's once in a lifetime." He pulls me close, and I know precisely what he means—I feel it too.

"When I got back, I settled into life over there. Which wasn't always bad. The guys were family to me. Being with them felt like it was where I was meant to be. Over there I was able to zone out—focus on the mission. I didn't pine over a relationship because we didn't have one. It was what I needed when I was there."

Everything he was saying made sense. But it didn't explain why he didn't call me when he got back. It had been *six years* of silence. "Jack, I get all that. But why didn't you come find me?"

"I had a friend, Peter. My best friend that I told you about. We'd grown up together, Peter, Nate, and me. We were like brothers. Nate's dad died in the towers on 9/11. Changed my life. His dad was like a second dad to me. His parents were best friends with my parents. The loss of him destroyed us. Peter and I joined the Air Force when we graduated from college. Nate stayed behind. He couldn't put his mother through the worry. She'd lost enough. But Peter and I, man, we were made for the Air Force. We loved every minute of it. Genuinely. Anyway, Peter and I were in the same squadron, although I flew and he worked on the planes. Being in the Air Force doesn't always mean you get to fly, and it was a bit of a sore spot with us. We'd play cards together, fight over the last dessert, hell, we'd fight over everything. It was always a competition with him. I got to fly, and he was always back on the base, on the ground, never in the sky. So our fights consisted over who sang better at karaoke and who got a girl's number the quickest." Jack smiles and his eyes are somewhere else. It's as if he's back in the past with his friend.

"I'd won the last bet and gotten the girl's number. It wasn't anyone I was even interested in—I just liked to one-up him." He rolls his eyes now and shakes his head.

I lift my hand up to his chin and pull his eyes to me. "Hey, if this is too hard, it's okay. We don't have to talk about this."

But he shakes his head again. "No. I *need* to tell you this."

I nod and let my hand drop from his chin into his hands.

"I was so excited that I won. I was an ass about it. Showing him the number, waving it in his face. Peter was so red. He really liked the girl. I threw the number at him and told him he could have it; I was going flying. And I walked out of there like a cocky ass. I never saw him alive again. The base was attacked while I was gone."

"Oh, Jack. I'm so sorry." At a loss for words and broken at the sight of him, I pull him close, and his body which normally towers over me crumbles into my arms.

"I have nightmares that I get back in time, only to hear him screaming in pain…but I never heard him scream. I was too late. It's my screams—the bloodcurdling, painful screams that I hear every night—they're mine from that day."

I stroke his hair, wishing I could take all his pain away. "Shh…I'm so sorry, Jack." It occurs to me then that I've never heard him scream at night. We've slept together almost the entire trip, and not once have I felt him stir in his sleep or cry out at all. "Do you still have these nightmares?"

He looks at me sadly, as if he feels guilty that they've stopped. "Not since you. You give me hope, Charlotte. You make me believe that maybe I can be normal again. That I can live the life that Peter and I always wanted. But if I'm honest, I'm scared I'm not capable of it all." The weight of his words and the tears in his eyes bring me to tears.

"Jack, you give me hope too. You've opened my eyes, pushed me to be brave. You don't have to be scared, because I'm right here by your side."

His eyes fall. "That's just it though. I'm not sure I can be brave like you. I don't know if I have it in me to let you down like I let Peter down."

I brush the tears from his face, pulling his gaze toward mine. "Jack Fitzpatrick, I don't need you to be anything. You're not my knight in shining armor, and you don't control my happiness. You enhance it. Stop putting all this pressure on yourself. You don't need to do anything special. You don't need to be perfect. I don't need anyone other than you, Jack. I just need you to keep showing up—to keep choosing us, to take it day by day with me. Can you do that?" My heart races as I wait for him to respond. As I wait for him to choose us.

Jack looks off in the distance, staring out at the blue lake, giving real thought to my words. "I took a job in Las Vegas. I leave when we get home." He looks back to me, as if he's waiting for me to give up.

I allow myself five seconds to breathe—to consider—and then I jump, because I believe in us. I trust him. "Is that what you want? To move to Las Vegas?"

He blinks. "No."

I let out an exasperated laugh. "What do you want, Jack?"

He shakes his head then looks down and meets my eyes. "I want everything. I want a future with you."

Smiling, I reach up and loop my arms around his neck, pulling him closer. "You have me. Years ago you ran without giving me a choice. Give me a choice now, and let me tell you I'll be there for you. Just tell me what you want, and I'll stand beside you."

The breath he lets out sounds like my heart sighing in relief. "Fuck, Charlotte, you're a dream come true."

Smiling, I shake my head. "No. I'm just me and you're just you. But together, Jack, *together*, we are amazing. Do you trust me?"

He nods. "It's not that easy though, Charlotte. I'm damaged. I'm screwed up. I get scared, I have nightmares, I have breakdowns. And I can't promise I won't run. I want to promise that. I want to tell you that I can give you everything. But you have to know, I'll probably fuck up."

This poor man. I had put him through the wringer with my distrust. And yet he kept showing up for me. Kept proving to me that he was worthy—that our relationship was worthy. "Then I'll chase you. I'll be there when you come back. I'll be *here* for you, Jack." I put my hand to his heart and offer him a smile, hoping that he understands that I don't just want the fun guy or the sexy man. I want *him*, imperfectly perfect as he is.

Jack's arms move around me, and I feel the wetness of his face against mine as he kisses me. We stand there holding one another on the bridge where Antilla and her shepherd stood, crying, and I can't help but hope his blue tears and my brown ones are somehow more magical than theirs and that we have a different ending than they did. A happy one.

CHAPTER 37

Jack

Lying in bed, I can't help but be hopeful. Today was not at all as I expected. I thought it would be harder to open up to Charlotte—to talk about Peter's death. But somehow I feel lighter now. The weight of holding it all in had taken such a toll. Even if I don't yet know what it all means, or what I want to do about my job, having told her about my fears, about Peter, about Las Vegas, makes it so that I can breathe easier. *She* makes it easier to breathe.

Shifting in the bed, I reach over for my phone. It's the same one from six years ago. I couldn't bear to get rid of it. This phone houses all the texts between Peter and me. I'm sure the phone company could probably help me transfer them into a new phone, but I'd never felt confident enough that they wouldn't somehow get lost.

It'd been a few years since I'd had the guts to look at the

messages again. I scroll back and see one of the last video messages I sent him. It's dated March 17, six years ago—the night I met Charlotte. I turn the volume down on the side so that I don't wake her—she's sleeping soundly next to me—and I pause before hitting play, nervous to hear what I said.

The phone lights up, and I stare at twenty-six-year-old me. I'm wearing a Red Sox hat and my face is clean-shaven—I look *young*. I thought I was so wise back then. Thought I had everything figured out. But I can see now that even after a tour in the Middle East, I was still just a cocky asshole who had no idea how much life would change. "Hey, man." I wince when I hear my voice. "I gotta be quick, but I just wanted to let you know I met the most incredible woman today...I think this is it...like the real thing. I know I sound like a fool, and you're probably rolling your eyes, but she's incredible." I shake my head now. I have no memory of recording this, but I *do* remember those feelings. "Oh, shit...she's walking back." The phone flips from my face and turns to Charlotte—twenty-two-year-old Charlotte whose light brown hair is wet from the rain, wavy around her face like she's been styling it all week, with jeans clinging to her curves. She walks with a bounce to her step, and the big smile on her lips causes her dimples to tighten in joy. The whoosh in my stomach right now is the same one I felt back then—I remember *that* like it was yesterday too. I pause the video and stare at her and then look next to me. I don't have to live in the memories anymore—she's right here.

I click on the next video, and there's Peter, his red hair shaved close to his head, and his blue eyes are turned up from his laughter. "Dude! She's hot! Can't wait to meet her!" And then he laughs, his signature loud, goofy laugh, and for the first time in a long time it doesn't hurt to hear it. I know he would be happy for me. I know he would have been proud that I finally found her. I can't change the past, and I wish I could turn back time and keep Peter safe. I wish I would have kissed Charlotte back then and not missed out on these last six years together. But I'm no longer angry about it. I can finally look at him and not feel the vise-like guilt around my chest. Instead, all I feel is grateful. Grateful to have known him, to have had his friendship, and beyond grateful to have Charlotte beside me so that when things get hard again, I have someone to lean on.

Shifting in bed, Charlotte turns and wraps her arm around my chest but doesn't wake up, just makes a slight sigh in her sleep and she's silent again. I put the phone down and curl my body into hers. No matter what happens in the future, I know I want to have her by my side.

The next morning when I wake, she's gone again. When I wander down to the kitchen, I spot her sitting with my aunt, talking quietly. "What are you guys being so sneaky about?" I tease, joining them at the table and settling myself down next to my aunt. I wink at Charlotte, who appears a bit uneasy.

"Just catching up." Charlotte stands and busies herself getting both of us coffees. But I'm not buying the distraction.

"What's going on?" My calm mood from the night before is gone—I can sense the tension in the room, and I'm tired of secrets. Charlotte doesn't even turn around to look at me. "You said no secrets," I remind her.

My aunt grabs my hand, drawing my attention back to how fragile she looks. "Don't you get an attitude with her. She's just keeping me company."

I turn around to look at Charlotte again. I know if she looks at me, she won't be able to lie. But she keeps her back to me, her gaze focused on the sea out the window. "Charlotte." My voice is stern now. Her shoulders flinch, but she remains in place.

My aunt huffs. "Fine, you big bully. I was just talking to her about my cancer diagnosis."

Whipping my head around, I look into her eyes, and the blueish gray that I've known all my life tells me everything I need to know. She's sad and she's scared. I don't have the words to respond, so I just wrap my hands around hers and look at her, waiting for her to tell me more. The silence continues—all of us waiting for the other to speak. Finally, Charlotte clears her throat. "I'll give you guys some privacy." She walks by me and places her hand on my shoulder, squeezing. I want to stop her, but I'm so shocked by my aunt's confession that I let her leave.

"What kind of cancer?"

She shakes her head. "I don't want to talk about it. I didn't even want to tell you, but Charlotte thought it was only fair, since this will likely be the last time we get to see one another…" Her voice cracks but she continues, "She thought it was only right that you knew, and we got to say our goodbyes." Her eyes water, but the tears don't drop. "She's a good one you got there. Hold on to her tight."

Unable to respond to her confession, I just nod. "I plan to." Then I get angry. "Wait. What do you mean you don't want to talk about it? And you weren't going to tell me? We can take you to see specialists. You probably didn't even talk to the doctors in the US. I'm sure they have medications…" my voice falters and fades as she shakes her head, putting her hand firmly down on mine.

"Jack Ryan Fitzpatrick, that is *not* what I want. Now you listen to me, I am not going to spend the rest of my days being pumped with medication and sitting in a hospital. I have had a good life, *not long enough*, but a good one. And look at this view. I am going to live out the rest of my days looking at the ocean. I'm going to spend my time with family, and I'm going to laugh. So please, do not bring this up again." Her voice is stern, and I find myself nodding. Nothing that she says is anything different than I would decide if it were me—but it's hard to let someone you love go. I find myself choked up trying to tell her as much. She just pats me on the back, and we sit silently enjoying each other's company.

That afternoon, she tells us she wants to nap, but I'm pretty sure she just doesn't want us to sit around and stare at her. We head off to the Caldeiras and I sneak a call to my mom and sister, sure that they would want to know if this was the last time they were going to see our Titia, just like I would hope they'd do for me.

"You're a good boy, Jack," my mother says after I share the news. I feel like I'm five years old again and wish I could still fit into her lap. She promises they'll get on the next flight they can, and I'm buoyed by the thought that my family will all get to meet Charlotte now.

"What are you smiling about?" Charlotte asks as we walk into the forest. The Caldeiras are natural hot springs carved into the rocks. There are waterfalls and steaming pools that are supposed to have some healing powers that Charlotte was chatting about earlier. It's a private oasis in the middle of the island—one moment we are walking down paths surrounded by trees that reach the clouds, listening to the birds and monkeys have a party above us, and the next we are entering an area covered with steam, where water falls from the cliffs and into stone, and people swim around lazily. The largest one is cooler, only eighty degrees, but the smaller ones are hot, and it takes a few minutes to put our entire bodies in. Pat looks skeptically at the pool while Steph and Charlotte sit in the steaming water on a bench carved into the stone. "Are you sure this is safe?" Pat asks, staring at it like I did the rust-colored water in Furnas.

"I promise, it can't be worse than what I've already gone in."

Charlotte and I lock eyes and she smiles, both of us remembering falling into the rust-tinged pool. The smell here is only a bit better than in Furnas, the sulfur overpowering our lungs.

"It stinks," Pat says, once again stating the obvious.

I hop in and make my way to the girls. "It's good for your skin."

"It's what?" He looks affronted that he would get the smelly water anywhere near his face.

Steph splashes him, and one of the other tourists glares at her; we are ruining the quiet sanctuary that existed only moments before. "Sorry," she whispers and then breaks out in a giggle.

The next few days are spent like this. I wake up in the morning and have coffee with my aunt and Charlotte. We both help her down to the picnic table by the water, and Charlotte butters bolos or I pick up pastries and we just talk. Then in the afternoons while she naps, we go on adventures. One day it's the beach, the next it's cliff diving. It sounds a lot worse than it was, although I'm sure Charlotte would exaggerate the drop—it was like ten feet, so hardly a cliff. We go on a catamaran and visit the Villa Franco Islet which you can actually visit, unlike the one in Mosteiros. Tourists sit on the stone walls, swim in the center where there is great snorkeling, and some also cave jump. Not surprisingly, we don't do that.

In the evenings we make dinner at my aunt's house, sit out at the picnic table, and watch the sun escape below the sea. We sip wines from different Portuguese regions and eat more bread than I ever have in my life.

On the second to last night of our vacation, Steph, Pat, and I carry the dishes in while Charlotte, Belle, and Aunt Maria relax by the water. Charlotte tried to help but I told her to sit, since she'd already cooked all afternoon. "The least I can do is the dishes," I tell her as I plop a kiss on the cheek and steer Steph up the path with me.

"Why are you being so sneaky?" Steph asks, glaring at me, fully aware I want to do more than clean the dishes.

"Shhh, wait til we get inside."

Pat follows behind us, completely oblivious as always. "What's up?" Steph asks again once we reach the kitchen.

After putting the dishes down, I turn around with a box in my hand. "What the hell is that?" she asks, pointing at it like it's a poisonous spider.

"I want to be Charlotte's Jim."

Her eyes whip up to mine. She's silent for a moment and then starts to laugh. Loudly. "Oh my God. You *are* her person. You're both made for each other. This is ridiculous. She forgave you, and you're together—what more do you want?"

A bit aggravated now, I grimace. That is not the response I was looking for. "I told you already—all of her, for all the days of my life."

Steph looks dumbstruck. "You're serious, aren't you?"

Exasperated, I sigh. "Yes. But I need your help. And Belle's.

I want to give her the Pam and Jim romance she deserves."

She rolls her eyes. "What is it with you guys and that show? It wasn't a romantic TV show. It's a comedy about *work*!"

"What's more romantic than falling in love with your best friend? Maybe I didn't buy the ring after our first date like Jim, but I did buy it after our first night together. And in all honesty, that was after our first date now that I think about it."

I ran by a jewelry store after I got off the phone with my therapist, and when I saw the ring I knew that was something that I could do for myself that would make me happy. The ring was perfect for Charlotte. It was like it was placed in the window at the exact right time, meant for me to one day slip onto her finger. I believed that time would be a year or so from now, but if I've learned anything over the last two weeks—or the last six years—it is not to waste a perfectly good moment. And not to delay being happy. Charlotte makes me happy, so what is the point in waiting an appropriate period of time to ask her to marry me? The result will be the same. Either way I intend on spending the rest of my life with only her.

"You bought a ring?" Steph's eyes grow wide.

I shrug. "Yeah. You want to see it? I need to know if she'll like it." Pat smirks. "What are you smirking about?" I ask him in annoyance.

He laughs. "I've never seen anyone surprise Steph as much as you do. It's quite enjoyable seeing her tongue-tied." Steph turns around and smacks Pat playfully on the chest, and he laughs harder.

"Okay, show me the ring!" She grabs it from my hand and gasps when she opens the box.

A good gasp, right? "Don't hold back on me. What do you think?"

Steph's eyes water. "It's beautiful. She will love it."

My heart soars. "So you'll help me?"

"Yup. Just tell me what you need."

CHAPTER 38

Charlotte

It's our last full day in the Azores, and I wake up feeling more than a bit blue. Everything about this trip has been life-changing. Not only did I increase my tan exponentially, I am going home with a boyfriend. A *boyfriend!* Yes, there's that word again. Well, at least *I think* he's my boyfriend. He was my boyfriend before, and we made up...so I think it's safe to say he's my boyfriend again.

Also, even if I wasn't going home with a boyfriend—which I *so* am—I had things to put in my biography now. To recap, I jumped into a hot spring, snorkeled in an islet, scaled the walls of death—which Jack said was *so* not a real cliff but he clearly didn't see the drop from my point of view. Also, he's like a foot taller than me so mathematically, for me, it was a farther drop. I'd gone to whale watch and only seen dolphins and sharks, swam in rusty life-changing water—I've decided that's what it was—relaxed in Caldeiras, and even eaten a bloody shrimp. Okay, I didn't actually eat it, but I *almost* did. Oh, and let's not forget, I became a *lover.* I feel fairly confident that if I ever had to create an online paragraph about myself, I would sound far more interesting and well-traveled than most.

But for the record, I do not believe I will ever have to create an online dating biography because *I have a boyfriend.* Also, I'm convinced he is the last boyfriend I will ever have. The only wrinkle that remains is the job in Las Vegas. I haven't gotten up the guts to ask him if he's made a decision. Is he leaving when we get home?

I turn over and watch Jack sleep, his chest rising and falling to the rhythm of my heart. *God, I love him.* Of course, I haven't told him that yet because I am a *new* woman. The kind of woman who jumps off cliffs and wears red lipstick. It's only been two weeks—I can't possibly tell him I love him. Women who jump into hot springs do not fall in love with men this quickly.

Watching him sleep now though, I know that I really, really do. And if he wants to move to Las Vegas, if that's what will really make him happy, I'll support him. Hell, I'll move to Las Vegas. I'll do whatever he wants to make him happy.

I jump out of bed before I shake him awake to tell him I love him. Sneaking downstairs, I peek into the kitchen and find Aunt Maria reading her book, like every other day. "Good morning, how are you feeling?" I ask as I make my way to her, offering her a kiss on both cheeks as she prefers.

Her smile grows. "I am so happy that I have had this time with you all. I'll be sad to see you go." We both hold hands for a moment, expressing our gratitude for the friendship we've created. I try not to focus on the fact that she likely won't be here the next time we visit. Living in the present is a gift we've given her as well as ourselves.

"Is there anything in particular you'd like to do today?" I ask, hoping she'll join us for a few hours.

She shakes her head. "Tonight is the big feast. You are so lucky you'll be here to experience this. It's like stepping back in time."

Belle had told me about the feast the night before. It's held in the town square. The women wear traditional Portuguese dresses which consist of a white flowing blouse, a long red skirt, and a red-and-black apron. They often wear flowers in their hair, and the little girls wear braids. Men wear big black pants, white billowing shirts, and black vests. They have red belts which hang down their waist and black hats. There will be food brought from every household and sangria in every cup. Lively music will play, and those dressed up will perform dances in circular motions while the crowds cheer along. It sounds like the perfect way to end our trip, experiencing a local tradition just as those who live here do.

After spending the afternoon sitting on the beach and returning to Mosteiros to show Pat and Steph our favorite spot, we make our way back to the house to get ready for our last night. "Oh, I so don't want to leave." Steph stares wistfully out the car window. Even I am reveling in the beauty, ignoring the way the car whooshes around the curves, content in the knowledge that Jack knows how to drive, and we aren't going to careen off into the ocean.

Or at least I'm doing a really good job of pretending I believe that.

All my clothes have been packed, except one special dress that I've saved for tonight and my clothes for the flight home. "What are you wearing?" Steph asks when we get home.

I hold up the red dress, and she coos in appreciation. "Perfect."

I smile. "I know." Already I'm imagining Jack's reaction when he sees the low cut back—it is perfectly respectable in the front. I've left my hair wavy again. It's a look I've adopted on this vacation, and I wonder if it will work back home. Or is it just the tropical air and Azorean water that makes it look so good. Or maybe it's the new Charlotte. The girl that fell in love. I slip on the dress and turn to her. "How do I look?"

"Like a *damn* temptress. *Wow*. Jack is going to lose his mind." She whistles and I laugh out loud, too excited for the night.

Steph disappears to her room to pick out an outfit, and I make my way downstairs in search of my date. Belle is in the kitchen grabbing wine and glasses when I enter. "Hey, have you seen Jack?"

Belle motions with her head to follow me. "He had to run an errand. He'll be back soon. Let's go down by the water and have a drink while we wait." I like where her head's at, so I follow along.

"Do you have any big plans for the rest of the summer while you're here?" I ask as we walk.

"Nope. Just to lounge around and spend time with Aunt Maria until lightning strikes."

I laugh. "What? I thought you're supposed to be coming up with a plan."

We settle at the table, and she pours our wine before answering. "Cheers!" She tips her glass toward mine, ignoring my question.

"What are we toasting?"

She smiles at me. "To new beginnings." Her face lights up. "For you and for me."

"I'll drink to that." We both sip our wine and revel in the beauty of the moment. The sky is a brilliant blue, and I hate that soon we will witness our last sunset in the Azores. The sky will turn light pink, and then deep red will take over until we are left with blackness. It's so depressing. "I'm so sad we're leaving."

"Me too." She squeezes my hand, and I'm happy to say I've made a friend here, and fortunately she'll be coming back to Bristol in the fall so the friendship can continue. "Know any cute guys?" she asks with a devious smile.

"Ha. You don't want me to introduce you to anyone. I have the *worst* luck when it comes to dating." I laugh now just thinking of Ben, Calves, and the blonde aficionado.

Belle looks skeptical. "Um, you are currently dating my cousin!"

I laugh again. "I don't mean him. But before him—ugh, I had the worst taste in men. And honestly if Jack didn't pursue me, I never would have had the guts to go after someone so good-looking and cocky."

Belle furrows her eyebrows. "You say cocky as if that's a good thing."

"On Jack everything looks good."

We both laugh again, and I'm already yearning for when he returns from whatever errand he's off on. Steph and Pat walk down and join us for a glass of wine, and I see Jack's aunt standing in the window watching us. "Hey, I'm going to see if your aunt wants to come down."

"She's okay. She's going to have enough excitement tonight." I look at Belle oddly but shrug my shoulders. She's the family member, so I'll defer to her request.

My Fiat Panda rental pulls up, and my heart skips a beat, excited to finally see Jack's reaction to my dress. Maybe I'm foolish, but I love how he always exaggerates his excitement over how pretty I look. I feel like singing "I Feel Pretty" at the top of my lungs while sashaying in my dress like Maria in *West Side Story.*

Unable to contain my excitement, I excuse myself from the table and walk quickly in his direction. His eyes tell me how happy he is with my choice of attire. "Damn, woman, what are you doing to me tonight? You look gorgeous." Jack lowers his head to mine and kisses me softly on the lips, and then he spins me, and I really do want to start singing now.

My heart bursts at the seams, and everything feels like it's finally settling into place. *Don't jinx it*, I tell my inner fairy-tale princess, but no matter how many times I try to tamp down my excitement, the butterflies swirl around like they're attending Cinderella's ball. "Are you almost ready to go? I think your aunt is anxious to leave."

Jack turns toward the window, looking for his aunt, and then looks back to me. "I'm ready." He kisses me one more time and then heads in to gather everyone. I watch as he walks away, focusing on his calves which flex so beautifully. He's wearing navy blue shorts and a white polo shirt that highlights his golden skin.

When we arrive at the town square, Jack leads his aunt to a table and offers to grab us drinks. Loud music plays while a group of women carrying fruit on their heads skip in circles. "What is going on there?" Steph whispers in my ear out of the corner of her mouth.

I nudge my elbow into her, and she laughs loudly. Jack appears before us again with drinks and then leans down, offering his hand as if he were a prince, rolling it through the air. "May I have this dance?"

I glance up at him nervously. "Jack," I whisper scream, "I don't know how to dance to this music." I don't move to get up, instead looking at him like he's crazy. Truly, he looks a bit nuts as he's still bent over holding his hand out to me.

Meeting my eyes, he whispers back, "But it's *our* song."

Laughing, I realize this is in fact the song that was playing the night in our hotel room. The one he danced *The Carlton* to. I turn to Steph to give her an exasperated look and warn her about Jack's dance moves only to find that the entire table is empty but for me and Jack's aunt. I turn back to Jack, and he's staring at me with a mischievous smile.

"What did you do?" I ask, looking around for everyone. My butterflies go wild, sure that something is going to happen.

Over the speakers, I hear the music switch from the traditional Portuguese music to Bruno Mars. As the familiar first bars to "Marry You" start playing, my heart skips a beat. I finally accept Jack's hand and stand up, looking around. The dancers have all lined up like they did at the end of *Grease*, and couple after couple comes down the path, throwing flowers from baskets, dancing, and cheering, just like during *The Office* wedding. When Pat and Steph come down the path in between the Portuguese dancers, I almost fall over. Pat rolls his eyes as he comes toward us, but the smile on his face tells me he's really enjoying himself.

Behind me, Jack wraps his arms around my hips, swaying to the music and singing in my ear. The next couple down is more shocking than the last. It's my parents! My mother beams and does a little wave as she dances past us, and my dad gives a big cheesy thumbs-up. My stomach does a nervous flip. What is going on? I throw my arms around both of them quickly, and my dad whispers in my ear, "You've found a good one." He winks as they move out of the way.

Next up is a girl who I don't recognize. Jack explains, "My sister, Amelia," and I see out of the corner of my eye Aunt Maria has gotten up, and she grabs her in a hug after Amelia does a little curtsy in front of us. Then Jack whispers, "My mom and dad," at the next couple. His dad twirls his mother and then dips her. In my mind I hope one day that will be us. And I also know it will be because Jack is my Jim. I am his Pam. Only we're us, so it's so much better.

Jack turns to me now. "You asked me if it was really love at first sight, and back then I would have said it was. But it's nothing compared to how I feel now. It was chemistry—*butterflies*—this unexplainable feeling that told me you were *it* for me." Jack pokes me in the belly, pointing to my butterflies, and I smile.

"Back then I only knew that I *wanted* to love you—but I didn't know you. Now I know the feeling was completely explainable because I *do* know you. And Charlotte, I love you. I love every inch of you. Even the parts of yourself that you don't like. I love that you don't shut up. I love how you never let a single thought go through your head without it coming out of your mouth. I love your belief that everyone is inherently good and how you hope everyone will find their 'happily ever after.' I love that you never stopped looking for yours and that you were smart enough to be picky and wait for me." I laugh at his cocky smile. "Charlotte, I will do everything to make your happily ever after come true, because I love *you*."

My cheeks hurt from smiling so much. "I love your calves," I blurt out.

Jack starts laughing. "Alright. Not what I expected, but I'm going to put these calves that you love so much to work." He kneels down and pulls a box from his pocket.

Oh my God, it's happening. This is not a drill. It's happening!

"He bought it after your first date!" Steph shouts from the crowd. I look at her, confused, and give him a puzzled look.

He nods. "It's true. Charlotte Marie Chase, I knew from the moment I met you there was something about you. And although it took us a while to get to this point…"

"Six years!" Pat needles him from the crowd.

Jack laughs. "Yes, six years. Although it took me six years to get to this point, I don't want to waste another minute without you by my side. I love you, Charlotte. Will you marry me?"

"I love you too," I say through tears, pulling him up to me. "I love you too, and all those things you said, that's how I feel as well."

Jack gives me a knowing smirk. "So, is that a yes, Sassy?"

I laugh. "Yes! Yes, that's a yes." He picks me up then and spins me around, and I swear to God we are floating. It is the happiest moment of my life. Jack slips the ring onto my finger, and my jaw drops. It's everything I'd ever imagined and then some—although it could have been made out of lava stone and I would have said yes. Jack is the only thing I need. But let's be serious here, it's a gorgeous diamond, so I don't have to choose. "So, are we moving to Las Vegas?" I ask, preparing myself for his answer.

Jack smiles. "No, baby, we are going to live in Bristol. We are going to live my damn dream. If that's okay with you."

I throw my arms around him. "Oh, thank God! I really love living by the ocean. And my friends. And my students." He laughs as I list off all my favorite things.

"You were willing to give up all that for me though?" he asks, sounding surprisingly nostalgic.

Easily, I answer, "Jack, I'd give up everything for you."

His lips meet mine again and then he whispers in my ear. "Same, baby, same."

Moments later we are surrounded by family, everyone hugging each other as if they've known one another forever. Jack gets along well with my dad, which I guess is understandable since somehow Jack had to have spoken to him before now to arrange for their flights and pick-ups. I now know where he had disappeared to on his errands.

"Wait, you guys flew here for one day?" I'm exasperated that everyone would go to all this trouble for me.

"About that…" Jack says, looking down at me.

"Jack Fitzpatrick, what have I told you about keeping secrets?" I give him my most stern angry teacher voice.

He holds his hands up in surrender. "Okay, Ms. Chase. I extended our trip so we can spend more time with my aunt and go explore some of the other islands."

My arms fly around his neck again, and I jump up to hug him. "Thank you. Thank you. Thank you."

As I sprinkle his face with kisses, he laughs. "Don't you know I'd do anything to make you smile?"

The butterflies sing, my heart skips again, and I offer Jack my red lips. They are his for the rest of my life.

Steph wanders over and whispers in my ear, "Ask him his middle name."

I turn to look at her, suspicious and confused, but do as told. "Jack, what's your middle name?"

Jack appears just as confused. "Ryan, why?"

My heart skips a beat. He really is my Jim Halpert, my John Krasinski, my St. Patrick's Day and Mr. Perfect all rolled into one—he's *my* Jack Ryan. Steph gives me a knowing wink, and I laugh conspiratorially. "Who says fairy tales don't come true?"

THE END

WANT MORE CHARLOTTE & JACK

Visit www.brittaneenicole.net and sign up for my newsletter to receive Jack and Charlotte's epilogue FREE.

Want to find out what happens to Belle? Order now on Amazon!

KISSES SWEET LIKE WINE

It started with a lie. An innocent, white lie. Okay, it wasn't so innocent. I'd hit rock bottom. No career, no boyfriend, and I had accidently moved into a fifty-five and up community where my best friend was a short seventy-year-old white haired Italian grandmother with big hips and an even bigger mouth who was constantly trying to set me up with her grandson.

When I was offered a job as a private investigator working with the hottest man I'd ever seen, I may have fibbed a little and told my new boss that I've got the right experience.

Tiny problem. I don't actually know what investigators do. Googling corporate espionage and taking my seventy-year-old neighbor on stings while drunk on Limoncello probably isn't in the job description. Neither is falling for my assistant, the gorgeous Green-Eyed Luca, who is either trying to take me down or take me out. I absolutely, positively cannot date Luca but with sparks flying, how could something so wrong feel so right? And will he still want me once he discovers the truth?

Want to find out what happened to Jack's sister Amelia?
Order now on Amazon!

LOVE & TEQUILA MAKE HER CRAZY

Nate Pearson was my first everything.
My first friend, first love, and first heartbreak. Now he's just my ex-husband.

It's been three years. It's time to let go of the past. When a man covered in tattoos walks into the bar where I work, with a guitar case slung over his back and a determined swagger, I think I'm finally ready to move on...until I see his guitar. I'd recognize it anywhere. It was the last gift Nate ever received from his father.

The man holding the guitar is different than the one I left behind in Nashville, but one thing remains the same, Nate Pearson will always be the love of my life.

The reasons why I asked for a divorce haven't changed. Only problem is, Nate Pearson says he still loves me, and this time he's playing for keeps.

Authors Note: Love & Tequila Make Her Crazy is a small town, brother's best friend, steamy, full-length, stand-alone, contemporary second-chance romance filled with emotion, that features both Nate and Amelia's past and present.

Trigger warning: Death of a parent, 9/11, and sexual assault.

ACKNOWLEDGEMENTS

Releasing this book to the world has been quite the journey! I would not have been able to do it without the support of my husband and children. My son snuggled me last night and said "I'm so proud of you, Momma," and I swear that was all the encouragement I needed. And my daughter tells everyone she knows that her mommy is an author. I'm incredibly lucky to have all three of you and to be living my own happily ever after. I love you!

To my Beta readers, especially Janae and Marie who have read every one of my manuscripts and provided invaluable insight, thank you! This book wouldn't be what it is without all of the readers along the way.

My team at Cover to Cover Author Services has handled every aspect of this book launch from my cover, to my social media, to formatting this book and hyping me up when I need it the most! I feel beyond blessed to have found Monique, Jamie, and Kala. Thank you!

My fellow author, Daphne, who has given me more insight and guidance, and just listened to me freak out, thank you! Also, you should really check out her Havenport Series, it's incredible!

To Ann and Ann, my editors at Happily Editing Anns, I can't sing your praises enough! The professionalism and detail you bring to your job is nothing short of amazing!

My family and friends who have had to listen to me talk

about my books for the last year, you've supported me, laughed with me, and cheered me on. Thank you! I owe you all the Pina Coladas!

And to my readers, thank you! There is nothing better than hearing how I made someone laugh, or swoon! I love reading as much as I love writing. Getting immersed in another world, falling in love with characters, and exploring places both real and fake. My family travelled to the Azores two years ago, and we fell in love with both the scenery and the people. I hope you enjoyed a glimpse into the beautiful island as much as I enjoyed writing about it. And Bristol, Rhode Island, has my heart. If you want to read more about my amazing hometown, make sure to order Belle's book. We'll be travelling back to Rhode Island and many of the characters you've come to love will be along for the ride!

If you want to follow along on my writing journey and have sneak peeks into all the characters in Bristol, follow me on Instagram and my join my awesome Facebook group where we talk all things book related with a twist!

https://www.instagram.com/britdnicole/

https://www.facebook.com/groups/brittsboozybookbabes

And don't forget to subscribe to my newsletter!